This Scot of Mine
by Sophie Jordan

"The balance of heat and suspense will delight Regency romance readers." —*Publishers Weekly*

"The fourth fast-paced and fun installment in best-selling Jordan's Rogue Files series is another expertly calibrated mix of vibrantly etched characters and steamy sensuality that will delight both longtime fans and new readers alike." —*Booklist*

A Scandalous Deal
by Joanna Shupe

"Joanna Shupe vividly evokes 1890s New York, from glamorous restaurants to a Bowery boxing hall to the original Madison Square Garden." —*New York Times Book Review*

"Shupe has done it again . . . with stories this fun, readers won't skip any of Shupe's books." —*Kirkus Reviews* (starred review)

HOW the *Dukes* STOLE CHRISTMAS

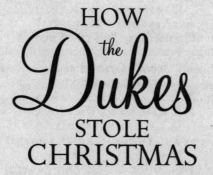

Also by Tessa Dare

Also by Sarah MacLean

The Bareknuckle Bastards
WICKED AND THE WALLFLOWER
BRAZEN AND THE BEAST

Scandal & Scoundrel
THE ROGUE NOT TAKEN
A SCOT IN THE DARK
THE DAY OF THE DUCHESS

The Rules of Scoundrels
A ROGUE BY ANY OTHER NAME
ONE GOOD EARL DESERVES A LOVER
NO GOOD DUKE GOES UNPUNISHED
NEVER JUDGE A LADY BY HER COVER

Love by Numbers
NINE RULES TO BREAK WHEN ROMANCING A RAKE
TEN WAYS TO BE ADORED WHEN LANDING A LORD
ELEVEN SCANDALS TO START TO WIN A DUKE'S
HEART

Young Adult
THE SEASON

Also by Sophie Jordan

Also by Joanna Shupe

HOW
the
Dukes
STOLE
CHRISTMAS

TESSA
DARE

SARAH
MACLEAN

SOPHIE
JORDAN

JOANNA
SHUPE

AVONBOOKS

An Imprint of HarperCollins*Publishers*

Originally published as *How the Dukes Stole Christmas* in the United States in 2018 by Rakes, Rogues & Scoundrels, LLC.

First Avon Books mass market printing: October 2019

Print Edition ISBN: 978-0-06-296241-6
Digital Edition ISBN: 978-0-06-296242-3

Cover photographs © PeriodImages.com; © ball2be/Africa Studio/ Vitalii Bashkatov/Pipochka/Brita Seifert/Shutterstock (six images)

Avon, Avon & logo, and Avon Books & logo are registered trademarks of HarperCollins Publishers in the United States of America and other countries.

HarperCollins is a registered trademark of HarperCollins Publishers in the United States of America and other countries.

19 20 21 22 23   QGM   10 9 8 7 6 5 4 3 2 1

Table of Contents

Note from the Authors

Dear Reader,

Thank you for purchasing *How the Dukes Stole Christmas*. We hope it holds a special place on your keeper shelves.

We are thrilled to share our holiday stories with you. When we first conceived of this anthology, we had so much fun collaborating and letting our favorite Christmas movies inspire us. It definitely put us into the holiday spirit and we hope these stories do the same for you. Also, please don't miss the MacLean family shortbread recipe in the back of the book!

So, relax with a hot cup of tea and a cookie (shortbread, perhaps?) and read on to enjoy our four surly dukes.

We promise, there's magic inside.

Happy reading,
Tessa, Sarah, Sophie, and Joanna

Meet Me in Mayfair

Tessa Dare

Chapter One

*C*hristmas just wouldn't be Christmas this year. A cloud loomed over the Ward sisters' bedchamber, and it wasn't the sort that dispensed glittering snowflakes. This would be their last holiday in Mayfair. That was, unless Louisa managed to work a miracle.

Tonight.

Thanks to her friendship with Miss Fiona Carville, she was invited to attend the Carvilles' lavish holiday ball. *If* she managed to attract a gentleman tonight, and *if* said gentleman was both wealthy and generous, and *if* he fell sufficiently in love with her to propose marriage within the next two weeks—then and only then could Louisa save this Christmas, and all her family's Christmases thereafter.

No pressure, she thought wryly. *None at all.*

She drew a deep breath and regarded her half-coiffed reflection in the mirror. She couldn't afford to indulge her nerves. Not with flame-hot curling tongs mere inches from her scalp.

"Here. Eat this." Kat thrust a plate under Louisa's nose.

Without turning her head, Louisa arrowed a glance at the scorched, misshapen lump of . . . something. A cautious sniff made her stomach turn. Her youngest sister's experiments in baking could be downright vicious. When you took a bite, they bit back.

"It's delicious," Kat sang, waving the shortbread back and forth under Louisa's nose.

"It's burned."

"Piffle. What's a bit of brown on the edges?" Kat whisked around her, attacking from the opposite side. She held the plate in front of her mouth and mimicked a tiny, chirping voice coming from the shortbread. *"Eat me, Louisa! Eat me!"*

"No, thank you."

"Let her alone, Kat." Maggie leveled the curling tongs in warning. Although she was the middle sister, the role of family disciplinarian came naturally to her.

Unfortunately, twelve-year-old Kat took just as naturally to the part of irrepressible hellion. She was not so easily deterred.

"You *must* eat it, Louisa," Kat said. "While I was packing the books into crates, I found the recipe in a moldy little collection of Scottish folklore. One bite, and every man you meet will fall in love with you. It's guaranteed to make you irresistible."

"Guaranteed to make me vomit, I warrant."

"But this is our last chance," Kat pleaded. "The whole family is depending on you."

Really. As if Louisa needed the reminder.

Ages ago, their father had borrowed money from a generous friend—a friend who just happened to be a duke—to purchase the Mayfair row house they called home. For decades, the old duke had ignored the debt on account of their fast friendship. Then he'd died last year, suddenly and without warning, and the mysterious new Duke of Thorndale had called in Papa's debt. He demanded not only the original amount, but also decades' worth of compounded interest. Papa had sent letters to the Thorndale estate in Yorkshire, even swallowed his pride and visited the duke's

London solicitors, but no amount of pleading had persuaded the man to leniency.

At the New Year, this house—their beloved *home*—
would belong to a stranger.

Kat thrust the shortbread at her again. "Just one bite. If
you're going to catch a husband at the ball, you need all the
help you can get."

She sighed. "Thank you, poppet, for your faith in my de-
sirability."

"Louisa would be an exceptional catch for any gentleman." Maggie pulled a hairpin from her clenched teeth to
secure one of Louisa's chestnut-brown curls.

And yet, she silently lamented, thus far the gentlemen
had failed to agree.

Louisa's parents had raised her to believe in her own
worth. She was clever, she loved to laugh, and she was
pretty enough that Mama's friends would occasionally comment on it—but she didn't possess the kind of beauty that
would make a man cross the room, much less convince him
to overlook her "flaws." She'd discouraged more than one
would-be suitor with her free opinions and straightforward
manner. In the Ward family, the three daughters were encouraged to read and learn and speak their minds in equal
measure with their three brothers. A difficult habit to break.

Tonight, she must try.

If she could snare a wealthy husband—one sufficiently
generous to pay Papa's debts—the Ward family could remain in London. If she failed, they would be forced to
leave within the month. Not to live in a charming cottage
in the Cotswolds or a sleepy village in Surrey. Oh no. Papa's
sole employment prospect would take them to the Isle of
Jersey, of all places.

Jersey.

It might as well be a thousand miles away.

"I tell you," Kat said, "this marrying scheme is balderdash. If I were the eldest, I'd be carrying out a different plan tonight."

Maggie sighed. "We've discussed this. Murdering the duke is not a plan."

"Of course it isn't," Kat replied. "Murdering the duke is an *objective*. A *plan* requires specifics. A concealed pistol. A hidden dagger. Poison-tipped darts."

"Shortbread," Louisa suggested.

In retaliation, Kat gave her arm a savage pinch.

"Promise me one thing." Maggie tied an emerald-green velvet ribbon at the base of Louisa's neck. "If you're invited to display an accomplishment tonight, please do not recite scandalous poetry."

"Byron isn't scandalous. Well, not *terribly*." Louisa reconsidered. "Very well, I'll play the pianoforte."

Maggie winced. "Never mind. Recite the poetry. Keep to Milton or Shakespeare, at least?"

"Milton, at a party? Good Lord."

"And don't blaspheme."

With a sigh, Louisa rose from the dressing table and moved to the full-length mirror. She corrected her posture, smoothed the ivory satin of her gown with gloved hands, and spoke to her reflection. "I will carry myself with quiet grace. I will give every appearance of a docile, compliant bride. And I vow it, I *will* hold my tongue."

Kat flopped onto the bed with a groan. "We're doomed."

Her little sister was right. In one way or another, Louisa was doomed. She had always expected to marry for love. To be courted by a gentleman who admired her for her mind and spirit, not despite them. A gentleman whose intelligence and principles deserved her admiration in equal measure.

Someone who loved her for herself, not for what society wished her to be.

It wasn't a duke who'd be murdered tonight, but Louisa's own hopes of a loving marriage. And the man holding the sword to her breast was the cruel, heartless Duke of Thorndale.

Oh, how she loathed the man.

Louisa glanced at the lump of burned shortbread. Perhaps she ought to give it a try, just in case. If some ancient Scottish superstition had even the slightest chance to save them, who was she to decline?

Before she could reach for it, however, their younger brother Harold called up from the bottom of the stairwell. "Lou-EEE-saah! The Carvilles' carriage is here for you."

It was time.

"Try not to look so glum," Maggie said. "It's nearly Christmas."

"Lucky for us it is." Kat propped her chin in her hand. "Because this family needs a miracle."

Chapter Two

Louisa's pulse quickened as she entered the Carville House ballroom. How she would miss this—the lively music, the company of friends, the holiday scents of nutmeg and evergreen in the air. Most of all, she'd miss the atmosphere of excitement and possibility. There was nothing like a ball to make one feel alive.

She prayed this ball wouldn't be her last.

As soon as they could safely escape, she and Fiona withdrew to a corner of the ballroom. Upon Louisa's arrival, they'd exchanged the usual pleasantries. But with Lord and Lady Carville nearby, they hadn't had an opportunity to properly *talk*.

And oh, did Louisa need to *talk*.

If this snag-a-suitor plan was to have any chance of success, she needed her friend's help. As the daughter of a lord, Fiona's connections were far superior. She could introduce Louisa to the most eligible wealthy gentlemen in attendance. Many of the landed gentry had gone to their country estates for the holidays, but the best of the rest would be present tonight. First sons, widowers, new-money families without country estates of their own. Surely *some* of the gentlemen would be in the market for a wife.

"Fiona, please. I must beg your assistan—"

Her friend clutched Louisa's wrist. "He's here."

Louisa blinked, confused. "Who's here?"

"Ralph. He's here. I saw him just outside."

"*Ralph?* Surely you don't mean Ralph-Your-Father's-Land-Steward's-Son Ralph."

A rosy glow brightened Fiona's cheeks. "Yes, that Ralph. *My* Ralph."

Dear Fiona. As the son of her father's land agent, Ralph was hopelessly beneath a lord's daughter in class—but hearts didn't obey society's rules. The two had been in love for years.

"This is our chance," Fiona whispered. "We're eloping tonight."

"*Eloping?*" In Louisa's surprise, she forgot to lower her voice. After a hasty look about them, she continued in a murmur. "Why didn't you tell me this?"

"You're my closest friend. But as much as I trust you, I didn't dare let slip any hint of our plans. Not to anyone. Please don't be cross with me. Tell me you understand."

"I could never be cross with you. And of course I understand."

Louisa understood better than her friend could know. She'd been keeping her own secrets from Fiona—namely her father's dire financial situation and the Ward family's likely departure from London. The first was too embarrassing to admit, and as for the second . . . She'd been so hoping that a miracle would save them.

Her miracle was slipping away by the second. If Fiona left the ball, who would introduce Louisa to eligible gentlemen?

"I need your help." Fiona pressed her dance card into Louisa's hand. "Please. Will you take my dances? Tell my partners I've retired upstairs with a headache. That way they won't search for me and bring my absence to Mama's attention. She's too occupied with hostess duties to notice otherwise."

"But—"

"Just until the midnight supper. Midnight is when the Royal Mail coach departs. It's the fastest way to the Scottish border. Once we've left London, they'll have no hope of catching us."

"Oh, Fiona."

"Don't worry. Mama and Papa will forgive me. I know they will. They've always liked Ralph. And it's nearly Christmas. Who can be angry at Christmas?" Fiona looked over her shoulder. "I must leave at once. He'll be waiting on me."

"But—"

But what? What could Louisa say to her friend? *Throw away your own long-awaited happiness to give me a slim chance at my own?* No. Of course not. "Go, then. Run to him. I'll make excuses for you."

"What a good friend you are." Fiona gave her a quick, fierce hug. "I only wish you could be at the wedding to serve as my maid of honor."

She smiled. "I demand to be godmother to your firstborn instead."

"Done." With one last squeeze of her hand, Fiona slipped away.

Once her friend disappeared, Louisa was left holding the full dance card. Dread crept through her veins. Fiona always made a habit of engaging the least eligible, most undesirable dance partners. No potential suitors. With her heart already given elsewhere, she'd been trying to *avoid* a proposal.

Louisa looked down at the list. It proved even worse than she'd feared.

The quadrille was promised to Mr. Younge, an aging widower with no plans to remarry. Fiona had given the country dance to a fourth son of an earl with no inheritance, destined for the clergy. And her third set belonged to Mr. Haverton—a dear man and "confirmed bachelor" who would have no interest in Louisa, nor indeed, any lady at all.

After Mr. Haverton's dances came the supper set, a waltz just before midnight. Fiona had promised to dance with . . .

She peered hard at the name written in close, severe script.

No.

It couldn't be. The man was all the way up in Yorkshire, wasn't he?

Louisa blinked hard and looked again, hoping the scrawled letters might have rearranged themselves in the meantime. Fate couldn't be *this* cruel.

The midnight waltz was promised to none other than—

"His Grace, the Duke of Thorndale."

Chapter Three

H is Grace, the Duke of Thorndale."

For a long moment, James didn't move. To the assembly, he probably appeared haughty or displeased. In truth, he needed a moment to recognize the grandiose title as his.

God, how he wished it wasn't.

He was never meant to be a duke.

Never meant for London, never meant for the *ton*, never meant for restrictive tailcoats and pinching boots. He was too big, too rough-mannered, too impatient. He belonged in an oat field in the North Riding, his sleeves turned up to the elbow and his boots six inches deep in mud.

St. John ought to have been here tonight. While James was learning how to manage his father's land, his brother had been prepared to assume their uncle's title through years of education and training in comportment. But St. John was dead, and James was the duke, and no amount of wishing or praying could change it. Lord knew he'd tried both.

Get on with it, then.

He'd avoided balls since arriving in Town, but the Carvilles were distant relations. Their invitation was one he couldn't decline.

He took a wineglass from a passing servant's tray and downed the contents in a single, uncouth gulp. Already, he heard rumors buzzing around him, pricking at his skin like wasps.

He had come to London for two—and *only* two—reasons. First, sorting out the estate finances. Second, suffering through his obligatory presentation at Court.

He explained these two—and *only* two—reasons clearly, repeatedly, to anyone who asked.

So, naturally, the entire *ton* had decided he was in London to find a bride.

And they made certain he didn't lack for candidates. Every marriageable lady he encountered flattered and fawned over him. They made excuses to take his arm and praised graces he didn't have. They declared a long-held desire to live a stone's throw from the barren Yorkshire moors. They'd been *yearning* for the rustic life, they all insisted. How *charming* it must be.

He knew what they wanted. It wasn't the country life, and it certainly wasn't him—it was the title of duchess. To a one, they would have leaped into his carriage the following day with nary an idea of what they'd agreed to take on.

And then, once they'd given him the requisite heir and spare, every one of them would have gone running back to London. If not to the other side of the world.

He knew what happened when a delicate butterfly was carried to the windswept north. She flew south with the next migration. His own mother had proved the rule. Whatever starry-eyed courting had caught her in London, it faded when Northern reality dawned. And nothing in Yorkshire had been enough to make her stay.

James hadn't been enough to make her stay.

Infatuation, romance—they had no place on his list, this year or any year. When he eventually married, he would only marry a woman he could trust. Someone who said what she meant, who would be loyal to her promises, and who understood what it would mean to share his life.

While the musicians tuned their instruments, he withdrew to the side of the room and stole a glance at the inside of his left cuff, consulting the list of names he'd scrawled there. It was truly unjust that the ladies had dance cards, but the gentlemen were expected to recall their partners from memory.

He'd specifically arranged his dances in advance, calling on the few families in London with whom his family claimed some sort of connection and asking whichever daughter or sister was conveniently present to reserve him a set. He didn't want to find himself ambushed again, the way he had been at the Hadleigh party. How was he to know the man had nine daughters? He wouldn't have dreamed a man *could* have nine daughters.

James lumbered through the first few sets without incident. A miracle. Then again, those were the easy ones, the dances where everyone stood in two lines and moved with painful stodginess, and he could muddle through by watching the gentleman next to him.

Next, the true test: the waltz.

Fortunately, his partner was to be Miss Fiona Carville, his hosts' daughter and his second cousin, thrice removed. Or was it his third cousin, twice removed?

He scanned the ballroom. Miss Carville was a wisp of a young woman with coppery hair, if memory served. He would have to take care not to tread on her foot, lest he crush her toes to splinters.

"Your Grace?"

James turned on his heel. He found a young woman standing before him, and she certainly wasn't Fiona Carville. Her hair wasn't copper, but a glossy, rich chestnut brown. And though she was small of stature, there was nothing wispy about her whatsoever. She claimed the space she occupied, without apology.

And by God, she was fair. Her features were appealing in a way that defied passive admiration. He found himself chasing down her beauty, his gaze roaming from a wide mouth to pink cheeks to dark eyes framed by even darker lashes. James couldn't quite identify the source of her loveliness.

Then again, where was the beauty of a Yorkshire moor? Hiding in a patch of sky? Behind a craggy rock or beneath a bit of heather? No. The effect came from all of it, all together. The way it made his chest expand. The way it scrubbed all worries from his mind.

The way it took his breath away.

"Your Grace." She made a deep curtsy.

He nodded in return. "I am at your service, Miss . . ."

"Ward," she said. "Miss Louisa Ward."

"Have we been introduced? I can't place the name." He was certain it wasn't written on the inside of his cuff. If he'd met this young woman, he would recall her.

"No. We haven't been introduced." Something tugged at her lips. A smile of sorts, or an attempt at one. More of a berry-pink curve with no feeling behind it. It set him on guard. He'd seen a great many of those thin, false smiles lately, and he was learning to despise them. Sincerity was rarer in London than Bengal tigers, he'd come to believe.

He had a sinking feeling about Miss Louisa Ward.

"I'm a friend of Miss Carville's," she said. "She's retired with a headache, I'm afraid, and she asked me to take her dances."

And there it was. The transparent excuse. However, this particular maneuver was new.

"How convenient," he replied.

"Convenient? That's not the word I'd use to describe a friend's illness."

"I simply meant it's rather fortunate, isn't it, that you would be unpartnered for this set and willing to step in for her. Rather a coincidence."

Too great a coincidence to be believed.

Breathtaking or not, she was like all the others he'd encountered since arriving in London. Insincere, scheming, and angling for a chance at a duke. The only difference?

For once, James was disappointed.

"Miss Ward, I'm certain your friend is heartened to have your assistance, but there is no need to sacrifice your supper set for my benefit. I will release you, and you may choose a partner of your liking."

"Your Grace is most generous to suggest it, but—"

"Truly, I insist."

The woman refused to take the hint. Instead, she dug the heels of her silk slippers into the parquet. "You don't seem to understand, Your Grace. Miss Carville asked me to take her dances. I promised my friend, and I always keep my promises."

He nearly laughed aloud. In the middle of this brazen ruse, she would paint herself as loyal and honest? A fine joke, that.

The music began. He didn't suppose there was any way to escape this without creating a scene. Unpracticed as his manners were, even James knew that to walk away would be the height of ungentlemanly behavior.

"Well, then." With a sigh he didn't attempt to suppress, he offered her his arm. "Shall we have it done with?"

Chapter Four

$\mathcal{A}$s they joined the waltz, Louisa seethed in three-quarter time.

Shall. We. Have. It. Done. With.

The Duke of Thorndale had actually spoken those words. Aloud. To her. All of them, in that order, without a hint of irony.

Really. *Really.*

And of course he couldn't place her name. Why should he know the name of a family he stood on the cusp of evicting from their home? He probably ruined so many lives, he couldn't recall them all.

An indignant growl rose in her throat. She wrestled it down.

Louisa, you must control your emotions.

Fiona's future depended on this, she reminded herself. Nothing less could have convinced her to waltz with this callous, horrid man. Unjustly enough, his outward appearance didn't reflect the man inside. Which was to say, he lacked horns, a forked tongue, and festering boils.

He was, much as it pained her to admit it, handsome. Not overly so. His looks were less tufted velvet armchair and more country church bench. Solidly crafted and made to age well over decades. His brown hair was a touch overgrown, curling behind his ear. Had he no valet to tell him it needed cutting?

He caught her staring. She wanted to disappear.

The next quarter hour stretched before her like a sentence of fifteen years' hard labor. Worse, afterward he would take her in to supper and attend her throughout the meal.

Unless, that was, he showed his true colors before the entire assembly and abandoned her with no regard for ballroom etiquette. She wouldn't put it past him. He wasn't making the slightest attempt to converse with her, merely pushing her about the ballroom like a mulish schoolboy forced into dancing with his sister.

After a seemingly endless silence, she couldn't hold her tongue any longer. She perked and said brightly, "Why, yes. I *am* enjoying the evening. Thank you so much for asking, Your Grace."

"I didn't ask anything."

"Precisely." Louisa sighed. "A bit of conversation is typical in such settings, no matter how perfunctory."

"Yes, I suppose you have the usual questions for me. All the ladies do. 'Is it true I've inherited half the North Riding? Do I mean to marry this year? How do I find London?' I'll spare you the trouble of asking. No to the first, no to the second. As for Town, I find I detest it."

"*Detest* it? That's a rather harsh judgment."

"It's an accurate one. The place is rife with scheming and rumor. Every encounter is composed of innuendo and pretense. No one says what they truly mean."

Louisa was suppressing several of her own true opinions at that moment. "What a pity you've formed such a poor opinion of London society. Perhaps you should be meeting different people."

He gave her a withering look. "No doubt."

Insufferable man.

When the dance began, Louisa had harbored a sliver of hope that the duke might prove more generous in person than he had been in correspondence. Perhaps she could explain her family's situation and persuade him to give her father a reprieve.

That hope had been foolish, clearly. The duke was not more generous in person. He was worse. Imperious, arrogant, inflexible. And *proud* of it.

"You've grown quiet," he said. "Has my honesty shocked you, Miss Ward?"

"To the contrary, Your Grace. I'm not shocked by you in the least."

"Good. I wasn't raised to tell falsehoods."

What was he insinuating? "Neither was I. And I'll thank you to not insult my parents with the suggestion. They are the best of people. Kind and decent. They don't deserve your scorn, nor your—" Louisa bit her tongue so hard she tasted blood. "Kindly forget I suggested conversation. There's no need for it."

"I concur."

"We've nothing in common, and little to discuss."

"Agreed."

"After all," she went on, "it's not as though either of us wishes to establish an acquaintance."

"I—" He cut off abruptly and peered down at her. "Wait. You said you *don't* wish to establish an acquaintance."

Louisa wasn't sure how she could possibly be clearer. "After this dance concludes, I doubt we shall ever see one another again, and I imagine we will be equally relieved."

He stared at something across the room. "Interesting."

She laughed a little. "Something *interesting*? In *London*? How shocked you must be."

"Indeed." He tilted his head. "You see, I *thought* I would be relieved to part ways with you. Suddenly, I'm reconsidering."

Now Louisa was the shocked one. Reconsidering? What on earth could that mean?

She was saved from having to puzzle it out. The dance finally—*finally*—twirled to an end.

The duke made a rough bow. Louisa curtsied with relief. The ordeal was over.

Or it *would* be over, as soon as he released her hand. Which he showed no intention of doing.

Instead, he nodded toward the dining room. "Allow me to escort you in to supper."

"Thank you, no."

The guests would notice her absence, but Louisa would make some excuse. A torn hem, or a need for fresh air.

She could still salvage the evening. This was the final set she'd promised to take for Fiona. Surely other gentlemen would notice her now that she'd danced with a duke. She wouldn't lack for partners the rest of the night. It gave her some satisfaction to think the Duke of Thorndale would be doing her a favor, unwittingly.

Despite everything he threatened to take from her, she was stealing something back.

Maybe all wasn't lost.

"If not supper," he said, "save me another dance."

Another dance? Louisa was astonished. After a moment, she laughed, painfully aware of how girlish and nervous she sounded. "You don't want that."

"I know what I want." His intense gaze pinned her slippers to the floor.

The other couples had gone in to supper, leaving them alone in an empty ballroom. A cavernous space, with nowhere to hide. Only the servants remained, clearing away the drained punch bowls and picked-over trays of sweets.

And still, the duke had not released her hand. "I've been in London nearly a month, and I'm starved for honest conversation."

If he was starved for honesty, Louisa could have offered him a heaping plate. She would have loved to gut him with sharp words for calling in forgotten debts and excoriate him for his callous treatment of his uncle's dear friend. But if she started, she wouldn't know how to end—and she couldn't afford to cause a scene.

"Your Grace," she said quietly, "perhaps your recent arrival in Town has left you unaware of social custom. A gentleman does not ask a lady for two sets in the same evening. Not unless he intends to . . ." *Not unless he intends to propose.* The words were too absurd to speak aloud. "People will talk."

"I don't care what people say."

"It's all very well for a duke to shrug off gossip, but a young unmarried gentlewoman does not have that luxury."

"Surely a young unmarried gentlewoman would only be elevated by a duke's attention."

He left her no excuse but the bluntest one. "I don't *want* to dance with you," she said through gritted teeth. "I find you insufferable and arrogant. You say you detest London? Well, I detest people who detest everything."

"Hold a moment. I never said I detest *everything*."

"I suppose you don't. You clearly have a high opinion of your own character. You believe yourself above everyone in the room."

"Not above them. Merely apart from them. I don't belong in this place. I've no patience for empty pleasantries."

"That explains why you skipped over them and went straight to unpleasantries." She tried to master her anger, with little success. "You insulted not only me, but my friend, my family, and the place I call home. As for your attentions, there are doubtless many young ladies here who'd eagerly queue up to experience this dizzying 'elevation' you describe. I am not one of them."

He regarded her for a long moment. "I believe that you aren't."

"I'm glad we understand one another." She tried to slide her hand from his.

He held her in place. "Wait."

She stared at their linked hands, baffled. His grip was firm. Not so firm as to be controlling, but strong enough to communicate resolve.

When he spoke again, his manner was entirely different. Not stiff and disapproving, but open and familiar. "Listen, we've begun all wrong, and that's my fault. You are correct. I treated you abominably, to my regret and my shame. But if you grant me another dance, I promise to behave myself. Or at least, to misbehave in different ways."

A half smile played about his lips. One that made distressing hints at warmth and humor.

No, no. Thorndale wasn't warm. He wasn't amusing. He was a villain with a heart of ice. A cruel, unforgiving man who meant to take her family's house—sagging floors, worn carpets, and all—out from under their feet.

"Your Grace, I don't—"

"You say you want nothing to do with me. Strange as it must sound, that makes me want to know everything about you. I can't speak for the strutting peacocks of Mayfair, but I appreciate a woman who speaks her mind."

Please don't say that.

Louisa's chest squeezed. Those were the words she'd been longing to hear—from any other man in England.

She had to leave. He had her utterly flustered. She needed to hide, compose herself, and return to the ballroom ready to be someone different. A demure, compliant lady who could catch the interest of a marriageable gentleman.

"The retiring room," she stammered. "My air is torn. That is, I need some fresh hem. I can't—" She swallowed hard. "I just can't do this."

She tugged hard, yanking her hand from the duke's, then made a drunken spin in her quest to escape. Her flight was impeded by an unsuspecting manservant bearing a cut crystal bowl half emptied of its contents.

Its red, sloshing, liquid contents.

As she and the servant collided, Louisa caught the scents of cloves and cinnamon and claret. Mulled wine.

The wave of red crashed upon the white shores of her gown. And her hopes of a Christmas miracle drowned.

Chapter Five

*D*amn and blast.

James had seen it coming. He'd reached to catch her by the shoulders and draw her back before the wine made its inevitable cascade.

Unfortunately, he'd been an instant too late.

The panicked servant mumbled something about fetching bicarbonate of soda before fleeing the scene.

James turned Miss Ward to face him. She stood frozen with shock, lips parted and eyes unfocused. A red droplet caught in her eyelash, then quivered and fell, trickling down her cheek. He whipped out his handkerchief and attempted to blot the dark liquid soaking into her gown. He only succeeded in smearing the wine about. No amount of bicarbonate of soda would remove this stain.

Miss Ward stiffened beneath his hand.

James realized that in his efforts to remove the stain, he'd been vigorously patting her bosom. God, he was a lumbering ox. This was why he belonged in an oat field, rather than a ballroom.

What would a proper duke do in this moment?

Damned if he knew. Anything else, he supposed.

"Right." He wadded up the handkerchief. "Which apology should I start with? The wine or the groping?"

"Don't bother with either of them." She took his handkerchief and dabbed at her gown.

"Then allow me to help."

"There's nothing to be done. I'll have to go home."

"If you give me your dance card, I'll make excuses to your other partners."

"I don't have any other partners. And it wouldn't matter if I did. It's over." She stared numbly at her gown. "It's all over."

"There will be other balls."

"Not for me."

James sincerely doubted that would be the case. She was much too pretty and lively to sit home alone. "Did you arrive with your family?" he asked.

"The Carvilles sent a carriage for me." She put her fingers to her temple and muttered a mild oath. "They're busy hosting supper. I don't want to trouble them."

"I'll call for my own carriage, then."

"But—"

"I insist."

She exhaled with resignation. "Very well. I don't seem to have any alternative."

"Is there someone to accompany you? A companion, a chaperone."

She shook her head.

"What about Miss Carville?"

"She can't." Her reply was swift, sharp. "She's taken ill, remember?"

"Yes, of course. A headache." James winced, recalling his rudely expressed skepticism. Neither Miss Carville nor Miss Ward had deserved his scorn. "If there's no one to accompany you, I'll see you home myself."

Her eyes flared with alarm. "You can't. *We* can't."

"No one will notice we've gone."

"Of course they will notice we've gone," she hissed. "This is London society. People here *live* to notice such things."

He steered her back into the entrance hall. "Calm yourself. I'm not going to try anything untoward."

"If you did try something untoward, you would regret it. I have three brothers. I know how to throw a punch."

"Warning received. And heeded." James smiled to himself. The more she challenged him, the more intrigued he became. He wasn't afraid of a few prickly edges. In his experience, the thorniest flowers were usually the ones most worth picking. "Where's your cloak?"

"The servants took it when I arrived."

"No matter." He shook off his tailcoat and wrapped it about her slender shoulders.

"You don't have to do this."

"Oh, but I do." He tugged the lapels, drawing the coat tight. "You might know all about London society, Miss Ward, but you don't know me. When responsibility falls into my hands, I see matters through. Rest assured, your honor will remain intact. I'll whisk you home, return before they've even finished supper, and explain to Lady Carville afterward."

"But—"

"Anyone who dares to draw salacious conclusions will answer to me." Her gown and her evening had already been ruined. He'd be damned if he'd allow her reputation to be ruined, too. "And I'll make the situation clear to your father, if that's your concern."

"My father?" Her head jerked in surprise. "You mean to speak with my father?"

"Of course I do. If I'm delivering a young, unmarried woman home, I could scarcely do otherwise. Do you expect me to merely slow the team and heave you out onto the pavement as the carriage rolls past? Even I'm not *that* ill-mannered."

She studied him. "I suppose you're right. No one's that horrid. Not even you."

James was vaguely aware of the insult, but his attention was occupied elsewhere. She held the two sides of his coat together with one hand, and her middle fingertip worried a single brass button. Tipping it back, then forth, and then back and forth again. A subtle, unconscious gesture on her part, but one that set continents shifting in his chest. Somehow his mouth watered and his tongue dried simultaneously.

He'd promised he wouldn't *try* anything untoward. He hadn't said anything about not wanting to. If kissing her was anything like conversing with her, it would drive him mad in multiple ways.

After a pause, she straightened. "Very well, then."

Well, hark the herald angels sing. It had taken her long enough.

James escorted her out into the brisk, wintry night. The carriage wasn't standing at the ready. It wouldn't be, only halfway through the ball. He led her down to the corner and around to the mews, where the horses and carriages waited. There, they faced down an endless row of black coaches. In this lighting, they all looked identical.

Damn it.

James shuffled forward in the dark, inspecting the side panel of each carriage they passed.

Miss Ward hunched next to him. She whispered, "Why are we creeping along like this?"

"I'm looking for my coach."

"You don't know what your coach looks like?"

"Of course I know what my coach looks like. It looks like a dashed coach. Black, wheels, sides, doors. At home, it's the only one for miles around. I've never needed to sort it out from a crowd." He moved on to the next carriage. "I'm searching for the one with the Thorndale crest."

"I'll help. What does the crest look like?"

James tried to remember. Was it two lions? A lion and a

dragon? Good Lord, the crest could have featured a pat of sheep dung, for all he knew. "I'm not certain."

"What kind of duke doesn't know his own crest?"

"The kind of duke who was never supposed to be a duke at all," he grumbled. "That's what kind." James often felt out of his element these days, but he seldom felt quite this stupid.

She tugged on his sleeve and pointed. "That must be it."

He squinted. Yes, that one was his. He recalled it now. No lions, no dragons, no sheep dung. Just roses. Three of them, intertwined. "How did you know?"

She shrugged. "Roses, *Thorn*dale . . . They go together."

Fortunately, his team was hitched—and impatient, judging by how the carriage jostled on its springs. Unfortunately, the driver was nowhere to be found.

"Where's the coachman?" she asked.

"God knows." Annoyed, James set his jaw. "I'll go in search of him. Wait in the coach. You'll be warmer inside."

He reached for the door latch and flung it open, preparing to hand Miss Ward into the cab. However, when he pulled the door open wide, they were met with a startling sight— a bare arse, humping enthusiastically between a pair of fleshy female thighs.

"Close the bloody door," the humping arse's owner shouted. "I told you, you'll have your turn at her next."

Beneath him, the unseen woman moaned with feigned delight. "Ooh. Ooh. Come to me, you magnificent stag."

James shut the door.

Good God. He blinked at his hand on the door latch, not knowing how to look at Miss Ward. He'd coaxed her away from the ball alone, vowing not to damage her reputation. And less than five minutes later, he'd led her skulking down a darkened alleyway and exposed her to a bawdy scene that would no doubt leave her shocked, confused, and possibly scarred for life.

"Oh goodness." Behind him, she broke into giddy laughter.

Perhaps she was not quite scarred for life, then. The tightness in his chest eased. His anger, however, did not abate. James didn't know how a proper duke would handle this situation, but the rough-mannered Northerner in him had a few ideas.

"Kindly face the other direction, Miss Ward." He turned her by the shoulders to face a brick wall. "And cover your ears, if you will. Matters are about to get ugly."

Chapter Six

When the Duke of Thorndale issued his command, Louisa promptly disobeyed it. Not only did she *not* cover her ears—she turned to peek over her shoulder, too. She wasn't going to miss out on whatever "ugly matters" might happen next.

"Get the fuck off her." The duke reached into the carriage and yanked the coachman out by the collar of his livery, tossing him to the ground the way laborers slung bushels of coal. "What the devil do you think you're doing, you rutting swine? And in my coach, no less."

The coachman's lady love slipped out of the carriage, gathered her rumpled clothing about her, and scurried off down the alleyway. Louisa hoped the woman had demanded her fee in advance.

"Y-Your Grace." The man scrambled to right himself and hike his lowered breeches—two activities that did not lend themselves to being accomplished simultaneously. "Let me explain. I . . . We was just—"

The duke only had to nudge him with the toe of his boot to send him sprawling on his bare backside again. "What you're doing is getting out of my sight, you reeking bastard. I advise you not to return. It won't go well for you."

The coachman stumbled off, holding his breeches up with one hand and clutching his aching ribs with the other. Louisa struggled not to laugh.

Then the duke turned, and she whipped her head around so as not to be caught spying. As she did, her cheek grazed the fine wool of his tailcoat. The warmth was a welcome balm for the air's frosty bite—and oh, the coat smelled heavenly. Not of any cologne or fussy pomade, but simply of soap and the night wind. The scent of a man's embrace when he came home from a journey in cold weather, charging through the door red-cheeked and stamping his boots.

Drat. She had to stop thinking like this. She didn't want to accidentally *like* him, in even the smallest degree.

He peeled off his gloves and tossed them into the cab. "At this rate, I'll owe your father a great many explanations."

Yes, Thorndale owed Papa a great many explanations, indeed. Such as why he'd so cruelly called in their debt, with years upon years of interest, ignoring the wishes of his own uncle. And when the duke delivered her home, he would be forced to enter their house and confront the kindhearted, honest man whose entreaties he'd ignored for months. Then he could offer whatever weaselly excuses and explanations he wished. In person.

"I'll have to find another carriage to take you home," he said. "I'm not placing you in a cab that's been defiled that way. It smells like cheap scent and the pox."

"We can take a hackney," she said.

"A *hackney*? I'm not taking you home in a hackney." He made an impatient noise. "Surely we can do better than that."

She stiffened. "A hackney is how I usually travel. My family doesn't keep a coach and team. I know you're a wealthy duke. One who doesn't have to worry about the costermonger's bill coming due. But not every family in London is so fortunate. My father is a third son. No inheritance. He's done better for us than anyone could expect. I'm not ashamed of my family or our circumstances."

"That's not what I meant." He put his hand on her lower back, brusquely guiding her down the alley. "We should do better than a hackney because you deserve better, after this farce of an evening. That's all."

"Oh." Well, with that she would not argue. Her entire family deserved better treatment from his quarter.

"I'm a second son myself," he went on as they ambled down the alleyway. "I wasn't raised with the promise of an inheritance, either. In fact, I had no expectations beyond the life of a gentleman farmer, until . . ." His voice trailed off.

"Until your brother died," she finished for him.

If he was a second son, and now he was the duke, that must mean he'd lost an older brother. Perhaps that fact shouldn't pull at her heart, but it did. People died. Most of her friends had lost a sibling, if not two—some in infancy, some later. But the Ward family had been blessed with good fortune, and Louisa had never known that pain. She couldn't imagine the desolation of losing one of her beloved brothers or sisters. She wouldn't wish it on her worst enemy.

The duke *was* her worst enemy, and her heart ached for his loss anyway.

She allowed her arm to touch his. "I'm so sorry."

A brusque nod was his only reply.

Louisa was left to wonder how grown men found the smallest words the most difficult ones to say. "Thanks," "please," "sorry" . . . From the way their tongues tripped over the syllables, you'd think those words were Latin names for species of exotic fungi. When it came to "love," some of them lost the power of speech altogether.

They reached the main thoroughfare at the other end of the alley. A few hackneys passed by, but none of them slowed at Thorndale's signal.

"At this time of night, I suppose they will all be occupied," she said.

"There must be something." He pushed his hand through his dark hair, dislodging a flurry of white crystals.

"Oh," Louisa breathed. "It's snowing."

She raised her arm and watched as twirling snowflakes came to land on the dark sleeve of his tailcoat. The sight sent an irrepressible, childlike happiness through her. She'd always loved snow. They seldom saw it in London this time of year.

She arrived at a sudden decision. "I'll walk home."

"What?"

"Truly, you've made every attempt at gallantry. I'll release you from the rest of it. You should return to the ball. You will leave the rest of your partners—and their mothers—disappointed indeed. Never mind me. I can walk on my own."

Louisa truly *could* have walked home on her own. She knew Mayfair. She loved Mayfair. A walk through falling snow would be a bittersweet farewell to the place she'd always called home.

However, a solitary stroll wasn't quite what she was angling for at the moment.

"Walk on your own?" he echoed. "Don't be absurd."

"My house isn't so very far from here."

"I don't care if it's a distance of ten paces," he said with gruff impatience. "I won't allow you to walk home unaccompanied."

Oh, I know you won't. In fact, I'm counting on it.

"But, Your Gra—"

"Stop arguing. I told you, when I'm decided, I am decided." He took her by the wrist and drew her arm through his. "If you insist on walking, I'm walking with you."

She sighed theatrically. "If you insist."

Inwardly, she cheered at the small triumph. She curled her fingers over the crisp linen of his shirtsleeve. His forearm was hard as rock, but perhaps there was softness in him somewhere.

Like Papa, Thorndale was a younger son. He'd known the pain of loss. He had *some* measure of generosity in his character. Of course, offering a lady his coat was one thing, and forgiving a debt of several thousand pounds was quite another. But even though he had refused her father's written petitions, maybe—just maybe—the duke might be persuaded to reconsider face-to-face. It was almost Christmas, after all.

Knowing his poor opinion of London ladies, Louisa didn't dare explain the situation and plead with him outright. If she tried, Thorndale would think their ballroom meeting was some kind of ruse. He would accuse her of lying and scheming to achieve her own ends.

But if she could make him understand, in even the smallest part, what their home meant to the family, and what Mayfair meant to her . . . Perhaps by the end of their walk, when he met with Papa, his stony heart might be moved.

Perhaps.

Louisa knew she was piling all her eggshell-fragile hopes into one last duke-shaped basket. But this was her only remaining strategy. She couldn't give up without trying, no matter how small the odds.

From the outset, she had known it would be tonight, or never.

Well, tonight wasn't over.

Not quite yet.

Chapter Seven

$\mathcal{F}$or once, the city was quiet. Empty. Cold swept through the streets like a broom, leaving the air clear and fresh. No fog or choking soot.

Looking around, James could almost deem this small corner of London pretty.

Then again, perhaps it only seemed pretty because Miss Louisa Ward was nearby.

As they walked, James found his gaze drawn to her, no matter how he attempted to train his eyes elsewhere. He couldn't help himself. The chill made pink cheeks pinker, red lips redder, and bright eyes brighter. She'd looked fetching in the ballroom, but now he felt dangerously close to . . .

Fetched.

He gave himself a little shake.

She glanced at him. "Do you want your coat back?"

"No." James recoiled at the mere suggestion. He'd eat a Christmas dinner of pickled slugs before asking a lady to return his coat. "What kind of gentleman do you take me for?" After a moment's pause, he added, "Don't answer that."

"I only asked because you're shivering."

"I am not shivering."

"Oh please. It's cold. There's no shame in saying so. No use denying it, either." She ran her gloved fingers over his exposed wrist, where every last one of his hairs stood on end. "I can feel your gooseflesh."

That's not from the cold, love. "I'm a North Yorkshire man. This is tropical for me. What I can't comprehend is why you want to walk home in this weather."

"It's my last chance to enjoy Mayfair in the snow."

"Does that mean you're leaving London for the remainder of the winter?"

"I am leaving London for the foreseeable future. Perhaps forever."

Forever?

That was quite a word to leave dangling without explanation, but James wasn't the sort to pry. He despised gossip. Unless she chose to share them, her private family matters should remain precisely that—private.

"I'm envious," he said.

"How could you be envious? If I had your means, I should never leave London."

He scowled. "What can you find to like about it? It's filthy, it's crowded, it smells. One can't see the sky. I can scarcely breathe—not in the streets, nor in a ballroom. My only purpose in coming was to complete some business. I have a few properties to sell, a few matters to settle. Then I can go home to Yorkshire having rid myself of all ties to the place. I intend to leave this city without looking back. I could never feel easy here."

Perhaps he should reconsider that last part of his statement. He was feeling easier by the moment. It was a relief to unburden himself of his thoughts, after weeks of being polite.

"You only hate London because you don't know it," she said. "It's more than balls and parties and teas. So much happens. Museums, parks, concerts, the theater. To judge the city so meanly on so little experience . . . Well, it's stubborn and ignorant." She bit her lip. "I warned you, I was raised to speak freely."

"Yes. That's why I'd rather be here with you than back in the Carvilles' ballroom."

"In my experience, most gentlemen don't appreciate a lady who voices contrary opinions."

"In *my* experience, ladies of the *ton* don't offer opinions, contrary or otherwise. You can't imagine how much 'oh yes, Your Grace'–ing I've endured in recent weeks. It's driven me mad with boredom. When everyone hops to agree with you, conversation is dull indeed."

"I suppose I'm never boring, at least."

He chuckled. "Certainly not that I've seen."

She lapsed into silence, and he took the opportunity to gaze at her. As many glimpses as he'd stolen, he was becoming a habitual thief. Every time they passed under a streetlamp, her skin glowed like a Dutch artist's masterpiece.

"So you claim to appreciate argument," she said, "but are you open-minded? Are you willing to let your opinion be swayed?"

"On rare occasion," he admitted grudgingly. "But only when presented with sound reasoning and compelling evidence."

"That's settled, then." Her chin lifted. "I'm going to present my most compelling evidence, make my soundly reasoned argument—and prove that you're wrong about London."

"How do you mean to do that?"

"I'm going to give you a tour of Mayfair. Tonight."

"What? No." He drew to a halt and planted his boots on the snow-dusted pavement. "I am delivering you home at once. It's already grown unforgivably late."

"No, it's perfect. This might be my last chance to see the

places I love." She arched an eyebrow, and a smile touched her lips. "Besides, you can't take me home if I haven't told you where I live."

Damn and blast. She had him there.

He didn't know their destination, and honor wouldn't allow him to abandon her. If she wished, she could drag him all over London like a dog on a leash.

What was worse, he couldn't bring himself to be disappointed about it. The prospect of spending more time with her—alone—warmed his body in ways no woolen tailcoat could do.

Her eyes gleamed with self-satisfaction. "It would seem you are at my mercy, Your Grace."

In more ways than you could know, Miss Ward.

"If we're going to do this, you must promise me one thing. I don't want to hear 'Your Grace' again for the remainder of the night."

"Then how would you have me address you? As Thorndale?"

"God, no. Call me James."

"Is that your family name?"

"No, it's my given name."

Her surprise was evident. "Really?"

"Don't sound so shocked. James is a common enough name."

"Well, yes, of course. But I didn't think dukes were ever addressed by their Christian names. Not by mere acquaintances, anyway."

He made a show of looking up and down the empty street, and then leaned close to murmur his reply. "I won't tell if you don't."

She smiled. "Very well then, James."

Hallelujah. Hearing his name from her lips set him free, somehow. He felt like a boy shedding his school uniform on the last day of Easter term.

"Come along, then." She took him by the hand and tugged. "Prepare to be amazed."

He already was, rather.

And if he wasn't exceedingly careful to keep himself in check . . . ? Before the night was out, he just might amaze her, too.

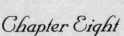

Chapter Eight

*I*f she was going to show him Mayfair as she lived and breathed it, Louisa decided she might as well begin at the beginning.

"This way, then." She waved him down the street, around a few turnings, and halted in front of the church. "St. George's Hanover Square."

He stared up at the columned edifice, unimpressed. "You know, we do have churches in Yorkshire. Ones that aren't penned in like chickens and stained with soot."

"Yes, but this church is ours. My parents were married here, as were my grandparents, and my eldest brother just last year, a few weeks before his regiment was sent to Canada. It's a family tradition, I suppose you could say." A tradition Louisa wouldn't be continuing, sadly. She'd be married in some tiny chapel in Jersey, if she married at all. "I was christened here, too. All of us Ward children were."

"All of you? How many are there?"

"Six. Three girls, three boys. Francis—Frank—is the oldest. Then me, Margaret, and Katherine all in a row. Poor Frank despaired of ever having a brother until Harold finally came along. William's the youngest, just seven." They turned and walked on. "And yourself?"

"I don't have much family to speak of. My father's gone, and my brother, as well."

"Your mother?"

"Departed, in the noneuphemistic sense. She wasn't happy in the match. Once she'd done her duty and given my father two sons, she ran off to New York. I haven't seen her since I was a young child."

"I'm so sorry."

His arm tightened beneath her hand. "I won't bore you with the details."

"You're not boring me. Were you close to your brother?"

"When we were boys, yes. But then St. John was sent to live with my uncle, so he could prepare to assume the title. I stayed with my father and learned to manage the land."

"Goodness. That sounds terribly lonely."

"Not really."

"Just the two of you on a farm in the middle of Yorkshire?"

"It was the two of us on a respectable holding in the north of Yorkshire, with tenant farmers, a village nearby, and a market town eight miles down the road."

"*Eight miles* to the nearest market town?"

"It's an easy distance. With a cart and team, it's less than two hours of travel."

"Two hours, there and back?"

"Two hours each way."

She was aghast. "How can it possibly take two hours to travel eight miles in a cart?"

He scoffed at her question. "I'm going to guess you've never seen a road in Yorkshire."

Yes, he guessed correctly. With the exception of a few visits to friends in Surrey, Louisa had never seen a road outside Middlesex.

Imagine. Two hours' travel, just to reach the nearest market. If he was so deluded as to deem that an easy distance, Louisa knew what the next stop on this tour must be.

Bond Street.

The shops were closed at this time of night. Since there

was no traffic, they strolled down the center of the street. As if the world, and all its treasures, belonged to them alone.

The shop fronts had been decorated with swags of Christmas greenery and golden stars. When combined with the glistening layer of snow, it made for an impressive sight, even with all the windows dark.

"Look." She swept her arm in an extravagant arc. "Goods from all over the globe, crammed in this one street. You could purchase a fine Madeira, an exquisite Indian shawl, and a plume from an Australian emu, all in one afternoon."

"I can't imagine *wanting* to buy wine, scarves, and feathers all in one afternoon." His voice deepened. "Not unless I had a very interesting evening planned."

What a rogue he could be. Louisa suspected he was trying to shock her into a missish fluster. She would not give him the satisfaction.

"It's not all exotic wares, of course. There are plenty of boring, practical things to buy, too."

"I can get all the boring, practical things I need in Yorkshire."

"Oh yes," she teased. "At the easy distance of eight miles away. Only two hours by horse and cart!"

Abandoning the argument for the moment, Louisa wandered to the side of the lane. There, she approached a familiar display window and pressed her forehead to the glass until her breath melted a circle in the frost.

"What are we looking at?" He came to her side. "A confectionary, judging by the way you're salivating."

"No." She heaved a wistful, yearning sigh. "It's books. All books."

He knocked a crust of snow from the sign. "So it is."

"It's not the largest of bookshops, of course. The Temple of the Muses and Hatchard's have much wider selections. Nevertheless, this one is my favorite."

He cupped his hands and peered through the window. "It looks a shambles."

"I know. Isn't it wonderful?"

"Must be impossible to find what you're searching for."

"That's why it's wonderful. If it were easy to find the books I *want*, I'd never find the books I didn't know existed, but once I've found them can't live without."

With one last, lingering sigh, she pushed off the window, and together they strolled on.

"If you were going to be stranded on an island," she asked, "what three things would you take?"

He answered without hesitation. "Food, water, and a boat."

"Don't be purposely obtuse. You know what I mean. Assume the island has plenty of food and water, and a ship will be coming to your rescue within the year. Now, what three items would you choose to take with you?"

He jammed his hands in his waistcoat pockets and squinted at the sky for inspiration. "A mermaid."

Louisa rolled her eyes. "That's one. What are the others?"

"Two more mermaids."

"That is a ridiculous answer."

"It isn't, really. It's a much better answer than wine, a shawl, and ostrich feathers."

"Emu," she corrected. "They were emu plumes."

"If you say so. Regardless, it's an absurd question. You should expect an absurd answer."

"It's not an absurd question for me. It's a quite real and pressing dilemma. When we leave for Jersey, I—"

"Jersey? The more-than-halfway-to-France *Isle* of Jersey?"

"Yes. That's the very real island in the question, you see, and within a month I'll be stranded there. When we leave, I'm allowed three trunks, no more. I'll be forced to use one for frocks and stockings and such. For the second,

Mama insists I bring my trousseau. Which will be useless, as there couldn't be any—"

Louisa bit her tongue. She'd been about to opine that there couldn't be any interesting or attractive farmers there, but she happened to be walking with an interesting, attractive farmer at present. One with a devilish sense of humor, a liking for opinionated women, and the brute strength to toss a bare-arsed coachman down the street.

And he smelled divine, too.

Oh dear. She pushed those thoughts aside. Very far aside. All the way to the edge of her mind, where they would hopefully drop off a cliff.

"Anyhow," she went on, "I'm left with exactly one crate in which to fit the remainder of my worldly possessions. It will be books top to bottom, of course. But which ones? I've been in fits trying to choose." A new idea came to her. "Perhaps I'll take the *useful* pieces of the trousseau— some handkerchiefs, a quilt—and then hide books beneath it. Who needs embroidered table linens, anyhow?"

"I couldn't say. But if you want my advice, any modest night rails can go, as well. No newlywed groom wants anything to do with those."

Louisa hoped the darkness concealed her fierce blush. "I suppose I'll always have my family. They'll keep me from dying of boredom, one way or another. We amuse and torment one another endlessly." She laughed to herself. "My sister Kat, alone. She has the wildest notions. Just yesterday, she dug up some book of Scottish witchcraft and made an appalling shortbread."

They walked in silence for a few moments.

"The Isle of *Jersey*," he blurted out. "Why is your family moving to Jersey, of all places?"

Because of you, she wanted to cry. *Because you called in an old debt that was understood to be forgiven. Because my father is insolvent now, and he was forced to take the first situation he was offered. Because our entire family is one of those pesky little business matters you're desperate to have resolved, so you can leave London and never look back.*

She didn't dare speak a word of it aloud. Not now. Not yet. Thus far, she hadn't succeeded in convincing him to rethink anything. Not even his shopping habits.

They stopped where Bond Street ended at Piccadilly.

"St. James's Palace is just down that way." She pointed. "If it were daytime, you could see it from here."

"I've seen it already. From the inside."

"Truly? Was it as grand as they say?"

"I suppose. I chiefly wanted to leave as soon as possible. I prefer the grandeur of nature."

"Nature? Well, then. Let's make a turning here. You can't have a proper tour of Mayfair without a stroll through Hyde Park."

He grabbed her by the arm, holding her back. "No, no, no. We're not going any farther. I've humored you long enough. Now I'm taking you home."

"You can't take me home. You don't know where it is. We've established this, James."

He groaned.

"Now, on to the park."

He stopped her again. "Not yet. At the least, we're finding a place to warm you first. Your nose is red, and your teeth are chattering. When I finally do take you home, it won't be with pneumonia."

"There's nowhere to go at this hour. All the establishments are closed."

He peered down the street in the other direction. "What about down that way? Seems to be a fair bit of coming and going."

"Well, of course, but that's St. James's Street. It's home to all the gentlemen's clubs. White's and Boodle's and so on."

"Ah, yes. They made me a member of one of them. Can't even recall which, honestly."

"You're a duke. I'm certain you'd be welcome in any of them."

"Then let's pay a visit to one, by God. Warm you up."

"Visit one? I've never even walked down St. James's Street before. My mother would never allow it. Too scandalous."

His gaze issued a devilish challenge. "In that case, you have a choice. You can be a good girl and give me your address, so I can take you home to your mother directly. Otherwise, this tour of yours includes St. James's Street, and we're walking down it together. Now."

Chapter Nine

Strolling down St. James's Street on the arm of the Duke of Thorndale . . . Now this was truly something. Sounds of pleasure filtered out from the row of clubs, heightening the excitement of encroaching on the forbidden.

"I think this is the one," James said, stopping on the pavement opposite the club in question. "I seem to recall receiving a notice of some kind. In honor of my uncle's longstanding membership, they'd be pleased to extend me an invitation to join, and so forth. I never did reply, but I suppose they'll admit me just the same." He moved toward the door.

Louisa stayed in place.

"What are you waiting for?" he said. "Let's go in for a bit."

"I'm not allowed to go in. No women are permitted. Well, perhaps some women are permitted, but they wouldn't be respectable women."

"They'll admit you if you're with me. I *am* Thorndale, and that must be good for something."

She stood firm. "I am not the most conventional of women, but even for me, that is a scandal too far. There's too much risk of being recognized. Some kinds of gossip can follow a woman even so far as Jersey."

With a muttered oath, he pushed a hand through his hair.

"Then wait here. I'll be two minutes. If anyone or anything frightens you, shout."

"Shout what?"

He made an aimless gesture. "'Help,' I suppose. Or 'fire' or 'murder.' In a pinch, 'James' would suffice."

She nodded. "'Come to me, you magnificent stag,' it is."

He looked at her and laughed softly. As though he weren't laughing at her joke, but at some joke he'd told himself long ago. "I knew I liked you."

And then he just left her with that staggering rhinoceros of a statement, giving her no choice but to rearrange her heart and mind to accommodate it.

I knew I liked you.

Did he, really? How much would he like her once he learned how they were connected by debt and circumstance? Was she being disloyal to her family if she liked him in return?

She was in so much trouble, and it had nothing to do with standing alone on St. James's Street after midnight.

He conferred with the doorman at the entrance of the club before disappearing inside. True to his word, he emerged moments later with a bottle of brandy under his arm. "Let's go."

Once they'd turned a corner and walked a safe distance from the clubs, they tucked into a darkened doorway that offered some shelter from the wind. From his pocket, James produced a cordial glass and poured her a thimble of brandy. "Here. This should warm you."

Not wanting to look missish, Louisa accepted the glass and downed its contents in one draught. That was a mistake. She very nearly coughed it right back up. She sealed her lips and swallowed with great concentration, forcing the liquid fire down her throat. Her eyes watered. So much for appearing worldly.

He drew a pull of brandy straight from the bottle, and

she found it ridiculously manly and attractive. By the time he poured her a second glass—she sipped it this time—she was growing warm indeed. A blush heated her from the outside in, and the brandy heated her from the inside out. She was hot all over.

Oh Lord. Louisa, stop.

The doorway they shared seemed to be shrinking, pushing them closer and closer together. She felt his gaze on her, and it made her nervous, so she stared into her cordial glass. When she could bear it no more, she lifted her head. Their eyes met and held. Her breathing quickened.

It's the brandy, she told herself. *It's only the brandy that makes him so desperately attractive. It's only the brandy that has you yearning for a kiss.*

No, not *a* kiss.

His kiss.

He took the glass from her and tucked it between two fingers, balancing it easily in the same hand with which he held the brandy bottle.

You can't, you can't. He's the enemy.

The enemy was touching her hair, then her cheek. "You are remarkable."

Remarkable. Not *pretty* or *fetching* or any of the few superficial compliments she'd fielded from men over the years, all of which were quickly followed with the word *but.* Pretty, but outspoken. Fetching, but too forward.

James had called her remarkable, full stop. "But" nothing.

His gaze settled on her lips. He moved toward her with dizzying swiftness, tilting her face to his. She sucked in her breath.

The door to the house swung open, revealing a man in a nightcap and nightclothes. "What's this? Who are you?"

They jolted apart. In wide-eyed panic, they looked to the gentleman, then to each other, and then back to the gentleman again.

Louisa swallowed hard. "Ohhhh . . . G—"

"God rest ye merry, gentlemen," James sang out in a robust baritone. "Let nothing you dismay."

She blinked at him. His elbow dug into her ribs.

In a reluctant soprano, she sang the next line of the carol. "For Jesus Christ our Savior was born on Christmas Day."

He joined in again, and they sang in unison, their voices gaining strength. It was as though they'd reached an understanding—they'd launched into this madness, and they had to finish it. They might as well do so with the full holiday spirit. "To save us all from Satan's power when we were gone astray. Oh tidings of comfort and joy, comfort and joy . . ."

By the end of three verses, they were singing in parts with confidence. Mr. Nightcap's entire household had gathered at the door. At their audience's urging, they followed the first carol with two others, and were forced to exchange many hearty Christmas greetings before making their escape.

They made it all the way down the lane and around a corner before bursting into laughter. It was several moments before either of them could talk.

Louisa wiped tears from her eyes. "That was brilliant. Very quick thinking."

"It would have been a disaster had you not played along."

"For that, you can thank the brandy. Where did you learn to sing like that?"

"Well, the North Riding isn't London. We don't have performance halls, but we do manage to make our own concerts." As they walked, making footprints in the thin layer of snow, he nudged her with his elbow. "You weren't so bad, yourself."

"What fulsome praise."

"I meant it."

She turned to him. "We did sound well together, didn't we?"

She was thrown back to the moment before their impromptu performance, when he'd nearly kissed her in the doorway. Would their lips meld as well as their voices did?

She changed the subject. "We must have done well enough. We got pudding out of it." She held up a slice of dense, plum-studded cake, wrapped in brown paper. "When we reach Hyde Park, we'll have a proper picnic."

Chapter Ten

*T*here now." Once they'd reached the park, Louisa spread her arms and twirled, indicating the glittering splendor of the new-fallen snow. "Even you cannot deny this is splendid."

"Very well. I will concede that London has *some* beauty."

His eyes fixed on her with unnerving intensity. Louisa felt the power of that stare, all the way to her core.

"And now," he said, "you must permit me to have my turn. In the spirit of fair play."

"Your turn? What can you mean?"

"To prove the superiority of the countryside."

She laughed. "I don't know how you mean to accomplish that. I am not in a particular hurry to return home, but I think even my parents would object if I disappeared to Yorkshire."

"We don't have to go to Yorkshire. I can show you right here."

He crouched and began to draw figures in the fresh snow, breaking through the wafer-thin crust of ice with his bare finger. Louisa crouched beside him, balancing on the toes of her slippers and drawing her gown about her knees.

"The estate is situated like so. The hall, of course. Right about here, on a prominence overlooking the valley. On a clear day, the southern vantage stretches for miles of green farmland. To the north"—he pushed snow into a rough plateau—"are the moors. Craggy and sparse and endless. I can't describe it, but it's beautiful all the same. A kind of magnificent emptiness. The wind whips and buffets you. You're helpless to stop it, but there's a feeling to pressing against it. As if you're utterly insignificant, but invincible at the same time." He shook himself from his reverie. "I'm explaining it poorly."

"Not at all." She never would have said so, but his description sounded terribly romantic.

He crafted two elongated heaps of snow. "Here's the valley. The Rye runs all the way through it."

He grew more animated, adding furrows and creeks to his model. Louisa couldn't help but smile as she watched him. A certain boyish enthusiasm had caught him up, tempered by an engineer's eye for planning.

"It sounds beautiful," she said.

"Aye, it is that." His Northern accent bled through. "Beautiful to the eye, at least. To the farmer, it's a bloody difficult place to be. The problem is here." He drew his finger through a long, winding stretch of virgin snow flanked by makeshift hillocks. "It would be rich soil for planting, if it didn't flood with every hard rain."

"And this being England . . ."

"Hopeless. Exactly. What with the failed harvests of the recent years, we're in desperate need of more arable land." He cocked his head and looked down at his handiwork. "I've drawn up plans for a system of drainage canals." With a stick, he slashed diagonals across the fields he'd sketched in the snow. "Custom hollow bricks are the most durable material. If we can't manage to finance them, it will have to be pebbles and straw."

He abruptly looked up. He gave Louisa a sheepish smile. "Sorry. Didn't mean to go on about drainage and property values. I'm boring you."

"To the contrary. I found it fascinating."

To be truthful, Louisa wasn't particularly fascinated by drainage, but she was fascinated by the way he talked about the plan. He cared deeply about his little piles of snow—or rather, for the vast sweeps of land they represented.

Yorkshire was home for him, the way Mayfair was home for her.

If only James's efforts to save *his* home didn't put Louisa on the brink of losing hers.

"It's no small undertaking." He dusted the snow from his hands as he stood. "I need capital. That's why I've come to Town, you see. There are a few properties I mean to sell as soon as possible. I need to return to Yorkshire by planting season."

One of those properties, of course, being her family's home—once he removed them from it. Her chest tightened.

"Surely that's rather sudden," she said. "For the current occupants of those properties, I mean."

"Most of them are storehouses, I gather."

"But most isn't all. Surely some are businesses and homes."

He shrugged. "Property is the solicitors' concern. My concern is for people."

"People?" Louisa couldn't conceal her emotion. "You care about your tenants in Yorkshire—to the degree that you no doubt know every last farmer, wife, and child by name—yet you have given no thought whatsoever to the tenants you may have here in London."

"London is full of buildings. Too many buildings. Houses are crammed cheek to jowl on every square. My farmers have nowhere else to go. Would you have me go back to Yorkshire and tell them all, 'Sorry—I could keep you from starving next winter, but I have to spare a few Londoners the inconvenience of moving house'?"

"Naturally, you can't allow people to starve, but that doesn't rule out compassion for everyone else. Losing one's home is more than a mere inconvenience. City or country, south or north."

He made an impatient gesture at his snowy sculpture. "I just explained what is at stake here, and you seemed to understand. But perhaps you were merely pretending to listen. I know the way young ladies are trained to smile and nod."

"You know well that I am no empty-headed, fawning young lady. For that matter, empty-headed, fawning young ladies are not nearly as common as you seem to believe. As for the women who *do* stifle their opinions to gain a man's approval—perhaps you should consider they might be compelled to do so by their families, by their poverty, or simply by virtue of their female sex." She drew a quick breath. "If women were afforded one-tenth the freedoms men enjoy, we would never need to abase ourselves by nodding and smiling while a duke drones on about farmland and drainage."

"Drones on?" His eyes caught a sharp glint from the snow. "You called it fascinating."

"What fascinates me is your hypocrisy. I thought you preferred a woman who speaks her mind. But you only seem to enjoy it when her opinions mirror yours."

He shook his head. "I should never have indulged your suggestion that we walk."

"There would not have been any need to walk if you hadn't drenched me in wine."

"I didn't drench you in wine. You drenched yourself."

"Oh, I wish I'd never danced with you."

He threw his hands toward the heavens. "It's a Christmas miracle. We've found something on which we agree."

Louisa growled with irritation. The lovingly drawn, painstakingly constructed model of his Yorkshire estate lay at her feet. She lifted her head, caught his eye, and arched one eyebrow.

His voice dropped a full octave. "You wouldn't dare."

"Wouldn't I?" She pointed a single gloved finger toward one lump of snow. "What was this again? Thorndale Hall?"

"Thorndale Abbey."

"Hmm." She scooped it up, slowly molded and packed the snow with her cupped hands. And then she lobbed the icy missile straight at his head. On impact, it burst into a satisfying firework of sparkling white.

As he wiped the snow from his face, steam rose up around his ears. "I warn you, I am on the verge of an exceedingly ungentlemanly response. Push me further, and I will not be responsible for the consequences."

Louisa bent over, gathered another handful of his ancestral home, crafted it into a second snowball—this one even icier than the first—and threw it.

He dodged it easily, then bent for his own handful of snow. "Very well. If it's a fight you want, you shall have it."

"You *bounder*."

That was it. The battle was on.

His aim was sharp, and since Louisa was wearing an evening gown, she couldn't hope to match him for nimbleness. Just one more unfair advantage belonging to men. He fired off two snowballs with astonishing speed. One caught her on the shoulder, spinning her to the side, and his next shot hit her between the shoulder blades.

"You shot me in the back!" Louisa ducked and bolted for cover behind a tree. "That's hardly sporting."

"Games are sporting. This is war."

They played cat and mouse, circling the tree trunk in wary steps.

"Surrender," he demanded.

"Never."

She feigned a lunge to the left, then sprinted right. Apparently, her strategy failed to confuse him, because within ten paces, he'd snagged her by the waist. She shrieked with laughter as he tackled her into the snow.

He rolled over and plucked her off the ground, arranging her on his lap and drawing his coat around the both of them, like a blanket. "There," he huffed. "I've caught you. Don't try to escape."

Louisa hadn't the breath or the heart to try. His arms held her captive in a firm embrace. His masculine strength called to some deep, womanly part of her being, and her body responded. Exhilaration coursed through her veins.

Could this be how it felt to stand on one of those wind-swept moors he described, looking out over a boundless expanse and facing into the wind? Invincible. Vulnerable. Breathless.

There was so much she hadn't experienced of the world. So much she suddenly yearned to explore. And it all started here, with the wildness between them.

He pushed an icy wisp of hair from her face. "What was it we're arguing about?"

"I've forgotten."

Inevitability coiled between them like a spring. The closer they drew to one another, the more the tension built.

And then—at last—a kiss.

Chapter Eleven

*J*ames was no poet. He had no particular talent for expressing tender emotions with words. Kisses, though . . .

Kisses were a different kind of language.

He brushed a series of light, tender kisses against her lips, giving her time to warm to the embrace. Only when her mouth softened beneath his, and her breath mingled with his own, did he deepen the kiss, taking her with barely restrained passion.

She tasted like Christmas. Brandy and plummy pudding and mulled wine and crisp snow. He still didn't like London, but he liked Louisa.

Her arms went about his neck, clinging tight.

Yes, he liked her very well indeed.

He gathered her close, bringing her against his body. Perhaps he could excuse it away under the guise of keeping her warm. In truth, he wanted to feel her. Needed to feel her. The shape of her body, the quiver of her pulse.

Their lips parted, and their foreheads met.

Reluctantly, he said, "I shouldn't be doing this."

"We're both doing this."

"Yes, but I didn't ask."

"I don't object."

He was running out of excuses. And he needed excuses, or he was going to take this much too far. "We scarcely know one another."

"We can remedy that. Dogs or cats?"

"What?"

"Do you prefer dogs or cats?"

"Dogs," he said. "Tea or coffee?"

"Tea. Autumn or spring?"

"Autumn. What's your favorite color?"

"Orange."

"*Orange?* No one's favorite color is orange."

"That's why it's mine. My siblings claimed all the others, and I was determined to set myself apart."

"You've succeeded at setting yourself apart." He caressed her cheek. "Magnificently."

He thought she might be blushing at his compliment, but the moonlight didn't reflect any shades of pink. Her skin, her lips, her eyes, her hair—they were painted in shades of silvery violet.

Violet was *his* favorite color. Which was strange, because until this moment, he'd always believed it to be green.

She bit her lip. "James?"

"Yes?"

"I think we know each other well enough now."

She pressed her lips to his, and he took the invitation. And then, God forgive him, he began to take more. He trailed kisses down her neck. He let his hands stray, vowing to himself he'd rein them in the moment she stiffened or pulled away.

She didn't pull away. As he drew his hand down her spine, her breath caught. Then her breathing resumed— quicker than before, and hot against his lips. Her fingers dug into his shoulders as he slid his hand upward, grazing the side of her breast. Then he moved his hand between them, cupping her breast in his palm, warming her flesh and soothing her hardened nipple. Desire had him stiff and aching.

You are a beast. Like a wolf pouncing on a snow-white hare.

He hadn't planned to take so many liberties, but all his thoughts and plans had melted like snowflakes in the warmth between them. They'd built their own little fire, and it licked like flame all over his body. Inside his body, as well.

There was something between them, and there could be more. So much more. She would fit well, both beneath him and beside him.

James put his arms around her again, drawing her into a less scandalous embrace—if not exactly a chaste one. They kissed, and kissed, and kissed some more. The way of young sweethearts with time stretched before them and nothing else to do. Exploring.

"I wish we could freeze time," she said.

He chuckled. "There are bits of me sure to freeze if we stay here much longer. And I really do need to take you home."

"Yes. But that's just it. Once you take me home, it's over."

"Why does it have to be over?"

"I'm leaving for Jersey in a fortnight, and you—"

Bong. In the distance, a bell tolled. He cursed. "It's already one—"

Bong.

"No, two o'clock."

Bong.

They stared at one another in horror.

Bong.

Bong.

Silence, finally.

"Oh no." Louisa pressed her hand to her mouth. "Five o'clock in the morning? My family will be beside themselves."

"No doubt. And the gossips will be thrilled."

"Are you worried you've ruined me? I'm moving to Jersey in a fortnight. My social life is over anyway."

Be that as it may, he owed her father some explanations, and—

Good God. Perhaps he would owe Louisa the offer of his hand.

Oh, it was madness. But James began to think that might not be so terrible.

It just might, in fact, be the best thing to ever happen in his life.

Chapter Twelve

$\mathcal{T}$he first snow of winter was all well and lovely, until it iced over. Rather than racing home, they were forced to skate over the pavement at a frustratingly slow pace. Louisa's ballroom slippers—with their soles fashioned to glide over a dance floor—slid out from under her on every third step, forcing James to stop and catch her before she could fall.

When her foot skidded and slipped for the hundredth time, Louisa cursed under her breath. James tightened his grip on her elbow, preventing what would have been a bruising fall.

"It's not far now," she promised.

He shook his head. "This is my fault. Somehow I thoroughly lost track of time."

"No, it's my fault. I'm the one who dragged you all over Mayfair."

"Well, that was my pleasure."

"I'm glad to hear you enjoyed the sights."

"Louisa." He stopped at the corner, and she reeled on her slippers. Putting his hands on her shoulders, he swiveled her to face him. Those hazel eyes, which she'd once thought cold, were warm and caring as they stared into hers. "You know it's not the sights I enjoyed."

Oh.

Her heart squeezed with bittersweet emotion. Here they

stood, a stone's throw from her house, which was about to become his property.

After the night they'd spent together—walking, talking, arguing, drinking, caroling, snowball fighting, kissing—she had true reason to hope. It was possible he'd understand their plight and be generous.

And now she couldn't go through with it.

Papa did owe the money, after all. James had every right to collect it. He wasn't motivated by heartless greed, but by the desire to help his Yorkshire tenants. Ambushing him this morning and prevailing on him to reconsider . . . Well, it wouldn't be fair. Especially not when Louisa had been hiding the truth.

And as for Jersey . . . Would it be so terrible to see a bit more of the world?

Perhaps James was right. She would always love London, but maybe she could benefit by expanding her horizons. Taking in a bit of the blue sky and fresh air he described with so much affection. She could picture a summer afternoon. Maggie helping Mama in a garden overflowing with flowers. Harold and William racing each other barefoot through green fields. Kat tucking a book under her arm and disappearing into the hayloft.

Louisa might dip her toes in the sea.

How ironic. She'd spent a full night trying to change his mind, and instead he'd succeeded in expanding hers.

"My house is just up the way," she said. "We should say our goodbyes here, I think."

He nodded gravely. "Yes, best to do that before I find myself staring down the barrel of your father's rifle. We may not have another chance."

She stuck out her hand in game fashion. "Farewell, James. I wish you the best of luck with your drainage."

"Wait, I thought we were joking about the rifle. But you speak as though we'll never see one another again."

"I don't expect that we will." She swallowed a lump in her throat. "Jersey's quite a distance from Yorkshire."

He took her hand—not to shake it, but to hold it in his. "I need to see you again."

"But I'm—"

"You're clever. You're warm. Lovely. Best of all, you're honest. Genuine. That's rare. I can't let it go once I've found it."

Her heart wrenched. She would have loved nothing better than to see him again. To be able to call him friend, at least—if not something more. But it simply wasn't possible.

"Louisa! *Louisa!*" Kat waved at her from the bedroom window, before disappearing back inside. "Louisa's back! And she's brought a man!"

She cringed. This was going to be a disaster.

Louisa turned to James. "Please just go," she said hurriedly. "Don't worry about me. I'll explain everything, make some excuse."

He looked affronted. "No one's going to make excuses for me. I'll see you safely inside and introduce myself. To start."

He meant to introduce himself. To start. Oh Lord.

"Really, I'm fine." She put her hands on his shoulders, attempting to turn him about and send him off in the other direction before it was too late.

But it was already too late.

The whole family—or most of it—poured over the threshold. They mobbed her, chiding and hugging at the same time. Chaos.

Once they'd let Louisa go, they all turned to stare at her companion.

"I beg your pardon." James cleared his throat. "I know this is all very untoward, bringing your daughter home at this hour. However, given the chance, I mean to make every explanation to Mr. Ward. Is he inside?"

"No," Mama said. "He's out searching for you, Louisa. He went to the Carvilles', and they were all in a flutter about Fiona, and then when you didn't come home—"

"I'm so sorry, Mama."

"The apologies are mine to make," James said. "Mrs. Ward, might I take the liberty of waiting on Mr. Ward to return?"

"Yes, of course. Of course." Her mother waved him inside. "Do come in. There's tea in the kitchen, and I'll have Nancy bring it in to the parlor."

"Please don't put yourself to the trouble. The kitchen is fine."

"That's very accommodating of you, Mr. . . . ?"

"James," Louisa interjected. "His name is James."

"Thank you, Mr. James." As she turned, Mama gave Louisa a questioning look and lifted an eyebrow.

Kat, on the other hand, hopped up and down with poorly concealed glee. "You did it!"

Louisa grabbed her sister by the elbow and yanked her aside.

"Oh, I'm so happy," Kat squealed. "We're saved! I never thought you had it in you."

"We are *not* saved," Louisa whispered. "He has *not* proposed."

"Well, I didn't think he would have proposed yet. He's waiting to speak with Father first."

"He is not *going* to propose."

"So he needs a bit of encouragement. Say no more."

Louisa set her teeth. "Kat. Your understanding of the situation is completely opposite of the truth, and if you do not hold your tongue, we will be in an even greater muddle."

"But—"

"Hush. I mean it. One word, and I will march you upstairs to the attic. And lock you there."

Grumpily—but quietly—Kat followed her into the kitchen. James was already seated at the table, accepting a cup of tea with milk and sugar, talking with her mother and making no objection as Harold shamelessly emptied his pockets. William pulled the watch from James's waistcoat, shook it, and held it to his ear.

He looked so very . . . at home.

Louisa slipped her arms free of his coat and draped the garment over the back of his chair, brushing his shoulder with her fingertips. *Thank you for sharing your coat.*

Holding his teacup in one hand, he used the other to pull out the chair next to his. *Sit next to me.*

She accepted with reluctance, edging her chair aside to create space between them. *I don't want to give my family ideas.*

Beneath the table, he caught her chair leg with his boot, dragging her close. *Let them have their ideas.*

Her heart fluttered in her chest. They hadn't shared a single word in the entire exchange. Not even so much as a glance. Yet as Louisa poured herself a cup of tea, he casually pushed the sugar in her direction, as though he'd been doing so every morning for years and years.

"Tell me, Mr. James," Mama said. "Have you been long in London?"

"No, I only came to Town a fortnight ago. I hope to return to Yorkshire as soon as possible."

"So soon?"

"Once my business is concluded. I've a few propert—"

"Bread?" Louisa shoved a plate heaped with rolls at him.

He stared at the plate with bemusement. "Thank you."

"Oh!" Kat hopped up from her chair. "If you're hungry, you must try the shortbread. It's divine."

Louisa choked on her dread. "Kat, no."

"Don't you like shortbread, Mr. James?" Kat put on her

best doe-eyed, guileless look. She could be angelic and charming when she wished to be.

"I do like shortbread," he answered.

"I made it myself." Kat beamed.

"Then I wouldn't dare decline." He took a square of burned shortbread from the plate.

Louisa ducked her head and put a hand to her brow. She didn't want to watch.

But she couldn't help watching anyway. Within the hour, this pleasant scene would crumble into tragedy, one way or another. If he choked on a bit of shortbread, it might be the least painful ending possible.

When James bit into the dreadful biscuit, his jaw froze. She could see the war going on inside him. His manners wouldn't allow him to spit it out, but his mouth refused to chew.

The conflict, however, was resolved before anyone else could notice.

He chewed thoughtfully, swallowed, and then gave Kat a slight smile. "Delicious."

Oh Lord. Perhaps that Scottish sorcery worked after all. Maybe the shortbread truly did make a person irresistible to the opposite sex.

Because when James swallowed that dreadful shortbread and smiled—that was the moment Louisa fell in love with him.

Her father burst in, hair and clothing askew. "Louisa."

She rushed to him, stopping just short. "Papa, I'm so sorry. There was a mishap . . . then no cabs . . . and I'd no idea how much time had passed—" She slapped her palms to her gown. "It's only wine."

"The explanations can wait, my dear. Let me look you over first. Are you here, and well, and safe?"

She nodded.

"Then that's all that matters."

She flung her arms around his neck. Other fathers might have scolded, but Papa never would.

However, he wasn't above a stern question or two. "Now. Where have you been?"

James stepped to her side. "She was with me."

"And you are?"

"He's Mr. James," Kat said.

"It's just James, actually." He cleared his throat. "James Standish, Duke of Thorndale."

The kitchen went silent. And Louisa felt everything slipping away.

"Oh, Louisa!" Kat flew across the room and hugged Louisa around the waist. "You've done it. You've convinced him not to take our house!"

"The house?" James looked baffled.

"Kat, hush."

Sadly, telling Kat to be quiet was like telling water to be dry.

Her little sister twirled in circles. "Isn't it wonderful? We won't have to move to Jersey after all. He'll let us stay, and Louisa didn't even have to murder him."

William stood on his chair, jumped on Harold's back, and the two of them galloped like horse and rider about the kitchen, whooping and cheering. Maggie caught a toppled teacup just before it met with the floor.

Amid all the din, James looked at Louisa. "What did she say?"

"Oh, that's Kat. Never mind her."

"She said that I've changed my mind. That you can stay." He looked around the kitchen. "Do I . . . Do I own this house?"

"Yes." She sighed. There was nothing left but to tell the truth. "Or you will own it, in a few weeks. Papa was in the old duke's debt. You called it in, and he has no way to pay, and so . . ."

"Jersey."

"Yes."

He nodded slowly. "I see."

The look in his eyes made her heart wrench. When he learned the truth, Louisa had expected he would be furious. But what she saw in his gaze was so much worse.

He was hurt.

"And so this was your aim," he said quietly. "Manipulation. Getting what you want from me. Or, alternatively, murdering me. I suppose that explains the shortbread." He stood, reached for his tailcoat, and pushed his arms through the sleeves. "I believe I must be going."

"James, wait. I know how it must look, but—"

But he was already out the door.

Drat. Louisa gathered her wrap from a peg by the door, threw it about her shoulders, and shoved her feet into Maggie's boots. She caught up to him a few houses down.

She clung to his coat sleeve, panting for breath. "Please, at least let me explain."

Anger and hurt mingled in his gaze. "And here I thought you were the first genuine person I'd met in London. How stupid I was. It was all a ruse. Switching dances with Miss Carville. That 'accident' with the mulled wine. Your insistence on walking home, traipsing all about London to while the night away. The park."

Louisa bristled. "Don't you dare imply that what we shared in the park wasn't real."

They squared off, staring at each other and huffing small thunderclouds of vapor.

She closed her eyes and searched herself for a measure of calm. "Here is the truth. I hoped to catch a wealthy suitor last night. One who might pay Papa's debts. It seemed the only way of saving our house. But I never had any thought of ensnaring you. I didn't even know you would be at the ball."

"I find that difficult to believe. You're friends with Miss Carville. It was her family's ball. I'm her cousin."

She jerked with surprise. "You're Fiona's cousin?"

"Third cousin, twice removed. Or second cousin, thrice removed. I can never remember which, but it doesn't matter. The point is, you knew I'd be there. So you set your cunning little trap."

Louisa threw up her hands. "I declined a second dance with you! When you insisted on seeing me home, I tried to refuse!"

"And then you led me on an hours-long walk through Mayfair. That is hardly the behavior of a woman eager to be rid of her companion."

"I know. But that came later. After you insisted on taking me home and speaking to Papa. I thought that if we spent a little time together first, perhaps you'd understand that I feel the same love for London as you feel for Yorkshire. That one's home is one's home. Maybe you could be persuaded to reconsider calling in the debt. But then you turned out to be so likable and decent, and to have such good reasons for needing the money. And . . . and somewhere along the way, I realized home wasn't about this house, or this street, or this city—but about being with the people I love, and who love me."

He shook his head, ignoring her rambling confessions. "I nearly fell for it, too. God, what an idiot. I was ready to marry you."

Louisa's eyebrows soared with disbelief. *"What?"*

"We were out together all night, alone. I felt obliged to protect your honor. You must think me a fool."

"Not at all, I . . . I think you rather wonderful."

"Spare me the flattery."

"It's not flattery. None of it was flattery. I swear, I had no expectations of a proposal. I wouldn't even want you to offer for me. Not because I don't like you. But because I like you a great deal, and it would be much too soon, and . . ." She pressed a hand to her forehead. "This is coming out all wrong. Come back inside and have a cup of tea, and I'll explain it properly."

"I understand well enough, thank you."

"James—"

"Don't call me that. That degree of familiarity is reserved for friends."

She recoiled, stung.

He made a curt bow. "Farewell, Miss Ward. I wish you and your family all due happiness on the Isle of Jersey."

So. That was that.

Tears pricked at her eyes as she watched him leave. She followed his shrinking silhouette as he walked down the lane in brisk, furious paces—and then turned the wrong way at the corner.

"Left," she called out. "You want to make a left turning."

He stopped, made a resentful about-face, and stalked left.

But he didn't once look back.

Chapter Thirteen

"*L*ady Carville." James bowed deeply as he entered the drawing room of the Carvilles' residence later that day. "Forgive me for coming by unannounced."

Lady Carville paled. "Oh dear. Don't tell me word is about already."

Puzzled by this greeting, he stood in place. "I have no word of anything. I expect to be leaving London soon, so I came to make my farewells. And to ask after Miss Fiona's health, if I may."

"Oh no," she moaned, pressing a handkerchief to her mouth. "I suppose it was the Waterfords who told you. I knew they couldn't be trusted."

Trusted with what? The knowledge that Fiona went upstairs with a headache? Londoners loved their gossip, but surely a headache, whether real or feigned, wouldn't merit notice.

"I didn't hear about her illness from the Waterfords. Miss Ward informed me." As he spoke her name, his heart clenched like a fist.

"Louisa Ward?" Lady Carville shifted in her seat like an agitated hen ruffling its wings. "Do not mention her name. I am excessively put out with that girl."

"You, as well?" James muttered.

"That dreadful, dreadful girl. She ought to have told me."

Lady Carville blew her nose into a flowered handkerchief. "Fiona is my only daughter, and now it's too late."

Too late? Even if the headache was real, surely it wasn't that dire.

He pulled a chair close and sat down. "Tell me what's happened, precisely. Perhaps I can be of assistance."

"Oh, there's nothing to be done. Carville wanted to go after them, naturally, but I put a stop to that. They'll be halfway to Scotland by now. He could never catch them in time."

"Halfway to *Scotland*. You can't mean she's eloped?"

"You may as well know the truth. You are family, after all, and there won't be any hiding it soon."

James was stunned. "I was told she left the ball with a headache. I called to inquire after her health."

"Lies." Lady Carville's breath caught on a sob. "All lies, put about by that scheming Miss Ward." She drew a crumpled paper from the depths of her bosom and passed it to him.

He reluctantly accepted the thing, plucking it from her hand with a single finger and thumb. Laying the unpleasantly damp sheet of paper on his thigh, he managed to smooth the creases sufficiently to read its contents.

Dear Mama,

 By the time you read this, I will be on the mail coach to Scotland with Ralph Bettany. We are in love and have been for years. I cannot be happy without him, and I can only hope that in time you will understand. Do not be concerned, and don't let Papa make a useless journey in pursuit. The elopement is my decision, and I've gone willingly, with all my heart. You can ask Louisa if you doubt it—

but don't be severe with her, please. She is such a dear friend.

Your loving daughter,
Fiona

James set aside the letter. "Good God. This Bettany fellow must be the worst sort of bounder."

"No, no. He's the son of Carville's land agent. He was brought up well. The Bettanys are a good Christian family."

"Is he after her dowry, then? Perhaps he's in financial difficulty."

"If that were the case, he knows Carville would help." She sniffed. "It's not greed—it's foolishness. The two were childhood friends. It was only natural that Ralph would be taken with her, but we thought Fiona would be more reasonable than this. She could have done so much better."

James wondered about that. Could she have done better, really? Or had she done what was best for herself? If this Ralph Bettany was a decent, honest man who loved her, Fiona certainly could have done worse. Naturally, her parents' shock would be keen. For a baron's daughter to marry the steward's son was a bit of a scandal. But in time, James suspected the Carvilles would come to accept the match.

At the moment, however, Lady Carville was a sobbing shambles. She jammed the letter back into her bosom and twisted her handkerchief in her lap. "Oh, that Louisa Ward. I will be as severe with her as I wish. This is all her fault."

"How is Miss Ward to blame?"

"Why, she aided their escape! Fiona must have slipped away early in the evening. But no one noticed. Carville went to the card room, as always, and I conversed with the guests. And that dreadful Louisa Ward put about some tale of a headache and took Fiona's dances so that no one would inquire. The impertinent girl. Her parents always were too indulgent." She fluttered her hand on her breast. "Oh! Merely speaking of it sends me toward apoplexy."

While Lady Carville rang for tea and a medicinal powder, James reckoned with this new information.

So Louisa had been telling the truth. She hadn't schemed to take Fiona's dance card, and she couldn't have known his name would be on it.

She hadn't deceived him.

Or rather, she *had* deceived him. But she hadn't lied with the object of attracting his notice—she'd been drawing notice away from her eloping friend. He recalled the way she'd dug in when he insultingly suggested she find another partner. No doubt she would have rejoiced in doing just that, considering how he'd treated her. But she'd stood firm.

I promised my friend, and I always keep my promises.

All his accusations from earlier that morning . . . They rang in his ears like the braying jackass sounds they were. What had he been thinking? That Louisa had *planned* to collide with a bowl of mulled wine, then arranged for his coachman to be tupping a prostitute in the Thorndale carriage? Oh, and she'd put in an order for softly falling snow, as well.

She was a clever woman, but that would have been quite a feat.

James didn't often reconsider his opinions, and once he'd made a decision, he seldom had cause to regret it. But from the moment they'd met, Louisa Ward had him reconsidering everything.

And if he didn't right this mistake, he knew he'd regret it for the rest of his life.

Chapter Fourteen

And so Christmas was still Christmas, after all.

On the twenty-fifth of December, the Ward family awoke in a house that, within a week, would no longer be theirs. And yet that didn't stop Louisa, along with her brothers and sisters, from racing down the stairs in their socks and dressing gowns, greeting Mama and Papa with warmest hugs, and sitting down to a veritable mountain of breakfast. Piping hot drinking chocolate, sweet buns and butter, sausages crisp on the outside and juicy within. Even oranges.

Heaven.

By necessity, the Christmas presents were small. No one had room to spare in their trunks for anything larger than a butter mold. But there were songs and games and books and teasing. Merriment, of all the best kinds.

In a quiet moment, Maggie nudged Louisa's arm. "Don't despair. We'll come back for visits."

"I'm only woolgathering." Louisa squeezed her sister's hand. "I'm fine."

In truth, she *was* a touch heartsick, but not on account of the house. Home could be Mayfair, or home could be Jersey. Wherever the Ward family went, she knew love would travel with them.

Even better, love didn't take up any space in Louisa's trunks.

However, she couldn't stop thinking of James. It was the most idiotic thing in the world, to worry over the man evicting her family from their home. She ought to be furious with him—and some part of her was.

But other parts of her felt differently. Even though they'd only spent the one night together wandering Mayfair, there were couples who courted for months and shared fewer honest conversations. She felt she'd come to know him, and that he'd come to understand her.

He must have believed it, too, if he'd been willing to *marry* her.

Whenever her mind wandered out of her keeping, she saw that flinty spark of anger in his eyes. His instinctive recoil when she'd reached out, and the cutting chill in his voice.

He'd erected a wall of ice between them.

But walls were built for protection, weren't they? Perhaps he wasn't merely angry with her, but angry with himself. He was a man who didn't trust anyone easily, and now he thought his own judgment had betrayed him.

Oh, James.

Emotions were so much easier to sort through one at a time, or so Louisa supposed. She wouldn't know. Her life always delivered them in bundles, tied with impossibly knotted string.

"Lou-EEE-saah!" Harold tromped in from the entryway. "Someone's brought a letter for you."

Louisa snatched the envelope from her brother's hand. The letter could only be from Fiona.

After the night of the ball, Louisa hadn't dared call on the Carvilles herself. But Mama had learned that the new Mr. and Mrs. Ralph Bettany were honeymooning in Scotland through the end of January. Presumably, the newlywed couple hoped a bit of time and distance might soften the blow. Little could they know, Lady Carville was already redecorating the nursery in anticipation of her first grandchild.

Once she'd nestled into the chair nearest the fire, Louisa worked her fingernail under the wax seal. However, a closer look at the envelope had her confused. The letter wasn't addressed properly—only her name, no direction. It could not have come from Scotland. It could not have come through the post at all.

Stranger still, when she broke the seal and opened the envelope, it didn't contain a letter. Not even a jotted note of explanation. Just a frightfully long document written in a close, almost-indecipherable hand.

As she scanned the paper, her fingers began to tremble.

Kat peered over her shoulder, impatient. "Don't be greedy. What is it?"

Louisa couldn't be certain. She'd never seen one before. But she thought it just might be the deed to a property.

This property.

She elbowed Kat aside and leaped to her feet, rushing into the entrance hall. "Harold?" She stood at the base of the stairs and called up. "Harold, who delivered this?"

"I did."

The rich, deep voice came from behind her. Louisa's heart pounded as she turned in place, already knowing who she'd find.

The Duke of Thorndale stood in the doorway, hat in his hands.

James.

She opened her mouth to speak. He motioned for quiet.

"Don't alert the cavalry just yet," he whispered. "I need a word with you, alone. If that goes well, then I'll go to your father."

"My father?"

"Not to ask for your hand."

"Oh."

"Not yet, at any rate."

She was thoroughly befuddled.

He looked at the ceiling, drew a deep breath, and then returned his gaze to hers. "Let's begin this again."

"That seems best."

"I mean to declare my intentions to court you. That is, if you agree. I couldn't blame you if you don't. The things I said to you . . ." He shook his head in self-censure. "A visit to Lady Carville set me straight that very afternoon. When she told me of Fiona's elopement, I knew at once that I'd been an ass. I wanted to come back and see you straightaway, but I forced myself to wait."

"Why?"

"Because it would have been too soon, too rushed, too muddled with questions. If a proper courtship revealed we didn't suit one another, you'd have feared letting down your family. And much as I hate to admit it, I'd always have wondered if it was the house you truly wanted, or me." He fidgeted with his hat. "It doesn't speak well of my character, that I'm so quick to suspect others' motives. But for the longest time, I was rather on my own."

"I know."

"My mother left. My brother went to school. My father was a good man, but I didn't have"—he waved his hat toward the cheerful din in the parlor—"anything like this. And then suddenly I'm a duke and everyone scrambles for my notice. It's too easy to believe people want what they can get from me, rather than . . . Well, rather than wanting me."

Her heart gave a sharp twist in her chest. "James."

"So I decided to do away with the doubt entirely." He nodded at the deed. "This house is yours. It can't be taken back, either, so you're not to feel obligated. If you agree, we'll start slowly. Perhaps you'll let me take you for a drive in the park. If I don't cock that up entirely, maybe an evening at one of those theaters you keep telling me about."

Louisa smiled. "That sounds lovely."

He hung his hat on a nearby peg and stripped off his gloves, jamming them into his pocket. "I must be clear. My intent is to win you, and patience isn't one of my strengths. But I swear not to rush you. You deserve the chance to think hard before making any decisions."

"What about *your* decisions? I should think you could use some time, too."

"Me?" He laughed a little. "I was decided the first night. I've had time to think on it since. Long nights of walking through Mayfair alone and forlorn, swilling bottles of finest Madeira and staring through bookshop windows."

"What a pathetic image."

"Indeed. Even the thought of three mermaids offered no comfort."

Louisa startled. "Oh, but the farmland. If you've given me this house, what about your drainage plans?"

"I decided you're lovelier than field drains, and a great deal more pleasant to kiss."

"But I know how important it is to you, what it would mean for your tenants. You shouldn't put me before their interests. It's not—"

He shushed her by pressing his fingers to her lips. "Louisa. I'm teasing. You were right—I have people to think about here as well as in Yorkshire. It's not right to be selling off properties with no thought for the occupants. I still mean to raise the capital, but I'll go about it a bit more carefully. You know, since I'll be in London for a time."

"How long a time?"

His gaze held hers. "As long as it takes."

Her heart melted like a new frost in sunshine.

"And even if all goes well here, you must visit my estate before accepting me. Yorkshire isn't an island, but it's a fair distance away. You'd be stranded without hope of rescue if you decided you couldn't bear my face."

"I like your face."

He cradled her cheeks in his hands. "I like yours, too."

"Oh Lord," she whispered. "But you're a duke. And if I married you, I'd be a duchess. I can't possibly—"

He tsked. "You're not one to doubt yourself, my love. Don't start now."

He brushed her lips with his thumb as he slid his hand to the back of her neck. His fingers sifted through her unbound hair, sending soothing waves of pleasure through her body. Her eyelids fluttered with bliss.

Then he leaned in to kiss her. Gently, chastely. Her family was in the next room, after all. Innocent as it was, the kiss sent a sweet thrill all the way to her toes.

His kiss tasted like shortbread. Buttery, sweet. Irresistible.

As they parted, someone in the parlor took to the pianoforte and banged out the first chords of a Christmas carol.

Louisa reached for his hand and tugged him forward. "Come in and join the family. We could use a baritone."

Epilogue

*I*t was the quintessential Mayfair wedding.

Announcement in the *Times*. A date set for the first week of June. Ceremony at St. George's Hanover Square. Wedding breakfast catered by Gunthers'.

And a wedding night in London's finest hotel.

As soon as he'd closed the door behind them, James swept his bride off her feet and carried her to the bed.

"What about dinner? Aren't you hungry?"

"Oh, I'm hungry." He pulled down the bodice of her gown and swept his tongue over her breast. His other hand went to her skirt.

"I've rose petals for my bath," she gasped. "A silky negligee."

"I don't care."

"I went to a great deal of trouble choosing it. You had better care."

"I'll care later. I promise." He kissed her neck, laying her back on the bed. "Louisa. I need you."

He'd promised her a proper courtship, and he'd done his level best. He'd made do with kisses and the occasional stolen caress. Once, in the theater box, he'd managed to slide his hand beneath her petticoats, all the way above her garter to her bared thigh. The way her breath had quickened had made him wild. He'd known they would be just as explosive together in bed as they were everywhere else.

James had waited months to have her. He couldn't wait another hour.

She was his wife now. His to explore freely, inside and out. This being Louisa, she'd demand to make her own explorations, and he was eager for that part, too.

He slid his fingers along the soft furrow between her legs. "Don't be anxious. I'll go as slowly as you wish."

"And if I wish you to go faster?"

He looked down at his wife. "I love you."

Surely, she knew it. She had to know. But he had been saving the words for today, just as he'd been saving all the sweetest pleasures.

As he kissed her, heat and determination charged through his veins. A few hours past, he'd spoken his vows in church, numbly repeating the words after the curate. He hadn't truly absorbed their import with his muddled brain. But his blood had been paying attention.

Love, his heart pounded as their bodies joined. *Honor. Cherish. Protect.*

And of course, there was the one vow most applicable to the current moment:

With my body I thee worship.

He took his time coaxing her pleasure to its peak, and then he found his own release with an alacrity that would have been embarrassing, if she weren't a virgin with no point of reference to judge.

Afterward, he gathered her in his arms, rolling onto his back so he wouldn't crush her beneath his weight. "Promise me we'll make bushels of babies."

She laughed.

"I mean it. I want a big family."

She sat tall, bracing her hands on his chest. "James, darling. You've just married into one."

His whirling thoughts came to a standstill. That was true, he had. And they'd welcomed him into the fold with surprising warmth for a family he'd nearly evicted from their home. Spending time with the Wards had required a bit of adjustment on his part. The laughter, the arguing, the sheer noise of it all. But to no one's surprise so much as his own, he was learning to enjoy the chaos.

Learning to love them, and to be loved.

When it came time to share a house with them—*that* would be the true test. He'd promised Louisa they'd always come to London for Christmas, and that the Wards would be welcome each summer at Thorndale Abbey.

He reached for her, gliding his hand down her arm, reveling in her skin's unbearable softness before catching her hand. With the pad of his thumb, he polished her wedding ring.

She admired the square-cut emerald set in gold. "You spent too much on it."

"Impossible." He brought her hand to his lips for a kiss. "You deserve it. You are a jewel among women."

Her brow wrinkled.

"What? I thought I was being romantic."

"Yes, but . . . I don't like to be praised in ways that deprecate the remainder of my sex. The world has countless jewel-worthy women. I'm not the only one."

He groaned in complaint. "For once, take a compliment. Am I not allowed to say you stand out from the throng?"

"Well." She stroked a single fingertip back and forth, teasing a path through the hair on his chest. "I suppose I'm the only bride in the world who was compromised by mulled wine and bewitched by shortbread."

"You're unique in another way."

"Oh?"

"You're the only bride in the world who's mine."

Her fingertip stilled.

Ah, there was that shy smile and blush he'd been hoping to see. For all her outward brazenness, Louisa had her moments of doubt and her fragile places. She needed the embrace of strong arms from time to time, and it pleased him mightily to provide it.

"I love you so," she whispered. "You do know that, don't you?"

He nodded.

"Promise me you won't doubt it. Even when I'm sharp-tongued or stubborn or forget to say it for a few days." She tilted his chin and stared into his eyes. "You must never doubt my love for you."

James could scarcely breathe, let alone speak.

In place of a reply, he drew her down for a kiss. She kissed him back with sweetness and passion and need.

"I seem to remember mention of a silk negligee," he murmured.

"Mmm-hmm. You said you didn't care about it."

"I said I'd care later." He broke the kiss. "It's later."

About Tessa Dare

TESSA DARE is the *New York Times* and *USA Today* bestselling author of more than twenty historical romances. Blending wit, sensuality, and emotion, Tessa writes Regency-set romance novels that feel relatable to modern readers. Her books have won numerous accolades, including Romance Writers of America's prestigious RITA® award (twice) and the RT Book Reviews Seal of Excellence. *Booklist* magazine named her one of the "new stars of historical romance," and her books have been contracted for translation in more than a dozen languages.

A librarian by training and a book lover at heart, Tessa makes her home in Southern California, where she lives with her husband, their two children, and a trio of cosmic kitties.

To receive updates on Tessa's new and upcoming books, please sign up for her newsletter at www.tessadare.com.

The Duke of
Christmas Present

Sarah MacLean

Chapter One

Christmas Eve

The Duke of Allryd was impressively drunk when he heard the ghost in the kitchens.

The irony of the situation, of course, was that on any other night of the year, he would have been sober as a judge. The Duke of Allryd was a notorious nondrunk.

Half of society thought him too rigid for it, the other half thought him too strange—though it should be pointed out that such an assessment was something of a chicken-and-egg conundrum for, when pressed, that same half would point to his teetotaling as proof of the strangeness that inspired his teetotaling.

The truth was that the Duke of Allryd didn't have time for drinking. He barely had time for sleeping. He had time for working. He had time for eating and breathing because he could do both while working. While building and rebuilding his vast holdings, while checking and rechecking his vast accounts, while summoning and resummoning his vast array of solicitors and estate managers.

At least, that was the truth he claimed.

It wasn't the actual truth.

The actual truth was that drinking welcomed memory, and he had no interest in resurrection of memory.

Or resurrection of ghosts, though the one in his kitchens seemed eager for it.

It should be said that Eben James, Duke of Allryd, did not believe in ghosts, generally. In fact, there were a dozen other reasons why the sounds that pulled him from his cups should not have been considered ghostly. Foremost, ghosts did not exist. At least, Allryd had never seen indication of such a thing.

Additionally, any otherworldly spirits lacking in corporeal existence should also lack interest in the culinary arts, which would have certainly occurred to his ordered and logical mind, if not for the influence of half a bottle of Scotland's best whisky.

Indeed, on any other night, Allryd might have considered the possibility of ruffians, highwaymen, Bow Street runners, street urchins, or (most likely) his own staff. But in that moment, minutes before midnight on Christmas Eve, Allryd could not conjure a single explanation for the noise in his kitchens save one—a ghost.

So he did what any self-respecting lord of the manor would do in that same scenario: he went to confront it.

Halfway down the pitch-black main staircase, it occurred to Allryd that he should arm himself for what might be a battle for the ages, and when he landed in the main foyer, he collected a shield and rusty sword from an exceedingly helpful suit of armor. Properly outfitted, he headed off to banish the spirit.

The house had been deserted, the dark, silent back hallway to the kitchens reminded him. Lawton had spent weeks convincing him that decent employers allowed their staffs time away for a Christmas holiday and, finally, the duke had succumbed to the guilt—like stone to incessant water. The house was silent as two dozen servants basked in feast and festivity—whatever that might mean—elsewhere for seventy-two hours, leaving Allryd to his own work.

His work, and the same activity he'd taken up every Christmas Eve for the last twelve years. Drinking himself into oblivion.

This was better, he thought as he headed for the kitchens, armed with ancient weaponry to battle the ghost who had interrupted his plans to avoid Christmas at all costs.

Light flickered, warm and tempting, spilling in golden chaos at the end of the hallway, and he edged toward its source, knowing he'd snuffed every candle before he'd taken to his rooms. He lifted his shield and saber—a soldier storming a keep.

A mighty crash sounded from within the kitchens, followed by a firm "Dammit!"

This gave Allryd pause. The ghost was foulmouthed. And female.

He reached the doorway, his attention immediately on the other side of the room, where a figure teetered atop a small wooden stool, reaching for a high shelf. It vaguely occurred to him that a ghost should not require such a feat of balance.

Nor should a ghost have such vibrancy: not hair that gleamed like dark fire, cascading around her like magic; not skin, brown from the sun; not full, welcome hips, flaring beneath rich green velvet the color of sun-drenched pines.

Nor should he be instantly attracted to a ghost.

Ergo, this was not an ordinary ghost.

The tip of his saber clinked as it dropped to the stones beneath his feet.

The specter looked over her shoulder at the sound, unsurprised, as though she'd known he was there the whole time. She was nothing like a ghost, all bright eyes and freckled skin and wide, welcoming lips the color of a blush. The color of *her* blush.

Then she smiled, that grin that had always won him. The

one that had always wrecked him. And he wasn't a grown man any longer. He was a boy, eighteen and with a single, wild purpose.

Her.

She wasn't specter; she was worse.

She was memory.

A shimmering, golden memory that slammed through him on a flood of surprise and knee-weakening desire. But he was a man—a duke, for God's sake—and he'd be damned if he let her see what she did to him.

"Oh good, you're here," she said, as though it weren't the dark of night on Christmas Eve, and they weren't alone in a Mayfair town house, and he weren't drunk, and she weren't returned after twelve years away. "I can't reach the chocolate pot. Do you mind?"

But Allryd didn't seem able to forget all those things. So he stood, rooted to the spot, and said the only thing he could. The thing he'd sworn never to say again, because it always felt like a broken promise. "Jack."

Her brown eyes crinkled at the corners—barely there proof of the years that had passed. "No one has called me *that* in a decade."

Of course they hadn't. It had only ever been his name for her. Pulled from a storybook about pirates that had come from Lord knew where. And Lady Jacqueline Mosby, the girl who lived next door—two years younger and thoroughly exasperating—had been a pirate, stealing into Allryd's life and looting what she wished.

He'd let her, of course. He'd given her everything she'd wanted—until he couldn't be what she wanted and she'd left to find someone who could.

"Did you think to run me through?" He tightened his grip on the saber in his hand as her lips curved. "That thing looks like it hasn't been sharpened in a century or two. I'm not sure it would do much damage."

Nothing like the damage she could do in return.

"Eben," she said after his lingering silence, using the name no one had called *him* in a lifetime. His eyes flew to hers as the past crashed through him. "It shall boil over."

Somehow, he understood her meaning, looking instantly to the stove, where flame licked at the bottom of a saucepan of milk.

He set his saber on the worktable and propped the shield against it, moving toward her before he realized that once he reached her, he would have to be near her. He hesitated, missing a step, setting him off balance for a heartbeat—not long enough for anyone to notice.

Jack noticed, tilting her head in a tease of movement. Movement no one would notice.

Allryd noticed.

It was ridiculous that they noticed each other, of course. It had been twelve years—too many for them to even imagine that they still knew each other. That they had any cause to notice each other. So, he made an effort not to notice her as he approached, even as she remained on the stool, her hands now clasped at her waist as she waited for him to reach her.

No, not her. *It.* Reach *it.*

What was it he was reaching for?

The chocolate pot.

He could fetch a damn chocolate pot without noticing her. And he almost did. But then he was in front of her, extending one long arm up to the shelf. If he hadn't had to navigate around her, he might not have had to lean so close to her.

Then he might have been able to not notice her warmth, like sunshine. Or her scent, sunshine and lemons. Or the sound of her breathing, close to his ear, as he struggled to grasp the handle of the damn pot.

There. Got it.

He pulled it down from the shelf, intending to back away. To put distance between them and forget all those little things before they resurrected memories best left dead.

They touched.

Maybe he'd been careless. Off balance. Maybe he hadn't left enough space between them. Maybe it was his fault they brushed against each other, the velvet of her bodice scraping against the chambray of his shirt, rough enough to catch the thin fabric. To tug it. To heat it and with it, him.

Maybe. He might have believed it had been his fault.

Except, she inhaled. It wasn't an ordinary intake of oxygen. It was longer than necessary. Deeper. It made enough sound that he couldn't stop himself from turning toward the sound.

Her eyes were closed. Her lips were curved. And she looked . . . pleased. When she exhaled, it was with a little, nearly imperceptible sigh.

Allryd perceived it. All of it.

His eyes widened, and he was barely able to restrain his jaw from dropping. He could not restrain the part of him that went hard as steel. He'd never been able to, with her.

He could restrain the rest of him, however, and he did so with immense personal pride, as though he'd fought a battalion of enemies or saved the Queen from attack. Both actions would have been easier than what he did do: he backed away from Jack as though she were aflame, and tossed the tall silver chocolate pot alongside his orphaned sword. For a brief moment, he considered retrieving the weapon. It seemed his drunken preparedness had not been without purpose—his home was under siege, after all.

He would have preferred the ghost.

He placed the table between them and turned back to face her. She had moved, now stirring her pot with a flat-bottomed wooden spoon. He watched the slow, steady motion, imagining the milk swirling under her calm preparation, and for the first time in his life, he resented a liquid.

Because he was in no way calm, especially when she said, as though discussing the weather, "You smell the same."

So did she.

He shook his head. "What?"

"I said you smell the same, which seems impossible, honestly. Like sage and cedar. Like you've been in the country." She raised her voice to speak, as though he couldn't hear everything she said. Every rustle of her skirts. Every scrape of that spoon on the bottom of her pan.

His pan.

His kitchen.

"What are you doing here?"

"Have you been in the country?"

"No."

"No, of course you haven't."

And there it was, the harshest of the memories, like a blow. Her disappointment. A keen awareness that he could never be what she had wanted him to be. But this was worse, in some way. Because there was no disappointment in her words today. Only honesty. Awareness. And acceptance.

She had been his future once. Then he'd inherited a dukedom and a massive estate deep in debt, and he'd had to make choices based on the responsibility and future of a dukedom and not the mad wishes of a young boy.

And that was that. But it didn't change the fact that she was making chocolate in his damn kitchen. Uninvited.

He repeated himself. "What are you doing here?"

"Would you believe it's a Christmas miracle?"

"No."

She watched him for a long moment. "Pity. There was a time when you might have believed it."

He shook his head, a futile attempt to clear it. To clear her from view. "That was a long time ago."

She turned back to the milk, and they both watched as she stirred. "Surely you missed me?"

Like cold missed warmth. "Again, what are you doing here?"

The soft scrape of the wooden spoon whispered between them. "Making my own excitement."

She had always been able to make excitement—more than her share. She'd been the one to discover the secret passageway between their houses. Not even a passageway, really. A door, locked from both sides, leading from the far corner of his conservatory into the far corner of the Mosby library. One day, Jack had pulled her father's vast collection of atlases down to explore the Southern Hemisphere when she'd noticed a handle in the wall behind them.

Young Allryd had been at his daily practice at the violin when knocking had commenced behind a nearby oil painting of satyrs at play, and his excitement had been entirely of Lady Jacqueline Mosby's making.

And then he'd opened the door, and she'd become the entirety of his excitement. Every day. Until the day she'd left.

The day he'd run her off.

She lifted the saucepan from the stove and came to the table with a bright smile. "If you must know, I am here because we don't have any chocolate in our kitchens."

"And so home invasion is the next logical step."

"Please," she scoffed. "It's not invasion if the door isn't locked."

"I haven't thought about that door in a decade."

Lie.

Her lips twitched. "And besides, you're well armed. Any

intruder would positively cower in the face of your rusty sword and a shield that was certainly the best of its kind in the Dark Ages."

He looked down at the shield by his feet and said the only thing that came to him. "I thought you were a ghost."

She tilted her head. "Are you soused?"

"I don't know."

She blinked. "Have you been drinking?"

"Yes."

"I think you are soused."

"It's possible."

"Why?"

"Because it's Christmas."

They both froze at the words—the product of a whisky-loosened tongue—and Eben meant to look away, except he couldn't. So instead he watched as dark brows rose and full lips parted on a little, soundless *oh*, as though she understood exactly what the words meant.

The room grew warmer, and Eben rushed to cover the truth. "Must I have a reason? It's my home. It's the dead of night. And I thought I was alone. You're lucky I didn't find you skulking through the conservatory."

"Or what? You might have struck me with an oboe?"

"I don't own an oboe, but the bow of a violin might smart."

She watched him for a long moment, and he could have sworn she was remembering. And then, a flash of a care-free smile. "Again, Eben, if you don't wish for intruders, you should lock the door."

"You're the only one who knows that door exists."

"Then I shall take it as a personal invitation." When he scowled, she added, "Somehow, it seems even worse that you're soused in your own home in the dead of night, alone."

"Worse than what?"

"Worse than being soused with someone else."

Had she been afraid of finding him with someone else? No. He wasn't good at other people. Wasn't that why she'd left?

"Are you offering your companionship?"

She wasn't, of course. Her companionship hadn't been available to him for twelve years. Not since he'd refused it one too many times, and she'd been proud enough and strong enough to walk away.

She didn't say any of that, though. Instead, she offered him a little smile and said, thoughtfully, "We've always been better friends at night, haven't we?"

The words unleashed a flood of unwelcome memories, but before he could decide not to speak, she had changed the topic, somehow making him feel even worse. "My milk shall get cold."

"How do you know I have chocolate?"

That soft smile again. "You always have chocolate, Eb."

Perhaps it was the diminutive that no one else had ever used with him. Or maybe it was that she remembered how much he enjoyed chocolate. Or maybe it was that smile, that he'd always been willing to do anything for. Or maybe it was the alcohol. Whatever it was, Allryd was already in motion, heading to a nearby shelf to retrieve a small porcelain pot, returning to slide it across the table to her.

She set the saucepan on the table and opened the pot, peering in. "This is . . ." She sniffed, then looked up at him. "What is this?"

"Chocolate powder. They make it in Amsterdam. It's sweetened. Easier to mix."

She smiled at him, and something came into her eyes that felt like the past. "You always liked it too sweet."

He scowled at the words, as though they were old friends. *Weren't they?* He ignored the thought. "No, I didn't."

She ignored him, scooping it into the saucepan and stirring for a bit before lifting the spoon from the mixture and touching it to her tongue, before closing her eyes and sighing, "Delicious."

Allryd sucked in a breath and, desperate to avoid her, the memory of her, the promise of her, he moved to fetch cups, along with a tin of biscuits that he'd been planning to eat for Christmas luncheon. When he placed the tin on the table, he realized that the biscuits would prolong Jack's midnight visit. Which he shouldn't wish to do.

But he'd always wished for her, and it had never been enough. That was the problem.

"I suppose there's no need for us to stand on ceremony, after all," she said, bypassing the silver pot he'd fetched and instead lifting the saucepan toward the cups.

He nodded his permission, and she poured two cups of chocolate, the steam curling up between them, directing his gaze over the bodice of her dress, the swell of her breasts, the golden locket that lay there like it was home.

She hadn't worn that locket when they were younger.

Ignoring the thought, he reached for a cup as she set the saucepan aside and sat, opening the biscuit tin. "Oooh," she said, "I've missed shortbread."

He raised a brow. "Is shortbread a thing to be missed?"

"Of course, it is," she said around a mouthful of biscuit. "It's delicious."

He lifted his chocolate to his lips, hiding his smile at her enthusiasm, forgetting for a moment that she wasn't here every day. That this wasn't their private ritual. "It's butter and sugar and flour."

She waved her hand in a little flourish. "Precisely."

Allryd supposed she had a point. He reached for a biscuit. "Where have you been that there's no shortbread to be had?"

She swallowed and took a sip of chocolate before she replied. "Everywhere, really. Well, everywhere Aunt Jane wished to go. Every country on the Continent—France, Spain, Italy, Greece. And then all the other places—North Africa. Turkey. Persia. Russia."

He knew all of that. He'd followed her travels. Jack had left London twelve years earlier as a companion to Lady Jane, Baroness Danton, a notorious widow who had once been scandalous and was now eccentric—beloved by the scandal sheets. He'd lingered over the gossip columns, waiting for their news, and when he was forced to break bread with the aristocracy, Jack's name was the only one he cared to listen for.

Not that he'd admit it. Instead he said, "I've never been to any of those places."

She met his gaze, her brown eyes full of too much past. "Your traveling has been in estates and ledgers."

Perhaps he imagined the judgment in the words, but he did not imagine the way he loathed them. The way they shamed him. The way he felt the need to defend himself against them. "I am responsible for hundreds of people."

"I know."

"That's what happens when you inherit a dukedom. You inherit the responsibility. You inherit the sins of the past. You inherit the mistakes. And you have to stay and sort them out. You don't have the choice to see the world. Not at the beginning."

What began as defense ended with a keen desire to rile her up. To remind her that she'd left him. That he was still here, in the same house he'd been in on the day they'd met, and she'd been the one to leave. He wanted her to rise to the bait.

She didn't, though. Instead, she gave him a small smile and said, "There's more than one way to see the world."

He hated the words, the reminder of their past. Of her leaving and his staying. He hadn't been enough for her. That had been it, no? She'd wanted more from him. He'd worked to build a home and a title and a life worthy of her, and it had never been enough. And still, here she was, returned and comfortable despite the years and the past.

And here he was, uncomfortable beyond imagining with the way she shone a light on all the dark places he'd learned to ignore.

Before he could give voice to that discomfort, she spoke. "In Egypt, they make a kind of candy from boiling mallow plants. It takes two days to make it. It's fluffy and white, and so sweet you can sweeten chocolate with it. I think you would enjoy it."

There was a long silence, during which he did not know what to say. He was half-drunk, and it had been twelve years, and she was back and talking about candy in the dead of night.

She smiled and said, "You would have enjoyed many of the things we saw."

And there it was, the hint of the future he might have had. The one he could have no longer. "Are you back?" he asked, irritation flaring.

She hesitated, and for a moment he clung to the pause, equal parts hope that she'd returned and desperation for her to leave. "Not for long."

He nodded; the words ached in his chest. Why should it matter? He had no right to her time. No right to her. He'd relinquished it years ago, in every arena but the damned papers he couldn't help but clip. Still, he asked, "For how long? You seem unprepared for Christmas if you haven't any chocolate in the house."

She smiled. "I leave on Sunday."

On Boxing Day. It made sense. She'd spent twelve years traveling the globe, and London's was not the most pleasant of Januaries. But still, two days seemed . . . fleeting. "Leave for where?"

"We are for Scotland."

"Your aunt does not seem the type who wishes to winter in Scotland." The baroness was rarely in Britain for all the world traveling she did, thanks to the ancient husband she'd buried not three years after their marriage had begun.

Jack drank deep, and when she set the cup down, it was to reveal a chocolate mustache along her upper lip. She licked at it, long and unladylike, and Allryd felt the movement on every inch of his skin. The temperature in the cool kitchens was suddenly impossibly hot.

Like the fires of hell, which was surely where he was going for thinking of all the things he might do with that tongue.

And then she said, "She's not. In fact, she leaves on Sunday, as well. For Constantinople."

"Without you?"

"With a new companion. A younger one. Someone able to keep pace with her." The words were weary.

His brow furrowed. "I don't believe you cannot keep pace with her. I've never met someone so ready for adventure as you."

"You always thought that was a fault," she said, softly.

"I didn't," he said.

She cut him a disbelieving look.

"I didn't," he insisted. Jack had always leapt into the world feet first, assuming she would land on a soft cloud of opportunity. And she had landed on that cloud. Every time.

Every time but one.

He cleared his throat. "If not Aunt Jane, then who is your companion for Scotland?"

"My . . ." A pause, and then, ". . . husband."

Allryd stilled, barely controlling the flinch. "You are married?"

"Soon to be," she said, and he heard the hesitation in her voice, as though she didn't want to tell him. Or perhaps it was his hesitation. Perhaps he didn't want to hear.

"I haven't seen banns." Not that he went to church, but that wasn't the point. Jack couldn't marry another.

"We shall marry in Scotland," she said quickly, selecting another biscuit from the tin as though she hadn't just fired a cannon in his kitchen.

"Why?"

She took a bite, chewed, and swallowed. "We're back from Greece, and headed to Fergus's estate there."

Fergus.

It was a silly name. The kind of name one gave a hound. A great, hairy one with a long lolling tongue.

She couldn't marry *Fergus.*

Nevertheless, she continued to talk as though the deed were, in fact, to be done. "As we will marry there, there is no need to post banns here."

"Not why no banns. Why marry?"

"It is not so uncommon, is it? Unless you reference my advanced years?"

"Of course not." She was thirty-two, not eighty-two. Thirty-two and beautiful and sun-soaked in December, which seemed impossible. Eminently marriageable. "I only meant—" He stopped. He did not know what he meant. And still he spoke. "I thought you wanted something other than marriage."

Her brows rose. "No. I wanted something other than marriage with a man who cared less for me than he did his estate."

The words were ice, sobering him. Anger and frustration and something he did not dare name coursed through him at the clear reference to their past. "I didn't care more for it."

Silence fell for long minutes, until he could no longer bear it. "Fergus would not like you being here in the dead of night."

She opened her mouth, and he saw the hesitation as she

considered her words. And then, "Fergus knows we are old friends."

He met her gaze. "Is that what we are?"

I know the sound of your sighs when you're properly kissed.

I know the sound of your moans when you fall apart in my arms.

I know you. Every inch of you.

You were mine before Fergus ever dreamed of you.

But he couldn't say any of that. And he couldn't stay here with her. Not when she was pure past and no hint of future.

He stood and made for the door. "Clear your mess before you leave. Take the shortbread with you. And the chocolate. With my best wishes on the occasion of your engagement."

Chapter Two

Christmas Eve, fourteen years earlier

*L*adies were not supposed to sneak into gentlemen's homes in the dead of night.

That went double for young ladies.

Triple for young, unmarried ladies.

It did not matter that it was Christmas Eve. Nor did it matter that the young lady had been sneaking into the gentleman in question's house for years.

Jacqueline Mosby, youngest child of the Earl of Darby, had always been more certain of her place in the world than most grown men—and that place had ensured that she never cared much for what she was or was not *supposed* to do. She'd never been very interested in how things should be. No, Jack had always been more interested in what *could* be. What *might* be. And that, of course, was her downfall.

Because Jack had always been the kind of girl who climbed to the top of a tree to see the view, only worrying about the consequences once she'd reached the canopy and found she couldn't get down. Of course, even then, Jack saw the best of a situation, snacking on apples and taking in the wide world from her new vantage point until she sorted out just how to extricate herself from the treetop.

It was that openness, that optimism, that willingness to

tackle any challenge that had made the secret door between the Mosby library and the Allryd conservatory more Jack's than Eben's.

For Jack, the door was freedom—to hide from her governess, to escape her brothers and sisters, to sneak a treat to Eben when she'd had a particularly delicious sweet at luncheon, to curl up with a book on the conservatory settee while he practiced his violin.

For Eben, however, the door was escape.

Most nights, his father drank until he could not stand and fell asleep in his study, with only his tears to comfort him. But on the bad nights, the duke either did not drink enough, or his sadness took a turn from melancholy, and he went searching for someone to punish for his misery. Misery for which he blamed Eben, his heir and only child, all that was left of the wife he'd once loved beyond reason.

On more than one occasion, Eben had sneaked through the secret doorway in the conservatory, to hide alone in the dark Mosby library until day crept into the sky like pale, lavender hope.

Or, at least, he'd been alone until the night Jack—ten years old—had come to sit next to him, tucking her knees up under her nightgown, her toes peeking out beneath the lace hem. They'd sat in silence for what seemed like hours before she took his hand in hers and bent her head to his shoulder, willing him to feel a fraction of the comfort she had. A hint of the certainty that she, even then, had known was an uncommon privilege.

They hadn't spoken, and Jack had fallen asleep, not stirring when Eben put his arm around her, breathing her in, reveling in her peace, until dawn came and he woke her to send her back to bed before they were caught.

But on the nights that followed, they'd talked. They'd played chess. They'd pored over maps as she'd showed him all the places she planned to visit when she was older.

She'd read him stories of the world's greatest privateers and they'd decided that someday, they would hire a ship and travel the world. She wanted the future, and he wanted to be far from the past.

They'd become friends.

Good enough friends for her to miss him when he left for school. Except, missing him soon gave way to something else—something more powerful. Something that made her heart pound when she thought of using the door to see him when he returned for breaks and holidays. Something that made her too eager to wait for him to use it. Something that made her use it herself, sneaking about his silent house to find him.

The first time she'd knocked on the door of his bedchamber, she was fourteen, and he, sixteen. He'd told her she couldn't stay. After all, he was a marquess and she was a young lady, and they weren't babies anymore. Bedchambers were not appropriate settings for their meetings. Certainly not bedchambers in the dark of night, but to be safe—bedchambers in any lighting scheme and at any time of day should likely be avoided.

It had only taken a heartbeat or two of convincing before Eben had tossed aside those silly rules. They were friends, after all, and he was so rarely home from school—Eton, and soon to be Oxford—and the late-night visits were clandestinely perfect, not because they were scandalous, but because they were theirs.

After that night, scant seconds passed between her soft knock and his opening of the door. They would take to the chairs by the fireplace in his chambers, and Jack would tuck her knees into her nightgown, her long pink toes peeking out, and he would pour her chocolate and they would whisper in the dark, reliving their months apart. Eben would tell her long and elaborate stories, answering every question she had—even the scandalous ones—and Jack lived vicariously through them, remembering the names of all the other boys in his class and the wild things they did when proctors and instructors and deans weren't watching. And Eben remembered, too—the minutiae of the books she'd read and the dresses she'd worn and the ridiculous things her older sisters had done to win this earl or that marquess.

On it went, for years, until his father died, and eighteen-year-old Jack had flown through the dark halls of All-ryd House, desperate to reach him. But that night, she'd knocked on the door, and he hadn't come to open it.

So she'd opened it herself—knowing, even as the handle turned beneath her grip, that everything had changed.

Eben was lying on his bed, staring up at the rich, velvet canopy. He didn't look to the door as she slipped into the room and closed it behind her. Nor did he look to her when she ignored the chairs by the fireplace.

Nor did he look when she climbed onto the bed with him, fitting herself against him without hesitation, stretching one long arm across his waist. An anchor in the storm.

His arm came around her, clutching her to him. "You shouldn't be here."

"I don't care," she whispered.

"Not in my room. Definitely not in my bed."

Again. "I don't care."

Silence. Then, barely there, "I don't want you to leave."

She'd never leave him. "Michael wouldn't let me attend the funeral," she said. Of course, her brother hadn't; funerals weren't a place for girls. "I raged, of course, but no one would listen."

"It's best you weren't there," he said, though it didn't sound like he believed it.

Jack certainly didn't believe it. "I wanted to be there. I wanted to be with you."

"You wouldn't have been with me," he said. "I was at the front. You . . . wouldn't have been with me."

She tightened her grip—enough to pull him from his stupor, eager for his beautiful green gaze. "You would have known I was there. That's how I would have been with you." She stopped, unable to look away from him. Wanting to be closer. To touch him. To reach him. "Eben . . . I should have been with you."

The words were an ache in her chest. Her own parents had died years earlier, tragedy striking when their carriage careened off course on an icy road in the middle of a winter storm, and Eben had been away at school—too far to return for the funeral. But he'd written. She still had the letter, filled with miles of words, words she now understood beyond measure.

She repeated them with reverence. "I should have been with you."

He did not reply except to tighten his arm around her, which was enough. She put her cheek to his chest, the heavy thrum of his heartbeat beneath her ear. She was with him now. And she'd stay all night if he'd have her, hang what her aunt and her brothers and sisters had to say. Eben needed her.

She'd stay all night. The next day. And the one after.

Until he found the words she knew he had to speak.

They lay in silence for a long time, until the candle at his bedside was barely a stump. Until Eben took a deep, shattering breath and told her his darkest secret. The one she already knew.

"I'm glad he's dead." The confession came on a whisper of fear, as though his father might hear him and take up haunting.

Jack did not loosen her grip. "As am I."

"He was a drunk."

"He was broken, unable to be mended." Eben looked down at her, and she gave a little shrug. "And a bastard."

His lips twitched at the forthright assessment. "That he was. Also a bad father. And a bad duke."

"You shall be a better one."

"You say that like it's a foregone conclusion."

She lifted her head, turning on the bed so she could rest her chin on his chest and tell him the truth. "It is."

He let out a long breath and looked up at the velvet canopy once more. "Everything is going to change."

"Nothing important." Not this. Not them, together. *Please. Not us, together.*

"I'm a duke now."

"I always thought you weren't impressive enough to be a marquess."

He laughed, and joy spread through her at the sound. That hadn't changed. She loved his laugh—like a secret between them. "You know dukes are higher than marquesses, don't you?"

She matched his smile. "Yes, but marquess has such a stylish ring to it. I'd much rather be a marquess."

"Well, I'm both, now."

"And there you are, already an insufferable braggart." She tucked herself closer to him.

His arm tightened again, and he whispered, "How am I to do this?"

The question heralded the change he'd foretold. It heralded the fear. The panic. The responsibility. Adulthood. She settled her hand on his chest, over his heart. "I shall help."

"Do you have a great deal of expertise in being a duke?"

She didn't like the question. Tried for levity. "No, but how difficult can it possibly be? Men bow and scrape to you and women wish to woo you."

"That seems a fine assessment of the whole situation."

"You shall be eternally grateful that I shall be there to keep you firmly on the ground." He huffed a little laugh, and Jack worked to keep him there, in freedom, just for a moment. "How shall we begin? Shall I follow you about and remind you that you once struggled to find Constantinople on a map?"

"I did not. The map was upside down."

She smiled at the well-worn argument. Solid ground. Equal footing. "Oh yes, Turkey does move about on the map when viewed in reverse."

"You think that my lack of geographical skill will impede my ability to woo women?"

She stilled at the question, time seeming to slow. "Are you interested in wooing women?"

"Isn't everyone?"

What kind of women? She didn't ask it. It wasn't her business. Especially not tonight. After all, it wasn't as though she hadn't expected there were girls who had caught his eye. It wasn't like she hadn't imagined there were girls with whom he wished to . . .

But she hadn't *liked* imagining them. That was all.

She'd *hated* it.

Not that it meant anything. It didn't mean anything. He could woo women if he wanted. Good Lord, she wished she'd never invoked wooing. They were friends. And friends did not care about things like this.

Except, it seemed Jack cared very much about precisely this kind of thing. She closed her eyes tight and willed everything returned to normal. Except perhaps he was right. Perhaps everything was going to change.

And then he said, quietly, "Jack?" and she was a runaway carriage, unable to be stopped.

"Jacqueline," she whispered.

"What?"

She did not look away from her hand on his chest. "I'm not a child, playing pirates any longer, Eben."

He was still for a long moment, long enough for her to feel like she might perish from mortification. She looked up at him, into his wide eyes, confusion and surprise and something else—something like understanding dawning.

Oh God. It was mortifying.

She put her head down. "Never mind."

But it was done, and suddenly neither of them was a child anymore. And not only because he used her full name. "Jacqueline."

She didn't look at him, not even when she whispered her reply. "Yes?"

"I missed you today."

She closed her eyes tight. Told him the truth. "I missed you, too."

Quiet again. Then, "I don't want to win women."

Her heart began to pound. "Why not?"

"Because I don't need them."

She held her breath. "Why not?"

"Because I have you."

She lifted her head at that, her eyes finding his, her lips parting on a little surprised breath when he dipped his head and stole them, just as he'd stolen her heart.

It was the first kiss of dozens, hundreds, thousands over the next two years, kisses that would blend together into a sea of memory, of clandestine moments and desperate desire. But that one—that first one—was not a part of that sea. It was memory distilled, singular because it was first.

For the rest of her life, Jack would remember every fumbling second of that kiss: the way he pulled her against him, the wild thoughts that tumbled through her as his fingers slid into her hair, holding her still as they explored each other, the warmth of his long body against hers, the rough scrape of his unshaven cheek, the firm planes of his torso, the certainty that this moment was perfection warring with uncertainty—could he possibly want her as much as she wanted him?

Except when his tongue traced the seam of her lips and she opened for him, letting him into her for the first time, he growled, low and deep, the sound like nothing she'd ever heard before. And, in a flash, the friend she'd once loved was gone. In his place, Jack found the man she would always love.

The man who made her wild.

Jack cast off her inexperience with gusto and leapt into learning, pushing against his chest to slide up and kiss him back, playing with pressure and sensation, her own tongue licking out to test the fullness of his wide, bottom lip, the softness of it.

Soft like heaven. Sweet like it.

When she sighed her pleasure into him, Eben went stiff, moving to release her. She pulled back from the kiss, her eyes flying open, meeting his clear green gaze with complete certainty. "Don't you dare stop. This is my first kiss, and I don't want it done until it's done."

A beat, and then a slow, easy smile. One she'd never seen before. One that had her stomach turning with wild pleasure. "You're awfully imperious, you know. It's my first kiss, too."

The wave of pleasure nearly knocked her over. "It is?"

A flush spread over his cheeks at the question. He cleared his throat. "It's not as though I haven't had the opportunity . . ."

She grinned. "Oh, of course not," she replied, wanting to kiss his rosy cheeks. "But you haven't done it."

He cleared his throat again. "I haven't." He paused, then added, "So, don't I get a say in how it goes?"

She shook her head, her gaze flitting down to his mouth,

her lids half-closed, wanting more of him. "You don't, as a matter of fact."

"Why is that?" he asked, the low rumble of his voice deliciously unrecognizable.

She tore her attention from his mouth. "Two reasons. First, because you'll probably summon some misplaced sense of duty and stop."

"I am delighted that you think so highly of my sense of honor."

She shook her head. "I don't. I think it's bollocks tonight."

He pulled her tighter against him. "Understood. And is there a second reason you're to take charge?"

She nodded, happily. "Because girls dream of their first kiss with a duke, so I have to make sure this one measures up."

His lips twitched. "Girls have fantasies of kissing dukes?"

"Oh yes," she said, eyes twinkling. Was there anything better than kissing and laughter? "What with how old and powdered so many of them are, how could we not?"

"But I'm not old or powdered."

She nodded, feigning disappointment. "As dukes are thin on the ground, I suppose you shall have to do."

"You have a smart mouth."

"Aren't you lucky you are able to kiss it?"

In response, he rolled her over, pressing her back to the bed, leaning over her, staring deep into her eyes as her fingers threaded into his hair. "I can't believe this is happening."

She pulled his head down to hers. "Perhaps you'll believe it with more practice."

They practiced until the wee hours of the morning, when that familiar purple light spread across the horizon and he walked her through the dark halls of the house that was now his by name and right. When he opened their secret doorway and stole another kiss, it was the first morning of their second life—the one that had begun with that first kiss that neither of them would ever forget.

He'd nearly closed the door behind her when she put a hand to the painted oak and whispered his name.

When he looked to her, she smiled. "Happy Christmas." And then she vowed, clearly and perfectly, "Nothing will change. I'm still here. We're both still here."

Of course, she was wrong. Everything changed.

Chapter Three

Christmas Day

She was soft and warm and naked in his arms, like a gift, just where he'd dreamed of her forever. He pulled her close and breathed her in, an impossibly lush garden in the dead of winter. She whispered his name like sin. "Allryd . . ."

Thump. Thump.

He rose over her, pressing her back to the soft bed, burying his lips in the crook of her shoulder, tasting the sweet-salt of her skin, licking over the round of her shoulder as her hands stroked along his body.

"Allryd . . ."

His name again. A prayer. A promise.

He growled and explored lower, over the swell of her breasts, seeking and finding one straining brown tip, taking it between his lips and worshipping it with slow, languid pulls, knowing how much she loved him to play there . . . long and lingering until she was writhing with want.

Thump. Thump.

Her fingers were in his hair, fisting with a roughness she could not restrain, pushing him lower, directing him over her impossibly soft skin, past the warm, wonderful swell of her belly, to where he ached to be . . . His mouth watered as her thighs fell open.

Thump. Thump. Thump.

Was that his heart? It must be. Pounding in desperation. Christ . . . How long had he ached for this? For her? For his love to return?

"Allryd . . ."

Wait. Something was wrong.

No. He tightened his hold.

She never called him that.

She was slipping away from him. Her warmth was disappearing. He lifted his head to find her eyes. If he could just find her eyes, maybe she'd stay.

Thump thump thump.

He couldn't find them. He couldn't feel her. She was gone.

"Fuck!" he roared as he opened his eyes, clutching the bedsheets, hard as steel, head and heart pounding, filled with fury and desperation and something dangerously close to madness.

Alone.

"Christ," he whispered, rubbing his hands violently over his face.

He rolled himself up to sitting, letting his bare legs hang over the side of the bed in the cold room, and paused, leaning forward, capturing his pounding head in his hands. They'd had ham for luncheon two days ago. Surely there was something to eat in the icehouse. Of course, that meant he had to go downstairs and outside.

And risk seeing her.

Not that seeing her would matter.

He didn't care if he saw her.

And even if he did see her, he'd made it more than clear that he had little interest in seeing her again. That, he remembered. It was the bit after that was . . . uncertain.

Because he'd gone back to drinking.

Christ, the room was cold. He groaned, realizing that the fire had died in the hearth. The room wasn't merely cold, but frigid.

Christmas meant no servants, and no servants meant no food or heat unless he summoned it himself. Which he was more than able to do, if only the room would stop spinning.

Perhaps the cold air would temper the ache in his head. And the one in his cock.

He stood, cursing his choices from the night before and desperate for clear thought, which twelve years of Christmas Day experience told him he would not have for at least another six hours. Which was fine, because he planned to be alone, with his ledgers. He would find cold food and hot drink and he would check the accounting of his estates, as he did on the twenty-fifth of every month. December should be no different.

It did not matter that it was Christmas Day.

And it certainly did not matter that she was next door.

Thump thump thump.

Allryd whipped around at the sound, an echo of the dream now disappeared. His attention fell to the door to his chambers, upon which a massive beast seemed to pound.

Thwack thwack!

Likely not a beast if it had climbed stairs and knocked on doors.

Maybe it was Jack.

It wasn't Jack. He'd made it clear she wasn't welcome here. That, and she wouldn't have knocked. She would have entered and climbed into his bed, like she'd done a hundred times before.

Desire returned, the cold unable to combat the thought of her in his bed.

Except, she wouldn't have climbed into it this time. This time, she had a fiancé. Who no doubt had his own bed.

And damned if the thought of her in another man's bed didn't make Allryd want to tear down walls to stop it.

Thwack! Thwack!

"Goddammit! Enough!" he called out, hating the sound of his own voice, the way it clamored through his skull like an ax. Maybe it was a beast at the door. Maybe it would put him out of his misery.

The door opened. "You look like proper hell."

It wasn't a beast. It was Lawton. Tall, broad, clean-shaven, and impeccably outfitted as the clotheshorse always was, boots shined to perfection, his cravat gleaming white against his black skin in elaborate folds and swirls, his crimson-and-gold waistcoat no doubt a nod to the date.

"What are you doing here?"

"Have you forgotten I have a desk below? Right next to yours?"

"I thought you had a holiday to observe," Allryd growled.

"I thought so, too," the other man said, leaning casually against the doorjamb, "but I work nearly as hard as you do, so I haven't anyone with whom to observe it."

Charles Lawton's brother owned a tavern in Marylebone, where many of London's dockworkers spent their evenings. The brother came with a fine wife and two boys who routinely turned up at Allryd's house to boisterously hang about the trouser leg of their all-too-cheerful uncle.

Allryd narrowed his gaze. "That's a lie."

Lawton flashed a smile. "Joan doesn't want you alone on Christmas."

"Why is everyone so concerned with my holiday solitude?"

"Everyone?"

He certainly wasn't telling Lawton about Jack's arrival in the dead of night. His business partner was an old woman at a church tea when it came to gossip. "You."

"I don't give a damn where you spend the holiday. And,

truthfully, I think it's less that Joan is concerned about you and more that she likes to tell her friends about the duke who comes to dinner. That, and the boys like it when the 'strange toff' comes."

Allryd grunted, ignoring the hint of satisfaction that came at the words. The boys were fine, he supposed. Most of the time, he liked them better than their uncle, who was still speaking, to the detriment of Allryd's pounding head. "Their affinity for you is perplexing, I know, as there's not a thing about you that's agreeable, but they're children and therefore fairly dimwitted."

Allryd ignored the dig. "You've wasted a visit. You should have told them I was busy."

"It's Christmas Day, Allryd. No one is busy."

"I am. I am working."

"At what? Sleeping until all hours and struggling to stand?" Lawton said, coming into the room. "It's freezing in here. And it stinks of stupor." He moved to the window and threw open the heavy drapes there. "I should open this window and air you out."

Allryd closed his eyes and turned his back to the sky beyond. "Goddammit, it's December. Why is the sun so damn bright?"

Lawton turned to face him. "It's snowing."

He stilled. *Jack would be elated.*

No. He did not have time to think of Jack. Nor was he interested in how she might react to the snow. He cleared his throat. "Then you'd best get back to your dinner; you won't like it if the snow keeps you here. As you convinced me to let the servants have the holiday, I've nothing to feed you."

Lawton cut him a look. "Leaving aside the fact that I know the larder is stocked full, I assure you that your current state—naked as a babe and stinking of gin—is no kind of incentive to stay."

Allryd reached for his dressing gown. "It was whisky."

Lawton stilled. "*My* whisky?"

"As it was in *my* home, its ownership is not exactly precise."

The other man narrowed his gaze. "Was its location precisely on *my* desk?" When Allryd moved to cover himself without replying, Lawton made a noise of disgust. "You don't even drink. It was wasted on you."

"I drank last night, and it did the job," Allryd said, tying the knot of his dressing gown. "I've the head to prove it."

"A day with my too-loud nephews is the punishment you deserve," his devious partner replied, already heading for the door to the chamber. "Get yourself presentable. My sister-in-law expects us at two. I shall meet you in the kitchens. If you're lucky, I'll have made coffee."

Lawton left, slamming the door behind him, exacerbating the throbbing pain in Allryd's head—a pain made worse when the duke shouted a wicked curse at the closed door.

Goddammit. Why anyone drank was beyond him. It was a stupid habit that served little purpose. After all, on the one night of the year he drank to forget, the thing he'd attempted to eradicate from memory had been made flesh in his kitchens.

And what glorious flesh it had been.

She was the same as she'd been when they were young, long and curved, with those bold eyes and that bright smile and freckled, bronzed skin from too much time in the sun.

Not too much. Just enough.

He'd thought of those freckles for years—lain awake at night and counted them as sleep teased at the edges of his consciousness. He'd dreamed of running his tongue along the dusting across her nose and the apples of her cheeks, of kissing the constellation of them on her left shoulder, of finding all the others, hidden beneath satin and linen, waiting for his arrival.

There were more of them now, on her chest and shoulders, a kiss from the sun, along with creases at the corners of her eyes and the deeper swells of her curves—all proof of her time away. He wanted to explore every one of those changes.

The thought of exploring Lady Jacqueline Mosby made him hard again, even as his head pounded with the after-effects of the night before. He cursed and moved to the basin at the far side of the room to strip and wash, splashing cold water on his face and willing away the results of his misplaced desire.

The strategy failed. He'd spent every day of the last twelve years trying not to remember her. Trying not to imagine how she'd grown. How she'd changed. How she might be the woman she'd become—a richer, fuller, more perfect version of the girl he'd known.

The girl he'd loved.

The girl he should have married.

Now he did not have to imagine. He knew.

Not that it mattered. She was to marry another. Fergus, the long-tongued, cabbage-headed Scot.

Allryd violently splashed frigid water on his face, rubbing his hands over his skin as though he could erase her from his thoughts. Finally, he plunged his entire head into the basin, enjoying the shock as he scooped liquid over his hair and the back of his neck.

He supposed the Scot did not deserve the descriptor . . . He couldn't imagine that Jack would tie herself to someone who lacked a brain in his head, but it helped to think that the man who was to have his life was less than he was, in some way.

His life.

He surfaced at the thought, hands fisted on the table that held the basin, droplets of water falling to the bowl, unseen.

Jack wasn't his life.

She might have been, once, but he'd chosen differently. He'd chosen responsibility and an estate in debt to the rafters, along with a title that had been left in shambles. She'd deserved better than what he could give her—no money, no comforts, and even less time.

She'd been right to leave.

Even though she'd stolen his heart from his chest when she'd gone.

Not that he'd noticed until he realized she'd never come back.

He shook his head, willing memory to fly with water, scattered in all directions.

Fucking holidays and their maudlin nostalgia. Getting out of Mayfair was a damned good idea.

He ran his fingers through his hair, vaguely taming it before cleaning his teeth and rinsing his mouth. Lawton had promised coffee and a hot meal. More importantly, that meal would be far from Jacqueline Mosby and the demons that followed with her.

Except, as Allryd made his way down the rear servants' staircase to the kitchens, fairly proud of how he'd turned himself out without a valet to do the job, he realized that he was not going to avoid Jack and her partner demons that day.

Because she was once more in his kitchens.

And this time, she was more dangerous, because she was laughing. Eben hadn't heard that laugh in twelve years. In longer. At some point, during their faraway youth, she'd stopped laughing.

Or he'd stopped hearing it.

But there it was—a sound he'd missed so much, he hadn't realized he'd forgotten it. It was rich and full like a miracle. Or a curse. Yes. A curse. She was a damn Christmas curse.

He paused at the entrance to the kitchens to find her

looking like she belonged there, in a functional, pale day dress covered by an apron, wide smile on her lips as she slid a teacup across the table toward Lawton.

She did belong there.

Eben resisted the thought as his business partner peered into the cup for a long moment before looking up at her and saying, "I didn't know there was chocolate here."

Her smile widened, and she reached down to wipe her hands on her white apron. "Now you may have it whenever you like."

Over the years, Eben had had his frustrations with Lawton—a man as carefree as Eben was careful. He spent money as though it was water on ridiculous frivolities like gold-threaded waistcoats and high-gloss phaetons. He routinely mocked Eben for his fiscal caution and his foul temper, and half the actresses on Drury Lane were liable to turn up for luncheon on any given weekday because women came to Lawton as easily as funds seemed to, and the man was happy to welcome them.

But watching his associate on the receiving end of Jack's brilliant smile made Eben want to do serious damage to him. Business partnership and friendship be damned.

Her smile wasn't for Lawton.

It wasn't for others.

Except for her fiancé.

Ignoring the insidious thought, Eben schooled his features and said, "He may not have chocolate whenever he likes, as it is mine."

"Consider it a trade for my whisky," Lawton drawled smugly into his cup.

"Was it your whisky that got him soused?" Jack asked cheerfully. "It did an excellent job."

"Did it?" Lawton asked, curious brows rising in Eben's direction at the revelation that Jack had witnessed him drunk at some point. Eben scowled a warning and the other man added, "How's the head, Duke?"

Eben ignored the question. "As neither of you were invited, would one of you please explain what in hell you are doing in my home this morning?"

The words were threatening and cold—enough that any number of others across London would have cowered in the corner or turned tail and run.

Neither of the intruders were moved.

Instead, Jack turned that wide smile on him, and it was he who considered running. She was far more threatening with her heat than he was with his cold—her smile instantly warming his freezing house as though fires roared in every hearth. "Happy Christmas, Eben."

He ignored the words and the way they claimed his heart for a beat. "Was I unclear about your welcome?"

She lifted a spoon from a pot on the stove. "I made chocolate."

"Because you don't have it in your own house?"

She tilted her head, the expression doing strange things to him. "Perhaps." She paused. "Does it help that I'm also cooking you Christmas lunch?"

"No." So that was the delicious smell. "Go home."

She shook her head and turned back to the stove. "No."

Before Eben could remove her bodily, Lawton smirked. "Imagine my surprise when I discovered a beautiful woman hard at work in your kitchens this morning, *Eben*."

Eben growled at the emphasis on his given name, a name Lawton had never used before this moment. A name with which no one but Jack had ever been wholly comfortable, not even Eben himself.

Irritation and frustration flared. "She's not beautiful."

He regretted the words the moment they left his mouth, even before Lawton's brows knitted together in instant, deserved censure. Even before Jack's breath caught on a little hitch, so soft that he shouldn't have noticed it. Of course, he did notice it. He noticed everything about her, now that she was no longer his to notice.

But he already hated the words before he even realized they'd hurt her. Because they were such a damn lie. He would have done anything for them to be the truth . . . Maybe if she weren't so damned beautiful, he might have a chance of surviving her.

As it was, he couldn't look at her. It was like staring into the sun.

"On the contrary," Lawton replied. "Lady Jacqueline might well be the most beautiful thing I've ever seen on Christmas—and when I was a boy, my father gave me a tin soldier the likes of which you've never dreamed."

He winked at Jack, and she offered up a little giggle. "I have never been compared to a tin soldier, but I shall take it as a high compliment."

"As well you should," Lawton said, lifting the cup from the saucer in front of him. "It was my favorite toy for ages."

"No longer?" Jack teased, and Eben hated the instant, easy rapport between the two. The rapport that used to be his, a thousand years earlier.

"I've graduated to better toys."

"For example?"

Lawton winked over the edge of his cup. "Well, this Christmas, I happen to be partial to pretty brown-haired angels."

She blushed, and Eben considered upending the table when she replied, "You're a terrible flirt."

"Really? I've always thought myself rather a good one," Lawton replied.

Their shared grin was enough, goddammit. "You can stop barking up this particular tree, Lawton. She's engaged."

His partner put a hand to his chest. "Holiday dreams dashed."

Jack laughed. "Believe it or not, there is another who finds me more than repulsive."

"I didn't say you were repulsive," Eben said. "You're not repulsive."

"Be still my heart," she retorted before turning back to the stove, where several pots boiled away. "It is a shock you remain unmatched, considering your way with words. Truly."

Feeling beastly, Eben looked to Lawton, who stared back and forth between them, jaw slightly dropped, which made Eben want to put a fist to it. "What is it?"

Lawton shook his head. "Only that I've never seen anyone less cowed by you than this woman. She could offer lessons for pay and we'd never make another sound business deal again."

"The duke won't like it if you ruin his business." The words came from behind Eben, the voice instantly familiar.

He spun around, a thread of something that might be called happiness coursing through him. "Aunt Jane."

The older woman cut him an uncompromising look. "That's Lady Danton to you, boy." Eben's jaw went slack. He'd never called the owner of the town house next door Lady Danton. She'd always been Aunt Jane to him, just as she'd always been Aunt Jane to Jack.

Though, he supposed he couldn't claim Jack anymore, so he should not expect to claim Aunt Jane, either.

Perhaps it wouldn't have smarted as much if she hadn't looked to Lawton then, considering the tall man who had come to his feet when she entered the room.

"Jacqueline," she asked, all curiosity, "who is our guest?" Wait. *Our?*

Eben blinked. "These remain *my* kitchens, do they not?"

Lawton bowed low. "Charles Lawton, my lady. May I say

it is an honor to meet you; your reputation precedes you."
He gifted her with his most winning smile—the one Eben
had seen win countless women.

The dowager baroness considered Lawton for a long
moment, then said, "And what reputation is that?"

Lawton inclined his head. "A woman with a discerning
taste for adventure."

Eben rolled his eyes. Aunt Jane was more than double
Lawton's age.

The baroness laughed, full and flirtatious. "You, my
dear, are welcome to call me Aunt Jane."

"I am deeply honored."

The older woman's lips curved softly. "You remind me
of a boy I knew a long time ago. He had a smile that made
skirts swirl."

"Aunt Jane!" Jacqueline interjected from her place at
the stove. "You'll scare the poor man off!"

"Nonsense," came the reply. "He's faced worse than me."

Lawton chuckled, leaning back on the table, black eyes
twinkling as though he'd never had such fun as this mad
crew. "Indeed, you shall have to do much worse to scare
me off, my lady."

"My point, exactly. After all, he works with Allryd."

"I beg your pardon," Eben said, feeling as though he
ought to defend himself.

"Oh, are you offended by my assessment of your company?" Aunt Jane asked.

"I am, rather," he said.

"Good."

Lawton guffawed, and a long-buried instinct had Eben
turning to Jack—for defense, perhaps? Or perhaps to see if
she, too, was laughing at him. She wasn't. She was transfixed by the simmering pot on the stove, gently stirring the
liquid within.

She was not interested in defending him. And he could not blame her. He did not deserve it.

Eben returned his attention to Lawton and said, "Don't you have a Christmas luncheon to go to?"

Lawton waved away the words. "I've time to stay and watch this play—it's rare to see a pair so uninterested in simpering before you."

"I've known Eben too long to simper before him," Jack replied.

"You've never simpered in your life," Eben shot back.

She turned her head at that, her brown eyes meeting his. "Fair. That might be why I never found a husband."

Did she simper before the idiot Scot who was taking her away from him?

The thought of the Scot grated. "Shouldn't you *also* be somewhere celebrating a holiday? With Fergus?"

He hadn't meant to snarl the name.

Actually, he had. Everything about their presence in his kitchens seemed like pain and punishment. Like penance for past sins and the promise of a punishing future without her.

"Who's Fergus?" Lawton asked, as though this were tea and cake with the vicar and not an invasion of his private space.

"Jack's fiancé," Eben said.

He didn't have time to consider Aunt Jane's disapproving harrumph before Lawton asked, confused, "Jack?"

"Me. Jacqueline," Jack clarified.

Not to Eben. Never to Eben. He wondered what hound-Fergus called her.

"He's Scottish," Eben said. "They leave tomorrow to marry there. On his estate." Good Lord. He couldn't shut up. What was wrong with him?

"Felicitations," Lawton said to Jack.

Another harrumph from Aunt Jane.

"Do you mind?" Jack said to the older woman before nodding at Lawton. "Thank you."

Eben wanted to murder something. He wanted to leave. But he wanted to stay more, and therein lay the pain and punishment. He hunkered down on the far side of the table, pretending not to notice when she set a steaming cup of chocolate in front of him. Pretending not to care immensely when he asked, "And so? Where is this perfect Scot?"

A pause. "On his way."

"Why not here already? Or rather, why not in *your* home already?"

She lifted one shoulder and let it drop. "He will be here for luncheon."

"If I were him, I'd be here now." He shouldn't have said it. The words were out, the product of his irritation, before he could stop them.

Before he could predict that they would draw the full weight of Jack's gaze. "To watch me stir plum sauce?"

To make sure I don't toss you over my shoulder and take you to bed.

He couldn't say that.

Eben lifted the cup and drank, the scalding liquid a punishment he refused to acknowledge. As if it were not enough, it came with the judgment of Aunt Jane. "You're not him, though, are you?"

Eben could not speak, and the burned tongue had nothing to do with it—the accusation in the words stung worse than the chocolate.

"Aunt Jane," Jack whispered, and he hated it. Hated the soft censure. Hated that she leapt in to stop her aunt's admonishment. Hated the quiet hint of past in her voice.

The older woman watched him for a long moment, then made for the oven. "My shortbread is ready to come out."

"You made shortbread?"

"Not for you," Aunt Jane shot back.

"Yes, for him," Jack said. "We ate his entire stock last night."

"It should be for Fergus," the older woman said.

The idiot Scot could get his own damn shortbread.

"But it is for His Grace."

His Grace. Good Lord. She'd never called him that. He wanted to leap across the table and make her take it back.

"You'd best be certain you *want* this batch to be for him," Aunt Jane said.

Jack sighed, and he recognized the sound, one he'd heard a thousand times before. She was exasperated. She turned back to the stove and opened another pot, this one larger. Drawn by the delicious aromas beckoning from within, he stood and went to look inside. At her elbow, he peered into the pot.

"Parsnip crème."

"Your favorite," she said quietly. "It seemed you should have it on Christmas."

How did she remember? Why would she make it for him now, after a dozen years away? Why would she remember that he loved chocolate enough to hide pots of it all over the kitchen? The answer was there, undeniable. She remembered just as he remembered the same—her love of treacle and raspberry tart.

Just as he remembered their taste on her lips when he kissed her.

And then he realized that he was staring at her lips, parted on an intake of air. He wrenched his gaze away from them, willing it to her eyes, only to find them focused on his mouth.

Had she been remembering those kisses, too?

"A Christmas curse," he whispered.

Her eyes flew to his. "What?"

"That's what you are."

Her brows furrowed. "Because I am cooking?"

"Because you are interrupting."

She raised a brow. "Were you very busy? It seemed to me you were sleeping away the day . . ."

"As is my prerogative."

"As it is *my* prerogative to cook a holiday meal."

The woman was infuriating. "It is your prerogative to do that in your own bloody kitchen!"

She lifted a shoulder and let it fall, as though they were disagreeing on proper outerwear for the climate and not home intrusion. "Yours is better stocked."

She was maddening.

No, she wasn't. She was the same as ever—quick and smart-mouthed and charming as hell and completely unruffled by him.

Christ, he'd missed her.

No. *No.* There was no missing her. He couldn't miss her. If he missed her, he might never not miss her, and that would certainly kill him.

It was bad enough he'd never stopped loving her.

He had to be rid of her. So, he did the only thing he could think to do. He ceded ground. "Either way, it is no matter." He nodded to Lawton. "I'm expected at Christmas luncheon with Lawton."

If he hadn't been so drawn to her, so focused on her, he might not have seen it. He might not have caught the tiny, barely there wrinkle in her brow. The nearly imperceptible tightening at the corner of her lips. The almost quiver at the point of her heart-shaped face.

Disappointment.

He must be wrong, of course. She was to be married to Fergus, the perfect Scot. She was for some place far to the north, where the land was unforgiving and the speech indecipherable. She was leaving tomorrow. It wasn't disappointment.

Except, it was.

He'd seen it for the split second it had been there before she schooled her features and it was gone. And then he heard it in the quiet *oh* that preceded, "Well, by all means, then. Don't let us keep you."

Another man wouldn't notice it, the little, dismayed syllable. Perfect Fergus wouldn't notice it. But Eben did. And he lingered on it, like a small child staring at tea cakes.

His chest tightened.

Did she want him to stay?

"You're not leaving." All attention turned to Aunt Jane.

"I beg your pardon?" Jack said.

"They're not leaving."

"I damn well am," Eben said.

Lawton spoke with slightly more aplomb. "I'm afraid we must, my lady. My sister-in-law awaits my return, duke in tow."

"That may be the case," Aunt Jane replied, "but I suggest you look outside." She waved a hand at one thick windowpane. "The storm is quite serious now. You shan't make it fifty yards, let alone—where is it you were going?"

"Marylebone," Lawton said.

"Oh no. You certainly shan't make it all the way there."

"We shall be fine," Eben said, desperate to be gone from this madness.

"No." Jack's single word came harsh and unyielding, and everyone looked to her. She was staring out the window at the world beyond—hidden by a wall of swirling whiteness, lost for a moment in the past.

Dammit. He'd spoken without thinking.

"The roads will be too dangerous." She looked to him, her eyes clouded, private.

Twelve years disappeared between them.

"We shan't go," he said to her, and he was rewarded with a single, long exhale, the tension running from her shoulders. His fingers itched to reach for her, and he couldn't stop himself from repeating the words, softly. "We shan't."

Unaware of what had transpired between them, Lawton said, "We shan't?"

He shook his head, his gaze not leaving Jack. "No. The carriage shan't be safe."

A long moment passed before Lawton shrugged. "If only you were the kind of man to have a sleigh, Allryd."

The dry statement distracted Jack, prompting a little chuckle, like sunshine in the snow. Eben looked to her. "What's so amusing?"

"Only the idea of you in a sleigh."

His brows rose. "Why?"

"I cannot imagine you in one."

"Why not?"

She raised a brow. "Well . . . I would have thought that you would consider them rather frivolous. And you've never cared for frivolity."

"That's not true." Silence fell, thick as the snow outside the window. He looked from one face to the next. "It's not."

"Name one frivolous thing you've done," Lawton said, arms crossed over his chest.

Eben's face grew hot. Christ, was he *blushing*? "I've done frivolous things."

Why in hell did it matter?

"Excellent. Tell us about one of them."

Eben stilled, a single memory flooding his thoughts. Consuming him. He looked at Jack, noting the color high on her cheeks and knew, instantly, that she was consumed by it, as well.

But he would be damned if he'd share it with the others. He stayed stubbornly silent.

After a long moment, Aunt Jane interjected, "Never fear, Charlie—may I call you Charlie?"

Lawton turned a ridiculous smile on her. "Nothing would give me more pleasure."

The old woman continued, "To make up for your tragic lack of family for the holiday, I shall regale you with stories of the duke, and the man he might have been." The words fell like lead in Eben's gut as Aunt Jane went on, a touch of smirk in her tone. "Did you know, for example, that he and my niece were once affianced themselves?"

Eben heard the hitch in Jack's breath from where he sat. Heard it and hated it. Hated that he, too, had trouble breathing at the question. Was that the word for what they'd been? Affianced? It had seemed like more than that. Like something that could not simply be dissolved. But dissolved it had been, like snow in sunshine, there one moment and gone the next.

Not so easily.

He met Jack's gaze across the kitchen, reading the past in her eyes and regretting the truth in them. Regretting, too, a different truth—that he'd never stopped loving her. That he never would. Not even when she was happily married to another.

He stood, desperate to be gone from this room with its cloying heat and memory. "If the snow keeps you here," he said to his partner, "so be it. And if these madwomen haven't anything better to do than to cook for you, so be that, as well. But I haven't any need to linger and hear silly stories of an ancient time. I have work to do."

With that, he left the room.

Chapter Four

Christmas Eve, thirteen years earlier

*T*hunder rattled the walls of Darby House, a wicked storm threatening to shake the place to its rafters, and Jack was shaking with it, teeth chattering as she raced through the darkened hallways to the library, not needing light to find the door tucked away in the back corner. She could find it in the dark, with her eyes closed, forever.

It opened before she could reach for it, and there he was, trousers on and shirt untucked, hastily dressed because he was coming for her. He always came for her.

She flew into his open arms and he caught her, pulling her close, tucking her head beneath his chin. "I have you," he whispered. And again. "I have you, love." He pressed his lips to the top of her head and tightened his arms around her.

"You—you c-came," she chattered.

"As soon as I heard the storm," he said, the words a deep rumble in his chest. "I shall always come for you."

The vow began to settle her. "It's so silly. It's just weather."

"It's not weather. It's the past." The night her parents had been traveling in a terrible storm, thunder had spooked the horses and sent the carriage sliding over slick cobblestones and into the icy Thames.

Jack had been barely fourteen and had never been able

to stomach thunder after that, seeking out Eben's company when he was home and pretending to be brave. But he'd always known the truth.

She took a deep breath. Released it. Allowed herself to feel his arms around her. The warmth of him. The truth of him. "You're here," she whispered.

"Thank God," he replied, his hands stroking over her, holding her tight. "Do you know how many nights I have spent lying awake and watching lightning flash? Listening to thunder roll through the countryside, and willing it to stay far from here? Far from you?"

She turned her face into his chest, his confession warming her. "You can't stop the weather," she whispered.

"That doesn't mean I can't try, love," he spoke to the top of her head. "And when I'm here—in London—I will always keep the storm at bay."

It was a silly vow. An impossible promise. And still, she believed him.

The rumble of the storm lessened as he held her, as though his will really could chase it away. When it was finally over, she lifted her face to his, clutching the loose fabric of his shirt. "You're here. I wasn't sure if you would be."

He brushed a lock of hair from her face, his green eyes dark and full of promise. "Of course I'm here. It's Christmas."

She blushed. "It's been seventy-three days since you were here."

He nodded, as though he'd been counting them, too. "I wish I could have been here sooner. I was going to surprise you tomorrow."

She smiled. "That would have made for a very merry Christmas, but I am happy you came tonight." She reached up, placing a hand to his cheek, where a hint of a beard threatened. Promised. "I want every minute I can steal with you."

He pulled away, taking her hand and leading her through the door and into the conservatory on his side. "If you're to thieve," he whispered, "do it in my house, where your aunt Jane won't have me strung up for tempting you to darkness."

Jack grinned and pulled the door shut behind her as he lit a small lamp on the pianoforte. "Everyone would know that it was *I* tempting *you*, you know."

He sat on a low bench and summoned her close, pulling her to stand between his long thighs. She turned his face up to her, taking in the dark circles beneath his eyes, the new lines around his mouth that aged him far beyond one-and-twenty. Running her thumbs over the dark slashes of his brows, she said, softly, "You look tired."

He pulled her closer, setting his forehead to her torso and inhaling, as though a breath of her might bring him strength. Then he leaned back and said, "The estates are in shambles. The tenants suffer. The herds are thin. Winter comes and with it the cold, and there's no money. They're angry and frustrated and full of sorrow—and he never did anything."

His father.

Jack hugged him close, curling herself around him, wishing she could make it go away. "You will, though."

Another deep breath. "I don't know how," he whispered. "The estate hangs by a thread. I've a list of necessities longer and more expensive than time and funds will allow. Each hour, some new repair comes due—each more urgent than the last. The mill in Wales is virtually falling down. The cattle on the estate in Surrey ail. Food for tenants in Newcastle is scarce."

And all of it at Eben's feet. Too much of it for him to solve at once.

He pulled her into his lap. "I can't fix it all. I'm as bad as he was."

She shook her head. "You're ten times the man he was. A hundred."

He put his forehead to hers, closing his eyes. "No one tells you how difficult it is to bear the mantle of responsibility." He opened his eyes, his gaze fixed to a point beyond her shoulder, and added, "No one tells you all that you must give up."

The words sent a thread of fear through her. She shook her head, reaching for him, as though she could stop whatever it was that was coming. "Eben," she said. "Let me help."

His gaze flew to hers, sharp. Understanding. "No."

She sighed. "There's plenty of money. Not enough to save a dukedom, but surely enough to help." She set her palm to his face again. Repeated herself. "Let me help."

He shook his head. "No. I won't take your money. Every mistake that has been made is mine to rectify. Every sin. This responsibility is mine. I have a plan. And I will not have you thinking I married you for anything but you. And I will not have you marrying me thinking I am anything less than you deserve."

They'd had the argument a dozen times. A hundred. In person and by post. And Jack knew better than to push. So, instead, she took his face in her hands and told him the truth. "You are the best man I know."

When she pulled him down for a kiss, he groaned, unable to keep himself from deepening the caress, his hands coming to capture her face, holding her still, taking control. "Christ, I missed you," he said, plucking the words directly from her mind.

"Seventy-three days are too many," she replied before he licked at the seam of her lips—a question barely needing an answer.

She opened for him and they kissed, long and slow and lingering; when they finally parted, both gasping for breath, he whispered, "I have a gift for you."

A thrill of excitement coursed through her. "What is it?"

Eben's beautiful lips curved in a devastating smile. "I can't remember."

She feigned a scowl. "Give it."

Another kiss, quick and delicious. "Come with me."

She followed him without hesitation, even as she teased, "I don't know if I should. It's two o'clock in the morning. Nothing good comes of two o'clock in the morning in the company of an unmarried gentleman."

He laughed. "I assure you, love, *everything* good comes of two o'clock in the morning in the company of an unmarried gentleman."

She cut him a look. "For the gentleman."

He lowered his voice. "I shall make it good for you, as well, Lady Jacqueline."

"Said the lion to the mouse," she replied, following without hesitation. She'd always follow him.

He led her through his quiet house, now empty of so much that had once mattered to him—things he'd sold for money to save the people who relied upon him.

He was a magnificent man. And someday, this house wouldn't be empty, Jack thought. They would fill it together—right to the brim with love and a future. And a family. Riches beyond imagining.

"I am sorry the house is so cold," he whispered. "No servants."

It was rare for an aristocrat to gift his servants a holiday. Too often, staff was required to work, putting another's celebration ahead of their own. But Eben had cut their wages that year instead of providing them with Christmas boxes.

His guilt over what he had to do to keep the staff employed had been the source of half a dozen letters between him and Jack. He'd offered them each the choice to stay or go, with his best references, and all but three had chosen to stay, trusting that the young man would serve them better than his father had done.

To show his gratitude, Eben had given those who remained the only thing he could—time away for the holiday. And with that decision, he'd tumbled Jack even further into love with him. She squeezed his hand. "I am happy for the time alone."

They stopped in the center of the home's great foyer, and he left her to light a dozen candles around the edge of the space. When she was bathed in golden light, he came to her, taking her hands in his and lifting them both to his lips, kissing one, then the other before saying, "In all the years we've known each other, it's never snowed on Christmas."

She raised a disapproving brow at that. "You needn't remind me, Eben."

He smiled. "I have no doubt you would have reminded me of just that tomorrow. Just as you've done every year for an eternity."

"It's *supposed* to snow on Christmas," she pointed out. "That's the whole *point* of Christmas."

"Well, I'm not certain that's the point of Christmas at all, but that's an argument for another time."

Thunder rumbled outside, and she moved closer to him. He wrapped one arm tightly around her, and she shook off her discomfort with a protest. "And to add insult to injury, it's *raining* this year."

He smiled. "Stay here."

Her eyes widened in curiosity, but she did as she was told, watching as he moved to the stairs, collecting a small box and climbing to the second floor. He stopped halfway up the stairs. "It's a silly gift."

Jack did not know what was in the box, but she knew, without question, that there was nothing silly about it. She looked up at him and said, "I want it."

But what she really meant was *I want you.*

He understood, if the fire in his eyes was any indication. Jack watched as the man she loved ascended to the top of the stairs in long, graceful movements before he took his place on the landing above, peering over the banister at her, twenty feet below in nothing more than a pink night rail and a matching velvet robe.

"You're not wearing slippers, Jack," he said. "I can see your toes."

She grinned. "Yes, your cold floor is reminding me of that. Now where's my present?"

"You're very demanding."

She nodded. "It's one of my worst qualities."

He laughed at that, a low, delicious sound that tumbled down to warm the very toes they'd been speaking of. "I rather like it."

Before she could answer, he lifted the box in his hands and called down, "Happy Christmas, love."

And then, he made it snow.

She squealed at the sight of hundreds of little ecru snow-flakes, each one painstakingly crafted, fluttering down to her, turning the air between them white. She reached up toward them and called out his name in pure, unfettered joy, and he laughed, rich and full and honest, and Jack thought she might never hear another thing in her entire life that she loved as much as that sound.

He was already on his way down the stairs, rushing to beat the snow. He reached her just as the last of the flakes did, capturing her midtwirl and pulling her to him even as she threw herself into his arms, kissing him once, twice, before he pulled back and picked a little paper disk from her hair, brandishing it toward her like a hero's prize.

She accepted it, eyes bright in the candlelight, and laughed again before breathlessly asking, "Where did you get them?"

His chest expanded, his eyes filling with pride. "I made them."

"You didn't! There must be hundreds of sheets of paper here!"

"Only fifty or so."

Still, it had to have been the most expensive thing he'd purchased for something other than the estate in months. She shook her head, twirling, watching the little snowflakes dance and scatter with her skirts. "When?"

"At night, in carriages, whenever I could find the time." He looked away, rubbing a hand over the back of his neck, blushing under her passionate scrutiny. "I would not recommend wielding a knife in the back of a carriage, however."

"I don't imagine you would," she said on a little, happy sigh before shaking her head. "Eben . . . this is . . ."

He waited for her to find the word.

It came on a wild, welcome laugh. "This is magnificent!" She plucked another flake from her hair and tossed it in the air above them, watching it flutter down and land on his shoulder. "You made me snow!"

"I'm sorry it is not more."

She was still staring down at their feet, where hundreds of little white paper circles lay, but his words drew her instant attention. "What did you say?"

"Another man—a richer man—would have given you jewels. Or fur. Or . . . I don't know . . . a vase."

She blinked. "You think I would have preferred a vase?"

"Well, perhaps not a vase."

"Definitely not a vase."

He laughed at that. "Fair enough. No vases. Ever."

She smiled softly, stepping toward him, taking his arms in her hands. "Not if I might have another snowfall."

He leaned down and stole her lips once more, before whispering, "I promise, you only have to ask, and I shall make it snow."

"You shall regret that promise."

He shook his head. "Here's one I shan't regret. I promise, I'm going to make you a fortune, and then I'm going to marry you and shower you with gifts. Jewels. Everything you desire."

Her breath caught, the words setting her heart to racing and her stomach to flipping and her legs to weakening, and all she wanted was this man in her arms forever and ever, weather be damned.

She put her hands to his face and pulled him down for a kiss. "If you marry me, Eben, I'll already have everything I desire."

If only he'd believed her.

Chapter Five

Christmas Day

S ome might say that it is *I* who should be avoiding *you*."

Eben looked up from his desk and over his shoulder to Jack, standing in the door of his study, holding a plate in one hand. "I am not avoiding you."

One perfectly arched brow rose in disbelief, and she came into the room. "No?"

"No," he growled, turning back to his ledger, leaning low enough to block his view of her with a towering pile of reports, and willing the lie away. "I've work to do."

"On Christmas Day."

"Yes. On Christmas Day. Every day," he replied. "I've responsibilities. Isn't that why you left me in the first place?"

"No," she said quietly. "It's not."

It wasn't?

Then why the hell had she left him?

He'd be damned if he was going to ask. He attempted to focus on the line of numbers in front of him, willing his brain to calculate the number of livestock on the ducal estate in Wales. It was a sheep farm, resurrected from the dead, once barely running for the debt of the estate, and now providing a significant portion of the Queen's wool.

Was it possible that significant portion came from only thirteen sheep?

Goddammit. Jack was ruining his mathematical skill.

He looked over his shoulder once more and fairly snarled, "Don't you have a meal to prepare?"

She did not blink. "Are you sorry that Mr. Lawton cannot get home?"

"Of course I am, though I don't see how that's relevant."

She leaned against the doorjamb, as though she belonged there. And Christ, she looked as though she belonged there. Enough that Eben was tempted to make a habit of drinking. "Or are you just sorry that you cannot go with him?"

Guilt flared, and along with it, irritation. "I don't want to go with him. There's nothing I want less than to spend the day playing the charming duke."

"Oh," she said casually, "I did not know you had charming in your repertoire."

He scowled at her. "I loathe holidays."

"You didn't used to."

That was before you left. "That was a long time ago."

She nodded, and he wondered if he could pay her to leave. He'd happily give up the lion's share of his fortune for the guarantee that he'd never see her again.

Lie.

The idea that he might never see her again was like poison. One day with her, and twelve years without her seemed to have disappeared.

"It occurs that Mr. Lawton might think you more than your title if he's come to fetch you for Christmas dinner."

He returned his attention to his ledger and grunted a response.

She pressed on. "One might think he considers you a friend."

"He likes the money we make."

A pause. Then, "Perhaps. How did you come to be partners?"

Eben had needed money. "He was running the most successful mercantile on the docks. He had a keen understanding of what sailors wanted when they disembarked after long journeys, and he was looking to expand."

The fact that Eben's money hadn't been good enough for aristocratic partners had been a gift of fate; Lawton was a brilliant businessman who hadn't thought twice about Eben's past, knowing that money from a failed dukedom spent as well as money from anywhere else.

"We worked well together." An understatement. They now owned a significant number of businesses at the dockside, and one of the largest overland transport companies in Britain.

"You must be very proud."

He paused at that. Pride had never been a part of it. He'd felt many things in the years since he and Lawton went into business together—determination, relief, gratitude—but never pride. He'd only ever been proud of one thing.

And then he'd lost her.

He pushed the thought away. "I am satisfied."

Her lips twisted in a wry smile. "So satisfied that you are working on Christmas Day."

He ignored the point, pretending to be riveted to his ledger, willing her to leave.

It did not work. "I am happy you have a friend, Eben."

That word again, so foreign. Something he hadn't even considered before she said it, as it had been so long since he'd had a friend. "I have a business partner."

"One with whom you would have spent Christmas dinner."

"Under duress. Thank goodness for snowstorms."

"Don't be so quick with your gratitude—now you're eating Christmas dinner with me."

He remained focused on his papers, hating the pleasure the verbal sparring gave him. "There's still time for you to change your mind and go home."

Her laughter was soft and surprised, barely there, and warmed him to the bone. Not that he would admit that to anyone.

After a long pause, she said, "I shall make you a deal, Eben. I shall leave you alone, collect my aunt, and return to our home, if you'll tell me one thing."

"Anything." Anything to end the torture of her presence. The regret that consumed him. The want. He repeated himself, desperate to be rid of her and the way she haunted him. "Anything."

"Tell me what you were thinking of when you insisted you'd done frivolous things."

No.

He might have thought he was willing to give up anything for her to leave, but answering that question would give up his whole self. It would require him to give voice to a memory he did not think he could suffer. Certainly not with her there, standing before him. "Nothing."

"We both know that isn't true."

He looked back at the ledger. "Stay then. I care not."

She did stay. Worse, she came closer. He could hear her skirts brushing against the carpet. Against her legs. And then, as though she'd been invited—as though she owned the damn place—she set the plate down smack in the center of his ledger and sat across from him.

For a single, mad moment, it occurred to Eben that she *might* own the damn place. That she might own him. Still.

He pointed at the covered plate with the nib of his pen. "What is that?"

"Shortbread."

He didn't want her baking for him. Baking made him think of her hands. And thinking of her hands made him think of the way she moaned when he kissed the inside of her wrist, and that wasn't productive at all. "I don't want it."

"I see the years have made you ever more gracious."

He met her eyes and said, pointedly, "I don't want it, thank you."

She sat back, altogether too comfortable with his unwelcoming demeanor, and picked at a speck on her skirts before saying, "It's a special recipe. It will help with your head."

He scowled. "There's nothing wrong with my head."

Her reply was under her breath, and he heard it nonetheless. "That is debatable."

"Will you leave if I eat it?"

She smirked. "A duke can dream."

He tossed the cloth from the plate and raised a biscuit to his mouth, taking an enormous, forceful bite, as though to prove to her that he was willing to do anything to get her to leave.

And immediately regretted it.

"Good God," he said, around the bite. "That's disgusting." He stood and went to the sideboard to pour himself a glass of water. After drinking deeply, he added, "Truly foul."

Her eyes went wide. "There's no need to be rude."

"It's not rude if it's true."

"It's absolutely rude if it's true."

He could still taste whatever horrid addition had been made to the innocent biscuit. "Blech. What did you do to it?"

She cast a sidelong glance at the offending plate. "It's a family secret."

"It should be kept as such."

Her lips twitched at that. "It can't be *that* bad."

"I assure you, it can be." He returned to the desk and lifted the plate toward her.

She rolled her eyes and reached forward, accepting a biscuit with misplaced bravado. When she took a bite, her own eyes went wide, and she offered a little cough around the cookie. "Mmmm."

He fought the urge to smile. "Delicious?"

She gave a forced nod, one belied by the watering of her eyes. "Very."

"At least now I know you weren't attempting to poison me."

"Would you believe it is a peace offering?"

"The only way I shall find peace today is if you and your aunt find your way back through your secret passageway."

"She doesn't know about the secret passageway."

He stilled. "She doesn't?"

"No. No one does. She came through the back door." She paused. Then, "I've never told anyone about it."

He hadn't, either. It had been their secret. He'd never wanted to share it with anyone but her. Not even now, years after the last time he'd used it. Still, he could not stop himself from asking, "Why not?"

She looked away. "I suppose I never wanted anyone to take it away."

An ache throbbed in his chest. "You haven't used it in twelve years."

She smiled a small, winsome smile. Sad and full of secrets. "That doesn't mean that I haven't wished to."

The words nearly stopped his heart. Had she wished to? Had she wanted to come to him? No. It was impossible. "I am to believe you thought about that doorway while you were wandering Pamplona? Climbing the Acropolis? Exploring Pompeii?"

She leaned forward, her fingers toying with the antique abacus on his desk. "Especially Pompeii."

"I suppose that is meant to be amusing." All that time, while she'd been off seeing the world, he'd been here, working. Missing her. Longing for her. Pressing his goddamned ear to the goddamned door and begging the universe to restore her to the other side. Willing the knob to turn. He'd have done anything for her to open that door. And she was making jokes.

"It wasn't meant to be amusing," she said.

"What was it, then?"

She hesitated, and he nearly lost his mind in the stretch of silence before she said, "When Vesuvius erupted, the people of Pompeii had no time to escape the volcano's wrath. Thousands of them knew what was to come, and they knew they had no choice but to surrender to it." She paused, sliding one ebony bead from one side of the abacus to the other. "While there, you cannot help but wonder how they chose to spend their last minutes. There's no way to know, but mothers must have cradled their children. Friends must have taken each other's hands. And lovers must have . . ." She trailed off.

No. She couldn't stop there. Not with his heart pounding in his chest for the first time in twelve years.

"What must they have done?"

She shook her head. "They knew they would die. They would have turned to each other. Faced it together." She met his gaze, her brown eyes swimming with tears. "They would have chosen each other."

Choose me.

Memory, preserved in ash.

"So, yes. I thought about the doorway in Pompeii."

She stood then and made for the exit, her words echoing around him like an explosion. Destroying him. At least, he thought they did, but there was something left to be wrecked when they were done, because she finished the job when she turned back, halfway to the door, met his gaze, and said, "I thought about the doorway, just as you thought about snowflakes."

The words pulled him from his chair, full of anger and frustration and the keen knowledge that no one would ever know him the way she did, no matter how hard he wished her ignorant of him.

Because he *had* thought of the damn snowflakes. Every moment of his life that was worth remembering had to do with her. Then she'd left him, going off to her future, to see the world and live her life and fall in love with another. And he'd remained here, alone, stuck in the muck of the past with nothing but the memory of her laughter and her joy and her kisses.

God, those kisses. They haunted him.

They haunted him, and he hated the memory of them. Almost as much as he loved it.

But he'd be damned if he'd let them haunt him any longer.

He bore down on her, half hoping that she would flee. Half hoping that she wouldn't let him reach her. That she wouldn't let him pull her into his arms. That she wouldn't let him kiss her.

She didn't flee, though. She was proud and strong and brave as ever. She stood at the center of his study, watching him come for her. And when he did reach her, all she did was raise her chin in pure, unadulterated challenge.

A challenge he met with agony and pleasure.

She didn't resist him. Instead, she melted into him, coming up on her toes to meet his lips with the same wild frustration he felt. His hands came to her face, tilting her up to him as he took control of the moment, as he claimed her with all the aching desire he'd held for her for years. Christ, he'd missed her so much. He'd missed her smile and her eyes and *this* . . . her stunning, free, abandoned kissing. This kissing that had always cracked him open and filled him with hope and joy and *freedom*.

She sighed into the caress, her hands coming to his arms, her fingers digging into his muscles there, using him as leverage to stretch up and kiss him back.

He tensed beneath those hands, giving her his strength, welcoming her using him. Never wanting her to stop using him. She could use his kitchens, his strength, his body, his mind—whatever she chose—as long as she did not stop this kiss.

He held her tight and licked over the seam of her wide, soft lips—an echo of a caress they'd shared a thousand times before. As she had done all those other times, she opened on a sigh, welcoming his entry as he sealed their mouths together and stroked deep, tasting her like spice, drinking her like wine.

And like wine, the taste of her had changed, grown deeper, richer, warmer. He groaned, every muscle in him tight as a bow, his blood pounding at this new discovery—that for all the times he'd dreamed of her in the past twelve years, he'd never once imagined she'd become more tempting.

But one taste and he was hard as stone, unable to think of anything but her. Of how much he needed her. He needed his hands on her, his lips on her skin, his tongue tasting the salty sweet of it. Decision made, he turned her without breaking the kiss, walking her back to his desk, and lifting her to sit on the edge of it.

A pile of paper dropped to the floor, the sound breaking their mutual concentration. Jack pulled back, her attention caught by the fan of documents against the thick, dark rug below. Eben did not look. He was too transfixed by the place at the base of her neck where her pulse thundered—proof that she was as moved as he was.

He dipped his head and licked that patch of skin slowly—once, twice. On the third slow slide she whimpered, the sound making him impossibly harder. He grazed his teeth across that skin and her fingers threaded into his hair, pulling tight as she gasped, "Your work . . ."

He'd worked for twelve years, without her. "Not important," he said, turning her to face him once more, stealing her lips for a long kiss.

Not long enough.

She pulled away, brown eyes full of the past. "Of course it is. It always has been."

The past, always between them. "Not today—" he began, and then, not knowing what to say, he stole her lips again, willing her to understand, even as he did not.

Not with you. No longer.

She kissed him back with a matching desperation, as though she hated the memories as much as he did. As though she wanted him as much as he wanted her.

Everything fell away—the holiday, the house, the history—and he reveled in her, this stunning, magnificent woman whose hands and mouth and body claimed him with a mere kiss.

She'd come back. And she was his once more. He could win her again. He had the funds now. He could give her anything she wished. *Everything.* Starting with the greatest pleasure she'd ever experienced.

He was about to make good on that promise when she pulled away abruptly, taking breath and heat with her, pushing him from her, the only sound in the room their harsh breath. And then, "Wait."

The soft, whispered word sounded like a gunshot, and he released her as though she was aflame. "Jack?"

She shook her head, transfixed by the papers. "No."

Confusion flared along with frustration as she pushed past him and made for the closed door, the gentle brush of her skirts stinging against his calves. He willed himself silent. And still, he spoke. "You left me."

The words stopped her short, those weaponous skirts

swirling about her legs as her shoulders shot straight. She spoke to the door, unwilling or unable to look at him. "You left me first."

The words settled unpleasantly between them. "I've been here the whole time. Every goddamned day for twelve years."

She whirled to face him then, a red wash vivid on her cheeks. Embarrassment?

Anger. "You were gone nonetheless," she said, the words vibrating around the room. "I tried so hard to keep you. To hold on to you. But you disappeared, a little bit at a time, every day. Lost to this"—she waved a hand at the room, at his desk, at the papers on the floor—"*life*."

She spoke the word the way he thought it, as though it were a pale approximation of itself and yet, there was no describing it any other way. He hated how well she knew it and lashed out to show her so. "I am sorry I could not surrender to your childhood whims," he said.

"My . . . *whims*?" There was incredulity in the reply. Incredulity and something like rage. "My only whim was you."

Was that true?

"You wanted the world. That's why you left. Because you wanted more than I could give you."

She nodded. "That much is true."

I can give it to you now.

"I was saddled with the responsibility of hundreds. The estate was crumbling, gambled away by my father, who never cared for responsibility as much as he cared for drink. I had to rebuild it. And *you* left *me*."

She looked to the ceiling as if for strength. "You wanted me to be invisible. Here, but not seen. For how long?"

"Until I had made enough!"

"Enough for what?"

"For you!" The words thundered through the room, angry silence quick on their heels. Did she not see? Everything he'd done was to make himself better. To make himself enough.

She shook her head. "No, Eben. I never wanted it."

It was a lie, of course. No woman wanted an impoverished duke. No wife wished to tie herself to debt and hardship.

But when she added softly, "I only ever wanted you," he almost believed it. "I only ever wanted to stand beside you and look into our future—whatever it might have been."

Or, rather, he believed it enough that he couldn't stop himself from asking, "Then why did you leave?"

She smiled, small and sad. "What was my love without your faith?"

Silence fell and he ached with it, every one of his muscles on edge, straining to go to her, to touch her again. To prove to her that he'd never been lost. That he had been here, frozen in time, longing for her. "Then why did you return?" he asked, because he didn't know what else to say.

Except, of course, the thing he could not say.

Why won't you stay?

"Perhaps I wished to see if . . ." She trailed off and he hated the silence—the absence of her that he had grown accustomed to and now, suddenly, could not bear.

When he filled that silence, his voice was hoarse and broken, as though he hadn't spoken since she left. "Why did you come, Jack?"

Her gaze flew to his, those beautiful brown eyes in that face he had missed so much and for so long. He ached for her answer. "Perhaps I wished to see if you were still here."

I am here. I will always be here. But he didn't say that. Instead, like a fool, he said, "I was always here."

She looked away, to the window, where snow swirled. "Do you remember . . ."

"I remember all of it." Every minute. Every second.

She turned back to him instantly. "Do you remember that you once vowed you'd always come for me?"

There could have been betrayal in the words. Hurt. Sadness. He would have accepted any one of them, because he could have hidden in defensiveness. But there were none of those things. There was only truth.

And that was worse, because it left him bare and filled with regret.

It was one of a thousand vows he'd never made good on.

"I came to tell you that we shall sup at two," she said.

He didn't want to eat. He wanted to kiss her again, to pull them both from the past and ground them here, once more, in the present.

But that was the problem with kissing her; it did not simply bring Eben to the present, it stole any hope of a future from him.

I love you.

The thought came, primitive and honest.

And irrelevant.

She was no longer for him. He had made sure of it.

Chapter Six

Christmas Day, twelve years earlier

"It is too hot to sleep." He was still working when she found him in his office, having sought him out in the dead of an unseasonably warm night, the weather more suited to a sunny day in May than a wintry holiday. The city had been the recipient of a heat wave and, with no one able to predict when winter would return, homes suffered without the moderate comforts that usually came with warm weather—windows remained fastened shut, their coverings heavy and oppressive like the air itself.

Jack shouldn't have been surprised . . . There was little festive about this year's holiday, anyway. Her siblings had all scattered from Town to their respective country seats and, though Jack had been more than welcome at any one of their holiday tables, she'd chosen to stay in London, in her childhood home, telling herself that she wished for one final holiday with her wild aunt before the older woman took to the wide world for what she referred to as her "Grandest Tour."

If she told herself that she remained in London out of a sense of niecely duty, she did not have to tell herself the truth—that she did not think she could suffer a round of familial idyll in the country, filled with happy marriages and laughing babes dandled on fathers' knees. Not when she was more and more convinced that such a marriage was not in her future.

And, if she told herself that she remained in London for Aunt Jane, she did not have to tell herself the other truth—that she remained in London for Eben.

She did not have to tell herself it was one final Christmas with him.

One final chance to win the man she loved, who she feared had already slipped away.

She stood in the doorway, a small box in hand, and watched him, brilliant and serious, focused, as always, on the ledger before him, working his sums, watching them increase as though by sheer force of will. Her chest tightened as she drank him in, the haphazard fall of his dark hair over his brow, the muscle flexing in his jaw, the strong forearms below the shirtsleeves he'd rolled up—a concession to the heat, perhaps, or to the late hour, or to both.

Gone was the boy she'd first loved. Two years and a lifetime of responsibility had turned him into a man, and she ached for him. For his warmth. For the smile that she had once been able to summon with ease.

She tried now. "I believe my Christmases are cursed never to yield snow."

He glanced up at her, then to the calendar wheel inlaid in the blotter on his desk. He did not reveal his surprise at the date, but Jack saw it, nonetheless. He'd forgotten that it was Christmas.

He looked back to his numbers. "You've clearly made some deity incredibly angry."

She huffed a dramatic sigh. "I've never even *met* Saint Nicholas."

He ran a finger down a column of numbers and absently replied, "Well, perhaps it's punishment for your obvious disinterest in him, then."

She came forward, tempted by the teasing. By the hint that he might be interested in playing. "I'm exceedingly interested in him! Perhaps it's *you* who is being punished. After all, you're the one working on Christmas. But you didn't realize that, did you?"

He scribbled a note on a paper nearby. "I suppose I haven't seen a servant in a while."

"The lack of servants was your only clue?"

Look at me.

He did, seeking her out in the shadows and failing. The candle on his desk had burned nearly to the end, the light unable to reach her—barely able to encompass the piles of paper spread across the workspace.

"The estate does not celebrate Christmas."

The words grated, and she could not stop the edge in her reply. "As a matter of fact, it does."

"The tenants, yes. The servants, yes," he said, calmly. "But someone must keep watch while they drink their toddies and dance their reels."

Her skirts rustled against the carpet as she came closer. "And you are that someone?"

"There isn't another duke to do it."

"You are a marvel," she said quietly to his bent head. "In barely two years, you've turned this ship around. There are full bellies this year, and more to come. They believe in you. Just as I do."

"It's not enough," he said.

Why not?

"Eben . . . You aren't through. It isn't finished. But there are things for which to be thankful. You are a better duke than your father could have dreamed."

He grunted a reply but said nothing else.

She took a deep breath. Launched herself into the fray. "But what of the rest of you? What of the man?"

He looked up. "I assure you, Jacqueline. I remain a man."

She came around the edge of the desk, leaning against it, taking the spot she'd claimed a hundred times before. "Are not men allowed to take a holiday once a year?"

He sat back, but remained silent, his gaze running over her. "Jack—"

A clock chimed from the hallway beyond. Once. Twice. Thrice.

"It's Christmas," she said, reaching for him, letting her fingers trail through his hair, loving its softness and the way he leaned into her touch. Hating the ache in her chest as she said, "Leave it. It will be here tomorrow."

Please. Please, this once, look at me. See me.

He shook his head. "I can't."

Disappointment flared, hot and angry and worse. Devastating. "I hate what this has made you," she whispered.

"You shall like it when you are a duchess and rich beyond your wildest dreams."

No, I shall always hate it. Because you will be gone.

And I, with you.

She withdrew her touch. Stood. Knowing what must be done, strength stealing through her. Strength and something more. "My wildest dreams have nothing to do with money."

"That's because you've always had it."

"No," she said after a long moment. "It's because of what I once had and have no longer."

The candlelight cast his face into stark angles and deep shadows. His eyes were black in the darkness. The shadows painted the line of his jaw like the edge of a knife. And his lips—when had he kissed her last?

"It's late," he said.

And because she knew there was nothing more to say, she nodded, and replied, "Will you come to dinner? Aunt Jane and I have plans for your favorites—the fattest goose we could find, potatoes roasted until they shall break your teeth for the crunch of their skin . . ." She looked away, to the window. "And a parsnip crème that is very well done, if I may say so myself."

"Tomorrow?"

"Today," she corrected. *Christmas Day.*

It took a moment for him to understand. "Yes, of course. Today. I shall be there."

Heart aching, she set the box she'd been holding—the one she'd carefully wrapped in paper and string, tied with a piece of holly—on the desk. With one finger, she pushed it toward him. He looked to it. "What is that?"

"It is customary for people to exchange gifts on Christmas." She forced a smile. "Which you might recall, as you did set the bar rather high last year—what with all that snow."

It was hard to believe it had only been a year earlier. It felt like a lifetime ago. She still remembered him pulling her close and promising to make her happy. Just as soon as the estate was sorted. Just as soon as he could crawl out from beneath the weight of his father's neglect.

He'd proved he wasn't his father in the last two years. His tenants had come to believe in him. The employees in his factories, as well. Twenty-two and with the strength and intelligence of any one of the other men who sat with him in the House of Lords, but he did not see it. Instead, he'd become consumed with the estate, with restoring the reputation of the dukedom, with securing the funds required to rectify the past—as though that was possible. As though there was not simply the present and the future to impact.

And whenever she asked him why—there was a single answer. "For you."

But it wasn't for her. It never would be.

The knowledge was punctuated when he shook his head. "I—I did not—"

There was no gift for her. She nodded. "I did not expect you would." But she'd hoped. "Perhaps you will play for me later." His brows rose in surprise, as though he'd forgotten he had ever played the violin for her. "I miss your music," she said, softly—the only confession she could bring herself to risk.

He looked back to the box. "I don't think—"

She interrupted him, not wanting the full force of his refusal, instead pointing to the box. "Open it."

When he did, the action lacked the excitement that receiving a gift should bring. And when he lifted the top from the beautifully wrought leather cube within to reveal her gift, she held her breath.

In silence, he lifted the gold pocket watch from its seat, turning it over in his hand to run his thumb over the fine filigree engraved there. "It's the finest gift I've ever received."

"It's inscribed," she said. She couldn't resist telling him so. "Inside."

He popped the latch and the back of the watch swung open, revealing the clockwork swaying and spinning within. He reached for the candle and held the light up, and she willed him to see more than the words: *For the time we yet have.*

More than the tiny, perfectly engraved snowflake below.

She willed him to see how she ached for him. How she loved him. How she wished for their future more than anything in the world.

He did not see it.

At least, he did not show it when he looked up at her and said, "Thank you."

Her face fell in the shadows, but he did not see. He was already looking away, back to the ledger. He was already forgetting the gift. Already forgetting her.

"Happy Christmas," she said softly. The words were

lost the moment she spoke them. Disappeared in the darkness.

I love you. But she didn't say it. She couldn't say it.

"I shall be at dinner," Eben replied.

And he was there. Promptly at two.

Jack, however, was not.

Chapter Seven

Christmas Day

$\mathcal{T}$hey'd already begun to eat when Eben arrived to luncheon.

He was deliberately late, telling himself he wanted to keep them waiting . . . wanted them to care whether he arrived or not. No. Wanted *her* to care whether he arrived or not.

But, in truth, he was afraid she might not be there.

He paused outside the doorway, knowing he shouldn't. Knowing that skulking about in the hallway and eavesdropping on the conversation in the room beyond would not end well. But he did it anyway, and so he supposed it was only fair that when he came upon the dining room, it was to discover the trio in raucous laughter, as though they had been friends for an age, and their past was filled with vibrant hilarity to which he was not privy.

"I don't believe you!" Lawton was insisting.

"I swear it is true," Jack replied, her laughter setting Eben on edge.

"I'm to believe that he plays—"

"Not just plays," she interrupted. "Has a superior talent for."

Eben held his breath. "Fair enough," Lawton joked.

"I'm supposed to believe he has *a superior talent* for the violin."

"Correct."

"Eben, Duke of Allryd."

The trio laughed again, loud enough to grate. "That's the one," Jack replied.

"And not simply Mozart or whatnot . . . lighthearted, raucous, *jovial* violin."

"I've never heard him miss a note," she said, her voice filled with memory. "I've never heard anyone play with the speed he plays, and I've never heard him miss."

Memory flashed. She'd danced to the raucous rhythm on more than one occasion, as he'd played faster and faster and she'd twirled and twirled until he'd nearly set the bowstrings aflame. And then she'd nearly set *him* aflame and they'd collapsed together in a sea of tangled skirts and heavy breath and happiness, and he'd had plans for her to dance for him every day for the rest of their lives.

Until he'd ruined it all.

"I'm sorry." Lawton's words interrupted his thoughts. "I'm having trouble imagining him at leisure at all, let alone at merry, entertaining leisure."

Eben scowled. He could be leisurely.

Silence fell in the room beyond. And then, her quiet reply. "I have trouble remembering him outside of merriment."

His heart threatened to beat from his chest.

"That's because you don't wish to, silly girl." The last came from Aunt Jane, short and with an edge of frustration. "But you'll recall that there was nothing merry at the end. Not for an age."

Eben hated the words and the silence that hung behind them, as though no one in the room would argue the truth of them.

And why would they?

There hadn't been play. There hadn't been entertainment.

He'd been too focused on building an estate and a title and a life, telling himself that it had to come first in order to make him worthy of her. And he'd been so worried about making himself worthy of her that he'd forgotten about her altogether.

What an ass he'd been. What an ass he continued to be. She would no doubt revel in the arrival of her Scottish fiancé, who was very likely not an ass.

If he was an ass, Eben would happily murder him.

The irony of that truth was not lost on him.

And then Jack said, "Well, perhaps people change."

Before he could consider the words, Aunt Jane and Lawton laughed, as though Jack had told the most uproarious joke anyone had ever heard.

Eben had had enough. He entered the room like a predator, prepared for a fight. Spoiling for one. Then he saw her.

She was cloaked in red velvet, having changed from her working clothes earlier in the day. He'd thought she'd looked perfect in green the night prior, but now in red—a deep, beautiful red shot through with gold—she looked like a Christmas box. Like something to be unwrapped. Like something to deserve.

He wanted to deserve her.

Putting the thought to the side, his gaze fell to the table, to the goose, already carved, to the wine, already poured, to the potatoes, already served, and he channeled his most ducal entitlement, lifting a brow and saying, "I see that we've chosen this Christmas holiday to do away with ceremony."

Lawton took a bite of goose and grinned around it. "We didn't think it worth things getting cold."

"Waiting for the owner of the house, you mean?"

"There was no evidence that you were coming at all," Jack said.

Did she honestly believe that he could have kissed her

the way he had—the way *she* had—and not be drawn to her like a dog on a lead? Of course, he'd come to dinner. There was nowhere else he could be, no matter the fact that he didn't deserve to sit at her table and eat her food. He had no place here, with her, on Christmas, basking in her merriment.

She was not his, even if he was forever hers.

She had chosen a different life. A different man.

Because of him.

And yet, in the back of his mind, there remained a thread of something immensely dangerous. She'd kissed him back. And hope had whispered like sin, a tempting, impossible lure.

"I am here, after all," he said, turning his attention to the end of the table, where he'd been seated as master of the house.

He stilled, his gaze landing on the instrument to the side of his place setting. A well-worn violin with a frayed bow.

His violin.

He looked to her, taking in her clear eyes and the curious, barely there smile on her lips. "You went looking for it?"

One side of her mouth twitched. "Not too hard. It was right where you left it."

In the conservatory, next to the music stand closest to the secret passageway. Where he'd left it the last time he'd been drawn to that dark room—that room that thrummed with the past. With her.

He only ever went there when the nights were too late and too dark and too full of regret. He would sit on the floor near that silly painting of mythical creatures and he would play for them and wish for them to summon her so he might make amends and begin, once more.

Then day would break, and he would return to his office, and he would remember that new beginnings were a fallacy. He would grow his fortune and try to forget her. And it would work, until it didn't, and he would repeat the cycle, making the instrument wail with his melancholy.

"I confess," Lawton interjected with a wave at the violin, "I am astounded by the revelation that you are a musician."

"I'm not."

"That's not true," Jack said.

"I'm out of practice."

"Perhaps you should return to practicing," Lawton said. "It would suit the staff well for you to work less."

Aunt Jane snorted at that. "Since the day he became duke, Allryd has worked. Do not expect it to change now."

"That doesn't make him less of a tragic figure," came Lawton's amused reply. "With his sad, lonely existence."

Eben blinked. "You realize I am standing right here, do you not?"

Lawton looked to him. "If you were to sit, you could eat some of this delicious meal." He paused, then added with a twinkle in his eye, "Or perhaps you would like to play? A feast such as this deserves entertainment."

Eben cut the other man a look, at once tempted by the delicious scent of roast goose and by the possibility of avoiding a meal with this trio, hell-bent on his discomfort, when Jack asked, quietly, "Is he lonely?"

For a moment, silence fell.

"No." Only when he thought of her.

"Desperately so," Lawton said at the same time.

Eben narrowed his gaze on his business partner.

"What?" Lawton cut him an innocent look, the bastard. "I'm merely answering the question."

God knew why, but he yanked back the chair at the empty place setting and sat. "I don't see how you could possibly have information relating to the question."

"I do not need information, Duke; I have eyes."

A plate appeared beneath Eben's nose, on the end of a lovely long arm that had been kissed by the sun. He focused on the meal rather than his embarrassed ire, noting the choice morsels of goose and the crusted edge of potato, next to the perfectly turned carrots and an exquisite parsnip crème.

She'd given him all the best bits—the bits she should have kept for herself—and for a mad moment, he imagined stealing her and that plate away to a quiet place and rectifying the injustice. Feeding her until she was full of the very best he could buy, and he was able to feast on the one thing for which he hungered . . .

Her.

He had clearly gone mad if a plate of roast goose had him thinking about kissing her. Of course, everything made him think about kissing her. Her voice, her laugh, that beautiful red dress with its beautifully cut bodice, revealing the long line of her, the rich swell of her breasts above it—deliciously freckled skin and that gold locket again— where had it come from?

The Scot, no doubt.

Eben scowled at the thought, his eyes rising to hers, which were full of curiosity. Somehow, he managed to look away, grumbling, "Thank you."

Down the table, Aunt Jane helped herself to the carafe of wine at her elbow and fired her weapon. "Tell us why you think the duke so very lonesome, Charlie?"

Eben willed Lawton silent. No such luck. The other man turned and looked to Aunt Jane. "Well, one cannot imagine anything but, what with how the man works all the time."

"You certainly like to spend the funds I make."

One of Lawton's brows rose in surprise. "The funds *we* make, friend."

Eben scowled. "Someone must do the research to bear out all the hunches you insist are good business."

Lawton smirked. "My hunches are always good business, but we'll leave that for another time—this conversation is about you."

Eben regretted ever entering into business with Charles Lawton.

"You, and the fact that you never do anything but work and count your money as if it keeps you warm."

"That's not true."

Except it was, of course.

"And is there a great deal of money?" Aunt Jane asked. It never failed—people of means were always interested in the means of others.

Eben stabbed a morsel of goose and ate. He might have thought it delicious if he weren't so consumed by the conversation. "There is, as a matter of fact," Lawton said, "a very great deal."

More than that, if they were honest. In twelve years, he'd turned the dukedom of Allryd into one of the richest in Britain. And Lawton had made enough to keep himself in perfectly tailored gold brocade for life.

"And does it?" Jack. Soft and steel.

He looked up, meeting her brown eyes. Too big. Too knowing. "Does it what?"

"The money. Does counting it keep you warm?"

I haven't been warm since you.

He remained silent.

Lawton answered for him. "Never so warm as it did last night, when washed down with my best whisky."

"No one likes a drunk," Aunt Jane said, toasting the table with another glass of wine.

"Allryd drunk is a rarity. He never drinks—except on Christmas Eve." Lawton looked to him, a knowing gleam in his eye. "Why is that?"

Eben's reply was like ice. "You overstep."

"I don't think so." Jack, now. Quiet and firm and terrifying in the knowledge he wished she didn't have. "You were in your cups last night. Why?"

In the hopes that I would forget you left me on Christmas Eve.

"A man is allowed to celebrate on Christmas, isn't he?"

She watched him, those eyes that had haunted him for twelve years seeming to see everything. *Don't care for me, Jack,* he wanted to say. *Don't you dare care for me and then leave to marry another.*

"But I thought you loathe holidays," she said, echoing their earlier conversation.

There was a time when her teasing tone would have tempted. "Perhaps I was celebrating my solitude."

She watched him for a long moment, her quiet inspection underscored by the heavy weight of their audience. Then she said, "What is past does not have to be future, Eben."

The words stole his breath, and he returned his gaze to his plate, where his food was invisible—as invisible as she was present, with her quiet truth. It was bad enough he could hear her when she added, "You needn't be alone on Christmas."

The words were a sliver of hope, more painful than he could have imagined, because it was wrong of her to promise such a thing. Wrong of him to hope for it. He'd been alone on Christmas for twelve years. He'd been alone ever since the Christmas she'd left.

He was alone even now. Because tomorrow she would leave to marry another, and what was past *would* be future. Set in stone.

The thought was a festering wound.

He might have been able to tolerate it if she hadn't decided to spend the last day of her spinsterhood snowbound with him, tempting him to touch her and talk to her and—even now—pull her into his lap and kiss her senseless.

"Ah, but I am not alone on Christmas. Behold my motley crew."

"How lucky you are to have us." She smiled, too brightly. Blindingly so.

"Is it luck?"

How did she have such straight, white teeth? "Not every duke can claim such esteemed company."

"Lawton, who would rather be in Marylebone, Aunt Jane, who would rather be on the high seas, and you . . . who would no doubt rather be with her fiancé."

Deny it, he willed. *Deny it and give me more of that hope you have in spades.*

What a fucking masochist he was.

Her smile softened. "Perhaps it is where we are *meant* to be that matters."

She was meant to be with *him*, dammit. She had always been meant to be at the other end of the table, with half a dozen children and a score of others between them. She was meant to meet his gaze and lift her glass and toast their life—past, present, and future all.

And he was meant to play the damned violin as she danced. He was reaching for the instrument before the thought was even complete, unable to stop the movement before three sets of eyes tracked it, and the room went still.

He froze.

Lawton was the first to speak. "Go on then, Allryd."

Eben lifted the violin, unable to tear his gaze from Jack's, riveted to the instrument.

Perhaps you will play for me later, she'd said to him all those years ago, on that last night, when she'd come to him and given him a final chance to make everything right. When he'd ruined everything. When he'd set all this in horrid motion.

What if he had played for her that night?

What if he played for her now?

It was too late.

He shook his head and returned the violin to the table. "You shouldn't have brought it here."

He ignored the silence that fell in the words' wake, the barely there exhalation from Aunt Jane, the sound of Lawton's jacket rustling as he sat back in his chair.

And from Jack, nothing. No movement. No response.

Not until she stood, without a word, and left, the sound of her magnificent red skirts sliding against her like gunfire in the room, punctuated by a soft *snick* as she closed the door behind her, the door latch sounding like a cannon.

And he, left ragged.

Of his own design.

"Well," Lawton said.

"Shut up," Eben replied.

Thank God, his partner did shut up.

"I should like to see you try to tell me the same," Aunt Jane interjected, her icy blue gaze finding his from her place down the table. When he remained silent, she said, "Ah, so some semblance of the sense you had as a child has remained."

She stood, seeming suddenly far taller than she was—looming large like the words she threw like a weapon. "That girl has spent twelve years with you in her thoughts. Most of them with you in her heart, as well. And you've spent twelve years here, without either thought or heart, it seems."

It wasn't true, he knew. She couldn't have possibly cared for him after she left. He'd promised her a future, full of everything she deserved. And all she'd had to do was wait for him.

You once vowed you'd always come for me.

He couldn't come for her. She'd left him. Didn't anyone see that? Why didn't anyone see that? *He* was the one who had been consumed with thoughts. It was *his* heart that had been heavy with the weight of lost love—a love who'd left him and returned only when she was about to marry another.

He did not say any of that, though, as Jane moved to the sideboard and lifted a plate laden high with foul shortbread. "Make no mistake, *Duke.*" She spat the title. "You don't deserve her."

"That's never been in doubt," he said.

"And you don't deserve my shortbread."

He had a feeling he very much deserved that shortbread. But he didn't think the old lady would appreciate his disagreement on that front, so he remained silent as she swanned from the room.

"I rather wanted that shortbread."

He looked to Lawton. "I promise you didn't."

His partner lifted his glass and leaned back in his chair, dark eyes hooded with judgment. "You're an ass."

Truth. "Because of the shortbread?"

Lawton did not bite. "What do you imagine your life is for?" When Eben did not reply, the other man pressed on. "The question is not rhetorical. Is it money? Because you've money beyond reason—more than you can spend in a lifetime."

"There is an estate to think of," Eben growled, knowing it was an idiotic answer.

"There's enough for that, too, enough to keep it healthy and happy long after you're gone—which won't matter, as you have no children to inherit it, so it will be another Allryd's problem. There's two off the list. It's not money, and it's not children."

There'd been a time when he expected it to be children— pretty, red-haired girls, and boys with big brown eyes, their mother filling their heads with dreams of the wide world, while he planned for them to see every inch of it.

"Shall I tell you what I thought it was for?"

Eben resisted the urge to stand and turn the table over. "No."

Lawton pushed back from the table and drank again, seeming to see everything. "I always thought it was for a woman."

The room went blazing hot. Eben shoveled potato into his mouth, though he could not taste it as his friend continued.

"No doubt, it was ridiculous of me to think that, what with your lack of social grace and the fact that the only time you leave the house is when there is a vote in Parliament."

"That's not true."

"You're right. You also go to the bank."

Eben ignored the truth.

"At any rate, the idea that there was a woman in play was madness, I told myself. And then lo, one turns up in your kitchens on Christmas morning. And not just any woman. One with a pretty smile and a prettier laugh."

"Neither of which are for you," Eben growled before he could stop himself.

Lawton tilted his head. "Are they for you, then?"

"No."

"And why not?"

"Because she left me."

"That's because you were a proper ass. Good Lord. The woman cooked you a goose. Unsolicited." He picked a piece of meat from his plate and continued around it. "A damned good goose, too."

"Not today," Eben said. "She left me twelve years ago. Walked right out of this house and was gone the next day, to a life that I was not party to."

Just as she'd be gone tomorrow.

"Were you not invited to that life? Or did you choose not to attend?"

"Does it matter? She left me."

Why did that feel like the worst lie he'd ever told?

"She found another," he added softly, a reminder to himself more than anyone else. He'd lost her.

Lawton nodded and stood. "Except it's Christmas Day, and she's here with you and not with him."

Eben sat in the empty room for a long time after his guests left him, turning Lawton's final words over and over, telling himself again and again that she was there because of the snow, until that simple, pure word was all there was.

Snow.

Chapter Eight

*H*e found her outside in the late-afternoon light, without a cloak, six inches deep in the snow, that stunning red gown getting more spoiled by the second, her face turned up to the sky, looking part angel and part ruin.

She did not turn to face him when he let the door to the kitchens close behind him, shutting out the empty house that had haunted him since the day she left. Instead, she remained still beneath the snow, and he found himself envious of the flakes that had permission to caress her face.

He watched her for a long moment, unmoving. Perhaps if he never moved . . . if he never spoke . . . perhaps then the moment would not end, and she would not leave, and he would not be alone once more.

But he had to speak. "I am sorry."

"For what?" She spoke to the sky, and somehow, madly, he turned and looked to the clouds, as though they might answer for him. They didn't, however. Perhaps because there was too much for which he must atone.

For everything.

"For being an ass."

Her full lips, kissed by snowflakes, curved in a tiny smile, there and gone before he could savor it.

Then she said, "Why haven't you married?"

"I've never wanted to." It was a lie.

"I'm sure countless women have courted you," she said.

"I'm sure they were beautiful and droll and rich and perfect."

They hadn't. And even if they had, it was difficult to imagine a woman more perfect than Jack. But he couldn't find a way to say that. So instead, he repeated himself. "I've never wanted to."

She looked to him then, her cheeks flushed red with the cold. "Not even to me."

Yes to you. Always to you. "What did you mean when you said people change?"

She turned away again. "Did I say that?"

"Inside. At dinner."

She smiled, small and knowing. "I wondered if you were eavesdropping."

"I wasn't eavesdropping."

She slid a look at him. "No?"

His cheeks grew warm. "No. It's impossible to eavesdrop inside one's own home."

"Well, that's absolutely incorrect."

When he did not reply, she seemed to consider her next words carefully—un-Jack-like. He hated that. He wanted the immediate answer and not the crafted one. The truth, and not the lie. "I suppose I meant that it isn't impossible to imagine that you might find happiness once more."

He didn't like that, either. Like he was a stray to be cared for. "So that's it? You're here to try your hand at mending me?"

She did not rise to the challenge in the words. "Are you mendable?"

"Not by you."

"Why not?"

"Because . . ." He let the words trail off.

Because I don't wish to be mended for another.

He sure as hell wasn't telling her that.

Her enormous eyes seemed to see it anyway, to see all

the bits he'd been trying to hide since he'd found her in his kitchens in the dead of night. Since before that. Finally, she nodded, turning back to the snow. "It's getting dark. Soon we shan't be able to see the snow."

He was riveted by the flakes tangled in her hair, his hands itching to pull it down and complete her transformation into a Christmas angel. "You always wanted snow on Christmas."

She smiled, breaking him. "And now I have it."

"Perhaps—" He caught the words before they cracked. Cleared his throat. "Perhaps it's a sign."

She turned to him. "Of?"

"That the future might bring you everything you want."

"Starting now?"

He shrugged. "Seems that a marriage is a good time to begin a future."

"So, tomorrow, then."

He nodded, hating the knot in his throat. "One more day of the past, and then, the future."

She faced him. "One more night, you mean."

Was she saying what he imagined she was saying?

We were always better at night.

He nodded.

Was there anything he wouldn't give to spend it with her?

What would she do if he asked her for it? For old times' sake. Or, better yet, if he reached for her and took it? He could. His fingers were eager for her. Eager to reseat themselves in her hair and scatter her pins and pull her close. How many times had he done it? What was once more?

It took every ounce of his strength to keep still.

She looked back to the gardens, her eyes full of secrets. "We were last in Greece. There is an island in the Cyclades, in the heart of the Aegean Sea, called Naxos. The water there is blue as sapphires, and the buildings white as clouds. The main town is a fishing village filled with old men who play table games with shiny, smooth stones, and children who shout and splash in the water, and young men who bring in the catch and young women who clean it.

"The town of Chora is built on a hill with streets so convoluted, they are a literal labyrinth—your travels might lead you to a home, or to the town surgeon, or to a bookshop, or to a restaurant, but they might also lead you right back to where you started—the locals say that the town chooses who may remain. At the center of the labyrinth, there is a market that sells trinkets and treats and honey candy and cones filled high with fish, and there must be a hundred cats, all waiting to weave through your ankles for a taste of your lunch. And it's the most beautiful place I've ever been."

He was jealous of that place, for having her memories. And angry that such a place was so much a part of her and he hadn't been there. Even though she made him see it as though they were there, toes in the warm sand instead of the cold snow.

"A half mile north of the town is the Portara, a massive marble door, rising thirty feet high from the sea into the sky. It's what is left of a temple that is no longer there, and no longer remembered. But those who live there call it Apollo's door." She stopped. "Do you know the story of Apollo and Daphne?"

"No." His voice was all gravel.

"Apollo was"—she waved a hand vaguely—"god of basically everything. The flock, the hunt, music, poetry, sickness, health, sun, knowledge. And a great warrior to boot."

"He sounds like a git."

She smiled. "As a matter of fact, he was a git. And a proper braggart."

"And did Daphne bring him down a peg?"

She turned back to the fast-darkening sky and spoke. "Apollo didn't like the fact that Eros received such accolades from humans—"

"Eros, as in Cupid? The portly baby?"

She cut him a sly look. "A portly baby with very sharp arrows."

Something came loose in him and he grinned, enjoying himself. He'd always loved her stories. "Go on."

"At any rate . . . It seems you'd best learn from this tale, as Apollo also thought Eros less deserving of respect than himself and told him as much."

Eben put his hands in his pockets and rocked back on his heels. "I'm guessing our infant friend did not care for it."

"In fact, he did not. He immediately strung one of his golden arrows and shot Apollo right in the heart—and the god fell madly in love with a nymph, young and beautiful beyond words. Daphne."

Eben could easily imagine the moment. "Lucky Apollo."

"You forget this is a Greek myth, Your Grace," she teased. "No one is ever lucky."

"Don't tell me. The baby strikes again."

She laughed, and he fisted his hands to resist pulling her to him to kiss the sound from her lips. "Quite literally," she said. "While Apollo stood, breathless, stymied by Daphne's beauty and his own nearly unbearable love, Eros strung a second arrow, this one of lead."

Embarrassing as it was, Eben found *himself* unable to breathe, stymied by a different beauty and her story.

"His aim was true, and the leaden arrow filled Daphne with a powerful loathing for Apollo."

Eben cursed, soft and muted in the snowfall, but Jack heard him and nodded. "Exactly. So Apollo chased the woman he loved, and Daphne ran from the man she loathed. And Eros laughed and laughed, for he had proven his power." She paused, then added, "They say that if you stand in that doorway on Naxos, you risk the same fate as Apollo and Daphne. You risk being struck by one of Eros's arrows."

"Gold? Or lead?"

She shook her head. "There's no way to tell. You must risk it. Give yourself up to love or hate. To the two clearest markers of our humanity."

"And did you? Give yourself up?"

She turned to face him, her eyes clear and beautiful. "I did."

"And so? Was it gold or lead?"

She held her hand out to the snow once more. Then said, quietly, "I wished for lead."

The words struck like the arrow. "And did you receive it?"

She shook her head. And Eben's breath grew harsher. They'd returned to England after that. To London. To him. "And what did you think of, inside that door?"

She remained focused on the snow in her hand, falling in wild flakes, melting into her skin. Becoming part of her. Christ. He was jealous of snow and Greece and cats and an ancient door that had seen the wind of the past whip her hair and skirts into a frenzy.

"I thought of the same thing I thought of everywhere we went." She paused, then, softly, "Every time we saw something beautiful. Or magical. Or unspoiled. Or flawed."

He drew closer to her, and she lifted her gaze to his, clear and honest. He raised a hand and placed his fingers to her cheek, rosy with cold. "What was that?"

Her eyes closed, and a snowflake landed on her lashes. He was consumed by that little white speck; it seemed the weight of it kept her eyes closed as she whispered, "I thought of you. I thought of you, and I came home."

Eben kissed the snow and the words from her lips, soft and full, lingering just enough to taste the cool liquid against his heated breath. When he lifted his mouth from hers and opened his eyes, it was to find her watching him again, eyes full of tears. "I missed you so much," she said again. "Every minute."

The words cracked him open. He pressed his forehead to hers and whispered, "Not like I missed you. Not like air. Not like heat."

She took a deep breath, letting it out on a long exhale, and he heard the tremor in it—saw it in the puff of air she released into the cold night. And then he was reaching for her, desperate to kiss her again, to hold her, to make her warm. To make her *his*.

He pulled her closer, as he had a hundred times before—a thousand if he counted his dreams—and she went, fitting herself to him, her fingers finding their place in his snowy hair, as he took her mouth again in a rough, searing kiss. The kind of kiss he'd wanted to give her for twenty-four hours. The kind of kiss that marked her. That marked them both.

She was his.

She had been, from the start. Shot with a golden arrow. Just as he had been. She was his, and it was Christmas, and he would have her tonight, and tomorrow be damned. For once in his life, he would have what he wanted.

And he would give her everything she wanted in return.

"Not like heaven." He kissed her again and again, his hands running over her skin, cold from the snow, pulling her tighter to him, kissing her until they were both gasping for air, and he pulled away enough to speak. "You are mine," he said, pulling back and finding her gaze, glassy and distant in the darkness. "Tonight, Jack, you are mine again."

She nodded without hesitation, pulling him down to meet her lips. "Yes," she said against him. "I am yours."

Then she was kissing him, and it was everything he had forgotten and everything he had remembered for twelve long, empty years—her magnificent taste, her wild enthusiasm, the way she set him aflame with the stroke of her tongue. Her little sighs, the way her fingers and teeth and tongue claimed him even as he claimed her.

He let her take the lead for a while, reveling in her touch and her kiss—in the proof of her passion for him, of the desire that matched his.

No. Not matched.

Nothing could match how he wanted her. How he'd longed for her.

Nothing could match how he ached for her now.

Nothing could match the pleasure he would give them both.

And then she was in his arms, and he was carrying her back into the house, letting the kitchen door slam behind him as he took the long strides to the back staircase and carried her up, up to the place she haunted every night, like a ghost.

But there was nothing ghostly about this Jack when he set her on her feet and they undressed each other, every movement a memory. His jacket and shirt were gone in an instant, her hands stroking over his shoulders as he pressed a soft kiss to the place where her neck met her collarbone.

He turned her and set his hands to the ties of her gown, unwrapping her like a gift, peeling away the red velvet and then the whalebone and linen, until he was staring at the long line of her back, mouth dry, fingers raised to touch her.

It was his turn to tremble.

For twelve years he'd ached for this. For free access to her. For another chance to touch her. To pleasure her. To love her. How could he let her go tomorrow?

He couldn't.

He'd never let her go again.

As he hesitated, she turned to face him, holding the fabric he'd freed to her, hiding herself from him. His gaze fell to the gold locket against her skin, and then lower, to the place on her chest where brown skin dusted with freckles shifted to white, the line stark and sultry, the border of what belonged to the sun and sky and what belonged to him.

He reached for that line, unable to resist setting his fingers to it, being singed by it. "I wish I'd been with you. I wish I'd known the sun that marked you here."

"I wish it, too."

"I want to take you back to that place. I want to stand in the door." Something flashed in her eyes—something like disbelief. And he kept talking, eager to keep it at bay. "I want to lie in the sun and count the new freckles it gives you."

A flush rose beneath his touch. "You're not supposed to like freckles."

"Says who?"

"Ladies' magazines. They say freckles are undesired."

He couldn't help the little laugh that escaped him. "Jack, I assure you, your freckles are desired."

She laughed, the sound fading into a sigh as he leaned down and brushed his lips across her sun-kissed skin, taking the fabric she clutched into his own grasp. She relinquished it, her fingers coming to his hair again, threading into it, her touch threatening to lay him low.

"Shall I tell you why I desire them?" he asked, his voice hoarse with it.

"By all means." Her voice was low and full of desire, and he grew impossibly harder at the sound.

"I want them because they show where you've been. The world you've seen. I want them because they are all the years I missed. I want them because I might learn them, and live those years again, but this time, with you."

He lowered his mouth to her skin and offered his own kisses there, worshipping every mark as he followed the line of them to the paler skin below, and then to the straining, aching tip of one breast. "Do you know how many times I've dreamed of this?" he whispered to the puckered skin begging for his touch. "Do you know how many nights I've imagined taking you into my mouth again? How many hours I've spent trying to remember the precise pitch of the cry I know I can wring from you here?"

"Eben . . ." she whispered, her fingers tightening in his hair. "Please."

"Shall we see if I remember correctly?" he said, dark and teasing as he set his mouth to her, suckling with long pulls, loving the way she threw her head back and gasped, then sighed, and then—when he ran his tongue and teeth over her sensitive flesh—cried out.

It was everything he remembered.

It was infinitely better.

He was hard as steel and threatening to come right then, at the sound of her pleasure, and he didn't care. Not as long as he could bask in her satisfaction.

Releasing her nipple, he took her mouth once more and brushed her clothes to the floor before lifting her to the edge of his bed—high enough to leave her legs dangling above the floor. She reached for him. "Come . . . join me . . ."

Not yet. Not after twelve years of forsaking her. And in truth, as much as he wanted to join her, he wanted something else more.

He wanted to worship her.

He went to his knees, pushing between her thighs, pressing kisses to the soft skin beneath her breasts and over the perfect swell of her belly, even as she moved to stop him, to hide whatever she perceived as imperfection on her perfect body.

He would not be stopped, settling between her thighs and pressing her back to the bed. She sighed again, her fingers sliding into his hair, another memory. "I've dreamed . . ."

she began, and trailed off as he tongued the soft crease where her thigh and hip met.

He lifted his head. "What, love?"

Her fingers tightened, directing him. Did she mean to? The thought made him ache with the need to spend. Christ, he hoped she meant to. He'd let her guide him for the rest of their days. He'd devour her whenever she wanted.

He set his lips to her.

"I dreamed of this," she whispered, lifting her hips to meet the touch of his tongue. She was so sweet—so magnificent. "I ached for this," she added, letting her thighs fall open as she confessed her need again and again above him.

All as he consumed her, holding her wide as he licked and sucked at her, making love to her with slow, savoring strokes. She tasted the same. Rich like wine, dark like pleasure. And he wanted to drink her forever. He was slow and gentle, exploring the soft, slick lines he'd dreamed of for years, rolling his tongue over the places he remembered she liked, again and again, over and over, until she was gasping his name and pulling him to her and pressing her lips to his, letting him devour her until she was wild with need, begging him for her pleasure.

And he gave it to her. Slow turning to fast, his tongue working in time to his lips, and then, when she lifted her hips to him and her fingers clenched in his hair, fastest—until she screamed his name and he held her and let her take her pleasure, and he reveled in his ability to give it.

He stilled against her, prolonging her climax with a gentle, steady suck, until she released the breath she held and relaxed onto the bed, boneless. Perfect.

His.

When he finally lifted his head, it was to join her on the bed, pulling her tightly into his arms and holding her, trailing kisses along her jaw until she turned to kiss him, bold and beautiful. Her fingers trailed over the planes and ridges of his torso, down to the place he ached for her. She hooked one finger in the waist of his trousers and said, "More, please."

He closed his eyes, thanking his maker for delivering her to him, and let her work open his trousers. He lifted his hips from the bed, so she could strip him and—*yes*—climb over him, straddle him, as though it were a thing they'd done a thousand times before, as though she'd been in his dreams every night when he'd imagined it.

"Jack," he whispered, his hands coming to her waist, sliding up to her full, beautiful breasts and back down, over her lush curves, to clutch her hips and fit her to him, the heat of her like fire against his hard, aching cock.

"Please, Eben . . . I want . . ."

"I know, love," he whispered, leaning up to meet her kiss. To lick over her full lips, to taste her. Christ, he wanted, too. He'd wanted her forever. Every day. Every hour. Every minute since the minute she'd left him. "I know."

He pressed himself to her entrance, easing just inside her tight, blazing sheath before he paused. She rocked her hips, and he held her still.

"Eben . . ." she complained.

"No," he said through clenched teeth. "I want to see. I want to watch."

"Watch later."

He grunted as she moved against him and stopped her again. "I shall watch now, thank you. I've been desperate to watch this since you left." He held himself still, reveling in the look of her, rising above him, tempting him beyond reason. He was so hard, and she was so soft, and God, it had been so long since he'd touched her.

Too long.

His gaze found hers. "I don't want to hurt you."

She put her hands to his chest. "You shan't. Dammit, Eben. *Please.*"

"Greedy girl."

"Only with you," she said. "Only ever for you."

He could not resist the words—the desire in them that so thoroughly matched his own—and he released her, letting her seat herself, tight and hot and so gloriously wet he nearly came with that single, magnificent movement.

No. Jack first. Jack always.

He reached between them, to the sensitive, straining flesh just above the place where they were joined, stroking and circling just as he knew she liked, stroking as she moved on him, adjusting to his length, sliding, gasping, giving him the greatest pleasure he'd ever known.

He wasn't letting her go tomorrow.

He wasn't letting her go ever again.

Desperation warred with pleasure, and his hands came to her hips once more, holding her still, filling her—filled with her. "Look at me."

She obeyed the command without hesitation and his chest ached as she saw him—as he saw her for the first time in forever. He shook his head. "I never should have let you go." She closed her eyes at the words, and he saw them hit her. Saw the longing in her. Recognized it as his own. "I should have put you first. Above everything."

She stilled. "I didn't want that. I only wanted to be a part of it."

Christ, he'd been a bastard. "I didn't know how."

She nodded. "I know. It's in the past."

Frustration. "No. It's not. It's here. Jack, you were everything. And when you left . . ." He lifted her, the slide of her softness a lash along his hard length. Maybe if he could make her feel pleasure, if he could remind her of how they'd once been . . . "You *are* everything. And without you—I'm nothing at all."

He rolled her to the bed then, fitting himself against her, cradling her in his arms, desperate to feel her everywhere.

Holding her face in his palms, willing her to hear him. To understand. "I've lived in the past for twelve years."

Her eyes—her beautiful eyes—went wet with tears, and she whispered, "As have I. So full of memories, there wasn't room to make new ones."

"Forgive me." He leaned down and kissed her. She understood. And she'd come back to him. "Please, love. Please, forgive me."

She lifted her hips to his and he hissed his pleasure. "Shall we make a new memory, now?"

Goddammit. *Yes.*

He began to move, memory taking hold. *Yes.*

"Eben . . ."

"Tell me."

"Deeper . . ."

Yes. "My love."

"Harder . . ."

Yes.

"Eben . . ."

He gave her everything she asked, leaning down to her ear, telling her his truth—all the things he'd wished he'd said before she'd left. "It's always been you. Everything has always been for you." And then, like a prayer, "I love you."

She cried out at the words, clenching him tight and bringing him with her. He groaned, thrusting deep, moving against her, wringing every bit of pleasure from her.

Jack. Past, present, and future.

Then she whispered her own truth, like a gift. "It was always you, Eben. It was always this."

Yes.

He pressed his forehead to hers, breathing her in, taking her lips in a long, lingering kiss—putting all of himself into the touch, wishing he could erase the past and begin again, from here. From this single, perfect moment.

Wishing he could start again, the man she deserved.

She clung to him like breath, sighing her dismay when he lifted himself from her. Not that he would leave her. Ever. He pulled the blankets over them in the cold room, and she moved into his arms, laying her head on his chest, tucking herself into the place that had been empty since she'd left. The place he had saved for her.

He trailed his fingers along her impossibly soft skin. She lifted her head and pressed a kiss to his chest. "Your heart is pounding."

Eben rubbed a hand over it. "It's been stopped for so long—it learns to beat again."

She watched him for a long moment before capturing his hand in hers and pressing it to her chest. "They shall relearn it together."

His gaze went to where their fingers entwined, marveling at the touch—at her presence—before sliding to the golden locket, inlaid with finely scrolled vines. He reached for the pendant.

Where had it come from? He traced the scroll with one finger. Had her perfect fiancé given it to her? A thread of resistance coursed through him at the idea that a gift from another man might find a home against her warm skin—that it had been here, against them both as they'd reveled in each other.

She recognized his focus and reached for the locket, taking it in hand, holding it tight in her clasp. He met her eyes, finding them wide and full of emotion. "I bought it the day we left London," she whispered. "A present."

Shame coursed through him. The gift he hadn't thought to give her. It was almost worse than discovering it was a gift from another man. "To begin your future," he said, the words coming on a low, harsh breath. A future without him.

A future he might have had, as well, if he weren't such a prat.

"No, Eben," she whispered, her eyes welling with tears again. "No. To mourn my past."

She fiddled with the pendant then, opening the latch and then the locket itself, to reveal the treasure she kept hidden inside, against her heart. He narrowed his gaze on the little compartment, considering the circle of parchment, small and yellowed.

A snowflake.

His heart began to thunder.

"I suppose I don't need it anymore," she said quietly.

What? She couldn't possibly think she was leaving him. Not now. She couldn't possibly think he would let her go. Not when he had a chance to win her again.

And he was going to win her, dammit.

He took the locket in his hand and closed it, protecting the small paper circle before setting it back to her chest and leaning down to kiss her before moving away from her, loath to release her even as he leaned over the edge of the bed and fetched his discarded waistcoat, working to disconnect the long golden chain at the pocket. He rolled back to face her and dangled the golden pocket watch from his fingers. Surprise leapt into her gaze as she focused on the pendulum—surprise chased by happiness, bright and welcome and making him feel like a king.

She looked to him. "Your watch."

"Not a watch. A talisman." He opened the back, revealing the truth of his words, showing her the place where the inscription had once been, where he had rubbed it smooth. And there, tucked inside, another yellowed snowflake. A match to hers. She caught her breath and reached for it, stroking the paper with a soft touch, as though it was as fragile as a real snowflake.

"It was all I had left of you," he said, his voice hoarse. "After chasing you away."

A tear streaked down her cheek, and he let the watch

drop, reaching for her, his chest tight with emotion. He could bear so much—twelve years without her—but not her tears. "No, my love. No. Don't cry. Not for me. I am not worth it. I was never worth your tears."

Her hands came into his hair, holding him to her as more tears came and, finally, she pushed him away, far enough to meet his eyes, and for him to recognize her emotion.

Anger.

"You have always made that decision for me. What you are worth. And I am tired of it." He reached for her again, but she brushed off his touch, rising like Venus, strong and beautiful, pulling a blanket from the bed as she stood beside it. "*You* decided we should wait to marry. *You* decided you had to be rich. *You* decided the estate had to be settled. *You* decided that I could not stand beside you while you worked. *You* decided that I could not love you while you were poor. *You* decided that you—" Her breath hitched, and he sat up, again reaching for her, again being rebuffed. "No—" He lowered his hand instantly, even as he ached to touch her, to erase the pain in the words that followed. "You painted me perfection. Set me high on a pedestal and told yourself I was too fragile to be yours."

The words destroyed him. He swung his legs over the edge of the bed. "What? No. It was never that." He'd always wanted her with him. He'd just—"I wanted it to be good enough for you. I wanted it all to be worthy of you."

"What proper bollocks," she replied. "I could have built it with you. We could have stood together. Built it together."

He stilled. How many times had he dreamed of just that? Went to bed hungry and tired and certain he could smell her and feel her against him?

But it had been too late. He'd run her off with his misplaced duty and his obsession with what he might one day give her—forgetting all the while what he could give her every day. Rich or poor. In sickness and in health.

As long as they both should live.

"Why didn't you come for me? After I left?"

He met her eyes. "I wanted to."

More than he'd wanted to breathe.

"You promised me you would."

"I wanted to," he said again. "But Jack—you were seeing the world. What could I give you here? A small life, mired in the past."

She gave a little exasperated sigh. "You could have given me the future with the man I loved, you dunderhead. Which was all I ever wanted."

The truth of the words rioted through him and he was through not touching her. He'd spent twelve years not touching her. He reached for her, snaking one hand around her, her bare skin against his arm like silk. He pulled her forward and she came, her hands coming to his head as he pressed his face to her midriff, breathing her in.

She whispered, "You could have given me everything."

He still could. "I bollocksed it up."

"You did, rather."

"From the start."

"No. Only from the middle."

It didn't feel like the middle, however. It felt like forever. No. It felt like the past.

He lifted his head and looked up at her. "You can't marry your idiot Scot."

She canted her head. "Why not?"

"Because he'll never love you like I love you."

Something softened in her gaze, and pleasure pooled deep within him, like ice cracking open on the first warm day of spring. "He never made me ache with sadness like you did, either."

Eben stood then, reaching for her, cradling her face in his hands. "I am sorry. Christ. Let me fix it. Tell me how to fix it."

"I only ever wanted you to choose me," she said. "I only ever wanted you to love me."

"I do," he said, taking her lips in a long, lush kiss, desperate for the touch of her. The feel of her. "Dammit, Jack. Everything . . . everything I have . . . everything I am . . . It's all yours."

"I don't want it," she whispered. "I just want you."

"You have always had me," he whispered. "Halfway around the world, with a decade between us, you had me." They kissed again, long and lingering until she shivered in his arms.

He went instantly to the hearth, turning his back on her as he crouched to strike flint and stoke flame. Once the fire was burning, he turned back, expecting her to be far from the bed, somewhere where they could talk—revisit the past—begin anew.

Except she was already where she belonged, in his bed once more, the covers pulled up to her chin as she watched him, the orange glow of the fire reflected in her eyes.

"Come back to bed," she said, soft and warm and delicious.

He shook his head, detouring to the desk at the far end of the room, where he'd left his violin earlier in the evening. Lifting it, he turned back to her. "I owe you a debt."

Her eyes went wide and she sat up, holding the sheets to her chest as a smile spread across her face.

"I have regretted not playing for you every night since that one," he said softly. "I used to lie in that bed and stare into the darkness and wonder if you would have stayed, if only . . ."

He let the words trail off as he lifted the instrument to his chin, set the bow to the strings, and played for the woman he loved. He closed his eyes the moment the music began, infusing it with his regret and his desire and his love for Jack, who had, by some miracle, returned to him. He played as though it was his only chance to convince her to stay, his only opportunity to win her back—his only hope.

And when the final strains of music faded into silence around them, he opened his eyes, immediately finding hers, seeing the tears staining her cheeks. "Eben." She whispered his name like a prayer, warming him from within. "I missed that so much."

He lowered the violin. "Happy Christmas, Jack."

A fat tear rolled down her cheek, and she whispered, "I love you."

Eben was already moving, dropping the instrument to the carpet and coming for her, climbing into the bed beside her, collecting her to him, kissing her.

She squeaked at his touch. "You're cold!"

"You're sunshine," he replied, pulling her close, loving her warmth.

Loving her.

She smiled, tucking her head to his chest, the weight of her warm and wonderful against him. He pressed a kiss to the top of her head. "It's snowing on Christmas."

She yawned, eyes already sliding closed. "A miracle."

He held her like that for what felt like an age, until her breathing went even and deep, and she was asleep in his arms in their warm cocoon, far from everything in the world beyond.

He lay awake for hours in the darkness, afraid to sleep. Afraid she wouldn't be there when he woke.

Afraid this miracle would not linger.

Chapter Nine

The Island of Naxos, two months earlier

*J*ack had been standing in the Portara, staring out at the Aegean Sea, unable to see the sapphire water or the gleam of the setting sun, when Fergus MacBride spoke from behind her. "Gold or lead?"

Startled from her thoughts, Jack turned to find the Scot leaning against the massive stone doorjamb, arms crossed and a curious smile on his handsome young face. She shook her head. "I don't—"

"Gold or lead?" he repeated. "Eros's arrows."

"Neither."

"Liar."

She huffed a little surprised laugh at the accusation. "I beg your pardon, it isn't a lie."

"A pity. I was hoping ye'd be shot straight in love wi' me, lass."

She couldn't help matching his wide, winning smile. "You're six-and-twenty and handsome enough to make a girl think the devil came direct from Scotland. You could have any woman you wished."

He winked at her. "Perhaps I've been looking for an older woman to take me in hand."

She waved toward the town in the distance, where she and Aunt Jane had lingered for the last month. "My aunt is reading on the veranda."

His laugh faded into the sea and silence until, finally, Fergus said, "Would you?"

She met his warm brown eyes. "Would I what?"

"Take me in hand."

Confusion flared. Fergus had been traveling with Jack and Aunt Jane for three months. Lady Danton was famous for collecting hangers-on, but what had begun in Constantinople as one of Aunt Jane's whims had ended with Fergus and Jack becoming friends. But never, in all the time they'd traveled together, had it occurred to Jack that Fergus might consider their friendship . . . more.

"Are you . . ." She trailed off.

He smiled, the expression more than a little sheepish. "You said you were growing tired of your aunt's travels."

It was true. Aunt Jane could easily spend the rest of her days living out of her well-packed trunks, never returning to London. But twelve years had been a long time for Jack—long enough that she found herself longing for home.

Longing for the man she'd once considered home.

The thought had her meeting Fergus's gaze. "I am, but . . ." Again, she lost her words.

"You're growing tired of being a lady's companion, and I canna travel around the world forever. I've a home in Scotland that calls me back—and I shall need a wife wi' me eventually."

"Eventually."

He lifted one shoulder in a carefree shrug. "No need to wait when I've found such a good friend."

"Friend."

He grinned. "Are ye having trouble hearing me, Lady Jacqueline?"

"No," she replied. "Just understanding you."

He straightened, coming to his full height, his too-long red hair falling low over his brow. "Let me make it more plain. I've need of a wife. And I think you've need of a husband. What say you we make a go of it?"

And there it was. Jack's first marriage proposal, spoken as the wind curled around them from the Aegean Sea, the gleam of the golden sunset turning the moment into paradise. Except, it wasn't paradise. Because it wasn't the proposal she wanted.

It never would be.

"It's a lovely offer."

He inclined his head. "But not one you're willing to accept."

She shook her head. "I can't marry you."

"Why not?"

"Because you don't love me."

He nodded in agreement, and something like relief chased through Jack. "I like ye plenty, lass. And fine marriages have been based on less than that, I'll tell you."

It was a good offer. Fergus was a good friend. Handsome and kind, and with seemingly endless funds and an estate in Scotland to boot.

"Why not admit the truth?" he said, pulling her from her thoughts.

She watched him for a long moment. And then, "All right. I don't love you."

The words held no sting. Neither did they deliver one, if the flash of Fergus's white teeth was any indication. "But you like me plenty."

She smiled. "When you're not behaving like a madman, certainly."

"Tell me this. How many times have you thought of returning to him?"

The question came from nowhere. Fergus shouldn't have known there was a *him* to ask about. There wasn't a *him* to ask about, was there? It had been twelve years, and surely all the wide world had moved on.

It wasn't like she'd asked to remain in love with Eben.

But she had. She had, and there was no man she would ever want like him—the boy who had held storms at bay, and given her snow, and made her believe in love. And like that, the tears came. The memory of Eben's arms, of his wide smiles, of his beautiful eyes and his broad shoulders and his soft kisses. The longing for him.

And she told her friend the truth. "I've thought of returning to him every day since I left."

There was no surprise in Fergus's response—only kind understanding. "And why haven't you done it?"

She looked to the sea, her words whispered to the wind. "Because . . . he never came to fetch me."

Fergus heard them nonetheless. "Well, he's a bawbag, clearly."

She gave a surprised laugh at the foul Scottish word. "He is, rather."

"But you've got a mind full of fluff," Fergus added.

Jack turned on him. "I beg your pardon?"

"Do you love him?"

"Yes," she said. "Yes. I love him."

"Still."

She took a deep breath, letting the sun and salt spread through her, her thoughts far away in London, where it was already turning cold with the crisp autumn air. She missed the cold, when the nights would grow longer, and she could creep about the house unnoticed. To the library.

To Eben.

"Always."

"Then why leave him?"

She watched the waves break and roll into shore for an age. Then, finally, "Because I could not stay and let him leave me first."

"Canna blame you for that. We all are running from something." Fergus was silent for a long time. "But the heart wants what the heart wants, I'm told."

Lord knew that was true. Softly, she said, "I don't want to love him."

"Seems to me that if you didn't want to love him, you would nae love him."

"He never came for me." Her heart ached at the confession. How long had she waited for him to turn up? To track her down and go to his knees and beg her to be his? And he'd never come.

Just as she'd never returned.

"That's because he's an idiot." She laughed again, wiping tears from her cheeks as Fergus added, "If he came, would you go with him?"

There was no reason not to tell the truth. "Yes. Without question."

A pause, and then, dry as sand, "Then you might be an idiot, too."

Only a sliver of the sun was left, turning the stone pink and orange, casting the whole town in a magical light, stealing Jack's breath. Setting her heart to aching, just as the rest of the wide world had. Twelve years of exploration, witnessing the beauty of the world, exploring its secrets and meeting its people, and Jack hadn't had a day of it that hadn't ended with her wishing for Eben.

She turned on Fergus, no small amount of fear coursing through her. "And if I go back . . . What if I'm the only one who remembers?"

"What if you're not?"

"What if he doesn't love me?"

"What if he does?"

What if he was there, waiting? Just as she was?

"What if I make a hash of it?" she asked her friend.

He smiled and spread his hands wide. "If you make a hash of it, there's always Scotland."

Fear gave way to hope. Wicked, wonderful hope.

"Can we get to him by Christmas?"

Chapter Ten

Boxing Day

*T*he Duke of Allryd shot awake in a cold room, blinding sun streaming through his window, certain that he had missed the most important morning of his life. He sat up, already reaching for the woman he'd held the night before, coming up with a handful of cool sheets and nothing else.

She was gone.

It was Boxing Day, and she was gone.

She was supposed to leave for her wedding today. For her life in Scotland. For her future.

Had he missed her future?

He was out of the bed, barely remembering to collect his dressing gown before he was out of the room, bare legged, belting the robe as he tore down the quiet stairs and into the kitchens.

Empty.

He spun on his heel and went for the other places she might be. The library. Empty. A knot formed in the pit of his stomach as he took to the dining room—perhaps she'd made breakfast already? Of course, he knew the answer. *Empty.*

Christ. Had she left him?

She couldn't have. She couldn't leave him.

Had he dreamed it? Her?

His mad thoughts were growing wilder by the moment, and he returned to the foyer, making for his study—perhaps she was there.

She wasn't, but Lawton was, seated at his desk, working. He looked up when Eben entered, his wild-eyed gaze taking in all the dark corners of the room. "I was not aware we were dressing so casually today," his partner said dryly.

"What time is it?"

Lawton's brows rose, but he looked to the clock on his desk. "Half past nine."

"Have you seen—" He paused, ridiculously, wondering if he had, in fact, dreamed her. He ran a hand through his hair. "Jack? Lady Jack? Lady Jacqueline Mosby?"

Lawton tilted his head, something like humor in his gaze. "I have not. Did you misplace her?"

Eben scowled. "Last I saw her she was right where she belonged."

"In her own home, preparing her wedding trousseau?"

"In my bed." Christ. What if he'd missed her? Panic flared. "Charles," Eben said, softly, "I can't lose her. Not when I just got her back."

A beat. Lawton rose, removed his spectacles, and set them on his desk, his mouth set in a determined line. "Well, then. It seems we ought to find her before she leaves."

Eben shook his head. "She's gone."

"She can't be. There's a foot and a half of snow outside and she won't have ventured out in it."

The snow. Hope flared. The miracle snowstorm that he'd thought was a gift from the universe to her. It hadn't been. It was a gift to him.

Lawton approached and clapped a hand to Eben's shoulder, adding, "We are snowed in. She's in the house, friend. She has to be."

Realization struck.

No. She wasn't in the house. But it did not mean she'd gone outside. Eben made for the conservatory, Lawton following, all curiosity. When Eben threw open the door and strode into the dark room with pure, unwavering purpose, the other man offered, "Do you intend to summon her with music?"

Eben ignored him and reached for the edge of the painting of satyrs.

"Allryd," Lawton added, too gently, as though he were speaking to a madman. "I'm not certain this is the best use of—" He stopped when the painting swung on its hinges to reveal the door in the wall. "Well. That was unexpected."

Please. Please be unlocked.

If she'd locked it, it would be a sign. It would be proof she'd left. Eben set a hand to the latch. Pressed.

The door swung open, and he exhaled on a barely there huff of relief before stepping through the door and into the library beyond, where Aunt Jane sat at a low window, staring out at the gray landscape.

She turned, unmoved by the fact that two men—one of whom was wearing nothing but a belted robe—were climbing through an unknown doorway into her morning silence, her knowing gaze finding Eben's without hesitation. "It's about time you used that door."

There was no time to be surprised that Aunt Jane knew about the secret door between the houses, as Eben was too busy using it. Just as he should have used it twelve years ago, the moment Jack left his office in the dead of night. Just as he should have used it every day since, until he found her. Until he fetched her.

"I'm marrying her."

One gray brow arched. "Not if he marries her first."

His heart began to pound. "Bollocks that."

She nodded to the door of the room. "Best be on your way, then."

And that was that. Eben left at a dead run, desperate to claim his love, and his future.

He found her descending the steps of the grand foyer of the town house, in an ordinary day dress, a beautiful navy blue that played at the neck with the rich bronze of her sun-kissed skin and caressed her lush curves through the bodice, until it fell in thick waves to the floor.

She looked like perfection. Like a queen.

"Christ, you're beautiful." It was pure, unadulterated truth, and she blushed, a wash of pink chasing across her cheeks and mottling the skin above the bodice of the dress.

Her gaze flickered over his attire, widening at his belted robe, her full, lovely lips opening on a surprised gasp at his bare legs and feet. She looked over his shoulder, to where Aunt Jane and Lawton lingered, an unwelcome audience to what was to come.

But Eben had had twelve years to do this correctly—to chase her around the globe and convince her that he deserved a second chance—and he was out of time. He moved toward her, desperation coursing through him. She couldn't leave to marry another. Not after last night. Not after letting him touch her. Not after letting him love her.

She couldn't leave him broken and empty, not when all he wanted was to fill his life with her and to fill *her* life with happiness.

"Jack." He had nearly reached her. She stood on the second-to-last step, rising up like royalty, and his gaze fixed to her chest, where the gold locket lay against her warm skin. The locket that held his snowflake. Their past.

Disbelief chased through him; she wouldn't carry him against her heart while she pledged it to another, would she?

"Eben . . ." she said, softly, and he was struck with twin emotions—a desperate desire to hear what she had to say and abject terror that she was about to tell him that he was too late and she had chosen another.

"Wait," he said, to stay her words. "When you turned up in my kitchens two nights ago, I told you I hadn't thought about the door in years. It was a lie. I thought about it every day. It was unlocked for you every day. Every night. Since the night you left. I never locked it. I never wanted to. I always wanted you to use it."

Tears sparkled in her eyes. "I wanted to come back and use it. But . . . I was afraid."

Fear coursed through him. "Of me?"

"Of the idea that you might not wish me to use it."

"I wish it," he vowed. "More than anything."

"Of you never using it yourself."

What a fool he'd been. "I used it this morning. Only tell me it's not too late, and—"

A pounding came, loud and insistent, behind him. Her gaze flew over his shoulder and he turned to follow it—to the enormous oak door, inlaid with carved vines. For a moment, silence hung in the foyer, as though no one present was quite certain what the protocol was for this particular moment.

"There's no staff today," Aunt Jane said.

Lawton replied. "Should I—"

"No," Eben said. "I'll do it."

He went to the door, dread pooling deep as he pulled it open, revealing the sky beyond—a perfect blue, accompanied by a gust of frigid air and powdery snow nearly knocking him back with the cold and billowing the fabric of his inappropriate attire.

There, on the step, was a tall, lean figure, cloaked in a black cape, the hood of which covered all but an angular, clean-shaven jaw. And propped over the figure's shoulder, a long-handled tool. A shovel.

And then the hood was pushed back to reveal a handsome, open face and a broad smile. "Mornin'!" came the thick Scots brogue. "I've come to rescue ye!" He looked down at Eben's bare legs and added, "Best let me in, man, before your lower half freezes!"

Somewhere behind him, Eben heard Lawton's shocked laughter.

Eben stepped backward, watching as the man came into the entryway, removing his cloak and shaking his head like a great dog, sending snow everywhere before he looked to those assembled and introduced himself. "Fergus Mac-Bride," he said, before his gaze alit on Jack and his eyes warmed with something horrifically like joy. "My lady, yer lookin' beautiful as a breeze."

Maybe Eben could've tolerated the jovial Scot at a different time and in a different place. Maybe he could have found him entertaining and friendly.

Likely not, but maybe.

Except Jack seemed to relax in the glow of Fergus's attention, and that was the end of any possible affinity Eben might have for the Scot because, dammit, she was his.

She'd been his since they were children. Since the first time he'd held her in his arms and she'd whispered her dreams—dreams he'd vowed to make real. Dreams he still had time to make real.

If he could just convince her he was worth it.

I only ever wanted you to choose me, she'd whispered the night before. *I only ever wanted you to love me.*

Surely that meant she loved him, as well, didn't it?

It couldn't mean she loved Fergus—Fergus, who was crossing the room to her, reaching for her.

No. She loved Eben. He was sure of it. Mostly. "Wait."

Four sets of eyes flew to him, but he only cared for one of them—his love. His heart, ripped from him twelve years earlier, made flesh in her.

"I love you," he said, the words ragged and desperate. He

moved toward her, ignoring their audience. Wanting only her. "I've loved you forever. I've carried you with me, the only light in my dull, dark life.

"I said it was for you. All that time. It wasn't. It was for me. To prove I could be the kind of man I wished to be when I was with you. And here is the truth. I will never be good enough for you. But I shall love you, Jack."

"Eben," she whispered.

He reached for her, brushing his thumb across her cheek. He shook his head. "If you choose him, I won't take that from you," he said, at once surprised and unsurprised by the words. "God knows I've never proved my worth. But know this—" He leaned in and put his forehead to hers. *She let him.* "I have never stopped loving you. Everything I am. Everything I have. It has always been yours. And it always will be."

Her hands came to his shoulders, holding him tight, and he closed his eyes, loving the touch even as it made him ache. "Jack," he whispered, "I've made such a hash of the past. Let me make it up to you. Let me give you the future. Stay."

Her tears were coming in earnest then, and his chest ached with every one of them. He pulled back to wipe them from her cheeks. He met her gaze. "Stay with me."

She took a deep breath.

"Stay with me, please," he whispered again. "Let us have the future we should have had from the start. Please, let me love you." He gathered her hands in his and went to his knees before her, like a knight pledging fealty to his queen. Her breath caught and her fingers tightened around his as he looked up at her. "I'm a selfish bastard, Jack. And a greedy one. And I want you. Forever."

Why was she shaking her head? She couldn't say no. His fingers tightened around hers, as though if he could just keep hold of her, she wouldn't slip away. If she said no . . . he'd have to let her go.

"Eben," she whispered, her hands coming to his unshaven cheeks.

She leaned forward and softly pressed her lips to his. Triumph coursed through him, making him weak, then powerfully strong—strong enough for his hands to itch for her, for his arms to ache to hold her.

Except, there were others assembled.

Most notably, the jovial Scotsman who was to have married her, but who seemed not at all unhappy with the scene unfolding before him. "Did ye ask him yet?"

"No," she said, and he heard the hesitation in her voice. "I had to be certain that he wished it."

"I wish it," Eben said. "Whatever it is. I wish it. I should have come for you. I'm here now. I will be forever."

"That seems promising," the Scot said, fairly bouncing in his boots. "No time like the present, Jacqueline."

Eben looked to Fergus, his brow furrowing. "Ask me what?" He looked back to Jack, still watching him, eyes shining, a smile on her face. "Ask me what?"

The foyer went quiet, and she swallowed. She was nervous. "I'm not marrying Fergus."

Relief coursed through him. "You're not . . ." Relief, and then something else. Understanding. "Wait. You're not?"

She winced. "I shouldn't have told you—but I was afraid . . ." she confessed, almost to herself.

He heard it anyway. She'd lied about Fergus. About the wedding.

Eben should be angry. But for the life of him, he couldn't find the energy. Of course she'd lied. She hadn't known what she was walking into.

No, he wasn't angry. He was elated.

Before he could tell her as much, however, she took

a deep breath and said, "Will you . . ." She stopped, the
words sticking in her throat.

Anything she wished.

He reached for her, taking her face in his hands. "Yes.
Whatever it is, Jack, it's yours."

She gave a little huff of laughter. *Perfection.* "You can't
say yes yet. I have to ask."

He nodded, not understanding, but wanting her to have
everything she dreamed. "Go on, then."

"Eben, will you marry me?"

His blood roared in his ears at the question, so unexpected. He would slaver after her like a dog on a lead if
that was what she offered him. Of course, he would marry
her. But *yes* didn't seem enough of an answer. So, he kissed
her instead, lifting her to him and taking her lips until her
arms were wrapped around his neck, and he was ready to
carry her to bed.

He didn't care about witnesses. She was to be his wife,
and husbands carried their wives to bed, dammit.

He was vaguely aware of the collective response of those
assembled—a wild hoot from the Scot, a deep-throated
laugh from Lawton, and a little sniffle from Aunt Jane, who
added, "I still don't believe you deserve her, but I suppose
if she's happy . . ."

Eben lifted his head, barely able to stop himself from
kissing Jack, and smiled down at her. "I absolutely don't
deserve her, but I promise to keep her happy forever."

"Then it worked!" came Aunt Jane's smug reply.

Jack rolled her eyes.

Eben's brow furrowed. "What worked?"

"The shortbread! That's what!" Aunt Jane crowed.

Jack laughed, the sound bright and perfect, cracking
Eben open and filling his darkness with light. "The shortbread nearly killed him, Aunt Jane."

"Nonsense. That shortbread has made love matches for generations."

Love matches.

The pieces clicked into place. Christmas Eve. The memories of their past. His favorite foods. "You came back for me," he whispered, unable to keep the awe from his voice.

She nodded. "I had to."

"You came back *to* me."

"I had to know if you might love me."

"I do."

Lawton interjected, confused. "And so there was no fiancé?"

Fergus jumped in. "To be fair, I did offer to marry her."

Eben did not look away from Jack when he replied to the Scot. "You're not marrying her."

Fergus grinned. "It's difficult to marry a lass so thoroughly in love with another."

"You're a good friend," she said to the Scot before turning back to Eben. "He was ready to have me, if I couldn't win you."

As though there was ever a chance she couldn't win him. "It's I who might not have been able to win you."

"Well, I'm afraid I'm no' offering to marry ye, Duke."

He ignored the Scot and the laughter from the others, focused only on his love. "Let me win you, Jack," he whispered. "Let me show you how it might be."

"I already know how it might be," she said. "I've been dreaming of it since the day I used that door for the first time."

His heart filled with something unfamiliar, cracking open, running over with joy. "You came back for me."

She smiled. "Do you forgive me?"

There was nothing to forgive. "Forgive you? I'm not sure how I will ever thank you," he said, pulling her into his arms once more. "I will have to settle for loving you beyond reason."

She smiled. "I shall allow it."

"I told you the biscuits worked!" Aunt Jane crowed again, and Jack chuckled against him.

He replied without looking away from his future wife. "We were already a love match," he said. "Your poison biscuits weren't necessary."

"Nonsense!" Aunt Jane waved his response away before adding to Lawton and Fergus, "Neither of you are leaving this house without the recipe." The old woman led the reluctant and altogether too-polite gentlemen away, back to the kitchens, no doubt to fill them full of the awful stuff.

"Better them than me," Eben said against Jack's laughing mouth, stealing it for another kiss.

"I don't know," Jack gasped after a long while, as Eben trailed his lips across her jaw to linger at her ear. "Perhaps it was the biscuits, after all."

"It wasn't," he said, lifting her high in his arms and starting up the stairs to the sound of her laughter. "It was you. My brilliant, beautiful past. My miracle present."

He immediately set about giving her the future she deserved.

Epilogue

. . . *A*nd it snowed every Christmas thereafter.

About Sarah MacLean

New York Times, *Washington Post*, and *USA Today* best-seller **SARAH MacLEAN** is the author of historical romance novels that have been translated into more than twenty languages and winner of back-to-back RITA® Awards for best historical romance from the Romance Writers of America.

A columnist for the *Washington Post*, Sarah is a leading advocate for the romance genre, speaking widely on its place at the nexus of gender and cultural studies. Her work in support of romance and the women who read it earned her a place on Jezebel.com's Sheroes list and led *Entertainment Weekly* to name her "the elegantly fuming, utterly intoxicating queen of historical romance." A graduate of Smith College and Harvard University, Sarah now lives in New York City with her husband and daughter.

To receive updates on Sarah's upcoming books and monthly recommendations of fabulous romance reads, please sign up for her newsletter at www.sarahmaclean.net.

Heiress Alone

Sophie Jordan

Chapter One

*T*hey left her.

Annis Ballister took another turn about the house to be certain, her steps echoing in the silence. The drawing room, the parlor, every chamber—all empty. Even the ghostly ballroom that hadn't seen use in decades and was in dire need of a good cleaning loomed vacant. Her younger sisters had liked to frolic over its stone floors, imagining they were debutantes at a grand ball in London. Anywhere other than here.

However, they weren't here now. The place was empty.

"Hello?" Her voice rang off the rafters of the drafty old Scottish castle Papa had won in a game of whist.

Her father had thought a holiday in Scotland's Highlands the perfect lark. An escape from Town. He'd hunted stag to his heart's content whilst Mama languished indoors, sipping her sherry, despairing of their exile to such a primitive location and rereading old scandal sheets.

Annis did not mind the respite from Town. Hardly anyone was about in the winter months anyway. Although, truth be told, even in the height of the season, she would have rather been in the country. Not that she ever got her wish on that matter.

She always felt judged and scrutinized and deemed lacking by good *ton* . . . Considering those were the only people Mama ever wanted to mingle with, life could be tedious.

Truthfully, Annis found the stark beauty of the Highlands, even if snow shrouded and bitterly cold this time of year, soul stirring. A fortuitous circumstance since, apparently, her family had forgotten her. They had left her and returned to that gilded cage for which Mama mourned.

She was well and truly alone. Abandoned.

"Unbelievable," she muttered as she lifted her skirts and made her way down to the kitchens. Yet she could not summon forth too much annoyance. As one of six children, she was rarely afforded solitude. A part of her relished the echoing silence. For however long it lasted. And it couldn't last long. They would return once they realized they had left her.

Annis took the winding stone steps carefully, minding where she placed her feet and shivering as the cold intensified. She pulled her shawl tighter about her shoulders and stepped down onto the damp stone floor of the kitchen, greeted by Fenella's humming. A sound she knew well as she had spent a good amount of time in the kitchens, enjoying the housekeeper's company. Fenella was an interesting person, full of colorful stories almost too far-fetched to be believed.

So—not totally alone then. Thankfully. Fenella stood with her back to Annis, working at something on the table before her.

"Hello," Annis greeted, her voice echoing off the walls of the cavernous kitchen.

Fenella screeched, flinging a mound of dough in the air. She spun to face Annis, one gnarled hand pressing against her thin chest. "Lass! Ye gave me a fright!"

"I'm sorry."

The housekeeper shook her head. "Wot are ye doing here? Ye should have left this morning with the rest of 'em."

Confirmation then. They had in fact departed whilst she slept. Improbable as it seemed, her family had forgotten her.

She supposed it could be understood. They were a large family with numerous staff, and they had apparently left in some haste. It was not even noon yet. Her sisters were notoriously late risers. The hand of God Himself would have had to drag them from bed. If she had not stayed awake so late reading by candlelight, she would have risen at her usual early hour.

"I did not realize we were departing today." They had planned to stay until tomorrow. Much to Mama's displeasure, Papa had secured her promise to stay here a fortnight and he would not be swayed to leave sooner. He'd wanted ample opportunity to hunt and he claimed they would have time aplenty to reach London by Christmas. He'd been resolute on the matter. Annis could not imagine what changed his mind and precipitated such an early departure.

Fenella waved an arm. "Did ye no' hear the commotion?"

Annis resisted pointing out that she occupied the farthest removed chamber on the third floor. That had been no random occurrence, either. She had selected the room for its very remoteness from everyone else, craving the rare privacy for herself.

Fenella continued. "Angus woke the house early this morn. Snow was rising high in the pass, and the rate it be falling, ye all risked being trapped here."

Ah. Annis nodded. Mama could not have borne being trapped here one day longer than necessary. She could well imagine the frenzied exodus of her family and their staff.

"Well, then. I imagine Papa will send one of the coaches back to fetch me once they realize I've been left behind." She smiled. She would have something to hold over her parents. Perhaps she could use it as leverage to bow out of the next ball or fete Mama attempted to force on her.

Just then the door leading outside from the kitchens opened, sending a gale of cold wind gusting into the room. Angus, the groundskeeper and Fenella's brother, shook the snow from his bent shoulders and removed his cap, slapping it on his trousers, pausing midmotion when his gaze landed on Annis. He straightened his wiry frame. "Och! What ye be doing here, lass?"

"They forgot 'er!" Fenella exclaimed, outrage high in her voice as she pointed a damning finger at Annis.

His wide eyes passed back and forth between Annis and Fenella before resting on his sister. "Well, what now? What we tae dae with 'er?" This he directed at Fenella.

"I am sure Papa will send a carriage to fetch me," Annis repeated for the benefit of Angus.

They stared at her.

She angled her head expectantly, awaiting their relief. Really, she saw no reason for such excitement.

"Nae," Angus returned, shaking his head slowly, his tone solemn. "There be nae getting through the pass. Yer stuck here until the snow melts."

"Melts?" she echoed, her stomach knotting. It couldn't be as bad as it sounded. "And when will that be?"

He shrugged and exchanged a dark look with the housekeeper. "Mayhap . . . March."

* * *

Annis moved her things into one of the larger chambers.

The room her parents had occupied touted a fireplace of gigantic proportions and the castle could be a bit drafty. She was quite certain she would want to be warm during the months ahead.

Months. She would be here for months. There would be no Christmas in Mayfair with her boisterous family. She had mixed feelings on this matter. She loved the trappings of Christmas in Town. Carolers. Boughs of holly. The fat goose on Christmas Eve. But her family was overwhelming. She welcomed the peace of a respite. Time to read uninterrupted. No one taking her ribbons or clothes. No terrible rows requiring mediation.

Sighing, she pulled back the coverlet and slipped beneath its heavy weight. She was tired, even though she had done little else than sit and stare out the window at the rising snow, waiting for a glimpse of her father as though Angus had been mistaken. As though Papa would miraculously appear to rescue her.

The keep did boast an impressive library, so she would have books to occupy her during her stay here. And she did have Fenella and Angus, so she was not utterly alone. Little comfort, however, when she thought about how worried Papa would be. He called Annis his most reasonable child, meaning she was not given to histrionics as were her sisters and mother. At least Papa would be comforted by the fact that she was not completely alone here. Mama, in her own fashion, would fret, too.

Snow-laden winds howled outside the keep and beat against the shutters of the chamber's single window. She leaned over and blew out the candle on the side table. Only the light cast by the fire saved the room from utter darkness.

Closing her eyes, she settled back into the big bed and waited for sleep.

Chapter Two

*A*nnis woke with a sudden jolt, sitting up in bed with a strangled gasp. Shivering, she pulled the bedcovers up to her chin. Heavens, it was cold.

She blinked into the darkness, struggling through the fog of her mind. It did not *feel* like her room in Mayfair. For starters, it was never this frightfully cold. Usually if she woke in the middle of the night it was because one of her sisters had invaded her room for one reason or another. The twins shared a bedchamber and when they came to blows, which happened frequently and at all hours, one of them would invade Annis's domain to escape the other— never mind that it meant shattering Annis's peace.

But neither Cordelia nor Deidra was around. She blinked into the gloom of her room. She was alone.

A distant shout carried from below, and her hands knotted in the thick coverlet. She swung her legs around, the balls of her feet brushing the ancient rug and it all came back to her in a rush.

She was in Scotland. Snowed in. Left behind with only Fenella and Angus for company.

Another shout carried from somewhere deep in the bowels of the keep. Concerned that either Fenella or Angus might have taken a fall or be otherwise in distress, she snatched up her dressing gown and slipped it on as she hurried from her chamber and down the curving stairs, hoping her imagination was getting the best of her.

Her bare feet padded down the faded runner of the corridor, her robe swishing at her ankles. At the second-floor landing, she peered over the railing down into the foyer below.

Clad in a heavy wool nightgown, Fenella conversed with a towering cloaked figure. Snow dusted his hat and the shoulders of his greatcoat. It was clear the man wasn't Angus. The groundskeeper looked frail and diminutive in comparison to this stranger.

Annis frowned and leaned forward, curious about a visitor who would arrive so late at night—in the midst of a snowstorm, no less.

She couldn't hear their words, but she gave a small start as Fenella suddenly threw back her head and shouted for Angus.

Annis called down, "Fenella? Is something amiss?" As her father's daughter and the sole member of her family present, she was the mistress of the house. It was a responsibility she should not take lightly.

Both heads snapped up to meet her gaze, but she only had eyes for the stranger.

Her breath caught in her chest, a great bubble locked inside her as the man's bright stare fixed on her. Except he wasn't a stranger. Unfortunately, she knew him.

Indeed, she remembered him well. The dark eyes. The handsome face. Oh yes. She knew this man. She'd know him anywhere. Mortification flooded her as she recalled his frosty gaze skimming her like she was a bit of vermin dragged in by the cat.

She pulled back her shoulders and lifted her chin. This was *her* home. He was the interloper here. She had no cause for embarrassment. Not this time.

She had never expected to see him again—especially not when she was in such a discomposed state. Her hair was unraveling from the plait she'd created hours ago and her nose was so cold she was certain it was berry red. And then there were her bare feet peeping out at the hem.

As embarrassing as her state of dishabille was, it couldn't be any more embarrassing than the first time the Duke of Sinclair laid eyes on her. She'd never live that memory down.

* * *

Nine days ago . . .

Annis stepped from the carriage and paused to inspect Glencrainn, the grand castle stretching to the skies in front of her. The pale gray structure was several shades lighter than the stormy winter sky above it. It made the castle Papa had won look like a modest manor house.

"Quit dawdling, Annis. We want down, too." A sharp jab in the back propelled her forward and sent her flying to the snow-packed ground. It was impossible to say which one of her sisters shoved her. Now that Imogen had secured a fiancé with a baronetcy, all the other remaining Ballister sisters were hungrier than ever to win a match. As though a gauntlet had been tossed. No manner of cutthroat behavior was above them. It was every heiress for herself.

Annis's hands saved her face from the worst of the impact. Her elbows, however, smarted from where they struck the ground. Her dignity was not spared, either.

Her sisters spilled out behind her, practically stepping on her in their haste. They pushed and shoved at each other, sniping like a quarreling nest of vipers.

"Really, Annis," Regan proclaimed in hot accusing

tones. Her second-youngest sister was largely considered the most beautiful of the Ballister girls. "Must you be so clumsy?"

Clumsy? No. She usually wasn't. *Odd duck out?* Yes. Almost always.

Annis blew at the snow flecking her lips. She looked up, freezing as she locked eyes on a pair of well-worn boots directly in her line of vision. She pushed up on her stinging elbows, following the path of boots over snug, well-worn breeches and up the long body to the humorless deep-set eyes staring down at her. Flat stare. Unsmiling lips. His square jaw was locked tight. He needed to shave. Bristle dusted his jaw, but even that did not detract from his handsomeness.

The man made no move to help her.

"You there," Papa announced, eyeing the stoic-faced man as he descended the carriage steps. "Fetch your master and see to our carriage." Papa started as he spotted Annis on the ground. "Daughter? What are you doing down there?"

Stifling an eye roll, Annis pushed up to her knees.

"This place is monstrous!" Cordelia tittered, rotating in a small circle in the courtyard, her mouth wide. "Can you imagine being mistress of such a grand place? It might make up for living so far from London."

"Yes, yes, I can imagine it perfectly." Deidra gave a toss of her curls. "You, however, should not bother stretching your imagination for you shall *never* be mistress of this place. The Duke of Sinclair would never want to marry a pinch-faced ninny like you."

"Stop saying that! We're twins!" Cordelia shrieked. "Identical!"

"Hardly. I'm the prettier. Everyone knows it," Deidra returned, squawking as Cordelia lunged for her with raised fists. Regan, unfortunately, stood in her path and caught a set of knuckles on the chin that launched her into an unceasing wail.

"Girls! Girls!" Papa wearily exclaimed.

"Papa!" Penelope, Annis's youngest sister of fifteen years, stomped her foot. "They're embarrassing. What if the duke sees?"

Papa rubbed a gloved hand over his face, no doubt regretting bringing his horde of unattached daughters along on this call. Not that Mama had given him a choice. In her mind, the only good thing about Papa dragging them to this far corner of the earth was that a duke happened to live in the area. Even if he was a Scot, a duke was a duke and Mama wanted each of her daughters to marry a title.

The rude man finally spoke. "The Sinclair is no' accepting callers."

As Annis made it to her feet and brushed off her clothing, it struck her as oddly irreverent for a servant to refer to his master so casually, but what did she know? Perhaps it was a Scottish convention?

Papa pulled his shoulders back in affront. He hadn't amassed a fortune without gaining a fair amount of arrogance. He wouldn't tolerate being turned away so abruptly by a servant.

Papa flicked his fingers toward the house. "Be a good fellow and let the duke know that his new neighbor, Evered Ballister, is paying him call."

Her sisters seemed to calm, as though they sensed they might not be getting their way. They stared expectantly at the servant, ready to fall into a pout or tantrum, whatever was in order.

The man didn't budge, and Annis couldn't help but wonder if he had even heard her father. His gaze skimmed the lot of them. "The Sinclair has nothing tae say tae any of you."

Annis blinked, imagining that his top lip curled faintly.

Papa's chest swelled at the servant's impertinence. "Now see here—"

Shockingly, the man turned, not even bothering to hear out her father's speech, and presented them all with his back.

Cordelia huffed. "What an insolent boor! The duke should sack him."

Papa's face flushed and Annis knew he was not quite certain how to proceed.

"Papa, perhaps we should go," she suggested. She'd never wanted to come along to begin with, but Mama had insisted. Annis was the second oldest. Although not a beauty like Regan or Imogen, Mama expected Annis to make a match for herself—whether she wanted such a thing or not.

"Leave?" Regan demanded. "Without meeting the duke? We can't! Mama said we must meet him. One of us will surely win him. Mama insists he will naturally fall in love with one of us as we are all passing fair and I'm the prettiest! I want to be a duchess!" She stomped her foot beneath her skirts.

Annis blinked slowly and shook her head, certain that the duke could hear them from wherever he lurked inside the castle. It was mortifying.

The servant was almost to the front door when he stopped, turned, and addressed them all. "I can assure you, Sinclair will no' fall in love with any of you. Extend your time and efforts elsewhere and return home."

"How do you know?" Cordelia demanded with a belligerent thrust of her chin.

He took his time answering, stepping forward a pace, and Annis couldn't help noticing the length of his well-muscled legs encased in wool trousers and boots. He towered over all of them. A bitterly cold breeze lifted and tossed his dark hair around his head. His stark handsomeness was so much like the surrounding countryside—wild and harsh and a little bit dangerous. "Because I'm the duke." The announcement dropped like a stone in the air between them. "And I'd just as soon kiss the arse end of a sheep as wed any of you lasses."

That said, he entered through the great wood door and shut it on them with a resounding thud.

Chapter Three

Present day . . .

*A*nnis could still hear the thud of that thick door shutting on them as they'd all stood in a shocked, frozen tableau. The sound had echoed through her ears these many nights.

Now that awful man was here, in her house. In *her* foyer.

Heat crawled up her face, and she was grateful for the distance between them. She was up here and he was all the way down there. Hopefully he could not detect her flaming cheeks. Perhaps he would not even recognize her. She had been one of five girls in his courtyard that day, after all. And she most certainly looked different now. She was wearing a nightgown and stood several stones' throw from him in a shadowy foyer.

"You." His deep voice rang out in the great hall.

Blast. He recognized her.

She gripped the railing and reminded herself that this was *her* home. *She* belonged here. Duke or not, he did not.

She lifted her chin. "What are you doing here?"

"I've come tae fetch Fenella and Angus." His brogue was a little less intense than the other locals. A fraction more cultured. She should have noted it that day when they assumed him to be a servant.

She scowled down at him. First he said he would rather kiss a sheep's backside than marry her or any of her sisters and now he was here to steal away her household staff and leave her truly alone in this great pile of stones. *No. Not happening.*

"What are *you* doing here?" he demanded. "I thought your family left." His gaze flicked to either side of her as though he expected her sisters to rise up beside her.

"Och, they did leave." Fenella darted a glance up at her. "But they forgot 'er."

Embarrassment flushed through her at the bold statement.

He looked between Annis and Fenella before asking of the housekeeper, "Forgot her? What do you mean they forgot her?" Bewilderment rang out in his voice.

Annis released a heavy breath. Her mortification intensified.

"I have a large family," she cried out in defense.

He stared up at her as though she possessed two heads. "So they forgot you?"

Why did that sound so much worse when uttered aloud? "They left in a rush. Snow was rising in the pass."

Fenella nodded sagely. "She's stuck 'ere."

He grumbled something in Gaelic and dragged a hand through his snow-dusted hair. He paced a small circle, tracking muddy snow over the foyer floor.

She eyed him warily. More refined brogue or not, it was still difficult to believe that this man was a duke and not a servant. She'd seen dukes in London; all from afar, but she had observed them and he bore no resemblance to those dignified well-turned-out nobles.

Her gaze raked his tall form. In his well-worn greatcoat, the man looked more like a common laborer than a nobleman. He was coarse and rough and . . . virile.

He stopped his pacing and glared up at her. "Verra well

then," he snapped, every line of him vibrating with hostility. "Gather a few things. You'll also have tae come."

She shook her head. "I'm not going anywhere with you, *Your Grace*, and neither are Fenella and Angus. Now if you would be so kind as to remove yourself from my home. It is quite late."

For a moment he looked amused, but then the gust of laughter that escaped him did *not* sound mirthful. "You're coming with me. A band of thieves is terrorizing the countryside, robbing all the houses locked up for the winter. I'm not about tae leave an old man, a woman, and a fool girl tae defend themselves against the unsavory lot."

"Thieves," she echoed. An image of wild ruffians bursting inside the castle filled her mind. She looked to the door that stood slightly ajar, wind and snow tufting inside through the slight opening.

"Aye, brigands." His deep voice recaptured her attention. "The vicar from a nearby village ventured out tae warn us. If you wish tae return home in the spring with your virtue and life intact, I suggest you return tae your room and garb yourself appropriately and pack for the ride tae my castle."

She couldn't move. His story of brigands could not be true. In this modern day and age such things did not happen.

And his suggestion—no, *demand*—that she come with him to his keep. Ridiculous. He was a surly boor, and she would not go anywhere with him.

She recovered her voice. "We appreciate your concern, but we will be fine. The doors have bolts and the windows—"

"Are you daft, lass?" Shaking his head, he stalked up the stairs toward her.

Annis backed away from the railing. "What are you doing?" He was *not* coming upstairs. He wouldn't dare. "Stop right there, Sinclair!" Yes. He was a duke, but the designation stuck in her throat. It was too polite, too formal, too gentle an address for a man such as he.

Still, he kept coming, his booted feet biting hard into the steps. She backed away from the railing, watching his head first appear, then his shoulders, then the rest of him. Heavens, he really was large.

He didn't relent until he reached the landing, where he stopped several feet from her. Then it was just the two of them.

"You shouldn't be here. This is vastly inappropriate." Was that strangled squeak her voice?

He pointed at her. "Dress for the journey. We're leaving."

"No, you're leaving."

"You selfish lass." His blue gaze blistered her where she stood. "If you haven't a care for yourself, then think of that old couple down there." He stabbed a finger to where Fenella stood below. "If you stay, they stay. I won't be able tae persuade them otherwise. And they will attempt tae defend this place. And you. What do you think those ruffians will do tae them?" His chest rose on an inhalation. "Or do you no' give a bloody damn?"

She released a shuddering breath, rattled at the scenario he painted. If there was even a kernel of truth to it, she couldn't remain here.

"What's it tae be?" he pressed. "Will you walk out willingly like a good lass? Or shall I carry you? Because I'm no' letting Fenella and Angus die for you."

His gaze held hers, hard and fast. Annis forced herself to not look away. She had never felt so . . . seen. With so many sisters, she was accustomed to being invisible.

"Well?" he prodded.

No. She didn't want them to get hurt for her, either. She didn't want anyone to get hurt.

She needed to put her silly embarrassment over their first encounter aside. The appropriateness of traveling alone with him, with only servants as chaperones, couldn't matter. This was a dire situation. Besides. No one need ever know that for a short while she had been alone with the unconventional Duke of Sinclair. Certainly the brigands would be apprehended and then she could return here with Fenella and Angus until the pass cleared.

She nodded, ignoring the small tremor of excitement rushing through her at the prospect of an adventure with this striking man. She was not like her sisters with a head quick to turn for a handsome face. "Very well. I'll change my clothes."

* * *

Calder remembered her well.

She was the one that was shoved from the carriage. She had been an undignified pile of ruffled skirts with several shrill females around her.

He couldn't recall much of the other Ballister chits other than that they'd made his ears bleed from all their painful caterwauling. Except he remembered her. She had been quiet. He recalled that about her. Her eyes had been as wide and blue as a spring sky, and her face had gone pink as the drama unfolded around her.

What kind of people forgot their own daughter or sister?

Shaking his head, he descended the stairs to where Fenella stood glaring at him.

She propped her fists on her narrow hips. "Now, lad, ye dinna have tae be mean tae her. She's a good one. No' like those worthless sisters of 'ers."

He shrugged, not liking that Fenella's opinion closely matched his own. This one was different from her sisters, but not different enough. She was still English. *Still* on the hunt for a duke. *Still* didn't belong here.

And he had no interest in marriage. Especially not to someone with a family like hers. He winced as he recalled the blaring mob of sisters. He hadn't even met the mother, but the girls had been more than enough. No way would he bind himself to that clan.

He addressed Fenella. "Are you ready?"

She pursed her lips. "Dinna pretend she's nae pretty. Ye ken it."

Calder shrugged. "A pretty face doesn't affect me."

Fenella released a rough laugh. "It affects every man."

"She could be the most beautiful woman in Scotland and I wouldn't—"

"Ye need a bride and Glencrainn needs new blood."

Her words fell like heavy weights on his chest, pressing and pushing the air from him. It wasn't the first time he'd heard someone voice such an opinion. Fenella especially was fond of telling him how to live his life and had done so ever since he was a boy. Only lately, since he turned thirty, those inclined to share such an opinion were becoming more vocal about it.

"Are you suggesting that lass and I . . ." Calder couldn't articulate the rest. Who could believe Fenella was suggesting such a thing? She wanted him to take a Sassenach to wife? For her, the English victory at Culloden happened yesterday and not a generation ago.

"Aye. Ye put it off long enough. How old are ye now?"

"No' verra old," he snapped.

"Mmm-hmm." She lifted her eyebrows dubiously. "Older than both yer parents when they died."

"Thank you for that somber reminder." She made it sound like he could drop dead any moment—and this from a woman who had been alive since the Magna Carta was signed.

"Life is fleeting." She snapped her fingers for illustration, her knuckles red and swollen from the labors of life. "'Twas a sign when all these lasses showed up 'ere." She looked heavenward. "And then they forgot *'er* . . . and she's the best of the lot! It's providential." She motioned to the stairs gleefully. "That lass is for ye. Dinna be stubborn and risk losing 'er."

He stared at Fenella's gaunt, lined face. Had she finally succumbed to senility? "You're mad."

She made a sound of disgust. "I'm sane as can be and see things perfectly. Better than ye. Och, I ken what ye need."

He sighed and glanced to the door. It was still cracked, the cold gusting through the small opening. He moved to shut it. They really needed to be on their way. They didn't have time for this delay.

Fenella continued, "I ken just the thing tae help ye."

He looked back at her warily. "What do you mean?"

She wagged a finger. "Wait 'ere."

"Wake Angus," he called after her. "And fetch your things. We need tae be on our way posthaste."

"Aye, I'll rouse him," she muttered. "That man would sleep through doomsday."

He watched her shuffle away, a tight anxiety gripping his chest. It had been there since the moment he'd heard about the brigands and realized Fenella and Angus were all alone here and at their mercy. Now, after finding the girl also here, the tightness in his chest squeezed harder.

He'd known Fenella and Angus since he was a boy and his cousin lived here—before his cousin lost his inheritance in some stupid card game to Ballister. He'd practically lived under this very roof after his parents had died, cleaving to his older cousin. That was until Dougall decided to go frolicking about, spending money he did not possess. Last he'd heard, Dougall was traipsing his way through Europe. Damn irresponsible fool.

He waited tensely, pacing a short line and glancing to the high window where snow fell against a backdrop of night. Calder doubted the uncomfortable sensation in his chest would relent until he was safely back at Glencrainn with his charges. He winced. Even if that meant he was now stuck with a title-hungry heiress. Taking the Ballister lass home with him would undoubtedly compromise her, but there was nothing he could do to prevent that. He couldn't abandon her here.

He cast another quick glance to the door. The brigands typically raided at night and he doubted they would leave this keep out of their sights, especially given its state of low occupancy. It would just be a matter of time before they struck such a plum mark. These thieves were ghosts. They clearly had friends willing to shelter them. Otherwise Calder and his men would have found them. God knew they had tried.

Even his home, which was more formidable and held far more occupants, was at risk. These brigands were bold and well numbered. He could only hope that tonight was not the night they planned to strike either place.

He glanced in annoyance at the stairs. Hopefully Miss Ballister wasn't packing anything more than a simple valise. He wasn't hauling a trunk atop his horse.

Finally, he heard the tread of steps. He turned to see Fenella lugging a bag and a book. Her gnarled hands patted at the worn leather skin of the tome she hugged close to her chest. "It's right in 'ere," she remarked, as though he'd asked.

He eyed the book dubiously. "What's that?"

She leaned forward and whispered, "Magic."

He blinked, an uneasy feeling rippling over his skin. "Magic?"

She nodded in satisfaction. "Aye, 'tis a recipe book that was given tae me many years ago by my cousin, Fergus." Her eyes sparked.

"It's necessary tae bring your recipe book?"

"Dinna ye 'ear me? There's magic in these pages. One recipe in particular." She tapped the well-worn leather.

"This thing is worth more than gold. I canna leave it here for those scoundrels tae steal." She stared at him in affront, as though he had suggested he leave her child behind. "As soon as we reach Glencrainn, I'll whip up some of my special biscuits and we'll fix ye right up and end this nonsense. One bite and ye'll see that ye and the lass are perfect for each other." She nodded in the direction of where Miss Ballister had once stood before the girl left.

"Fenella." He sighed, rubbing his forehead. "Are you telling me this is a book of . . . *spells*?"

"Bite yer tongue. I'm no witch." She looked over her shoulder as though someone might be lurking about to hear such a dire allegation. "I'm merely a housekeeper who puts a little something *extra* special in 'er food."

"Special? As in . . . magic?" he clarified.

"Indeed."

And she wouldn't call that witchery? These brigands, the unexpected presence of the Ballister lass, and now this? His head was starting to throb. "Don't tell me you think that book contains a recipe for . . ."

She cackled and nodded in satisfaction. "'Tis no ordinary shortbread, to be certain. *Love* biscuits. Aye. That be a more correct description."

She. Was. Daft. He really should keep her away from the sharp cutlery.

"I'm ready."

He looked up as Miss Ballister descended the stairs, her lofty English tones chafing his quickly fraying nerves.

She was dressed in a deep blue wool riding habit with jeweled buttons down the bodice jacket. She wore matching gloves trimmed with fur at the wrists. Fine leather boots peeked out from beneath her hem. He was certain she was the height of fashion. He'd seen nothing of the like in these parts—nothing of such quality in any of the local villages or even when he visited Inverness. If the thieves spotted her in her finery they would unquestionably abduct her for a ransom. Better than death, he supposed.

He looked away from her. She was dangerous. A title-hungry, marriage-minded English girl left without a chaperone in his company. She was a contagion he needed to avoid.

He knew the Ballisters were obscenely rich, each daughter an heiress in her own right. He had made certain to learn all he could about the people who were to be his closest neighbors. Not that he had to probe too deeply. His barrister in Glasgow had answered all his inquiries. Evered Ballister made his wealth in railways and Mrs. Ballister was renowned through British society for her determination to see her daughters wed into the aristocracy.

As Calder's grandfather had been awarded the title of Duke of Sinclair for his service at Waterloo, Calder knew it would only be a matter of time before the Ballister females showed up on his doorstep. A duke was a duke, after all. Even if his pockets didn't run as deep as the Ballisters. Even if he was Scottish and master of a mere run-down Highlands castle.

Staring at the most palatable of the Ballister daughters, suspicion niggled in the back of his mind. He could almost imagine they left her here on purpose. *Deliberately.*

If the scheming Mrs. Ballister knew anything of winter in these parts, it would not be too difficult to conceive such a plan. However, how could she have anticipated the brigands terrorizing homes throughout the countryside? That was too far-fetched.

Angus emerged with a small knapsack in tow. "No' keen on being murdered in m'bed. Let's be off then."

Calder nodded and relieved Miss Ballister of her bag, pausing as he noticed Fenella's rheumy gaze narrowing on the two of them. She doubtless read far too much into the simple courtesy. He recognized the cunning there. She was probably wondering how soon she could get her damnable love biscuits down his throat.

"I'll need use of yer kitchen," Fenella declared, seeming to confirm his suspicion. "Hope yer cook won't stand in my way." She gave a militant nod.

Fenella and his cook would definitely be coming to blows. His cook would not be a fan of another person invading her kitchen.

He turned for the door, more eager than ever to be on his way. He needed a respite from Fenella's ridiculous notions.

Miss Ballister arched an eyebrow as he pulled open the door. "Something amiss?"

"Nay," Fenella quipped, patting her book and stepping out ahead of them into the bitter cold. "Once ye each have some of my biscuits, all will be well."

Miss Ballister's smooth forehead knitted in bewilderment as she lifted her fur-lined cloak off her arm and slid it over her shoulders. "Biscuits?"

"Och, no more talk of yer love biscuits, woman," Angus snapped.

"Those biscuits are responsible for many a merry match," Fenella countered in indignant tones. "The vicar and the Widow Grant *and* the smithy's son? The lad can thank me for the Orson lass even looking at him."

"Love biscuits?" Miss Ballister echoed as she stepped outside, her voice twisting into a sharp gasp of shock at the sudden cold.

Calder lifted the flaps of his greatcoat to better ward off the bite of frigid air. "She speaks of shortbread. Nothing more. Ignore Fenella," he advised as Angus locked the keep's great front door behind them. A feeble precaution. With this place empty, the brigands would make short work of the windows.

"Much luck with that," Angus grunted, tucking the keys back inside his coat before turning and moving into the sharp angle of wind and snow. "Fenella is no' one tae be ignored on any matter."

"Words tae heed," Fenella chimed in with a hard nod, her pointed gaze flipping back and forth between Calder and the lass. "Words tae heed."

Shaking his head, Calder turned for the stable, but stalled as he glimpsed the twitch of Miss Ballister's smile on her full lips. Pink, plump lips parting enough to reveal her teeth—straight white teeth save for one incisor that was slightly crooked. That tiny imperfection fascinated and drew his gaze, tightening his stomach muscles. Her smile was a bit of sunshine amid this winter's night.

He looked away. No sense looking for sunshine in this storm. "Let's make haste."

Chapter Four

Of course there were only three horses. Sinclair wasn't counting on her presence.

As there were no other horses in the stables—her family took them all when they departed—four people would have to mount three horses. Mathematics had never been her strongest subject. She was much more suited to history and science and languages, and yet even she knew the numbers didn't compute. Two of them would ride *one* horse.

Annis knew that fate was to be hers even before she felt the duke's gaze land on her. She could do nothing more than squeak as his hands circled her waist and lifted her, plopping her on the saddle. He swung up behind her and gathered the reins.

She rode wedged snugly against him. There was no other choice, but that did not stop the awkward embarrassment. No man had ever held her this closely. Especially no man like him. A man that affected her senses.

Cold wrapped around them. If they took to a path it was not in evidence, eaten up in swirls of wind and writhing snow flurries.

The snow fell in a deluge, pelting hard at the exposed skin of her face and neck, heedless of her hood. She would be quite wet by the time she reached his home. That made her squirm uneasily. She'd read plenty of accounts of people who died when exposed too long to conditions like this.

Despite the elements, they forged ahead, traversing at a steady clip. Even with warm pinpricks of embarrassment rushing over her from the proximity of the duke's body to her own, she could not stop shivering. Her fur-trimmed cloak had been perfectly suitable in Town, but it wasn't enough to ward off this Highland wind.

Sinclair muttered something and pulled her against his chest. She'd been trying so valiantly to keep herself from leaning back into him. Now he brought her in closer, opening his greatcoat to snuggle her inside, sharing his warmth.

She parted her chattering teeth. "You don't have to—"

"Quiet," he growled.

She sniffed. "You don't have to be rude—"

"You're shaking so hard I can hear your teeth clacking."

She brought her gloved hands to her mouth and blew air into them, trying to do what she could to warm herself. They continued on through the winter night. It was almost eerily quiet, only the murmur of snow and the whisper of wind and hooves lifting and falling.

She thought about her family. They were undoubtedly tucked in for the night at some inn, warm under the covers. Her sisters were likely squabbling, the sheer number of them forcing them to share beds. She knew they were loathing every moment of that and not giving her a passing thought. Shaking off the grim reminder of the family who left her behind, she redirected her attention.

"How far is it?" When she'd made the trip with her family it had been by carriage and they had stuck to a road.

Sinclair didn't reply. She sought to fill the silence. "Fenella," she began. "She's . . . interesting. A bit eccentric."

"Aye. You could say that. Interesting. Eccentric. Possibly senile. Possibly a witch. She's fortunate she's well-favored enough in these parts and hasn't been dragged tae trial." Annis felt his shrug around her and it only made her more aware, more sensitive to the endless breadth of his chest. "Does one ever really know?"

"A witch? Surely you jest." She twisted around for a glimpse of his face to see if he was serious. She could read nothing of his expression. However, she was treated to the reminder of how very handsome he was. Blue eyes and midnight hair. His eyelashes would be the envy of any woman. She quickly faced forward again, her breath falling a little faster.

"What would you call a woman who believes in magical shortbread?" he asked with a snort.

She released a slow gust of air, rolling that question over in her mind. She rotated her shoulders and sneaked a glance at the old woman in question. Fenella wore a stoic expression, staring straight ahead, but her lips moved in private conversation, talking to herself. She wasn't close enough for Annis to hear the words. Were they some manner of incantation?

"You might have had the right of it with senility." Because certainly there was no such thing as magic biscuits. *Absurd.*

"Och. You mean you don't believe in spells or the power of love biscuits?"

Annis twisted one shoulder in a semblance of a shrug, suddenly feeling a little bad for Fenella. "To be fair, there are some things, many things in this life, that are beyond logical explanation."

"You do believe in such fanciful notions then?"

"I didn't say that." She bristled at the mere suggestion. She was not like other girls. She was not like her sisters. She did not believe there was a knight in shining armor out there for her. She didn't believe romance and love were fated. Nor was the dramatic fluff within novels the stuff of reality. "What brought about this talk of love biscuits anyway? What does a love biscuit even do . . . purportedly?"

"Oh, did you no' realize?"

Annis shook her head, for some reason nervous. The horse whinnied, jangling its bridle, as though sensing her sudden unease.

"She intends tae make these biscuits for me," he explained.

"For you?"

"Aye, tae make certain that I'm amenable tae your charms, Miss Ballister. Fenella believes her infernal biscuits capable of weaving some influence in matters of the heart."

Her mouth opened and shut several times, her mortification only deepening. She might have escaped Mama's matchmaking efforts, but now she had to contend with Fenella? Suddenly his bigger body beside her felt like a boulder, its shadow deep and impossible to escape. She leaned forward to sever contact between them. "What absurdity!"

Annis turned around as much as she could, glaring at Fenella who trotted a few yards behind them, her lips still moving in conversation. The momentary pity she felt for the old woman vanished.

Her gaze shifted to the duke. "Why would she do that? Why would she want us . . ." She couldn't even say it aloud. It was too far-fetched. This was worse than with her own mother. Mama had not attempted to match her *specifically* to *him*. She'd tossed all her unattached daughters at his head in the hopes one might ensnare him. Annis felt uncomfortably targeted.

"Apparently she likes you, Miss Ballister. She likes you a great deal."

She digested that. She had spent a good bit of time chatting with the housekeeper over the last fortnight. Fenella's company was an improvement over her sisters, after all. She hadn't realized it would plant such notions in the old woman's head. "And for that she thinks we should . . . attach ourselves?"

"Indeed, she does."

"We don't even know each other." *Yet.* She would be under his roof for months.

"That's of no matter to her. She knows us and she likes us both, therefore she has decided we would pair well."

"As soon as we reach your home, I shall persuade her to forget all about the idea of you and me." And all about her silly love biscuits.

He grunted in response to that and she felt him shift in the saddle against her. Heavens. He was hard. Solid. Definitely not like her soft and pudgy father. Even Imogen's husband-to-be was nothing like him. The baron might be young, but he was an inch shorter than Annis and as plump and squishy as a babe.

The difference between this man and the men of her acquaintance was glaring. However much she rejected the idea of him as attractive, her body wholeheartedly accepted his appeal.

She shivered, and this time she wasn't entirely certain it was a result of the cold.

"This cloak of yours is ill suited for this weather."

"I'm not as accustomed as you are to this clime."

"Did you no' explain that tae your parents?"

"My parents?" What did her parents have to do with the weather here?

"Aye, when they sent you knocking on my door in the hopes that you might win me, did you explain tae them that Highland winters did no' suit you?"

"Win *you*?" Indignation flared in her chest. It was bad enough Fenella was playing matchmaker, but he thought she was complicit in her parents' machinations?

Sinclair continued, "I confess I dinna see myself as such a prize, but this pesky title of mine is quite another thing. It's a yoke about my neck, but coveted by many."

"Well, not by me!"

"Indeed." The single word was rife with disbelief.

"Indeed," she agreed. "Your title is no lure to me, nor are *you*." Contrary to how attractive she found him. "It would take more than a title to induce me to marriage."

She tossed her head inside her overly large hood. Her ice-caked hair struck her cheeks in stinging pricks. She wished she had taken the time to pull the heavy mass up, but she had been in such a hurry.

"I should warn you," he said near her ear. "Dinna feel encouraged because you've charmed Fenella. If you've designs on me, it's pointless. No matter how long we are stuck together. I'll no' be bound tae one such as you."

"Such as *me*?" Oh, the arrogance!

"Aye."

He made it sound as though she were some devil come to corrupt him. How very wrong he was. The suggestion that she wished to be bound to any man was preposterous. She laughed, long and hearty. She could not stop herself.

"I've said something amusing?" the duke grumbled.

"Yes. You think me intent on marrying you. It is very amusing. My sisters would certainly think so. I'm the most unmarriageable of us all and that's by choice. *My* choice."

He snorted. "No eligible female is opposed tae marriage. It is a condition of birth, I suspect."

"I am opposed. I want to take vows."

"Take vows?" he echoed, his voice fraught with skepticism.

How she longed to dash that doubt. The truth should do that. Aptly so.

She watched his face, annoyed to see the doubt reflected there. He did not know her. Not in the least. He thought her cut from the same cloth as her sisters.

"Yes," she asserted. "I want to be a nun."

Chapter Five

 $\mathcal{H}$ er words rocked through him. She wanted to be a nun? Calder didn't know what surprised him more. The words themselves? Or the keen disappointment he felt? Disappointment that was not his right to feel. She wanted to live a life in service to God. He should hold her in esteem for that. Not begrudge her.

Even with an abbey not very far from Glencrainn, he had never known a girl to take the veil and enter its hallowed walls. None of the girls he grew up with had such aspirations. All of them wanted to be wives and mothers.

He'd encountered the nuns from the abbey on more than one occasion over the years. They were women of advanced age. He tried to imagine Miss Ballister among them. It was a difficult image to swallow. She was young and vibrant—and practically sitting atop his lap, affecting him in ways a nun should not affect him.

"Why do you want tae be a nun?" He knew it shouldn't matter. He shouldn't care. He also shouldn't be so aware of how nicely her body fit against his. Or the delicious floral aroma of her hair, wafting on the frosty air. He wanted to pull back her hood and bury his nose in the mass.

She wasn't a small female. Her proximity confirmed that. She was solid and nicely curved, built for pleasure. He was a big man, and she would fit him perfectly. To think of her shrouded in a habit and veil for all her days was unfortunate.

Damn it. It had been too long since he'd been with a woman. That was it. He should rectify that so he could stop thinking about what Miss Ballister, self-avowed nun-to-be, looked like out of her clothes.

"My days spent in thoughtful contemplation. No shrieking siblings. Time to garden. Tranquil walks. Time to read books on history and science. Abbeys boast impressive libraries, you know."

"And prayer," he reminded her, amused that she had failed to list that rather significant detail. "Dinna forget the hours devoted tae prayer."

"Yes. Of course. Prayer." She nodded somewhat agitatedly. "I know that," she snapped. Did she truly know that, though? Had she given that part of becoming a nun serious consideration?

"Do you? Because it sounds like you're contemplating a nunnery to escape your family."

"Well, you're mistaken. I'm a very spiritual person." Affront dripped from her clipped tones, and her body with all its pleasing curves stiffened against him.

"I must confess you do no' seem the type."

"Type?"

"Aye. The nun type." He grinned. It really was rather comical to imagine. She was too fiery. Not in the least serene. He'd gathered that within moments of meeting her.

"And what do you know of nuns, Your Grace? Or me, for that matter? Do I not *seem* a spiritual person?" Indignation hummed through her and her stiff body, leaning forward away from him. He tugged her back against him, quite liking the feel of her and loath that she should pull away from him even if he was being an ass and behaving as though her becoming a nun was a personal insult to him.

Calder suddenly realized he was smiling. It might be the

middle of the night and he might be freezing his balls off, but the lass was damned diverting. In fact, he had been smiling throughout this entire conversation. He could not recall a time when he had enjoyed a female so much.

He killed his smile. She was not enjoyable. She was unacceptable in every way. An English heiress with an insufferable family. She knew nothing of the Highlands. Not its customs, nor its people. Oh, and there was the not-so-minor fact that she planned to be a nun.

He needed to get his mind out of the gutter and stop enjoying the sensation of her against him. She would be on her way eventually. When this infernal snow melted, her family would reclaim her.

Not soon enough for his peace of mind.

She continued, "You may rest easy. Unlike my sisters, I've no designs on you. Papa promised that I could enter a convent if I've not married by my twenty-first birthday. Mama may not be pleased about that, but his word is final."

"And when is that?"

"When is what?" She twisted to look up at him, a backside that felt alarmingly lush grinding against him and sending a spike of arousal straight to his groin.

"When is your birthday?" he clarified.

"Six months hence."

Six months and she would enter a convent. The fact rubbed him wrong.

What a waste. The thought flashed unbidden across his mind. Unbidden and unwanted.

Why should he care what the girl sitting in front of him did with her life? He'd just met her. To be certain, she was his responsibility since her parents had left her behind, but there it ended.

He didn't even know her name—this lass who was occupying far too much of his thoughts and lap.

"What's your name?"

Her words were carried away on the wind, but still managed to reach his ears. "You know my name."

"Your Christian name. We're well past formalities." His hand flexed on her waist as though to remind her of the intimacy between them, but that was a mistake because it made him even *more* aware of how her waist dipped above nicely flaring hips—hips that rocked into him as his mount carried them toward his home. His grip tightened and he couldn't resist a slight spreading of his fingers over her ample flesh.

"Oh." She paused on a breathy sigh, clearly aware of his touch. "Annis."

"Annis." *Sister Annis.*

It had a wretched ring to it. Except she wouldn't be called that. She would adopt another name after she took the veil. Because she would be someone else then. Someone he couldn't think of in such a fashion. Someone who would never think of him or this time in Scotland, and damn it all but that bothered him because he knew he would not forget her.

Chapter Six

They rode into the night, the moon high overhead, snow falling and draping the land in a hush of white.

The horse's hooves sank ankle-deep in a succession of steps. Annis marveled that they did not become lost in the endless expanse of snow, but the duke guided his stallion with easy confidence. His long arms wrapped around her, hands holding loosely on the reins. She felt all of him like a never-ending embrace. She might be cold but she knew it would be so much worse if she didn't have his heat radiating through her.

She was glad for the shelter of his body. Truly. Despite the race of her pulse or the untoward thoughts running through her mind at his nearness. It was most disconcerting. She had felt his hand on her hip earlier like a brand. Through all their layers of clothing, his touch had singed her—the only point of heat on her body.

Annis was not one to let a handsome man turn her head. She'd always taken pride in that. She liked her books and walks and gardening—much to the gardener's displeasure—and her solitude, hard-won as it was. She didn't drown herself in scandal sheets or make eyes at every nobleman without a hump on his back and chronic foul breath. Her sisters' criterion wasn't too particular.

Once she had both feet planted on the ground again and some distance from the Duke of Sinclair, all her inappropriate thoughts about him would be a thing of the past. She was almost certain of that.

At times he stopped, turned, and checked on Angus and Fenella riding stalwartly behind them.

Dare she say it? He *cared*. He was solicitous of others. Grumpy but solicitous.

It was bewildering.

What noble *duke* left his home in the cold of night to fetch two servants from a nearby property because he feared for their safety?

She thought of the one other duke she'd met. Well, she had met him in a manner when they first moved to London. She had never felt so small as she had in that single encounter.

The Duke of Sommerton was as old as her father and much too puffed up with his own self-importance to speak to her on the single occasion they came in contact. Beyond slighting her, he had slighted Papa, too, which seemed the height of absurdity as the duke had deigned to invest in one of Papa's many business ventures, and they had met several times over the matter, but in the glittering drawing rooms of the *ton* Sommerton couldn't be counted upon to greet her father or his family.

He'd snubbed them cold publicly, mortifying Mama. In that moment, Mama vowed her daughters would have titles all and set about on such quest with dogged resolve. Much to Annis's chagrin, she and her sisters were plunged into an intense education on all things dealing with the aristocracy. They were called upon to cite from memory all the noble families in the land. They were drilled constantly on matters of etiquette, dance, flower arrangement, voice and pianoforte lessons.

It was misery, and that's when Annis decided she would enter a convent. It had struck her as a sound escape plan.

Papa hadn't been too difficult to persuade on the matter.

His own mother had been a very devout Catholic, and the vestiges of faith still adhered.

Annis only had to suffer six more months on the marriage mart. Six more months of living in a cage, of feeling like a piece of meat at auction, scorned by the likes of men such as the Duke of Sommerton.

According to Fenella, three of those six months would be spent here in the Highlands.

The man behind her shifted, reminding her that, while she would be spared her mother's last desperate efforts to find Annis a husband, she would not be spared the duke.

Of course, she would not be spared the duke. He would be part of those three months. At least for a little while. Certainly not the entire three months.

The thieves would be apprehended eventually, and she, Fenella, and Angus would return to their own home. It would be most unseemly to stay longer than necessary at Glencrainn. Especially with a duke who didn't want her around, who suspected she had orchestrated being left behind so that she might trap him into matrimony.

Despite that, he was nothing like Sommerton. He spoke to her. He saw her as a person. A person worth saving from the threat of brigands. There was that. He was very un-duke-like. A good thing, to be certain. He might have expressed a desire to kiss a sheep's arse rather than marry her, but there was something decidedly noble about him. He tugged his mount to one side and surveyed the older couple behind them again.

"Are they well?" she asked, her teeth gritting against the biting cold.

Fenella and Angus had wrapped their heads with heavy tartan, leaving only their eyes to peer out.

"Those old birds? They're fine. Between the two of them, they've lived over a hundred Scottish winters."

She nodded in understanding. They were managing better than she was because she was so cold now she couldn't feel her toes inside her boots anymore. But she didn't complain. They could only press on. There was no going back.

"And how many Scottish winters have you lived through, Your Grace?" she asked through shivering lips, teeth knocking.

"Is that your way of asking my age, Miss Ballister?" His deep brogue vibrated from his chest into her back. "You mean your mother left that out of her research?" He adjusted behind her, his broad chest bumping her back. The white puff of his breath flowed past her head and into the air in front of her. "And out here everyone calls me Sinclair."

Of course, he would eschew formality. He had done everything else in seeming opposition to ducal pomp and manners.

"My mother talks about a great many things. I confess I do not pay attention to all of them." When Mama started talking dukes, Annis tended to block out her voice. Sommerton had soured her that much.

"Well, I'm thirty."

"And yet unwed? Hmm. Perhaps you *should* listen to Fenella and wed. I have several sisters, as you know."

He made a noise that sounded suspiciously like laughter. It was pleasant—the sound deep and delicious. Like warm chocolate on a chilled morning.

"Which one would you recommend? The one who shoved you from the carriage? Or the one who punched the dark-haired one in the face?"

She fought back a giggle. It wasn't amusing. At the time, she had felt more like crying than laughing, but here she was, enjoying herself with him.

Suddenly, he fell silent. He pulled back on the reins and motioned for Fenella and Angus to stop and hold silent, as well.

He peered into the stretch of shadows.

She followed his gaze, seeing only a horizon of snow-capped mountains. She held her breath, staring into the night, grateful for the moonlight reflecting off the snow and saving them from complete darkness.

"What—"

He swiped a hand through the air to silence her.

"Come. Quickly," he whispered. Dismounting, he reached up for her, swinging her down beside him. She staggered a bit, unsteady on her feet, especially in the heavy snow. Fenella and Angus followed suit. They led their three horses to a small copse of trees, guiding the animals well within the gnarled trunks that poked up and peeked out from the snow.

He motioned for them all to crouch low. Angus's knees cracked as they sank down into the snow. Fenella muttered something in Gaelic, her words muffled with her thick tartan.

Annis shivered, peering out between the trees, not sure what it was they were waiting for, but her pulse hammered.

Then she saw it. Or rather *them*. At least a dozen horsemen.

"There they be. Thieving low-born scoundrels," Fenella grumbled, "forcing an old woman from her bed at night and out into the snow."

"Shh." The duke cast Fenella a reproving look.

Annis couldn't look away from the group of men. She'd never seen a criminal up close before and here were a dozen of them.

They were a motley band attired in dark clothing and faded tartan. Tufts of snow covered the heavy beards on their faces. They looked lean and hardened, heads bent against the onslaught of wind and snow as they rode at a steady clip.

"Heading right fer our home," Fenella whispered. "They'll make short work of the food stores."

Sinclair nodded grimly, not taking his gaze off them.

Her chest loosened and released a shuddering breath. Those men could have been her fate. If Sinclair hadn't come for them, she would have been left to face them with only Angus and Fenella at her side. She glanced at his face again, profoundly grateful right then.

A short bark attracted her attention. A sheepdog ran at the front of the horsemen. It paused and lifted its nose, sniffing, indifferent to the riders moving on without him.

Of course, dogs possessed a keen sense of smell. Could he detect them? Would he expose them?

Unthinkingly, she reached for Sinclair's arm. Warm fingers reached up to cover her hand and squeeze reassuringly. She should shrink from such intimate contact, but there was nothing circumspect about this situation. His touch, his nearness, made her feel safe.

One of the riders stopped and shouted a command. The sheepdog snapped his attention forward and trotted after the brigands.

She expelled a heavy sigh. Although the relief did nothing to ease her tension. She was too cold to relax. Her muscles were frozen stiff.

The four of them waited until the riders were well out of sight before pushing to their feet. Annis moved a pace before realizing that the duke still held her hand.

Awkwardness consumed her. The only time a man had ever held her hand was while dancing. This felt decidedly different. She stumbled a step, staring down at their joined hands. Even through their gloves she imagined she felt every line, every callus, and the very pulse at the base of his palm.

Odd, funny little flutterings swam through her middle. She yanked her hand free with more force than necessary and lost her balance. Her arms swung wildly as she tried to stop herself from falling. She took one more step back, hoping to find purchase. Instead her foot came down on a twisting bit of exposed root.

She went down with a sharp yelp.

She caught a flash of Sinclair's face, of his hand reaching to grab her. Then nothing. Not the cold. Not anything.

Blackness.

Chapter Seven

Calder carried her inside, not bothering to explain the unconscious woman in his arms to his perpetually stern-faced housekeeper, who rushed forward to meet them in the foyer. Miss Ballister was beyond cold, her dress and cloak solidly wet from her fall in the snow and crusted with ice. The fabric crackled against his gloved fingers.

"Mrs. Benfiddy, please see tae Fenella and Angus." He nodded behind him to where they followed closely. "And then bring more blankets tae my chamber."

He had no doubt the crotchety siblings would apprise his housekeeper of everything. Fenella and Angus were second cousins to Mrs. Benfiddy. In fact, the pair was related to most of his household staff. This part of the Highlands was tight-knit. Decades might have passed, but the effects of Culloden could still be felt. Those who hadn't died at Culloden, starved in the years following, or emigrated, had remained and banded together. They were still banded, even if his grandfather had been bequeathed with some ridiculous title by an English monarch. He was still part of this land and these people, no matter how many title-hunting misses showed up on his doorstep.

He wound his way up the stairs, Miss Annis Ballister a deadweight in his arms. Her skin had a waxy appearance that did not bode well. Calder took the steps more quickly.

The heavy scent of fir and pine filled his nose. The staff

had wrapped the banister in greenery to mark the holidays as they did every year. The entire castle was full of holly boughs and ribbons and greenery all in preparation for the Christmas Eve assembly Mrs. Benfiddy insisted they host annually. Everyone attended from the nearby villages. This year, however, with the recent robberies, there would be no such festivities. Mrs. Benfiddy was not happy with his decision, but it would present too grave a risk for his tenants to leave their homes unattended. He'd have none of his people victimized.

He carried Annis into his chamber and settled her on the very same bed that his great-grandmother had brought over on a ship with her from France. It was an extravagant four-poster beast situated at the center of the room. Perhaps he should take pause at placing her in it, but it seemed the place for her. It was the nicest bed in the castle, and she deserved that.

Leaving her side, he quickly moved to the fireplace. It was the largest in the keep, even greater than the one in the great hall. Several men could stand within it. He tossed several more logs into it, stirring the near-dormant fire to a crackling roar.

He turned back for the bed and started on her boots, but the laces were frozen stiff. They would take forever to unlace. With a grunt, he unsheathed his dagger and cut through them. He tossed them aside and stripped off her socks, gasping when he touched the cold blocks of her feet. And the lass had not uttered a complaint. "Ah, hell." He chafed his hands over them, trying to chase away the blueness from her skin.

"Och, make haste and let us rid her of all her wet clothes." Mrs. Benfiddy's efficient tones rang out as she strode inside the room with an armful of blankets. A maid followed fast, carrying ceramic hot water bottles. His housekeeper dropped the additional blankets on the foot of the bed and made short work of undressing Miss Ballister, snapping at him to turn away the moment before she and the maid slipped off the lass's chemise. "Now hand me more blankets."

Turning, he observed that she was tucked under his bedcovers, only her bare shoulders peeping above the edge. He swallowed hard and cursed under his breath. Now was not the time to yearn for a glimpse of her body. He was not some letch. He shook loose a blanket and covered her with it. Mrs. Benfiddy added another and then moved to examine Miss Ballister's head and the knot there she'd received when she tripped.

"She fell and struck her head," he explained anxiously.

"Looks like a right nasty bump." Sighing, she stepped back, her hands leaving Miss Ballister and falling to her sides.

He looked at her expectantly. "What now?" His gaze darted from the female in his bed to his housekeeper, a woman he estimated to be as old as the stone walls sheltering them. She'd been here long before his birth and he suspected she'd be here several decades longer yet. She looked precisely as she had when he was a lad of five. White-haired, worn skin translucent—thin and pale as milk. She was the wisest person he knew and had delivered more babes than there were stars in the sky. She'd raised him after he lost his parents and there was no one in the world who put him more at ease. Only right now, she was falling short in that regard.

Mrs. Benfiddy took several more steps from the bed and gave another shrug. "No telling if the knock tae her head did any real damage. If she wakes, she's fine." She waved a hand as if he were an overly fretful mother.

Hardly the most heartening advice. "That's it?"

"Keep 'er warm. Pray. And wait." That said, his housekeeper turned and shuffled from his bedchamber, shutting the door after her with no concern for propriety. As though her master brought strange unconscious Englishwomen home all the time and together they stripped them of their garments and tucked them into his bed. Just another day at Glencrainn.

Calder looked down again at the alarmingly gray pallor of Miss Ballister. *Wait and pray.* He did not count himself to be very good at either of those tasks. He'd prayed and waited as his parents and little sister fell sick from the cholera pandemic nearly two decades ago. It had been Christmastime then, too. He'd sat before the small nativity set that his mother put on display in the drawing room and prayed to the tiny baby Jesus. Still, he had lost them.

Every Christmas since was a gloomy stretch of days he simply endured. He permitted the usual festivities among his staff. He wasn't so much of a grump that he would stop them from celebrating. He said nothing as they decorated the castle from top to bottom. They celebrated. He did not. Christmas was a joy for others, but reminded him only of pain and loss.

He stared down at the lass in his bed, a strange thickness in his throat as he contemplated the possibility that she might die. Just as his family had.

She tossed her head and let out a pained little whimper, shifting so that more of her throat and shoulders were exposed to his view. Her light brown hair tangled loose around her shoulders. Her lips were still blue-tinged, and he knew that wasn't good.

He'd lived through enough Highland winters to know the signs of someone on the brink of freezing.

He touched her forehead. Still like ice. He glanced around his chamber. The fire was at full roar, but it wasn't helping fast enough. The cold had its teeth in her and didn't want to let go. Damn it. He glanced from her and down to himself, still fully clothed in his own snow-dampened garments.

He supposed propriety had ceased to be a consideration the moment he fetched her from her castle and brought her to his. Not that he could have left her behind. Certainly taking off her clothes and placing her in his bed, no matter the urgent need or that his housekeeper had performed the bulk of the task, pushed him well over the edge of propriety.

She looked tiny in his big bed. Small and very alone. He stared down at her wan face. Her body needed heat. She needed *him*.

"Damnation." With fierce movements he began yanking at his clothes. There was no time. He needed to act. Fabric ripped, but he didn't care.

He slid beneath the heavy coverlet and pulled her slim body against his. He hissed at the instant of contact. Her skin was like ice.

There was nothing like shared body heat to chase out the cold. He ran his hands up and down her back, chafing briskly, training his gaze on her face, willing color back into her cheeks and lips. "Come, sweet lass. Stay with me."

She moaned at his ministrations and he paused at the long, throaty sound. A bolt of heat speared through him and arrowed directly for his cock.

He muttered an epithet. He wasn't depraved enough to take advantage of an injured woman . . . no matter the enticing sounds she made. Or the fact that both of them were naked and wrapped around each other.

Determined to ignore her nudity and forget his arousal, he continued rubbing his palm up and down the slope of her back. God, had a woman's skin ever felt more like silk? She whimpered and burrowed against him, seeking his warmth. He swallowed back a groan at the soft swell of breasts mashing into his chest.

Bloody hell. This was punishment for all his many sins. He would endure it, though. Her salvation would be his hell. She clung to him like he was a bit of driftwood at sea, the only thing keeping her from going under.

He ignored all of his baser impulses that rose to the fore at her closeness.

This was instinct. He'd respond to any naked female pressed against him.

Closing his eyes, he blocked out the sight of her. And that only made him *more* aware of the shape of her. More miserable.

He opened his eyes and stared at a spot on the wall and fixed his gaze there. *I won't look at her. Won't peek.*

He would not take advantage of the situation. His hands continued to rub at the slant of her back, imbuing her with his own body heat. It was one thing to touch her for the purpose of saving her life and quite another to look at her, to want *her*—a lass he didn't want to like. And yet he feared that it was too late. He already did.

It was going to be a long night.

* * *

Oil-hungry hinges creaked loudly. Calder lifted his head as the heavy wood door thudded against the stone wall. He blinked awake, rubbing at his eyes, not feeling the least bit rested. Somehow he had managed to doze off even in his present circumstances.

Fenella strode into the chamber, holding a plate aloft in her hands, clearly unmindful and uncaring that she might be interrupting anyone's slumber. "Och, good." She ran her gaze over the length of the bed, assessing first him and then the girl next to him. She nodded in satisfaction. "Just as I 'oped."

"Fenella." He tightened his grip on the counterpane, making certain it hadn't dipped past his waist.

Her rheumy gaze slid over him again, noting the movement of his hands. "No need tae be so self-conscious, lad. I've seen yer bits before."

"When I was four," he said wryly.

She shook her head and snorted. "What's the difference?"

"I'd like tae think there's a good amount of difference since then."

She stopped at the side of the bed and squinted at him. Not only him, of course. Her gaze skipped to Miss Ballister before flicking back to him. "Changed or no', it appears ye made progress with our lass 'ere."

Progress? He glanced at the deathly still Miss Ballister and back to the old woman. "She's unconscious . . . and injured!" If he'd had any doubts regarding the soundness of Fenella's mind, he no longer did. The woman was daft.

She set her plate down on the side table with a clatter. "She's fine. Hearty stock. She will give ye many babes."

Calder sighed and rubbed at the center of his forehead where it was beginning to ache. He did not bother to deny her charge that Annis would bear him many children. No point arguing with that bit of absurdity.

He surveyed the sleeping female. She was still pale. He wished he could feel as confident as Fenella that Miss Ballister would be well. "Fenella, I'm no' in the habit of taking advantage of unconscious females."

"Och, man. The lass is fine. She will rouse soon enough and then ye may begin wooing in earnest." She tsked. "I've brought these tae help matters along. Eat a few . . . and once she wakes give 'er one, as well."

He glanced down at the plate. A dozen small biscuits

scattered over the surface. No buttery shortbread. They more resembled clumps of rock than edible fare.

"Fenella, are those your . . . biscuits?" One would think alleged love biscuits at least looked more appetizing.

"Aye, and yer cook was most unaccommodating. I had tae threaten her with a rolling pin tae use the oven." She shook her head ruefully. "She did no' understand I'm about important work 'ere."

"Fenella," he groaned. If Marie was unhappy, he would suffer charred food as a result. He predicted no fatted Christmas goose in his future. "Stop this nonsense." He motioned at the lass next to him. "She and I do no' suit—"

"Ye've said that about every lass tae toss her bonnet at ye for the last decade. Yer no' a lad anymore. Ye've a legacy tae provide. Ye owe it tae yer people and yer parents, rest their sweet souls."

He shifted uncomfortably in the bed. "My parents would want me tae be happy."

"Aye, *happily* wed. Now eat a biscuit, lad."

He looked in horror at the plate. "Be serious."

"Ye don't believe they have magical properties, aye?" She shrugged one bony shoulder. "Verra well. Then it won't matter if ye were tae eat one, will it?"

A valid point. Still, he hesitated.

"Go on, then," she prodded. "Do it and I'll let ye get back tae sleep, warming up the lass there."

He winced. Why did her words sound debauched? He was merely attempting to warm her . . . to imbue life into her.

"Fine," he snapped, reaching for a biscuit. It felt as hard as it looked, but he bit into it anyway—and somehow managed not to break a tooth. "Omphgf," he choked as the stone-hard pastry broke into smaller chunks of foul-tasting stone. "This . . . is . . . awful. Are you certain it's no' off in some way?"

She stared at him in affront. "I made it this verra night.

The ingredients came from *yer* kitchen and they were all fresh."

He worked the biscuit around in his mouth until he managed to break the chunks into bits small enough to swallow. He stared reproachfully at the rest of the biscuit in his hand and then looked defiantly at Fenella.

"All of it," she directed with a stab of her finger.

"Fine," he mumbled, and stuffed the last mouthful of dry pastry into his mouth. "I'll only eat one," he choked, managing not to gag around the vile shortbread.

She narrowed her eyes and considered the remaining biscuits for a moment. "Verra well. But when ye wake I want ye tae 'ave another one."

He nodded. In that moment he would agree to anything to get her to leave him in peace.

She dusted her hands. "I'll see ye and the lass in the morn, then."

The moment the door shut behind her, he dropped his head back on the pillow. The woman was a menace. He wouldn't feel safe until she and the Ballister chit were back in their own beds. Anywhere but here.

Scowling, Calder arranged the blankets so that they had a barrier between them and weren't skin to skin. Satisfied, he snuggled closer to Annis, so that his body heat reached her through the fabric.

* * *

Annis woke toasty warm. A marked improvement considering her last memory was only of stinging cold.

She felt snug, wrapped in a veritable cocoon. She opened her eyes and settled her gaze straight ahead. A great wall of firm skin yawned before her. A male chest. She could see little beyond it. She inhaled. If warmth was a scent, then this was it. It radiated from him. Salt on supple skin.

She glanced up and stared at the face of the sleeping man. Sinclair.

The back of her skull was tender. Yet even that dull ache couldn't distract her from the virile body sharing a bed with her. A bed. She glanced down, pulling back the cover for a peek. She was naked. She shifted, enjoying the sensation of warm sheets against her nudity. She should be alarmed. Horrified. She touched her tender head again. Her last memory was riding with Sinclair. They'd spotted the brigands. She must have struck her head sometime after that. Had she fallen?

Whatever the case, Sinclair had delivered her safely to his home . . . and his bed. But he hadn't touched her. He slept on the other side of her blanket, a blanket of his own pulled up to his waist, the material functioning as barriers between them. That spoke to his honor. He hadn't taken advantage of her. Not many men would have left a ready and available woman unmolested. He was a good man— even if grouchy.

She studied him at her leisure, knowing it was quite untoward of her. In fact, everything about this scenario was untoward. However, in this moment of unobserved freedom, she did not care.

He was quite the handsomest man she'd ever seen, and for the moment he was hers to enjoy. Dark lashes formed crescent shadows on his cheeks. His chest lifted on a soft breath. Asleep and not speaking, he was quite the amenable fellow, unlike during their previous encounters. She stifled a giddy giggle, pressing her fingers against her lips. The action made her sore head throb, and she winced.

Of course, she'd never shared a bed with a man before. She likely never would again. She wanted to absorb the momentous occasion for all it was worth. Years from now when she was at the convent she would have this secret memory. She hesitantly placed a hand on his shoulder, willing herself not to shake, but needing more, needing to expand on this memory. She craved the sensation of his skin.

She could imagine Mama instructing her to do just as she was doing. All the better to compromise herself and force his hand. For the sake of his title. For a dukedom.

Except she could care less about that. She shoved out thoughts of Mama.

This was about temptation. About all she would miss when she entered the convent. The realization made her frown. *Miss?* She had never thought about taking vows in such terms before. Before it had been about escape, about claiming peace for herself. It had never felt like deprivation. Never like she would be cheating herself of something. Now, though, with her body humming and her heart racing, she felt that keenly. She felt the temptation. The *need*.

So instead of hopping from the bed as she should, instead of disentangling her limbs from his heavier ones, she stayed put and let her hand meander over him. She sank a little deeper into the mattress and let herself have this. She let her gaze study the sweep of his long lashes. The nose that appeared to have been broken. The lips that in sleep looked too full, too vulnerable for any man. She looked and looked and looked.

She relaxed and touched him at will. She would make a memory for herself because she could. Right now.

Because tomorrow, next week, three months from now . . . she would not have the chance. A heavy weight settled on her chest, sinking, threatening to pull her down. This opportunity might never come again.

Now was her chance. Now she would seize the moment.

* * *

Calder came to slowly, bit by bit, his cock hard, aching, pushing against sweet feminine flesh, seeking release.

Damnation. Somehow his barrier of blankets had failed him and twisted free.

It wasn't the first time he'd woken at full mast—or with a woman in bed with him. He'd not lived out his days a monk, to be sure, but this was the first time he'd ever been in bed with a female with whom he was not at liberty to share intimacies.

This was a scenario that called for restraint.

His body was an inferno, burning beneath the blankets and his own scalding skin. He flung the covers off his shoulders and lifted up on his elbows, his gaze dropping to Miss Ballister, unprepared to find her so . . . awake.

Wide blue eyes gazed up at him, unblinking. His self-control slipped a dangerous notch and yet he clung to it. He wasn't like some men, lacking self-control. He was a man who held himself apart—even from people he knew well. His life was and always had been one of restraint.

Calder stared in silence for a moment before finding his voice. "Hello," he breathed.

"Hello," she returned in a small voice.

"How are you?" Were they truly exchanging niceties?

She moistened her lips and he followed the trail of that pink tongue. "Fine. I think." She inhaled and lightly touched her head. "What happened? I don't recall . . ."

"You fell and hit your head." He reached up and brushed the light brown hair off her forehead. He delved through the strands until he found the lump on the back of her scalp. "Does that hurt?"

She reached around, following his fingers to test the area herself. "Just a bit tender."

"By the time we arrived here you were soaking wet and freezing nigh on tae death. We had tae get you warm." He actually sounded conciliatory. There was no cause for that, however. He'd saved her life.

"Oh." Her gaze dropped between them, taking in her

state of undress. Her cheeks pinkened as she pulled the counterpane higher up her chest. "I suppose that explains this."

He waited, imagining her ladylike sensibilities taking over. He braced himself, waiting for the shrieking to start, something any proper soon-to-be-nun would do.

Only it never came.

Her fingers flexed on his shoulders, and that was when he realized she was touching him. Voluntarily. His mind might have been slow to process, but his body had known. It had recognized her closeness, her touch. He'd wager that was what woke him in the first place with a raging cock.

"I always wondered . . ." Her hands trailed down his shoulders to his chest, her eyes brightly curious. Perhaps dazed? Perhaps it was the lump on her head?

He needed to be sensible for both of them. He should climb out of the bed and put space between them. Put his clothes back on. Stride from the room until this inconvenient desire ebbed.

Instead, he asked, "What did you wonder?"

She looked up from his chest, her eyes hooded beneath her lashes. "I wondered how it might be . . . with a man."

He swallowed back a groan.

She didn't mean that. She couldn't. She was an innocent destined for the sanctity of the church. She'd been through an ordeal tonight and was undergoing the effects.

"You're clearly suffering from some sort of head injury."

A faint smile hugged her pretty lips. "Is that what you think?"

She was a siren.

Suddenly, he felt tied up in knots. As though he was the inexperienced one here and she the skilled lover.

Their lips were so close. Somehow his head had lowered. Or had she lifted her lips to his?

"You're supposed tae be a nun," he reminded her in a whisper, his words husking over her mouth.

"But I'm not yet one," she reminded.

He brought his head down then, sinking into her lips.

Just as he feared. She was the sweetest thing he had ever tasted. Unfortunately—*fortunately?*—their individual blankets were bunched between them, keeping all their most intimate parts from pressing flush. It was the only reason he wasn't already between her thighs. Had that been the case, he might not have been able to stop himself from driving inside her body the moment she invited him.

He slanted his mouth over hers and she parted her lips on a sigh. He took advantage, sweeping his tongue inside, stroking hers. She responded, tasting and licking him back until he felt even hotter than when he first woke up, blazing and afire.

He tore his mouth away.

She chased after his lips with a soft little whimper. He cupped her face with one hand and looked down at her, his breathing labored. This girl was unraveling him.

"Where did you learn tae kiss like that, Annis?" It was not how he expected a convent-bound girl to kiss.

She smiled coyly. "I have kissed a few boys . . ."

"Boys?" He hated the thought of that. Almost more than he disliked the notion of her becoming a nun. He far preferred the idea of her staying nearby—within reach—however impossible that was. Her father had won a castle for them to enjoy on holiday. There was no chance of her staying in proximity.

"Yes. When we lived in Bristol. Before we moved to Town." Her smile faltered, and she looked suddenly less confident. "I suppose you think less of me for that." Her tone turned indignant. "I don't know why it has to be that way. It never struck me very fair that men do all manner of vice and are excused for every single instance. How many girls have *you* kissed, Sinclair?"

She was lovely angry. Hot color splashed her cheeks. "Calder," he said.

She stared at him uncomprehendingly. "I beg your pardon?"

He brought his head back down. "My name is Calder, and I don't care how many boys you've kissed, Annis," he declared. "Because I'm the first man."

Chapter Eight

*A*nnis once had a governess who insisted she was the most troublesome of all her sisters. Naturally, Annis took exception to that. She didn't throw tantrums. She didn't pick fights with her siblings or treat any of the household servants with disdain. She never complained about the pudding or the tea or any number of things about which her sisters saw fit to complain.

You're the one I worry will dive off a cliff. When a notion takes you, there be no swaying you, miss. Such a headstrong lass I never did attend.

Dive off a cliff, indeed. It wasn't true, of course. She was the practical one. She might be headstrong, but she wasn't one given to flighty thoughts or impulses. She had chalked the remarks up to the governess's terrible judgment of character.

Except this moment, right now . . . This was impulsive behavior. No denying that.

Perhaps that governess had known her better than she knew herself.

This was reckless and completely out of character, but she'd already decided it might be her only chance. One time to surrender. One time she would always remember.

One time for her blood to sing. Already the faint light of dawn crept in around the thick damask curtains. Soon the light of day would be upon them and it would not be so easy to forget or pretend.

She felt his manhood, hard and jutting against her hip. She knew what it was. What it meant. She was a great reader of histories and scientific texts and that included the medical texts in Papa's library. Reading material she was certain would scandalize Mama if she only knew.

He ground against her and she couldn't stop herself from turning and rotating so that his hardness brushed the apex of her thighs. She didn't even want to stop. In the name of research, she had to explore this further. She craved that hardness right . . . *there*. She moaned softly as she pressed into him.

Just because she'd kissed a few boys didn't mean she had experience with matters of the flesh. Although, as she arched closer to Calder, she supposed she shouldn't underestimate the power of instinct.

With a move that ripped the air from her lips, he rolled over onto his back, taking her with him and settling her astride him.

She gasped and dropped her hands to his broad shoulders, steadying herself. The counterpane slid to her waist, leaving her exposed.

His deep blue eyes swept over her, taking in her full nudity before resting on her small breasts.

Self-consciousness seized her. Her sister Regan was quite well-endowed and liked to lord it over Annis and the others who were less developed. Annis's lack of assets had never bothered her before now. Now she wanted to be more. More for him.

She brought up her hands to shield herself, but he brushed them aside with a tsk. "No hiding these from me."

Then his hands covered her, his blunt-tipped fingers tweaking her nipples until they were hard and straining. She arched her spine, crying out and quite bewildered at the searing sensations shooting from her breasts directly to her core. She covered his hands with her own, exerting pressure, guiding him with that instinct that seemed to be serving her so well.

His hands left her for a moment, and she whimpered in disappointment. He grasped her waist and adjusted her until she was sitting perfectly aligned with his manhood. Her mouth parted on a quick gasp.

She felt every inch of him against her wet heat. Long and straining, pulsing at her opening but not breaching her. No, he made no move to do that. She held her breath, biting back further sounds as she gazed down at him.

His eyes, hungry and dark, watched her, waiting, she sensed, for something from her. She waited, too.

Until she couldn't wait anymore.

"Calder?" She heard the plaintive edge in her voice. She was afire. She started moving. Rocking on him. Grinding his hard length. The friction was delicious. A moan tripped her lips as she grew slippery.

He muttered encouraging words, his hands roaming over her, touching, stroking until she was mindless. Pleasure burned in her, swelling and growing. She started shaking uncontrollably, pleas for something, for more, falling from her lips.

A sob swelled in her chest, strangling in the back of her throat and suddenly her skin sizzled and snapped. She burst from the inside. For a moment her vision blurred. She could see nothing. Could only feel. Could only choke as ripples of pleasure rushed over her skin.

Then she was on her back, Calder looming over her, his big body between her thighs. His muffled words reached her ears, but it took her a moment to digest. His burr had thickened in a way that made her skin shiver. "Och, you are a hot-blooded lass . . ."

She opened her mouth to respond, but suddenly the door

flung open and a cheerful exclamation rang out. "Up with ye! No lazing the day away!"

Did no one knock in this infernal keep *ever*?

She squeaked and tried to shrink more fully beneath Calder's body. Thankfully he was a big brute of a man and shielded most of her from the woman's view.

"Impeccable timing," he muttered so low she could scarcely make out the words. He twisted his neck to look at the older woman standing in the doorway. His shoulders dropped with a great exhale and there was disappointment laden in the sound—a disappointment she felt, too. This lovely escape had come to an end. "Good morning, Mrs. Benfiddy."

* * *

After Calder politely requested her departure, Mrs. Benfiddy left so that they could dress. Nothing in the woman's stoic expression revealed what she thought one way or another of her master in bed with a naked woman, which only led Annis to wonder if this was a regular occurrence. And that made her scowl. She didn't want to be one of *many*. One of a slew of women to warm his bed.

What do you want?

Shaking her head, she finished dressing, averting her eyes from him even as she refused to answer that question—even to herself.

To say the mood had fled between them would be an understatement. It didn't take long for the embarrassment and self-recriminations to settle in. In the light of day, there was no pretending or hiding. She was Miss Annis Ballister, late of Bristol, now a resident of London and destined for the veil.

She had plans. Her future was decided. *She* had decided it. Not her parents. Not society. Certainly not this duke. She could not change her mind. She could not be having doubts now. She wouldn't . . .

Her hands shook as she finished her last button. Her gaze caught on a plate on the nearby side table and she froze. "Wait. What's that?"

He followed her gaze to the plate of what looked like . . . biscuits.

Biscuits! Her stomach knotted. *NoNoNoNoNo.*

"Ah. Nothing. Just a plate of . . ." His voice faded.

"Of what?" she quickly demanded, a sick sense of knowing making her stomach knot harder. When he held silent, she pointed at the plate, pressing for an answer. "Who left it here?"

Still, he hesitated, his expression oddly blank.

"Fenella did, didn't she?" At his continued silence, she pressed, "Those are the biscuits? The *magic* biscuits?" Not that she believed in such rubbish. She was of a scientific mind. Yet it was highly coincidental . . .

He shook his head with a sigh. "There's no such thing as magic—"

"Did you eat any?" It was vastly important for her to know. Suddenly his answer might be the most important thing ever. "Did you?"

His gaze traveled her face before he slowly admitted, "I might have had . . . one."

"One," she echoed, nodding. The knotting in her stomach gave way to nausea. He had eaten one of Fenella's love biscuits before they had very nearly—

She could not even think it. Not about what they had almost done. Not the chance timing of it all. As much as she rejected the idea of magic, this man's sudden and ardent response to her was baffling. She had lived all her life in the shadows of far more beautiful sisters. Her feminine wiles were not so substantial.

Perhaps there was something to this magical shortbread, after all.

He chuckled. "Come now. You dinna think this has anything tae do with what you and I—"

"I don't know," she cut him off, unwilling to hear him say the words. If she couldn't think it, she certainly did not want to hear him give voice to it. "And yet it is coincidental." *Too* coincidental.

Now everything about what happened between them felt suspect. *She* had been the initiator. *She* woke him with roaming hands. If the biscuits truly possessed properties that served as some manner of aphrodisiac, then that, combined with her assertiveness, might have rendered him vulnerable. It shouldn't matter since she was destined for the convent, but it still stung.

"I know what you're thinking and you're wrong." He reached for his boots. "Ridiculous even," he flung out.

She bristled, watching him tug on one boot, then the next. "You can't claim to know me or my mind."

"You wear your thoughts and emotions plainly on your face, and right now you're thinking Fenella's foul biscuits made me—" He stopped abruptly, looked at her. Looked away again.

Love. The word he wouldn't say. Of course. Because *that* would be ridiculous.

Emotion did not play into this—*love* did not. What they had done was physical. Frowning, she stared at his face. The sight sent flutters through her stomach. An ache started at the back of her throat.

He couldn't love her. Men could engage their bodies without engaging their hearts. She knew that. It was science. Biology. Like animals in the barnyard. He did not even want her here. And yet he'd acted like he wanted her here when they were in that bed together. There had been no derision or contempt from him then. He'd behaved as though she were his entire world. He'd behaved as a man obsessed—obsessed with her.

She turned and glared distrustfully at the biscuits again. Perhaps they had cast some spell over him. Her chest ached to think that what had transpired between them had not been real—that it had been wholly one-sided on her part. As illusory as a dream.

Humiliation burned in her throat. Her governess had been right. Annis had done just as she said and jumped off a cliff. She was lucky to have survived.

She'd not make that mistake again.

* * *

Annis spent the rest of the day in bed. Not by choice, but every time she insisted she was fine, she was just pushed back down on the bed by old women who were a lot stronger than they looked.

She was achingly conscious of the fact that it was the duke's bed and that he had occupied it with her the night before—and they had done things there that she'd never imagined herself doing with any man. She had long settled into the idea that she would never marry. Now, in the light of day, the fact that she had engaged in such brazen behavior—and had justified it at the time—left her reeling.

Annis had to get out of this room. What if he came back? What would he think if she was still lazing about in his bed?

She flung back the counterpane and paced the large space, her skin itching with anxious energy. Even when he wasn't here she imagined she could smell him—that hint of leather and wind and *man*.

She took a bracing breath. In six months she would enter the abbey and begin her year of postulancy. She should *not* be thinking about him so much and imagining she could *smell* him everywhere. *Feel* him even now, when they were not touching.

Especially after knowing he'd eaten Fenella's wretched biscuits.

The doubts were planted now. Even as irrational as they were, she could not shake them. She would always question his desire for her. She could never trust it. Never trust him. Not that it mattered, but—with a decided lack of promises between them—it felt *bad*. Crushing.

Her gaze darted around the room anxiously. She would feel immensely better in a space that did not belong to him. She would be more herself then. *Again*.

"What are ye doing out of bed?"

The accusing question hung on the air as she swung around to stare at the irritated-looking woman in the doorway. She had not even heard the door open, but Fenella stood there, her eyes sharpening on Annis. "Ah, Fenella. I am fine—"

"Nae. Back tae bed with ye." Fenella propped her bony fists on her narrow hips.

She shook her head stubbornly even as Fenella charged toward her. "I'm not staying one more moment in *his* bed."

"Tis more than likely he saved yer life, so stay that saucy tongue of yers," Fenella reprimanded as she pushed Annis back down on the bed and rearranged the covers around her, tucking her in as though she were a child. Annis didn't miss the sneaky glances she sent the plate of biscuits. A self-satisfied smile curled the old woman's mouth as she eyed the crumbs, remnants of the one he had eaten.

"I would like to be moved into one of the spare bedchambers."

"Ye should stay here where it's more comfortable. This is the warmest room in the keep."

"Fenella." She glared at the woman, quite aware of the game she was playing. Now Annis fully grasped what an expert manipulator she was. She'd baked her magic biscuits in the middle of the night and somehow managed to get the duke to eat one because she thought it would leave him lust-addled. "It is most unseemly. You must see that."

Fenella waved a gnarled hand dismissively. "Dinna be concerned with that anymore. Ye be well and truly compromised by anyone's standards. Yer papa will force Sinclair's hand, mark my words."

Her stomach dropped as she considered the veracity of that statement. If her parents were to learn of last night's happenings . . . *Heavens!* Her hand flew to her already-unsettled stomach.

If Mama knew, there would be no dissuading her from insisting Sinclair marry her. She'd begin organizing the wedding at once.

She dropped her head back on the pillow. "You are right. I am ruined." Yes, last night had not been a night for thinking things through fully, rationally, and now she could see that she was indeed compromised. A fact that could not be undone, nor as easily overlooked as she once believed. Circumstances, should they come to light, would dictate they wed, and one look at Fenella's resolved expression told Annis that she would waste no time informing her parents of her lapse with Sinclair. Good thing a slightly besmirched reputation wouldn't matter greatly as a nun. Convents were known to offer refuge to women with sullied reputations. She looked miserably at the plate beside the bed. The biscuits resembled rocks. "Why even bother addling the duke's head with your biscuits then?"

"Och, 'tis always better if yer happy and eager tae marry because ye believe yerself tae be in love and loved in turn."

Annis laughed weakly. "Funny. I did not think you were overly concerned with my happiness as you pressured the duke into bedding me." Not that she believed in the magical power of love biscuits, but on the off chance . . .

Fenella chuckled. "I suspect he was halfway already in love with ye before he ate the shortbread. I watched the sparks between the two of ye. 'Twas the same way of it with his parents, bless them both." She quickly made the sign of the cross. "The biscuits simply hastened matters." The old woman gathered up Annis's lunch tray and moved toward the door. "I'll have a maid prepare ye a bath. Ye will want tae look yer best when he returns this eve. He is busy today seeing that we are properly fortified against these rogues plaguing us."

"Thank you." She would happily accept a bath. Even if she did not require to look her best for him. "And what of changing into another bedchamber?" she called out, unwilling to give up on that quest, but Fenella was already gone, the door thudding closed behind her.

As promised, maids soon returned and poured steaming water into a hip bath with a high-angled back so she could actually recline. Annis declined their offer for assistance. Alone again, she stripped off her shift and sank into the steaming water of the copper tub with a sigh. After a moment, she leaned forward and dipped her head under the water's surface to wet her hair.

Reaching for the lavender-scented soap, she worked a lather between her hands and started on her hair, gradually moving on to the rest of her body until she was covered in bubbles and smelling of the fragrant soap. Using the full bucket sitting beside the tub, she doused herself with fresh water, rinsing off the soap.

Sighing, she relaxed her neck on the lip of the tub.

She wouldn't linger long. Even if she was reassured Sinclair would not return until this evening, she needed to see about moving into a different room and keeping as much distance from him as possible.

Chapter Nine

Calder spent the entire morning scouting the property and making certain Glencrainn was well fortified with no door, window, or exterior area vulnerable. After he had prepped the outside, he'd turned his attention to the interior of the keep. Two men worked beside him, searching for every potential weakness.

It had been a long time since this castle had to face invaders, but now that he'd seen the brigands with his own eyes and knew they were well armed and a dozen strong, he intended to take every precaution. His staff was not trained in arms, but they outnumbered this foe, a fact he would use to his advantage.

He remembered his father telling him stories of the castle and its long history. Of enemy clans attacking and how the Sinclairs had built a secret tunnel so that the family could escape in the event of an attack. The entrance to the tunnel was located in the kitchens. It was no longer a safe or viable means of passage, littered now with mostly crumbled rock and debris. Impassable or not, he'd barricaded it, several wide-eyed kitchen maids watching as they kneaded bread for the day's meals.

The tunnel was the stuff of local lore. The brigands could easily know or learn of its existence. He would leave nothing to chance and put none of his people at risk. The criminal mind was devious. If there was a crack in his defenses, they would find it. He stood back and gave the barrels stacked against the door a satisfied nod.

He felt more at ease knowing he'd taken the necessary precautions to protect his home.

"What ye doing there, Laird?"

Sheila sidled up to him, swaying her hips and giving the flimsy cotton of her bodice a good tug so that the swells of her prodigious breasts were better on display. The redheaded lass had often sent him inviting looks. Mrs. Benfiddy frowned on the interaction and had voiced her disapproval in no uncertain terms.

That lass is an ambitious one . . . has an eye on becoming the future lady of the castle.

He'd always been on guard with Sheila, having no intention of marrying the lass, no matter how beautiful her face.

"Seeing tae our safety," he responded. "You needn't fret."

Her hazel eyes flitted over his handiwork. "Ye think the reivers might try tae get in through the tunnel?"

He shrugged. "Possibly. 'Tis no secret it exists. Until they're captured I leave nothing tae chance."

She leaned in, pushing her ample breasts into him and covering his forearm with a hand. "It does comfort me, Laird, being under yer protection." She swayed her breasts side to side.

He lifted her hand from him and adopted an unyielding tone. "You have duties, no doubt, Sheila."

For some reason Annis's face flashed through his mind and that was peculiar. He wasn't engaging in anything untoward with Sheila, but he still felt a sense of loyalty to Annis. As though she was the only female allowed to lay hands on him—as though she were the only woman he wanted to touch him. *Because she was.*

The mere idea of dallying with anyone other than the female he'd left in his bed sat cold with him. And that was a sobering realization. He shifted uneasily, refusing to examine that too closely right now.

Sheila jutted out her bottom lip in a pout. "Is it that lass upstairs, then? I can be a fine lady, too. I will be one day. Ye will see."

"I'm certain of that, Sheila."

"Sheila!" Marie snapped. "Leave the master alone and get back tae yer duties before I box yer ears, ye cheeky lass!"

She scowled at the cook but did as she was told, backing away from Calder with reproachful eyes.

He turned, only to pause at the sight of his housekeeper looming in the kitchen doorway. He felt very much like a child caught at mischief.

"She is too much enamored of ye, Laird."

She wanted position, not him. Unlike Annis. What existed between them had nothing to do with his position . . . nothing to do with her angling for anything from him. Despite his earlier suspicions, he now believed that she cared nothing for his title, property, or wealth. Status mattered not at all to her. She wasn't matrimonially minded, and that very thing set her apart. Ironically, it made her more appealing. What he felt was more than lust. Annis. *Annis.* For God's sake, her name made him giddy.

Mrs. Benfiddy stared at him expectantly.

"Rest assured, nothing will come of it," he assured her.

The old woman stepped aside, allowing him to depart the kitchen.

Calder took the winding stairs to his bedchamber, passing down the long hallway. He rubbed at the back of his neck, his thoughts drifting to Annis yet again and the night before. She'd blamed the damned shortbread. She thought those foul biscuits were the reason he kissed her. Touched her. *Ached* for her. Fool girl. He was not under any spell.

He was a flesh-and-blood man who responded to a fetching woman pressed against him. Nothing more.

At least that's what he had been telling himself all day.

He pushed open his bedchamber door and immediately froze. He thought for certain she would have changed rooms by now.

Why was she still here? And why was he glad? Warmth hummed through him to find her here bathing in his tub. *Bathing.* Suds rolled down the smooth slope of her back. Shining skin peeked out between the bubbles and his mouth instantly dried.

Her hair was piled atop her head with tiny dark blond tendrils escaping and trailing down her nape. It was the most erotic sight he'd ever seen.

He must have made a sound because she twisted around and gasped, bringing her knees up to her chest, shielding her breasts from his view.

Her eyes flared wide, enormous and frightened as any animal caught in a predator's sights. "What are you doing in here?" she demanded shrilly.

"Er . . ." He cleared his suddenly tight throat as his gaze dragged over her, feasting on wet flesh. "It's my chamber. What are *you* doing here?"

"You weren't supposed to be back until later, and *I* am here against my will," she promptly replied. "I keep asking to be moved, but Fenella won't permit me and she prepared a bath for me in here."

Fenella. Of course.

Shrugging, he moved toward a bench positioned near the fireplace. Lowering down onto it, he began tugging off his boots. It gave him something to do besides gawk at her. Something other than looking at all that glistening pink skin. "Actually a bath sounds like a fine idea. Any room in there for me?"

He grinned at the sound of her sharp intake of breath and

the immediate sound of splashing water as she emerged from the tub.

"What's wrong with you?" she sputtered. "Haven't you any decency?"

He flicked a glance up at her and froze. She'd brought her shift up to cover herself, but the fabric was now wet and very nearly translucent pressed against her body.

His heart pounded savagely. Perhaps he was wrong. Maybe he was under some spell. But not a spell cast by magical biscuits. *She* had wrought this witchery over him. She alone. He'd compromised her the night before and he was quite happy to do it again. Damn the consequences. He wasn't without honor. He'd marry her. To have her right now, he'd do just about anything.

Free of his boots and socks, he stood and stepped closer, advancing in his bare feet over the rug as he contemplated her, this female who had thrust herself into his life, falling from out of nowhere. Quite literally.

"I rescued you from the imminent descent of brigands. Saved you from certain freezing. I think I've passed any measurement for decency."

She shook her head and his gaze fixed on all that glorious hair piled atop her head, his fingers craving to touch her there, bury themselves in the mass. Her mouth worked, seeking speech, but no sound came.

He continued his hungry perusal, subjecting her to a thorough examination, his stare lingering on her poorly hidden breasts. They were a handful, perfect, and his mouth watered. His palms itched. She was the most delectable woman he had ever seen, wet from her bath, her plump flesh exposed like a juicy fruit ready to taste.

God. He was hard. She need only look down and see the evidence.

As though she read his mind, her gaze dropped. Bright color fired to life in her face.

Damnation . . . Perhaps he wasn't decent. After all, he'd brought this lass here. He'd put a soon-to-be-nun in his bed and he'd done things to her no one should ever do to a virtuous woman with such holy aspirations. She was right. He was not a decent man because he wanted to continue right where they'd left off this morning and corrupt the hell out of her.

Staring at her like this, he didn't want to be decent—and that led him to several uncomfortable realities. Yes. He would make her his and even marry her. Because right now she was the epicenter of his universe. She was the only thing he could concentrate on. She and his raging, pulsing cock.

He advanced.

Her expression tightened as he neared her and she started to back away. Something sparked in him, a long-buried primitive urge to hunt and claim. To prove to this sharp-tongued lass that she didn't want a life of abstinence. She wanted *him*.

"Perhaps you're right and I'm no' good. Perhaps the true reason you haven't left my room is because you want tae be here. With me. Now. Again."

She shook her head, damp tendrils of hair skimming smooth shoulders. "No."

"You wanted me tae return." He gestured at the bath. "Perhaps you staged this entire enticing scene."

"Oh!" The red in her cheeks deepened. "I didn't. I was told you wouldn't return until this evening. And I told you I'm not after a title. I'm not like my sisters. I'm not trying to trap you—"

"I know that." He stopped before her. No. This was more problematic than that. If she were any one of her sisters she would be easy to dismiss. Easy to resist.

He didn't think she was trying to trap him into marriage. It was worse. She wasn't, but he wouldn't mind it anymore if she were.

"Then . . ." She shook her head and he caught a whiff of lavender. It only added to the headiness of her nearness. "What's happening?" she whispered, and she looked almost childlike in her bewilderment. Part of him wanted to soothe her, but that wasn't possible when this thing raged between them. Crackling heat, drawing him closer.

"This," he said, the word thick in the space between them as he reached down and tugged her shift free. He tossed it aside and she was left bare before him, her body damp and beautifully naked.

He touched her, starting at her collarbone and coming down between her breasts in one long stroke.

She trembled under his fingers. His hand was shaking, too. He felt like a green lad with his first woman. Not an experienced man.

His hand stopped, flattening between the swells of her breasts. Her pulse pounded under his palm.

She leaned forward slightly, the weight of her body pressing into his palm. She wasn't running away. It was all he needed. It was all he could bear.

His hand shifted to cup her breast, his thumb rubbing a nipple. Instantly it beaded, pretty and pink as a raspberry. He released a gust of breath at the sweet weight filling his hand. He cupped her other breast and she cried out, her knees giving out. She buckled forward. He caught her against him, gripping one sweetly rounded cheek as he claimed her lips. She moaned into his mouth, kissing him back.

He gripped her in both hands then, lifting her high against him, thrusting his hardness against her soft stomach. It was a pale emulation of what he really wanted to be doing.

He massaged her backside, delighting in the soft little moans and mewls escaping her.

"Annis," he growled against her lips.

"Yes," she panted.

The kiss deepened and he half carried, half walked her until he'd backed her against a wall. She gasped into his mouth and he swallowed her breath, taking it deep inside himself just as he wanted to take her and devour her until they were one entity. She appeared to be of like mind.

Her hands clawed at his shoulders and arms as though they couldn't get enough of him. As far as he was concerned the only problem was that he was still dressed.

"Och, pardon me!"

He whirled around to see Fenella standing in the threshold, a triumphant smile playing on her lips.

Damnation! Did no one knock on doors in this keep ever? Clearly he needed to call a meeting with his staff and cover this simple protocol.

Annis's fist beat on his shoulder. "Calder!"

He turned, mindful to keep his body blocking hers.

Still grinning, Fenella murmured, "I just came tae see if Miss Ballister needed help finishing her bath. I'm so *verra* sorry, Laird." Her smile revealed that she wasn't the least bit sorry. "I knocked, but no one answered and after Miss Ballister's condition last night . . ."

"Understandable. Don't fash yourself," he said tightly. "Miss Ballister is fine. Thank you. Would you give us a few moments?"

"Of course. Take yer time." Fenella slipped out of the room, closing the door behind her.

He gave a brief prayer that it would stay shut this time, and turned to face Annis as she slipped out from between him and the wall, moving like a burst of wind. She snatched up the robe on the foot of the bed and pulled it on, unfortunately covering up all her delicious curves.

"This is madness. I'm not . . ." She gestured vaguely with her hand and shook her head. "N-not this."

He nodded slowly. "You are. You're no' made tae be a

nun. You're made for this." *For me*. The words popped immediately to mind, but he didn't voice them. She already looked as skittish as a rabbit. He needed her to acclimate to the notion of them together. He himself was still adjusting to the idea, but the certainty was there. He wanted her. Wanted to keep her. Wanted her to want him back.

He couldn't articulate why or how he knew this, but he did. Just as for years he had felt certain of his bachelor status, certain that none of the young women in or around Glencrainn were for him, he knew she was. *She* was for him.

She held his gaze for a long moment. "That's not true. Either direct me to a different bedchamber or I'll find one on my own. This castle is big enough. I'm sure that won't be too difficult." Her gaze darted over his shoulder as though judging the distance to the door.

Did she think to lunge for it? Did she think he would imprison her in this room, in his bed like some kind of Viking marauder of old?

He stepped aside and gestured at the door. He wasn't that man and he'd show her even if it killed him. "By all means."

She hurried across the room to where her valise sat. She fumbled through it, sneaking him looks over her shoulder. With a handful of garments bundled in her arms she hastened behind the dressing screen. The soft sounds of her movements carried through the thin barrier. He inhaled and tried not to imagine her undressing. He grasped at his restraint. A female such as she would require skilled wooing. He was not confident he had it in him for that, but he would try.

Minutes later, she emerged, smoothing her hands over her wrinkled skirts.

His gaze tracked over her. She wore a modest day dress of rich burgundy trimmed in purple piping. She was the perfect London lady. Untouchable. But that did not stop him from seeing her as he'd seen her before with all her naked skin glistening fresh and pink. With his hands on that skin.

Her cheeks colored brightly as she gathered up her valise and started across the chamber toward the door, no doubt reading his thoughts.

He stepped in her path, blocking her escape.

She lifted those guileless eyes to him. How had he ever thought her a conniving title-hungry miss? There was no deception about her. No guile at all.

He lifted the valise from her fingers. "I'll escort you."

She nodded jerkily. He opened the door, gesturing for her to step out into the corridor. She stared at him uncertainly a moment longer, then passed through ahead of him.

Chapter Ten

*T*he duke led Annis to a different chamber without another word. Without another tempting, impossible word. He bowed politely over her hand and left her alone. Which was how she remained all day and into the night, discounting when a maid carried a dinner tray into her room.

As alone as when her family forgot and left her.

Melancholy wiggled its way inside her. She knew she shouldn't feel so . . . abandoned. It was not the same as when her family left her. Sinclair was not her family. Not by a long shot.

Besides. She wanted solitude. Blessed peace. No shrill, squabbling siblings. No mother who didn't understand her or care to try. Right now she could be crammed into a carriage, fighting for seat space and enduring her sisters' high-pitched dramatics as they journeyed home.

The following morning, a maid brought her breakfast, helped her with her hair and dress, and then left her. She wondered if this was to be how she spent her time here. Hidden. Forgotten. Blast it! She needn't care. It was for the best.

She should be grateful that they'd stopped before he'd divested her entirely of her virtue. Gads. He might feel compelled to marry her, then. She could think of no worse fate than being forced into a marriage lacking love and affection and respect simply for propriety's sake. Married to the Sinclair . . . A strange fluttering took off in her belly.

Left to her own devices, she availed herself of one of the books stacked atop a side table. She settled on a chaise lounge positioned near the window, draping a thick wool blanket over her legs. The fire in the room cast enough heat to reach her where she sat. The book, a treatise on the significance of the Magna Carta, was one she had not read before, but she had a dreadful time focusing.

She often lifted her head and stared out the crack in the heavy damask drapes, gazing at the snow-shrouded grounds. Her nose twitched at the scent of nutmeg and cloves. Someone was baking. Maybe she would get to eat the fruits of their labors? She inhaled deeply of the aroma. It smelled like Christmas.

She reflected on last night, brushing fingers over her lips, imagining Sinclair's mouth there and how it had felt. The man certainly knew how to use those lips.

You're not made to be a nun. What if he was right? Shouldn't she be more certain before entering into a life-long commitment? She had thought she was certain of her decision. Now she was not so sure.

She jumped, startled by a knock. Setting her book aside, she marched toward the door. Opening it, she came face-to-face with the duke, his hand poised to knock again.

"Oh." She stepped back, her hand fluttering to her throat. "You. Hello." *You.* The utterance felt foolish. *She* felt foolish. All of this was so new and strange. *Liking* a man—wanting him. Desire.

"Aye. Me." He shifted, actually looking nervous, and that would be the first time she had ever seen him nervous. "I thought you might like tae go outside." He motioned behind him.

"Outside?"

"Aye."

She glanced back toward the window. She could see snow flurries through the part in the cracked curtains.

"We won't be verra long," he added, running a hand quickly through his hair and sending the dark locks aflutter. "Mrs. Benfiddy claims we need more holly."

"Holly?" she echoed as though she had never heard of such a thing.

A corner of his mouth kicked up. "Are you going tae stand here and repeat everything I say or are you going tae join me outside? We won't take verra long. It's still frightfully cold, but we will bundle up."

She inhaled a quick breath. He really was handsome—especially when he smiled like that. She considered him, looking him up and down. He was asking her to collect holly with him as though this were an ordinary holiday. As though she were a welcomed guest and not someone foisted upon him. Warmth suffused her.

She should remember that he didn't want her here.

She should refuse and stay put in this room by herself until she remembered that peace and solitude were all she ever wanted. Not go holly picking with a man who made her blood hum faster in her veins.

Stay put. Indeed, that was what she should do.

"Very well. I'd be glad to join you." *Right off the cliff . . .*

* * *

Fenella saw them off, waving a gnarled glove-free hand, her eyes narrowing as they clattered through the gates. She was probably surmising that her infernal biscuits had worked.

Annis turned away from the castle and faced forward again. She counted eight riders accompanying them as they made their way in a small cart through the woods surrounding the keep. "We won't go far," Sinclair declared as though she were worried about the matter.

It had never occurred to her to fret. Although, with brigands lurking about, she supposed the issue of safety should
have crossed her mind. She sent Sinclair a measuring look.
She suspected she had him to blame—or thank—for her
lack of worry.

He made her feel . . . safe. Among other things.

She fought back a whole host of uncomfortable sensations as she shifted upon the bench. She would not think
about her time in his bed. It had been a dream. And like a
dream, it wasn't real. Even if a part of her—perhaps a very
large part—wished it to be.

They sat side by side on the bench. She folded her gloved
hands in her lap. The duke had draped a great fur blanket
over her, declaring her cloak and garments not enough. She
had not protested. After very nearly freezing to death, she
would take all precautions to avoid a repeat of that.

The last thing she needed was to end up naked in his bed
again.

Prickles of heat broke out over her body and it didn't feel
like the last thing she needed. It felt like the only thing.

The duke's men eyed the trees. Even the duke himself
kept vigilant, assessing their surroundings.

"You're worried," she pronounced.

He glanced at her. "Merely cautious."

She looked about slowly, searching as though she might
find a menacing face in the nearby branches.

"'Tis unlikely they would strike in the daylight. Or attack a party of this size. They are not highwaymen," he
reminded her. "They typically thieve empty homes."

Snow fell softly over them, lightly dusting her blanket
and his garments.

"Here we are," he declared, stopping before a stout hedge
of holly. The other riders pulled up, as well, waiting nearby.

He hopped to the ground and walked around to lift her
down. Then he plucked a basket from the back of the cart,

handed it to her, and removed a basket for himself. There was a lightness to his step as they approached the hedge.

He offered her a pair of shears and she accepted them, careful that her gloved fingers not brush his. Looping the basket handle over her arm, she managed to start snipping holly and dropping it in the basket.

"I'm surprised holly gathering falls among your priorities, Your Grace."

He stopped abruptly and looked at her in such a way that she knew her formal address of him rankled.

"Sinclair," she amended.

"It's important tae Mrs. Benfiddy. She still expects the house trimmed accordingly for Christmas, brigands or no brigands."

Her lips twitched. "So you're afraid of your housekeeper?"

"Should I not be? She wields a great deal of power. One word from her and I cease tae have fresh linens on my bed and warm kippers on my plate in the mornings."

Annis giggled. "Except, you are her employer."

Smiling, he shrugged. "I inherited her right along with the keep. She's no' going anywhere."

"Ah." She nodded. "She's legacy, then."

"Indeed. Practically raised me after my parents died."

As he was a duke, she had assumed his father was deceased in order for him to inherit the title, but she knew nothing of the rest of his family. She fell silent for a moment, feeling sudden pity. Here he was, essentially an orphan, and she had so much family that she was coming up with ways to escape them.

"Do you have siblings?"

"The cholera pandemic that took my parents also took my sister."

"I'm sorry," she murmured, feeling awful and selfish. What must he have thought of her when she told him she wanted to be a nun for the solitude and peace? He, who lost his family.

"It happened a long time ago," he replied, snipping a bit of holly and dropping it in his basket. "Christmastime, in fact. Twenty years ago."

"Oh." Her gaze scanned the red holly berries, a quintessential reminder of Christmas. "This must be a difficult time of year for you, then."

Sinclair shrugged, not denying the charge. "We carry on. That is what the living do. We live even when those we love do no'. We can only remember them and honor them."

He sounded so very practical. Wise, but also . . . cold. Detached. "Still. It could not have been easy," she remarked.

His gaze slid to hers. "What do you want me tae say? That I cried myself tae sleep for years? I did. That I wanted tae weep at Christmas without them? Aye. I did." He shrugged one shoulder. "Sometimes still do."

She blinked at that admission . . . at this vulnerable side to him she could never have imagined existed.

Snipping more holly, he went on, "But I owe it tae my family tae live the best life I can."

Stilling, she stared at him for a long moment, seeing him as if for the first time. He was thoughtful and brave and strong. Not at all what she imagined when she was sprawled in an ignominious pile in his courtyard as he unceremoniously ordered her family to leave. And now she could not unknow this information about him. She could not *unsee* it as she looked at him. Blast it. He was not only attractive. He was likable.

Forcing herself back to action, she snipped a sprig of holly and tucked it inside her hood, behind her ear. Immediately the aroma of holly berries filled her nose. "I'm sure they are looking down at you with pride."

"You're so certain, are you?"

He sounded less than convinced. "Of course. You're a good man." She seized his arm and squeezed, hoping to convey this to him.

He held her stare. Everything seemed to melt away as she looked into his eyes and wondered if, perhaps, it was excusable to kiss this man. To do the things she had done with him *again* and maybe more since he was undeniably likable.

He was leaning so close now. She was certain he was going to kiss her.

And she was certain she would let him.

His deep voice rumbled between them. "Still want tae be a nun, Miss Ballister?"

"Why do you ask?" she breathed.

"Kissing a man isn't exactly nun behavior." His gaze skimmed her face, pausing on the sprig of holly tucked behind her ear. He touched the tiny plant and then his gloved thumb extended to her cheek in a slow drag of leather. Her skin sprang to gooseflesh.

"Oh." She lifted her face a fraction higher, placing her lips closer to his. "And do you still find Christmas so objectionable?"

His voice husked over her mouth. "I might be developing a fondness for it."

Suddenly an explosion sounded near her and she was flattened to the ground, the snow cold at her chest, the great weight of him over her, pushing her down.

Shouts from the duke's men erupted all around them. It was madness. Feet pounded. Gunfire popped all around them. The duke cursed near her ear, lifting his head to peer around.

"Keep your head down." Seizing her hand, he dragged her, pulling her to the side of the wagon, where they were better shielded. He pulled a pistol out from his greatcoat.

"Seamus," he called, motioning to one of his nearby

men. The bearded man scuttled over to where they hunkered behind the wagon.

"Aye." Seamus brandished his own weapon.

Calder nodded at her. "I want you tae take the lass and get her tae the keep."

"What?" she gasped, grabbing his arm. "What of you?"

He did not even look at her as he addressed Seamus. "I will create a distraction, drawing their fire from you and the lass."

"What? No!" He could not remain here where he could be hurt or killed. Her heart clenched painfully in her chest at the prospect, and she knew then. She knew how very much he mattered to her.

He uncoiled her fingers from his arm and shoved her at Seamus. "Take the lass. Cut through the woods. Protect her."

She grabbed his hand. "No. I'm not leaving you out here to die. We can run for the castle together."

Sinclair shook his head, at last looking at her, but in his eyes she read a fierce determination that didn't bode well.

He peeled her fingers off him again and gave her a cheeky grin. "Don't worry. You won't be rid of me that easily." With one last look, he was gone, slinking low along the wagon and then around it. She surged to go after him, but Seamus wrapped an arm around her and kept her close to his side.

Then she heard Calder's voice boom across the air, his brogue deep and resounding with authority. "I'm the Duke of Sinclair, Laird of Glencrainn."

The gunfire ceased.

"That's our prompt." Seamus lifted her to her feet and pulled her into the trees and toward the castle as Calder continued to talk. His voice faded to an echo as they broke through the thick branches. She struggled to go back, to make certain he was safe.

"Come, miss. Don't make this any worse. Move yer feet. Ye want the laird fretting for ye? He'll manage just fine. Now let's see ye tae safety."

A fervent prayer passed her lips as she obeyed Seamus and forced her legs to move. Calder would be fine. *He would not be harmed. He would not be harmed.* Her heart did not cease to twist in her chest even as this plea rolled over and over in her head.

The guards at the gates were ready for them when they arrived at the castle, no doubt hearing the report of fire-arms. They quickly let Annis and Seamus and two other of the duke's men inside. The rest of their party remained in the woods with the brigands. A fact that made her sick. She paced a short line in the courtyard, feeling utterly help-less, still angry at herself for leaving Calder and angry at Calder for making her go. She wanted to grab a weapon and charge back out there. If he died, she would never for-give herself. Or him.

Mrs. Benfiddy appeared and motioned her to move in-side the great hall. "Come, Miss Ballister. Let's get ye warm within."

She shook her head. "I'll stay here until Sinclair returns."

The housekeeper frowned. "Dinna fash over the laird. He'll be fine, lass."

"We never should have gone out there."

Mrs. Benfiddy approached, her hands folded neatly in front of her. "Aye, well 'e thought ye might enjoy an outing and these brigands usually strike dwellings at night. Pick-ings must have gotten thin for them tae attack in daylight."

"He thought *I* might enjoy an outing?" She looked askance at the woman. "I thought you asked him to fetch more holly."

"Aye, so that ye could spend a bit of time together."

Annis closed her eyes in a pained blink. "So your match-making is the reason we went outside the castle?"

"Och, I'm no matchmaker. Dinna confuse me with Fenella. I merely saw the lad pining for yer company, so I gave him a reason tae see ye."

Pining for her company? Could that be true? She didn't have the time to digest that. She could only look to the gates, hoping they would open to reveal him safe and hale. She called to the men on the ramparts. "Do you see him?"

Lifting her skirts, she marched over to one of the ladders leading up to the parapet, ready to look for herself.

Suddenly there was gunfire directly outside the gates. Men atop the ramparts released fire down below.

"Calder." She breathed his name, uttering it like a prayer, and started climbing up the rungs.

"Miss Ballister, what are ye doing?" Mrs. Benfiddy called after her. "Get back 'ere!"

She was halfway up the ladder, ignoring the housekeeper, when the command to open the gates roared from somewhere above her. She froze, watching as the thick wooden doors cracked open and the duke's men stumbled in.

Her heart hurt inside her chest, twisting and pumping as she scanned the group for the duke's familiar form. A moment before the door thudded closed again she spotted him. He staggered through, an arm wrapped around one of his men who was clearly injured.

She climbed back down the ladder. Dropping to her feet, she surveyed the chaotic scene. Household staff surged forward, mobbing the group.

Calder snapped orders and servants appeared, quickly attending to the men.

Even as relieved as she felt, the fear was still there. She'd never felt anything close to it. She felt as though she was not getting enough air into her lungs.

Her gaze devoured him across the distance, assessing, making certain he wasn't injured.

He was accosted by a clucking Mrs. Benfiddy. He stood a

good head taller than the housekeeper, and he looked over her, searching the courtyard.

His gaze landed on Annis and there it stayed. Something flickered in his stormy eyes, speaking to her, pulling at something deep, where her fear lurked.

With a choked cry, she turned and fled.

Chapter Eleven

*A*nnis took refuge in her bedchamber, striding its length and rubbing her hands together as though that would rid her of some of her anxiety. It did little good. Her hands wouldn't quit shaking. Her fear. Her relief. It was all too much for her to comprehend. The door opened then, and she whirled around.

He stood there. Her heart took off, wild as a bird set loose from inside her too-tight chest. His eyes fastened on her and she couldn't move.

"You shouldn't have done that," she spit out shakily. All of her was shaking. "You shouldn't have sent me away while you faced those brigands."

Everything slowed to a crawl. Blood rushed, a dull roar in her ears. She imagined she could hear the muffled thump of her own heart.

"What was I tae do?" he asked thickly. "Risk you getting hurt?" He shook his head once, emphatically, and something quivered deep inside her, starting low in her core and spreading throughout her body.

"You could have died," she accused, wishing he would stop staring at her in that disconcerting way of his.

"I'm here," he responded. "Alive."

Indeed he was.

"I see that," she whispered, her heart so loud now that she was certain *he* could hear it.

Then he slammed the door shut behind him, sealing them in. They moved in unison, coming together.

Their mouths collided, fused, breaking only for the time it took them to tug their clothes off in a blur of wild motion. Everything was frantic. Desperate. Violent in its ferocity. Her cloak hit the floor followed by his. Her dress was hastily unbuttoned and the sleeves shoved down her arms.

It was utter madness and totally unlike her. Perhaps it was a release from the turmoil of the day and their near brush with death. Even as the fleeting thought crossed her mind, she knew it was false—a brief attempt at rationalization. This was about need. Desire. Affirmation of life.

They kissed and kissed and kissed.

Hot and feverish, tongues warring. It was senseless and wild. There was nothing smooth or civilized about it. It wrecked her.

He tugged the rest of her bodice down, revealing her corset-covered breasts. She gasped at the brush of chill air on her exposed flesh. His hands grazed over the crests, rough palms abrading the tender skin as his mouth ravaged hers. It wasn't gentle, but she didn't want him to be. He didn't treat her like some fragile piece of crystal, and she reveled in it.

His hand settled on her right breast, closing over the small mound and squeezing, making her feel like she was the lushest, most beautiful creature in the world.

He pulled back to untie the laces at the front, his hands shaking a little. Soon her chemise gaped open, exposing her breasts fully to the air—to him. He dipped his head, taking her breast into his mouth. She cried out, her fingers latching on to his head and threading through his hair.

They sank to the bed, his hard length coming over her. He pulled back, looking down at her, his hand gliding over her cheek, fingers buried in her hair, scattering pins. He gripped her by the head, kissing her again, his hot mouth consuming hers.

Her hands dropped to the front of his trousers, eagerly unbuttoning the falls of his breeches to free him. He adjusted to shuck off his jacket and shirt and shove his trousers down his hips.

She watched, devouring the sight of him, her breathing ragged and harsh between them. They came together again, bare skin slipping sinuously against each other. He pulled the skirts of her gown up to her waist and settled between her thighs. She gasped at the sensation of his hips wedged between her splayed thighs.

It felt so wicked and so right.

He kissed her breasts again and she whimpered, arching her spine, offering him more, *wanting* more. His mouth closed around one nipple, pulling deeply, and she moaned, her fingers clenching on his biceps. He shifted and nudged his manhood directly against her opening.

She panted, her hands moving to clutch the back of his neck, clinging, straining against him, pulling him closer as she rotated her hips, needing him inside her.

"Annis? Are you sure?"

Yes, yes, yes. This would be all she would have of him once the snow melted and she was gone from here. For now she would embrace this. Hunger. Raw desire. *Calder.*

Gasping, she rolled her hips and pushed up against him. "I want to. I want you, Calder."

His eyes gleamed fiercely. She looked down between them, watching as he took himself in hand, gripping his hard member and guiding it inside her. Her mouth parted on a cry, fascinated and aroused by the sight.

Calder wrapped an arm around her waist and hauled her closer, holding her steady as he sank inside her. His eyes locked with hers.

It was an unreal moment, staring into his eyes, feeling

his body joining with hers, filling her with a burn that wasn't entirely comfortable.

She wiggled, her body stretching to accommodate him. Choking little breaths escaped her as she molded to fit him.

"You're so bloody tight," he hissed, pulling her closer and mashing her breasts to his chest as his manhood pulsed deep inside her. "Am I hurting you?"

"No." Leaning forward, she wrapped her arms around his neck and pressed her mouth to his, kissing him for all she was worth. Squirming beneath him, she gasped into his mouth as shards of pleasure spiked out from where they were joined.

Her nails scored his back. "Keep going," she commanded in a voice that did not even sound like her.

He obliged, rocking his hips against her and she cried out, arching against him.

"Oh, you feel good." He withdrew and drove back inside her. "Sorry, lass. It will be better next time."

Next time? She could not even wrap her thoughts around that. Not whilst this felt amazing *now*. An aching pressure built inside her as he moved faster, increasing the tempo and friction and tightening that invisible coil low in her belly.

She writhed against him, desperate for release. "Calder," she pleaded.

In response, he hooked a hand under her knee and draped her leg around his waist, penetrated even deeper.

His next thrust shattered her and she cried out, fingers digging into his skin.

She'd never felt anything so amazing. Her vision blurred as he continued moving inside her, working a steady pace that left her wild and gasping.

"Annis," he growled in her ear.

Her palms roved over his solid flesh, loving the absolute freedom to touch him, to cherish him with her hands.

Shudders shook through her. His name ripped from her lips.

His hand delved into her hair. He held her there, peering into her eyes as he moved inside her, driving harder, reaching some hidden spot where all sensation seemed to begin and end.

Suddenly every nerve ignited and burst. She cried out, arching under him. "Ohh!"

His lips seized hers. She moaned into his mouth, feeling his own release follow and tremor through him, eddying into her.

They collapsed down to earth together, his weight atop her. As heavy as he was, she didn't want him to ever move. She could stay like this forever.

He rolled onto his back and tugged her against his side. She smiled dreamily, drowsy and replete in the aftermath of their shattering union.

"I feel as though I could sleep a fortnight," she murmured after some moments, smoothing her fingers over his chest.

"A fortnight? That's not going to work considering I'd like tae do this again. Verra soon."

"Again?" She lifted her head. "Do people do it again? More than once in a day?"

Calder chuckled and pulled her closer, kissing her nose. Smiling, she lowered her head back down and nestled her cheek against his chest, his heart a comforting and steady thud against her ear. Suddenly his stomach growled.

"Someone is hungry," she commented.

"Aye. You need rest, and I need sustenance before we indulge ourselves again." Despite those words, his broad palm slid down her back and curled around one cheek of her backside, molding and squeezing it in a way that sent a renewed spike of heat straight to her core.

"I think we skipped luncheon," she breathed, her blood stirring with desire.

"What if I ring for a tray? We can eat in bed. I scarcely even ate at breakfast, merely grabbed a couple biscuits."

She stiffened at that remark, letting it roll around her head. She tried to dismiss it, calling herself foolish and overly sensitive. And yet she could not shake loose the horrible feeling inside her that chased away and killed her euphoria.

She sat up, pulling the covers to her chest as she stared down at him. "You ate more biscuits? *Fenella's* biscuits?" The distinction was important.

He blinked. "God, no! I'd never put more of those foul things in my mouth. They were inedible."

She stared at him, the wariness still humming through her.

She knew that suspecting the biscuits of influencing him was ridiculous, but it almost made more sense than the alternative: that this beautiful man—*a duke!*—wanted her so desperately.

"Annis," he continued, "I'm telling you the truth. I've no' eaten one of those infernal biscuits since the first."

Yes, but could she believe him? He knew how she felt about the biscuits and their potentially damning curse on free will.

She continued to stare at him, her grip tightening on the sheets.

"Annis," he growled, canting his head, his eyes bright and alive as they fixed on her. "Don't be absurd. Even if I ate one of those biscuits again, they are no' magical. They did no' make me do anything I did no' want tae do."

And there was another consideration if she allowed herself to believe the shortbread possessed magical properties. How long did one of Fenella's biscuits hold its spell?

She moistened her lips. "I think I need to be alone."

Alone to think. Alone to reclaim herself away from him.

"Alone," he snapped. "Indeed. Your grand dream . . . tae be alone."

She flinched.

He shook his head at her. "This is unbelievable. Have you so little trust in me?" He waved between them. "In us? This isn't the result of a spell. It's real and you're terrified."

She sucked in a heavy breath. Fear knotted her stomach. He wasn't wrong. Fear was an accurate description. She'd had plans for her life, following this forced hiatus. Plans that did not involve falling in love. When she was able to return to her family, she would begin preparations to enter the novitiate. She would not think about him then. She would not *long* for him. Because she was not in love with him.

Love. Her heart seized.

No. It couldn't be. She didn't need romance. She was the one Ballister daughter with no intention of marrying. The one daughter who would not fall prey to her mother's designs and desperately attach herself to a nobleman.

But what if it was too late? What if you're already attached?

* * *

Calder stared at her, waiting for her to answer him. She stared back at him, a horrified look on her face. He blew out a breath and dragged a hand through his hair.

He had to squash her doubts and convince her he wanted her because he did. He loved her. There was no other reason. This was his single pressing thought as the door to the bedchamber burst open. The wood length collided into the wall with a bang and three rough-looking ruffians poured into the chamber wielding blades and pistols.

Annis cried out, pulling the sheets up over her nakedness. He lunged to his feet but didn't take a step before a pistol was pressed to his chest. He stared into the cold eyes of the man wielding the weapon.

How? How could they have gained entrance into the keep? He'd been so careful. The castle was veritably sealed from the inside.

He blamed himself for being caught unawares. As vulnerable as any man could be, naked in bed with the woman he loved beside him.

Yes. He loved her.

It had begun the first moment he saw her, when she landed on her face outside her family's carriage in his courtyard—so different from her army of sisters. Different from any woman he had known.

"Did no' think ye saw the last of us, did ye?" asked the ill-kempt man at the front of the group.

"How did you . . ." The question faded as he spotted Sheila just beyond the thief's shoulder.

The thief followed his gaze. "Aye, lovely Sheila is an accommodating lass. She let us in."

Calder glared at the maid. "How could you?"

She lifted her chin proudly. "I want more fer myself than this place. They're willing tae give me a way out. They're taking me with them tae America where I can be more than a servant, where I can make something of myself."

"Hush, lass," one of the other thieves snapped. "They dinna need tae ken our plans."

The leader simply grinned. "'Tis doubtful the grand laird here would follow us all the way tae America. I warrant he'll be glad of our departure from these parts."

Calder nodded. "Indeed." Good riddance.

The thief's gaze slid past Calder, beyond his shoulder to where Annis shrank behind him. "There's a fetching bit of baggage. Perhaps I'll take her with us, as well." A wide, roguish grin spread across his face. "What say ye, lass?" he called to Annis. "Want tae see the grandeur of America?"

"Take one step near her and I'll kill you," Calder said evenly, quietly. It did not matter that he was without weapons or clothes. It did not matter that several armed men surrounded him. He'd use his bare hands and kill anyone who tried to take her from him.

Annis's fingers slipped around his arm, tightening as though prepared to cling to him, if need be.

The thief chuckled. "I see ye are partial tae the wench. Well, never accuse me of tearing true love asunder." Still laughing, he left them, calling to his men. "Bring them downstairs with the rest of them."

They were given a few minutes to attire themselves whilst a few of the brigands lurked nearby. Annis was allowed a modicum of privacy behind the dressing screen before they were herded belowstairs where the entire household huddled in the great hall. Calder eyed his staff, satisfying himself that they bore no signs of mistreatment. He kept close to Annis, one hand on her arm. She clutched the neckline of her gown in an effort to preserve her modesty. Hastily donned, it still gaped at the front.

They waited as the thieves ransacked the keep. Several of the women wept and clung together. Others glared at the thieves left to stand guard over them.

Calder seethed, but held his anger in check, scowling at the bastards invading his home and frightening his people. At Christmastime, no less. He knew the distinction should not matter, but it did.

At any point in the year this act of thievery would have chafed him ill, but at Christmas, it felt worse. This was a special time for his people. It was for that reason he forged ahead and allowed them their festivities. He'd always ignored the painful memories surrounding Christmastime and focused instead on the happiness of others. This was the first time in many years, however, that he felt happy during Yuletide. And it was because of Annis.

He'd be damned if he let these brigands ruin it.

One of the thieves strolled into the great hall with his

arms full of rolled canvases, portraits, presumably, cut from the frames. Another marched in with a chest full of Calder's mother's jewels. The indignity of it soured Calder's stomach.

"Blackguards," Annis whispered.

He bit back his own ire and gave her hand a squeeze. "These are just things," he whispered, even if the words felt like jagged bits of glass in his mouth. "Things can be replaced."

What mattered was that everyone here—his people, *Annis*—remained safe.

Her eyes met his and he could see tears brimmed there. Tears for him.

The leader entered the hall, gnawing on a great leg of poultry. Sheila stood close to his side, a knapsack over her arm. The girl preened, not looking the least bit ashamed even with so many of the staff glaring at her.

"That's this evening's dinner!" Marie thundered. Someone shushed her, but it did little good. "He's eating my goose," the cook exclaimed, quivering in outrage.

"Oh, let them have it so they can be on their way," Fenella snapped, jostling her heavy leather-bound recipe book higher in her arms.

"Och, what ye have there?" One of the villains ambled toward Fenella.

The old woman hugged the tome and shuffled back a step, which was probably not the proper reaction in the hopes of dismissing interest.

Like a predator sniffing blood, the bandit slithered closer. "Come now, old dame. Give us a look."

"Nay," she moaned, twisting away to put the book farther out of reach.

The thief gnawing on the goose leg joined in on the advance toward Fenella. "Aye, what have ye there?"

Calder glared at that recipe book, little caring if they

took it. The damnable thing had caused him enough trouble. Annis doubted his desire for her because of it.

Seized with sudden inspiration, he heard himself saying, "'Tis a magical book."

"Magic?" One of the thieves scoffed.

"Aye, there's one recipe in there for magic shortbread. 'Tis potent stuff," he bluffed.

"Laird!" Fenella screeched, her expression twisting in affront. "This book is more valuable than anything in this castle! Dinna let them have it!"

"Aye, it is valuable," he agreed, hoping he looked convincing.

"Bollocks," a thief spat.

He nodded somberly. "Everyone knows Fenella is part enchantress."

The leader smirked. "Aye? Which part is that?"

"The part that will curse you tae eternal damnation if you relieve this castle of its riches, mark my words." Calder held his gaze unflinchingly. As long as that recipe book existed in their orbit, she would always doubt his love.

A moment of silence fell. The thieves exchanged uneasy looks with each other. One made the sign of the cross and took a step back. Calder fought down a smile. He risked a glance to Annis. She watched him with wide eyes.

The leader looked to Sheila. "Does he speak true, lass? Is the old woman an enchantress?"

Sheila looked apprehensive. "There are rumors of that, aye, and she's older than the hills. Only a witch can claim so many years."

"I wouldn't risk her wrath," Calder advised. He motioned to the loot they had assembled, his family's legacy heaped in a careless pile. "Tell you what. Take the book. With our blessing. The recipes in there do more than fill a man's belly. May it bring you fortune as you begin your new lives in America. In exchange . . . leave all else behind."

Fenella huffed.

The leader lowered his half-eaten goose leg and stepped closer for a better glimpse of the book, clearly intrigued.

His cohort tugged on his arm. "Ian, I dinna think we should . . ."

Ian reached for the book with one hand. Fenella squawked and batted him away.

"Come, Fenella," Calder scolded. "Give it over with your blessing now."

"Calder," Annis whispered beside him, "what are you doing?"

He leaned in and murmured for her ears alone, "I'm getting rid of that accursed thing so you'll know it's you I want. I want *you*, Annis Ballister, and that's the truth of it."

"Fenella! Cease your caterwauling!" Angus suddenly pushed forward, plucking the leather-bound volume from her hands and shoving it at the thief.

Ian caressed the leather almost reverently.

"Ian . . . Ye dinna ken what that thing can do. Leave it," one of his men advised.

"Nay." Ian shook his head. "It will bring us good fortune. I can feel it. Just as the laird said. As long as the old woman gives it with her blessing. I'll have no curse following me across the ocean."

"She will, as long as you leave everything else and harm no one else," Calder countered.

Ian nodded. "Aye. We'll not take anything else." He stared at Fenella hopefully.

"Fenella," Calder prompted.

"Aye, verra well. Take it with my blessing," she grumbled.

"Thank ye." Smiling and exposing stained, crooked teeth, Ian handed the volume to Sheila. "Keep it safe for us, lass."

Sheila wrapped her slim arms around the book as though she would never let go.

Fenella made a strangling sound in her throat to see it go, but she did not make a move toward it.

"Now go. You've gotten everything you've come for," Calder said.

"Right we have." Ian lifted his fingers to his forehead in a casual salute. "Men, let's ride. Laird, yer hospitality will no' be forgotten. I'll think of ye fondly as we make our way across the pond."

With that, he and his men departed the keep.

Chapter Twelve

*T*his shouldn't be happening. None of it. Annis's parents shouldn't have forgotten her. At least *one* of her sisters should have stopped being selfish for a fraction of a moment to look up and realize that Annis wasn't with them. She should never have crossed paths with the duke beyond that ignominious first interaction—much less ended up in his bed. This should not be her life, but it was. Here she was, thoroughly compromised, her heart fully and irrevocably engaged, her body longing for his.

Now she would be burdened with the memory of him. The memory of his kiss, his taste, his touch running through her mind nonstop. Perhaps even worse than all that was the memory of his words, repeating in her head: *I'm getting rid of that accursed thing, so you'll know it's you I want. I want* you, *Annis Ballister.*

He couldn't have meant it.

After the thieves absconded into the night, the staff busied themselves restoring the house to rights. She couldn't quite fathom what had happened to Fenella's recipe book. Calder had given it to the thieves. It was the only thing they'd taken . . . all because of his quick thinking.

The housekeeper ushered Annis upstairs with clucking words. She had one last glimpse of Calder talking with several of his staff. Their eyes connected for a brief moment before she was whisked away.

A hot shiver rolled through her as she remembered their bodies tangled together. It had been so intense. So incredible. Certainly it wasn't like that for everyone, was it? She closed her eyes in a heavy blink. Drat. She was starting to think what they had was special.

Oh, Annis. You're in trouble here . . .

She fell back on the bed, pulled a pillow over her head and groaned, the sound muffled in the plump softness. Immediately she was assailed by the scent of him on the pillowcase. Splendid. She lifted the pillow off her face and threw it across the room with all the strength she could muster.

"Impressive."

She bolted upright at the deep voice.

The duke closed the door after him and stepped deeper inside the room. "You have quite an arm. Hopefully, you won't toss anything more dangerous than a pillow at me."

Where did all the air in the room go? "What are you doing here?"

"Why wouldn't I be here?" He advanced on her.

Her chest ached at the sight of him. She moistened her lips. "You gave away Fenella's book." *The shortbread recipe . . . It was forever gone.*

"I'll hear no more of biscuits, of magic, of spells. The book is gone and good riddance to it. There are no biscuits. What was left of them was tossed in the scrap buckets for the pigs." He stopped before her and trailed his thumb down her cheek. "The only spell I'm under is the one you've cast upon me. I want you to stay here, Annis Ballister. With me."

She shook her head. "I—I can't do that. I have to go back. The thieves are no longer a threat. It's unseemly for me to stay—"

His hands came down on either side of her, forcing her to lean back on the bed. He followed, coming over her, his features stark and intent. "I'm asking you to stay. To admit that your goal in life isn't being a nun . . . that it's not solitude. Be with me." The words dropped in the space between them like solid objects.

She blinked up at him. He didn't. He couldn't.

The moment stretched. Endless. She knew she already loved him, but . . . could this happen?

She reminded herself that this wasn't what she wanted. Romance. Love. Marriage. At least . . . she didn't think so.

Staring at his face, so resolved, so heartbreakingly handsome, she thought of her boisterous family. She thought of all the days, all the Christmases. The loud revelry. The singing of carols. The tearing through food and presents as Mama smiled fondly, watching her children shriek and squabble with each other. It actually hadn't been so very awful.

Annis actually missed it a little. Very well. More than a little.

Christmas was about love and family.

So why was she running away from it? Why was she fighting it?

Would it be so terrible to have those things with Calder? She envisioned little babies with Calder's eyes. Future Christmases. Other holidays and harvests and christenings and birthdays. Her heart swelled. What was so wrong with having all of that? Especially if she could have it with this man? Was it so impossible that he could love her? That this could be real? Why couldn't he love someone like her? He was not the standard duke. And she was not the standard heiress. Perhaps Fenella was right, and they were suited.

She opened her mouth but only stammered.

He cupped her face in both hands. "Annis? Do you love me? That's all that matters. The only thing." His thumbs moved in small circles on her cheeks. "What are you really afraid of?"

"Loving you this quickly and this deeply," she whispered. "And you not loving me back. You later realizing this is all a mistake and you don't want me."

"Too late. I already love you. That isn't a mistake and it won't be undone. You can stay here at Glencrainn." He shrugged. "Or I'll follow you. Either way you're stuck with me, Annis Ballister. I would even follow you to England, if need be."

She choked on a small sob. "Bold words indeed."

"Indeed." He nodded somberly. "I would do that for no one else."

She released a short laugh. "You really must love me."

He stared at her solemnly. "Marry me."

A long breathless moment passed, and she flung her arms around him with a broken sound. Soon they were kissing between words of forever. Clothes were hastily shed as they came together.

"You know what this means, don't you?" she asked, gasping as he bit down on her earlobe. "You get my family, too."

She grinned at his muttered curse against her throat and merrily set about divesting him of the rest of his clothing.

About Sophie Jordan

SOPHIE JORDAN grew up in the Texas Hill Country where she wove fantasies of dragons, warriors, and princesses. A former high school English teacher, she's also the *New York Times* and *USA Today* bestselling author of more than thirty romances. She now lives in Houston with her family. When she's not writing, she spends her time overloading on caffeine (iced coffee preferred), talking plotlines with anyone who will listen (including her kids), and cramming her DVR with true crime and reality shows.

To receive updates on Sophie's new and upcoming books, please sign up for her newsletter and visit her at sophiejordan.net.

Christmas in

Central Park

Joanna Shupe

Chapter One

Save the leaves of your tea for a few days, steep them
for half an hour, then strain them. Use the liquid to
wash your varnished wood. It washes better than soap.
—Mrs. Walker's Weekly, *New York
Daily Gazette, December 1889*

*O*pinions, they said, were like elbows; everyone had one
or two.

Miss Rose Walker was fortunate. Not only was she full
of opinions, she was paid to give them out.

Rose stepped out of the elevator and into the noisy newspaper office located on Park Row. Reporters dashed to and
fro, the constant hum of typewriters serving as an undercurrent to the chaos. The men were writing stories and following leads, eagerly informing the public of corruption
and wrongdoing. How she longed to join this frenetic club
of male journalism.

Instead, she was the paper's best-kept secret—Mrs.
Walker. In her popular weekly newspaper column, the
reclusive Mrs. Walker provided elegant recipes, cleaning
tips, and relationship advice from her husband's mansion
in New York City.

Never mind that Rose was not married, could not boil
water, and lived in a tiny room at a ladies' boardinghouse.

Lies, she had quickly learned, always sold better than the truth.

Head down, Rose hurried to her boss's office, her latest column on spring gardening in her hand. She spoke to no one and not a soul recognized her. The editor in chief, Mr. Pike, was the only person on the *Gazette* staff who knew Mrs. Walker's true identity.

It was a start. Someday, she would have a desk here in the newspaper office, where she would reign as the best-known writer in the country. Then, at the end of the day, she would go to her fancy home on Central Park, like the one in which her mother worked, and relax with her handsome husband.

Keep your feet firmly on the ground, her mother often said when Rose's attention wandered. Yet Rose believed in dreams and lofty goals. There was more for her in this world than hiding behind a fictitious name.

Not that she was ungrateful for Mrs. Walker. Posing as the society matron had given Rose her first newspaper job and the column had developed a devoted following. Soon she'd work her way up, write other stories, and become a famous journalist recognized on the street.

Pike's door was partially ajar. When she peeked inside, she saw the gray-haired man putting things from his desk into a small trunk. Was he . . . packing? "Mr. Pike."

His head shot up. "Walker. Come in." He hardly ever spoke in complete sentences, his speech as rapid-fire as the pace of the newsroom. It was one of the things she liked best about him.

"Are you moving offices?"

"No." He straightened and put his hands on his hips. Bulky white sideburns could not hide his sullen expression. "Been fired."

"Fired?" Hadn't he been working here forever?

"Yes, fired. Sacked. Dismissed. Shown the door."

"I know what *fired* means. Why on earth have you been let go?"

He looked at her as if she were cracked. "Haven't you seen yesterday's papers? Any of them?"

"No. I've been writing my column." She held up the envelope containing her five hundred words. "I have it here."

"Leave it. I'll give it to another editor. Reese, maybe."

"Who?" Pike was her lifeline at the *Gazette*. "Please, tell me what happened."

Instead of answering, he picked up a newspaper and tossed it on his desk. It was a copy of the *New York World*.

GAZETTE TAKES BRIBES IN BLACKOUT EXPOSÉ
EDITOR PAID BY ELECTRIC COMPANIES
TO BLAME WORKERS

"Oh no." She glanced up at Pike. "This . . . This wasn't you, was it?"

"No, it was Frank MacHenry. But Havermeyer ousted me, too. Says it's my staff, my responsibility."

Duke Havermeyer III, the president of Havermeyer Publishing and publisher of the *Gazette*, was rumored to be ruthless and unforgiving. His great-grandfather had made a fortune in the copper mines of Montana before coming to New York City and buying a failing newspaper. He quickly turned it around, and an empire was soon forged after that first success. Havermeyer Publishing Company currently owned ten newspapers around the country—ten newspapers that all published Mrs. Walker's Weekly.

Havermeyer's harsh reputation aside, firing Pike hardly seemed fair.

"That is absurd."

"Havermeyer never goes back on a decision once it is

made." Pike continued throwing things into the small trunk on the floor. "And he's the owner. He wants me out, I am out."

"You're a great editor. I'm sorry to see you go."

He sighed. "Me, too. Spent forty-two years at this paper. Worked my way up under Havermeyer number two."

"What will you do? Work for another paper?"

"Doubtful. I'm too old. Spend more time with my grandchildren, I suppose."

Grandchildren? Rose had always been so focused on the work, she'd never inquired about his personal life. *Some reporter you will make, Rose.*

"Before I forget," Pike said. "Havermeyer wants to meet with you. I told him you'd be here this morning to drop off your column. So go on up to the top floor and his secretary will show you in."

Rose's stomach sank, like that time she had attempted Mrs. Walker's lemon loaf recipe for herself and forgot to add sugar. Why on earth would Havermeyer want to see her? Was she being fired, as well?

Oh God. She needed this job. She had no savings to speak of and the last thing she wanted to do was go into service, like her mother. Rose had seen firsthand the damage a lifetime of scrubbing, bending, and washing could do to a woman. She wanted a different life for herself, one that wouldn't work her fingers to the bone. And one that would allow her mother to quit before she dropped from exhaustion.

Moreover, Rose liked her job. People from all over the country wrote to ask her advice.

No, he is not firing you. You are Mrs. Walker. Why would he fire his most popular advice columnist?

She remembered the first time she saw Duke Havermeyer III. A tall, striking man in a smart suit had breezed by her at the elevators. The elevator operator had addressed him as Mr. Havermeyer and Rose had unabashedly stared, eager for a better look at the renowned publishing magnate.

Somehow, she hadn't been surprised by his handsomeness. He had broad shoulders and long legs, along with dark hair that curled just so over his collar. High, sharp cheekbones, the kind found only in those with excellent breeding. She had sized him up quickly, an arrogant and pretty package, one who lived up to his reputation as a cold and calculating scion of industry.

Then she had seen the scar, an unapologetic slash directly above his right eyebrow. The mark intrigued her. It made him imperfect, which she found much more interesting. He looked like a pirate in a morning suit, ready to run a cutlass through anyone who stood in his way.

This led to hours of research, with her devouring every newspaper she could get her hands on. She learned that, though Havermeyer was unmarried, he always appeared in the business pages, never the social columns. Was there no fiancée? No mistress? For all she could discover, he did nothing but work at his company. For some reason that fascinated her, as well.

Had she hoped for another look at him every time she was in the building? Most definitely. Worse, she made a habit of occasionally loitering on the walk, just to see him climb into his brougham and drive away. She fantasized that he would see her, stop, then approach her with a half smile on his face and ask to escort her to Delmonico's or Sherry's, one of the fancy restaurants where the elite New Yorkers dined.

Now he wanted to see her—and not to ask her to dinner. Probably.

A girl could always dream, of course.

She folded her hands. "What does he want with me?"

"No idea, but you'd better hurry. Havermeyer does not like to be kept waiting."

"Does he know . . . ?"

Pike gave a dry chuckle that lacked mirth. "No, I've stuck with our story. Everyone believes Mrs. Walker to be fiercely private, uncomfortable with public attention of any kind. Whether you choose to tell him or not is up to you, but after this scandal . . . Well, if you like your job you might want to stay quiet."

So she'd need to pose as Mrs. Walker, married society maven. She glanced down at her simple outfit of a cream shirtwaist and brown skirt. Not very fancy, considering Mrs. Walker's position as an elegant woman about town. And she hadn't painted her face today, which might have aged her a few years.

Well, nothing to be done for it now. She'd see Havermeyer exactly like this and hope for the best. Besides, hadn't one of her great-aunts worked as an actress back in Dublin? If Rose kept her poise, she could fool anyone. She could handle one meeting with the company owner.

Pike continued sorting through papers and she stood there, unsure what to do. This would be the last time she'd see his weathered face and gray hair. He'd been a mentor to her, the only person she'd known at the newspaper for two years. Moreover, she and Pike had invented the Mrs. Walker persona together. What was an appropriate send-off for an editor in chief? "Mr. Pike . . ." Her arms fell uselessly to her sides.

He stopped and offered a small smile full of kindness. "Now, none of that. You have a bright future ahead of you. Mrs. Walker is HPC's most valuable asset and I like to think I had a small part in that. Nothing but fond memories, Rose."

Nodding, she said, "I hope you will keep in touch. I'll miss you."

"Same goes to you, Mrs. Walker. Now, get up to see Havermeyer—or else we may both lose our jobs."

* * *

Duke Havermeyer tossed yet another competitor's newspaper on his desk. *Goddammit.* How much bad news could one man take?

It had started at breakfast yesterday when he learned of the bribery allegations involving a member of the *Gazette* staff. He'd immediately hurried to the office, where an emergency meeting of the Havermeyer Publishing Company's board of directors had been called. The board was furious over the scandal and the damage to the newspaper's reputation. Predictably, the stock price had plummeted. This would affect the company's bottom line, and if Duke did not fix it quickly, the board could replace him as president of the company.

A Havermeyer ousted as president of Havermeyer Publishing. It was unthinkable—but not impossible.

Not that he was apathetic about this scandal. Indeed, he'd been livid over the allegations. To lie, accept bribes, and cheapen the word of his family's newspaper? Unforgivable. Nine staff members had been fired in total, including his editor in chief, Mr. Pike. Duke liked Pike, a holdover from his father's days at the *Gazette*. He'd been sorry to see the man go, but the newspaper came first.

The newspapers always came first.

The Havermeyer men were raised to know this from birth. Duke had accepted it and learned all he could about publishing in his twenty-eight years. This resulted in an expansion neither his father nor his grandfather had been able to pull off. Thanks to Duke, HPC owned ten newspapers across the country—soon to be eleven.

And those eleven newspapers would thrive only if the news on their pages could be trusted. Otherwise they were printing sheets of garbage.

A man's only as good as his word.

How often had his father said as much? A hundred times? A thousand? Duke meant to restore that reputation by any means necessary.

His secretary appeared, her eyes glowing with excitement. Mrs. Jenkins was dependably even-tempered, so what had happened to cause such a reaction? "Sir, Mrs. Walker is here. *The* Mrs. Walker," she breathed, as if clarification were necessary.

It was not. Duke had been expecting Mrs. Walker, one of his publishing company's biggest stars—and a key element in his plan of attack to restore faith in the Havermeyer Publishing Company. "Send her in, please."

"Yes, sir. And you might try to smile. Put her at ease."

He stood and straightened his vest. Though he resented the reminder, he supposed Mrs. Jenkins was right. He needed Mrs. Walker's help and scaring her wouldn't do— unless she refused him, of course.

Forcing a grin on his face, he crossed his arms and waited. He was actually looking forward to this meeting. Mrs. Walker was quite the celebrity in town, a society maven that Pike had somehow convinced to write a column. Duke started reading her column shortly after it began, uncertain this sort of "news" was what the company needed. Serious stories, not fluff, had always appealed best to their readers.

How wrong he'd been. Mrs. Walker became an instant draw. Letters to her nearly overflowed the HPC mailroom after the first week. He'd soon understood why. She had a clever way with her words, putting the reader at ease and never talking down to them. Her columns were humorous, informative, and mature. In addition, she included personal details about herself as examples. It left the reader with the impression that he or she knew Mrs. Walker, as if the columnist were a close friend. Duke was no exception. Utterly charmed, he read her column each week and devoured these tidbits. He learned she lived uptown with Mr. Walker, the couple having no children. She adored baking and gardening, was apprehensive of dogs after a childhood incident, and struggled with needlepoint. And she had a wit and intelligence not found in most women.

In fact, he was counting on that wit and intelligence to help rescue HPC.

A young woman entered—and he glanced over her shoulder, searching for Mrs. Walker. No one else entered, however, and his secretary closed the door.

This was Mrs. Walker?

The smile died on his lips. She was a far cry from the sophisticated matronly type he'd expected. Not that she was unpleasant. Merely unexpected. There was nothing remarkable whatsoever about her appearance. Light brown hair was piled under a plain bonnet, and a modest shirtwaist had been paired with an unflattering brown skirt. The only visible adornment was the cameo pinned at her throat.

She watched him carefully, unabashedly, with piercing blue eyes that conjured images of calm azure oceans and cloudless skies. Many women found his stare disconcerting, but Mrs. Walker didn't glance away or bat her lashes. There was a challenge there, one he recognized but did not fully understand. It was as if she saw through him, everything he was, down to the marrow of his bones.

He fought the urge to fidget.

"You are very young," he blurted, then winced at his rudeness. *Good Lord, man. Get a hold of yourself.*

Instead of being offended, she held his gaze and cocked her head.

"How old should I be, then?"

Shaking off his surprise, he offered his hand in greeting. "Mrs. Walker, it is nice to finally meet you. I am Duke Havermeyer. Please, sit."

They shook and then settled into the armchairs near

his desk. She folded her hands in her lap. "You wished to see me?"

"Yes. I won't waste your time with pleasantries but rather get right to it. I have a request. Undoubtedly you've heard of the scandal surrounding the *Gazette*." She gave a brief nod and he continued. "The accusations are true, unfortunately, and the paper's reputation has taken a nasty hit. This has led to a much larger problem."

"Which is?"

Her demeanor was cool, reserved. Direct with no prevaricating. Exactly like her column. He liked that. Perhaps he'd merely been around reporters for too long, but he preferred someone who got to the damned point. "My board of directors. They are nervous and unpredictable on the best of days. After yesterday, they are downright skittish. They've lost confidence in the newspaper—and me. I need to win them back or there may be . . . unpleasant consequences. That is where you come in."

"Me?"

"Yes, you. Mrs. Walker is the crown jewel of the Havermeyer Publishing Company. You write our most popular column, and you're the woman everyone wishes to befriend. Who dispenses sage advice with one hand, and whips up extravagant meals with the other."

She narrowed her gaze as if she were suspicious of the flattery. Granted, he had laid it on a bit thick, but he hadn't lied. The woman possessed an impressive breadth of knowledge.

"And how does all that help you with the board?"

"I need for you to host a Christmas dinner party for the board of directors."

Her eyes rounded. "A dinner party? For the board?"

"Now, I know Christmas is only a week away, but I have every faith that you, a woman so comfortable with entertaining, will be able to pull it together."

"I couldn't possibly. It . . . It is not enough time."

He waved his hand. If anyone could work this miracle, it was Mrs. Walker. She was a household magician. "Nonsense. The woman who managed tropical plants and pineapple for her New Year's celebration? The woman who boasts of having the best, most organized staff in the city? I have full confidence in your abilities, madam."

"But this is your board, not some group of society wives," she said.

"Don't worry about that. You have an unlimited budget to work with and the board will undoubtedly be dazzled by anything you do. They'll be thrilled merely to meet you. Mrs. Walker is one of New York City's biggest mysteries and I am giving you to them for one evening." She didn't appear convinced, so he added, "I realize this is an imposition and that you are intensely private. However, I must insist. It's for the good of the paper."

She rubbed her eyes with her fingers. Time stretched, her chest rising and falling rapidly in the silence. A seasoned negotiator, Duke knew to remain quiet to let his quarry think.

"What happens if I refuse?" she finally asked.

A smart question, one he had anticipated. He cocked his head, his voice turning hard. "I am certain you have read your contract, Mrs. Walker, but in case you've forgotten, allow me to recall the fine print. You do not actually own the Mrs. Walker's Weekly column. We do. Specifically, *I* do. Therefore, I could hire anyone to answer those letters and write her column. It does not need to be *you*."

She swallowed, her delicate throat working. "A dinner party? With seven or eight courses?"

"Six? I realize I've sprung this on you without much notice. Now, this will take place on December twenty-second, so as to not take away from family celebrations."

"That's only five days from now!"

"As I said, I have full confidence in you."

"I appreciate your faith, Mr. Havermeyer, but I simply cannot. Why not hire a chef and tell everyone that I—"

"No." The one-word answer cracked through the office. "No subterfuge. This must all be aboveboard. You will prepare the menu, oversee the meal, and dine with us. Your staff will be on hand, of course."

"My staff?"

"The dinner absolutely must take place at your home, Mrs. Walker." Hadn't he been clear? When he imagined this conversation, she'd been much more amenable. How hard could this be for a woman who had once hosted the viceroy of India? "The board will love the peek inside your home at the holidays. It lends a more personal touch to the evening. Mr. Walker is welcome to join, as well, of course."

She paled, her hand shooting out to grip the armrest. "Of course."

He steeled himself and pushed aside any guilt over his unusual request and the disruption it would cause her. She was an employee and HPC should be everyone's top priority.

Still, perhaps he was being a bit harsh. He cleared his throat. "I would consider it a great personal favor—and I do not often ask others for help."

"I . . ." She drew in a deep breath. "Then how could I possibly refuse?"

Chapter Two

*Y*ou've agreed to *what*?"

Rose traced the edge of a black floor tile with her boot. She and her friend, Henry, were in the butler's pantry of the Lowes' large home on Fifth Avenue, where her mother had worked for over ten years. Henry was the second footman here and currently locking the breakfast dishes away while Rose filled him in on Havermeyer's request. The household was being shut down for the holiday, the owners on their way to Newport. "I told you. I had no choice."

"There is always a choice. You say no."

"And lose my position as Mrs. Walker? No, I cannot. You *know* why I cannot." As her oldest friend, Henry was well versed in Rose's plans for a better life, a freer life—for her *and* her mother.

He glanced up from the dishes, his expression full of sympathy. "Yes, I do, but she would not want this. For you to lie and swindle people."

Perhaps, but Rose would not budge. She and her mother needed the money from her job at the *Gazette*. "It is one dinner party. How hard could it be?"

He huffed a laugh and counted off on his fingers. "Let's see. You must find a cook, a husband, a staff, and a furnished home uptown to use as your own, one that no one recognizes." Shaking his head, he turned back to his dishes. "I wish you luck."

Only one year older than she was, Henry had been her friend for ages. Their families had been neighbors while growing up downtown and he was like a brother to Rose. Her mother had harbored hopes in regard to a match between her and Henry, but there hadn't ever been a spark, not even before he had proposed to Bridget, another housemaid in the Lowe home.

That made her think of Duke Havermeyer. Her stomach fluttered merely recalling his large frame and intense brown eyes. Mercy, he was even better looking up close than in the far-off glimpses she'd had of him over the last few months, not to mention younger. The man couldn't be much past thirty years of age.

And he would fire her if she did not find a way to make this dinner party happen.

She pushed down her panic and returned to the problem at hand. "I have been thinking on this—"

"Ah, hell."

She ignored that. "I have an easy solution. I'll come down with some horrible condition the day before and tell Havermeyer I must regrettably cancel."

Henry spun around, one dark brow cocked. "Are you serious? What if he merely reschedules?"

"Why bother after Christmas?"

"There is always New Year's. You cannot think to put him off forever, Rose."

Goodness, Henry was right. Havermeyer had seemed quite determined. Undoubtedly, he'd find some other way to back Rose into a corner. How on earth was she supposed to make this happen? "You must help me think of a way to pull it off."

"Absolutely not. You need to level with him and hope he's not too angry. Perhaps if you inform him of the situation—"

"No, it's too risky. He'll fire me on the spot." After all, hadn't he said anyone could write her column? If she wished to continue as Mrs. Walker, she must find a way for this to work.

Henry folded his arms and leaned against the counter, his disapproval clear in the flat lines of his mouth. "I told you not to make Mrs. Walker's life so grand. Inventing all those dignitaries and European aristocrats as your dinner guests merely built her legend up to unreasonable proportions. That you've eluded discovery before now is a dashed miracle."

"I still haven't been discovered—nor will I if we figure this out."

"*We?*"

"Yes, you must help me. I cannot go to my mother with this problem. Who else will I turn to if not you? Please, Henry."

The moment stretched, and he stared at her, his expression blank. She clasped her hands under her chin and held perfectly still.

Finally, after what seemed ages, he exhaled loudly. "Fine, I will help you. But let it be said I believe this to be a terrible idea."

"So noted," she said quickly, bouncing on her toes.

He rolled his eyes heavenward. "So, what's your first problem, Mrs. Walker?"

"An empty mansion with an owner no one's met."

He stroked his chin. "Wait, what if we don't need an empty mansion?"

"We do. We must have a place to host the dinner."

He waved the comment away. "What if the Walker home is undergoing extensive repairs and you are using the Lowes' house instead?"

"Henry! I cannot use this house." She lowered her voice, though no one was about. "I could not do that to your employers. What if you and my mother lose your positions?"

"You are right. It is too risky. I certainly don't wish to be fired. And you know how particular Mrs. Lowe is about her things. She'd find out somehow, especially if gossip circulates. Why not let Havermeyer host it?"

"Because he wants Mrs. Walker to show off her home for the holidays. It lends a more personal touch, he said."

"So his house is out. There's a place on Seventy-First Street that has a For Sale sign in the window. Right off Central Park. I walk by it every night. Still furnished and it's been on the market for the last six months."

"We couldn't use an empty house, could we? It belongs to someone."

"I cannot see that you have much of a choice," Henry pointed out. "And what does it matter, for a few hours? They've obviously moved elsewhere. If we slip the real estate agent a few bucks he might look the other way for the night. No one will ever be the wiser."

Havermeyer's generous allowance could help with this. And yet, it did not *feel* right. "What if one of the board members knows the owner? Or one of the neighbors?"

"Then you claim to have purchased the home recently and hope the truth is never discovered. Really, Rose. Unless you know of a mansion we may rent for the evening, I cannot see any other option."

"You are right, of course. It all just seems so . . ."

"Wrong?" Henry glared down his nose in that disapproving manner of his she knew so well.

"I was going to say risky. The lies are piling up on top of themselves."

"There is a surefire way to stop that. Tell Havermeyer the truth."

"You know I cannot. He'll fire me, considering all that is happening at the newspaper."

"So shall I investigate this empty house for you?"

She sighed. What other choice had she? "Yes, but I'll go with you. Think we might be able to convince any of the staff here to help? A footman and a maid or two would do. I'm able to pay them—or rather Havermeyer is able to pay them. He has provided a generous allowance for the event."

Henry stretched to put a crystal water goblet high on a shelf. "They'd appreciate that, though it's likely unnecessary. Most of the staff would throw themselves in front of a streetcar for you."

Rose had been a regular fixture in the Lowe home for more than a decade. Her mother worked as an upstairs maid for years, then transferred to the kitchens when her knees had started to ache. So the staff treated Rose as one of their own, celebrating when she had landed the job at the *Gazette*. They had also generously offered to answer questions for her advice column while keeping her identity a secret. She adored them all for it.

"That is everything but the cooking," Henry said. "You might ask Mrs. Riley to help. Her daughter's about to have a baby but she might spare the time. Then all you would need to do is let the footmen serve."

"Not quite everything." Inhaling a deep breath, she plowed onward. "There is just one more tiny, small, teeny thing I need."

Henry froze in the midst of picking up a fork. "No, no, no. Not me. Anyone but me."

"Henry, you must. Who else is there for me to ask?"

His eyes were wild when he turned around. "What about that Elmer fellow you went skating with last month?"

"You mean the man renting ice skates at the pond? Be serious. I haven't anyone else to ask." She placed her hands together, pleading. "Please, Henry. Please, I am begging you."

"I . . . cannot. I will muck it up for you, Rosie. I do not know the first thing about society and manners. I'm the worst choice for Mr. Rose Walker."

"Stop right there. No one knows the silverware and table

manners as well as you, and you see these society gents nearly every night. So you drink port with the men for a few moments after dinner . . . How bad could it be?"

He jerked a thumb toward the windows. "What about Bert? He'd be a fine choice."

"He is a *groom*, Henry, and he smells like old fish. No, it must be you. Besides, we've been friends for ages. Playing at an old married couple won't prove too difficult. Unless you think Bridget will mind—"

"Bridget is the least of our problems. I am terrible at pretending. You know this. I have never been able to tell a lie, not even little ones—and this is hardly little, Rose."

"No one will find out except for the few staff members we ask to help. You said it yourself—a few hours for one night, Henry. *Please*."

He dragged a hand down his face. "I am going to regret this, I just know it."

She hoped none of them had cause for regret. This had to go without a hitch—or her job at the *Gazette* and dreams of reporting were over. "Thank you, thank you, thank you!" She leaned in and kissed his cheek. "You are the absolute best, Henry."

He smiled at her fondly. "Are you going to tell your mother?"

"Goodness, no. We must swear everyone to secrecy, at least until it's finished. I wouldn't care to worry her."

"Not to mention she'd never let you follow through with it."

True. Mama still did not understand why Rose had to write as Mrs. Walker and not under her own name. But Rose had handled the family finances for years, and she hadn't the heart to tell her mother of the direness of their situation. They both needed to keep their jobs. "I'd prefer to wait and tell her when it's over."

"That's probably an excellent idea."

"See, I told you this would be easy."

He grimaced and resumed his polishing. "Rosie, I've known you almost all my life. You are stubborn and much too inquisitive for your own good. Nothing is easy when you are involved."

* * *

A light snow dusted the city's streets three nights later as Duke's brougham rolled to a stop. Turned out Mrs. Walker lived in a modest town house on Seventy-First Street overlooking Central Park. Modest, but welcoming. There was a tiny evergreen tree in a large pot on the stoop and fresh garlands wrapped the iron railing. Her Christmas tree, colorful and bright, shone through the front window. How festive. The woman really did think of everything.

He'd been right to let her host tonight. His home was not nearly this welcoming. In fact, he hadn't decorated for Christmas in years. There wasn't a point to it, really. The tree and holly remained for just a few short weeks, then were thrown out like trash. Only written words were permanent, archived for future generations. Everything else was a waste of time.

Besides, he had no family. No wife. Not even a distant cousin or great-aunt to welcome at the holidays. His father had run off all the relatives, mostly in fear they would try to claim an inheritance when the old man died. Now there was no one left. No one but Duke.

He didn't mind the solitude. It allowed him to focus on the newspapers, and the results had borne fruit.

If only someone would remind the HPC board of that.

The board and HPC investors had grown very rich off Duke's daring and foresight over the last ten years. Yet, at the first patch of trouble, they intimated that new leadership might be required—including *the president of the company*. It was insulting. He'd be furious if he weren't so terrified of losing it all.

He threw open the door and stepped out. It was imperative that tonight went well, that he wooed his way back into the board's favor and helped them forget the scandal.

The front door cracked as he approached. An older butler appeared and pulled the heavy wood open slowly. Duke took the last step and crossed over the threshold.

The inside was bright and cheery. Lemon polish scented the air and every surface was gleaming. Tasteful decorations were carefully placed to draw the eye but not overwhelm. Most impressive was the large chandelier hanging from the ceiling, its crystal pieces shining like diamonds.

The tension between his shoulders eased somewhat. He had barely entered and already it was everything he'd expected of Mrs. Walker's home. This dinner was his best idea yet.

"Welcome, me lord," the butler said through a heavy brogue. "A wee bit early, ain't ya?"

Duke blinked at the man's greeting, not sure if he was more surprised by the incorrect address or the rudeness. So, not everything was as expected. "Just *sir* will do. And I hope my early arrival does not pose a problem."

"Well, come on then. Lemme take your things and such forth."

"Mr. Havermeyer." Mrs. Walker appeared as he was shrugging out of his coat, her face flushed and a polite smile firmly in place. Then those startling eyes met his and he almost forgot to breathe. Her red-and-gold gown was clearly a nod to the season, and even Saint Nicholas himself would have glanced twice at that plunging neckline. A healthy expanse of bosom was displayed above the lace edge of her dress, her skin absolutely flawless.

Mr. Walker was one lucky man.

Duke forced his gaze firmly on her face. Married women were off-limits. Even fetching ones.

He bowed. "Mrs. Walker."

She smoothed a few stray hairs back into place. "Good evening. Won't you follow me to the salon?"

Duke offered his arm and she led him toward the right. On the way, Mrs. Walker leaned around his back, and he caught her mouthing something to the butler. Unfortunately, he couldn't make out the words. "Everything all right? I apologize for my early arrival, but I wanted to ensure you had what you needed."

"Never fear, all is ready. Your budget was more than generous. I couldn't possibly have spent all that money."

He nodded, recalling her impressive column on the benefits of frugal living. "I did not wish to stifle your creativity in any way, especially when the tight timetable was at my insistence."

"True enough, which was why I didn't hesitate in spending what I did." She nodded at the footman as they entered the drawing room. "We'll start the champagne now, Peter."

"Yes, madam."

Duke followed her deeper into the elegant room. Delicate French furniture, thick Persian rugs, and brass lamps abounded. The wallpaper, though clean, appeared a little faded—not that he judged her. He would never presume to know more about wall coverings than *the* Mrs. Walker.

"Your butler seems a colorful character," he said.

"He is, indeed. Been with the family for years and a bit set in his ways, I'm afraid."

A young brown-haired man dressed in a black evening suit walked stiffly into the room, his attention entirely on Mrs. Walker. Was this her husband? Duke hadn't spent any time pondering the type of man she'd married, but Mr. Walker's bookish appearance and reserved manner was somewhat unexpected. This was no gregarious charmer or boisterous industrialist. This was a scholar more tempted by lectures and experiments than dinner parties.

He wondered if theirs was a happy marriage.

Shaking off that inappropriate thought, he stuck out his hand. "Mr. Walker, I presume? I am Duke Havermeyer."

Mr. Walker pumped Duke's hand once. "Nice to meet you, Mr. Havermeyer. Welcome to our home."

"Thank you, and I must express my gratitude for hosting us on such short notice."

"Not a problem. Our staff is adept at these sorts of things."

Exactly what Duke had assumed, considering Mrs. Walker's columns.

"Your home is lovely," he said to them both, realizing he hadn't properly complimented their efforts when he arrived. "Exactly what I expected."

The couple exchanged a quick look. "Thank you," Mr. Walker said. "We moved in recently, so we are still settling."

"Mr. Walker," she said, "perhaps you would check with Cook to see how dinner's progressing." She then took Duke's elbow and turned him toward the well-lit tree near the window. "Mr. Havermeyer, have you seen our tree?"

The ten-foot tree was spectacular. He'd never seen one quite like it. Strategically placed amongst the boughs, ribbons, and ornaments were electric lights, a relatively new trend amongst wealthy New Yorkers. Stood to reason Mrs. Walker would insist on the latest innovation for her tree. "It is breathtaking. I cannot recall ever seeing a more festive tree."

"Thank you. I am proud of it. Is your tree similar?"

"Oh, I don't bother with a tree."

Her head tilted as she studied him. "A tree is hardly a

bother. Besides, I assumed you would have a team of decorators outfit your home for the holidays."

"I'm afraid not. Perhaps when I have a family one day." An event he could not begin to picture in his mind. He knew nothing of small children and even less about being a decent husband and father. His own father had certainly set a poor example.

Besides, short liaisons were best, with women who wanted nothing more than a quick tumble. Who would never complain when he put his business needs above his personal ones.

"Incidentally, what does Mr. Walker do?"

She waved her hand, gaze sliding away. "He is in silver."

"Ah, yes." Walker had probably struck it rich somewhere out in Dakota and traveled east. "We should swap stories, then. My great-grandfather mined for copper out in Montana."

"I'd heard that. Good, here is the champagne." She nearly lunged for the footman carrying a tray of champagne. Had Duke made her uncomfortable somehow?

He'd try harder to put her at ease. Just tonight, he needed her relaxed and friendly enough to impress the HPC board.

That reminded him. Reaching into an inner pocket, he withdrew a faded piece of paper. "Before I forget, I have another favor to ask of you."

She frowned, her expression suddenly wary. He forged ahead anyway. Undoubtedly, she wouldn't like the request, but he was the boss, after all. "I thought it might be fun for the board members to see you at work in the kitchen. You've written extensively about your love of baking and the recipes you have mastered. You make it sound easy. Something all women are able to do."

He was rambling. *Get to the point, man.*

Holding out the paper, he continued. "I have a Havermeyer family recipe for shortbread cookies that came over with my mother from Scotland. Perhaps after dinner you could whip these up while we watch?"

Her mouth opened, then snapped shut. She remained mute, staring at him with her startling blue gaze. He hadn't expected her to express joy at the request, but her silence concerned him.

"I realize this is an unorthodox request," he said. "However, there are but a few ingredients listed, and I am certain it'll be a snap for a woman of your talents."

"I . . . don't know what to say."

"Say yes. No one's made them since I was a boy, and I cannot even remember the taste. I'm dying of curiosity."

"What if I make them tomorrow and send everyone a box—?"

"No. It'll be far more memorable for the board to observe you actually creating them. Furthermore, that it's my family recipe connects the experience to me and to the newspaper."

"And that's important to you?"

"Very."

He decided to confide in her. She deserved to know the truth, given his strange requests. "You see, the board could, through some clever maneuvering, remove me as president of HPC, a company my family has built up and overseen for four generations. I need the board to equate me with the company." A non-Havermeyer running HPC? He could never allow that to happen. Tonight, it was imperative to remind everyone of his legacy, his family's roots in starting the company. Rose Walker could help him accomplish this. "Please, Mrs. Walker."

"The kitchens will be in disarray after the meal—"

"I'll give you a thousand-dollar bonus." A staggering amount of money, but he hardly cared. He wanted her to agree and he would cajole, bribe, and threaten to get his way.

Then he remembered his surroundings—the stunning tree, this house, and Mr. Walker's silver fortune—and immediately felt like an idiot. Mrs. Walker didn't need money; yet, she had cared about keeping her job at the paper. He blurted, "Furthermore, I won't fire you."

"Mr. Havermeyer—"

"Call me Duke, please. Now, do you plan to help me and keep your job?"

She blinked, her cheeks turning a flattering shade of pink. "It will be my pleasure."

Chapter Three

*R*ose's heart was galloping in her chest. The HPC board of directors, all eight of them, were now convened in the drawing room. Only three had brought their wives, but the group was still quite large. Duke held court, his tall frame the center of attention. The man was magnetic, his confidence and presence drawing everyone closer just to be near him—except for Rose. She was in no hurry to join the party. She was still attempting to understand how he kept maneuvering her into doing what he wanted.

No wonder the man had amassed an empire. Who could say no to him?

Not her, obviously. The beautiful man had stared down at her with his mesmerizing dark gaze, the rough scar making him somehow appear vulnerable, and her resistance melted like hot candle wax.

She blew out a long breath. Goodness, she hoped she appeared calmer than she felt, because her heart was threatening to skip out of her chest. She, along with a dozen members of the Lowes' staff, had pulled off a minor miracle getting them this far. After paying off the real estate agent, they had borrowed enough furnishings to decorate four rooms and the entryway, while the rest of the home remained barren and dirty, a housemaid's worst nightmare. However, as long as none of the guests wandered, the ruse should work.

Except for the cooking demonstration in the kitchen after dinner. How in God's name would she manage it? After Duke's unusual request, she had raced belowstairs. She instructed the kitchen maids to gather the ingredients listed on the recipe card and then clean the kitchen as best they could to make it presentable. Mrs. Riley had unfortunately already departed, so Rose hadn't even been able to ask the cook for advice.

How hard could it be to make shortbread cookies? All one needed to do was follow the instructions carefully.

Never mind that her last three attempts at baking cookies had all failed miserably, each time for a different reason.

"Breathe," Henry said quietly at her side. The two of them watched the board members from the entryway. "You'll figure out the cookies. Just stick to the recipe—and stop staring at Havermeyer. You're supposed to be happily married."

She sent him a sharp glance over the rim of her champagne glass. "I have no idea what you are talking about."

"You know exactly what I am talking about—not that I can blame you. He is striking."

The man was indeed striking. Her skin prickled with awareness whenever she was near him. "And unmarried."

"Staked a claim, have you?"

"Don't be ridiculous. He is my employer. And he thinks I'm married to you."

"Good point. Though I must say, I've noticed him watching you when your attention is elsewhere."

Duke Havermeyer, watching *her*? Likely to ensure she didn't screw up his campaign to win back the board. "Sure—and next you'll say you have a bridge in Brooklyn to sell me."

He chuckled. "Doubt if you must, but we shall see. What is the story behind the scar, I wonder?"

She studied the fascinating mark on Havermeyer's forehead. "Initially, I thought a circus accident, or perhaps a broken bottle in a saloon brawl. Of course, there is always the angry mob theory. My current favorite, however, is a crystal figurine thrown by a scorned lover."

"I can see you've hardly given this any thought at all," he drawled. "Is your journalistic heart quivering with desperate curiosity?"

Yes, it rather was. "If not for the scar, he would be too pretty. I just find it interesting, is all."

"If you say so. Shall we mingle?"

"I suppose—oh, I forgot. Havermeyer thinks you made your fortune in silver mining."

His body jerked in surprise. "He *what*?"

She patted his arm. "To be fair, I told him you were in silver. He chose to interpret it as silver mining. Don't be surprised if he asks you about it."

Henry began to sputter, but Rose ignored him, towing him into the room. "There she is," a booming male voice— Duke's—said. "There's our most popular writer."

"Good evening," she said to the room at large. "Welcome to our home."

One by one, the guests approached, hands outstretched and smiles in place. They all seemed genuinely happy to meet her, and she tried to play her part. Duke watched from a distance, arms folded over his chest, a proud expression on his handsome face. His eyes, though . . . His gaze burned with a raw intensity she could not name, one that warmed her in dark places, places an unmarried woman should not yet know about.

Yes, but you are playing a married woman tonight. Perhaps a little flirtation—

Heavens, from where had that thought come? Staring at her nearly empty glass of champagne, she promptly handed it off to Henry. No more spirits. She couldn't ruin the evening with inappropriate thoughts about her employer, even if he was the most compelling man in the room.

Besides, what did she know about men? She hadn't ever been seriously courted, too busy with her writing career to bother. There would be time enough for romance later in life, after she and her mother were financially secure. For now, her focus had to remain on her job as Mrs. Rose Walker.

The board members expressed admiration for her and her column, while the wives peppered her with questions and comments about Mrs. Walker's tips. Did cayenne pepper really work for mice? Could one truly remove stains on the skin by using the juice from a tomato? What did she think about using kerosene to prevent rust on silver?

She answered them patiently. After all, women were the reason her column had succeeded. Rich, poor, middle-class . . . It made no difference. Her readers came from all backgrounds. So the least she could do was share Mrs. Walker's wisdom with them in person.

"Havermeyer, you've got quite a marvel on your hands," one of the board members crowed to Duke.

"I could not agree more." Duke toasted Rose with his champagne glass, sending her a wink. "We are fortunate to have her."

Her breath hitched, a giddy sensation filling her chest. *A wink?* She hadn't seen that coming, not from such an imposing, serious man. She cleared her throat. "Thank you. I only hope you are equally as pleased with me after dinner has concluded."

Everyone chuckled, assuming the statement a joke. Rose was utterly serious, however. Mrs. Riley had prepared the entire dinner a few hours ago, unable to stay, seeing as her daughter was about to give birth. A kitchen maid would be managing the warming and plating. It was not ideal, but what else could they do on such short notice?

Unfortunately, there was no room for error tonight.

Henry leaned in toward her ear. "John's given me the sign," he said, referring to the footman who would lead the dinner service. "We should gather everyone to the dining room."

A weight settled in her stomach and she struggled not to grimace. "Here we go. Cross your fingers."

* * *

As they came to the long dinner table, Duke noted he'd been placed two seats away from Mrs. Walker. Before anyone saw, he switched the small card bearing his name with the man next to him, the person directly to her right. He should feel guilty about moving. He should sit in his assigned seat and allow another to be charmed by her.

Yet he wanted the chance to get to know her better, which confused him. She was married, and he had no need for a platonic friendship with a woman. Still, he found her fascinating, this young woman with an incredible wealth of knowledge at her fingertips. And was she not his employee, an HPC commodity he needed to cultivate and protect? He couldn't have her going off to another paper instead . . .

Decision made, he claimed the chair beside her, with no plans whatsoever to move.

Everyone settled, and Mr. Walker took the customary position at the opposite end of the table. Duke studied the man, purely out of mild curiosity. Were the Walkers happy together? They were solicitous of one another, friendly, but had it been a love match? And why in God's name did it matter to Duke?

The man on Duke's right, Mr. John Cameron, leaned over. "Cannot wait to see what she serves. This dinner party was a stroke of genius on your part, Havermeyer. Mrs. Walker is one of the city's most famous—and reclusive—residents."

"I merely wanted to show the board my appreciation," Duke said.

Cameron made a sound in his throat. "Please. We all know you're worried after what has happened. However, you cannot blame us for being concerned about the newspaper's reputation after such flimflam."

Mrs. Walker tapped her crystal wineglass with the tines of her fork. "Now, I must insist on no business discussions at the table." She lifted a pointed brow at Cameron and Duke. "Tonight is for pleasant conversations and festive harmony."

The guests beamed at her, nodding in agreement. She gestured toward a footman and he began pouring the wine at the table.

"I hope you don't mind my making an example of you," she murmured to Duke.

"On the contrary, the reminder was a welcome one. We should stick to proper etiquette in all things this evening."

"Yes, of course. Although I'm fairly certain that switching name cards defies proper etiquette."

Heat washed over him. "I hadn't realized anyone saw."

"Likely I was the only one. Do not worry—I won't tell."

He leaned in slightly. "You are not allowed to tattle on the boss. It is actually in your contract." That got a laugh out of her, and he found himself smiling in return.

"Clever of you. So, is that how you keep all your sins private?"

He opened his mouth to comment on said sins, but then closed it. This almost felt like flirting. Of course, it had been some time since he'd flirted with a society woman. Perhaps such interactions had changed in recent years, become more casual.

Somehow, he doubted it. Which meant the real Mrs. Walker might not be as rigid as the woman from the newspaper column. He contemplated the possibility. All that experience and wisdom combined with an adventurous spirit? Such a woman would prove quite a tempting package.

You cannot flirt with her. She is married.

And he was her employer. He never dabbled with women from the company. Not only did it put the employee in an awkward spot, he'd never know if she wanted him for himself or because he was her boss.

Thankfully, the man on her other side had garnered her attention, so Duke made small talk with Cameron and pushed thoughts of a bold and proficient Mrs. Walker from his mind.

The first course was served minutes later. "Are you a fan of horseracing?" Mrs. Walker asked, obviously overhearing him discuss plans to visit Sheepshead Bay Race Track.

Before Duke could answer, Cameron craned his neck toward her. "You could say that. Havermeyer's got one of the best stables in New York."

One of her brows climbed. "Is that so? I am afraid I know nothing about horses."

"Do you ride?" Duke asked.

"No. Never learned how."

A memory tugged at him. Hadn't she written a column with riding tips not long ago? No, he must've read that elsewhere. "Was there an incident in your past, such as what caused your fear of dogs?"

Her mouth opened and closed before she said, "You really do read my column."

"Of course. Why would I lie?"

"I thought you were merely being polite."

He resisted the urge to fidget with his collar, like he was a young man caught admiring the teacher. "I'm much too selfish for that. Anyway, I'd happily assist you with riding lessons." He added, "Along with Mr. Walker, of course."

"That is a kind offer. I'm afraid I spend most of my time indoors, however."

"Quite understandable," another guest said. "Considering the topics in your column. Doubtful many ladies would care to hear about tennis or badminton."

Her tone remained polite, yet deep grooves appeared between her brows. "On the contrary, many women are interested in physical pursuits—which is an excellent idea for my column. After all, how many recipes and cleaning tips am I able to provide? Perhaps an unexpected, unusual topic would be a refreshing change every now and again."

"I thought we were to refrain from speaking business," Duke said, unable to keep from teasing her.

He was rewarded when she chuckled. "Touché. A thought for another day."

The footmen began bringing in small plates. Cameron rocked back and forth in his seat, the man nearly apoplectic with excitement. One would think he was dining with *the* Charles Ranhofer in the Delmonico's kitchens—though Duke supposed that, to many, Mrs. Walker was equally as popular as the renowned chef.

"These are fresh Blue Point oysters from Long Island Sound," she announced as the plates were delivered. Each contained five shelled oysters, a lemon wedge, and a sprig of parsley.

Picking up his seafood fork, Duke loosened an oyster and brought it to his mouth. The shellfish was briny and firm, with a blast of sweetness after the swallow. Utter perfection.

Conversation died for a moment as the table commenced eating. "These are delicious," Cameron murmured, already on his third oyster.

"I agree," Mrs. Walker said. "Simple and flavorful. Perfect just as nature made them."

"We used to buy oysters right off the boats when I was a boy," Duke said. "Before the boats docked, a line of us would gather there and wait." Oysters and clams, the Newport cottage, sailing and running with the other lads . . . Those were good memories, the only few he had from childhood.

His finger automatically went to the scar above his eyebrow, feeling the puckered skin. It served as a reminder of his recklessness.

"Would you care for more wine, sir?" asked a footman at his elbow.

He nodded, eager to escape maudlin thoughts of days gone by. When his eyes met Rose's, there was a question there, as if she were about to start interviewing him. Straightening, he looked away and swallowed a healthy mouthful of wine, irritation slithering over his skin like humid air on a summer afternoon.

He didn't need anyone asking about his past. He presided over the largest publishing empire in the nation, dammit. That was all the world was required to know about him. The newspapers were what mattered, not his childhood or his scar.

He vowed to keep his attention on his agenda this evening—and nothing else.

Chapter Four

"What is your background, Mrs. Walker?" the man on her left asked. "How did you become such a talented writer?"

Rose smothered a grin. Her mother said she'd been born with a pencil in her hand, continuously writing as a small child. Later, she studied the classics and pored over newspapers to soak up as much information as possible. Then she saw an ad in the *Gazette* for a reporter and applied. Pike balked at hiring a woman reporter, but he had been thinking of starting an advice column. After they had concocted the idea of Mrs. Walker's Weekly together, Rose relished the challenge. She spent long hours researching answers, as well as using her mother and the other members of the Lowes' well-trained staff as resources.

Not that she could share as much with the HPC board.

Instead, she lifted a casual shoulder. "Oh, I've always been writing down my thoughts. Forever scribbling, my mother said. I had some patient teachers and studied hard."

"Will you ever branch out and write on some real topics?" Cameron asked as he finished his wine.

Real topics? Of all the dashed nerve . . . Her right eye began twitching. "I am not certain what you mean, Mr. Cameron. My topics are quite real."

Cameron leaned back and clasped his hands over his stomach. "I mean no offense. But they're filled with just

women's issues. You must admit, stains and recipes are
hardly as important as politics or the market—"

"I believe what Mr. Cameron is trying to say," Duke
broke in with, "is that you're incredibly talented and should
you ever want to explore other stories and issues, you only
need let me know. Havermeyer Publishing is happy to support you, regardless of topic."

She unclenched her jaw and murmured her gratitude.
Duke gave her a short nod, as if to reassure her. She appreciated it. No one had ever disparaged the topics of her
column before, at least not to her face—the blessings of an-
onymity, she supposed. The experience was not one she'd
care to repeat.

Yet she was loath to let the issue drop. If her topics were
so frivolous, she wanted to ask Cameron, then why was
hers the most popular HPC column? Why did her words
sell more papers than other writers'?

She pressed her lips together and swallowed her argument. She needed her job and antagonizing one of the
HPC board members—no matter how much he deserved
it—was unwise. Thank goodness Duke had switched plac-
ards to put Cameron farther away from her.

The next course arrived. Soup bowls were distributed
while John, one of the Lowes' footmen hired for the night,
rolled in a cart containing the tureen. When all the bowls
were full of soup, Rose picked up her soupspoon—only to
drop it when an unholy crash resonated from the floor beneath them.

Good heavens. That had come from the kitchens. Her
gaze locked with Henry's, and her fake husband appeared
equally startled.

Trying to maintain a calm veneer despite her panic, she
pushed back from the table and rose. "If you'll excuse me.
Please, continue your dinners."

The men all stood, including Duke. His brows were lowered in concern over his precious dinner party.

She shared that same concern.

Hurrying into the corridor, she caught up with MacKenzie, the groom they'd recruited to serve as the butler, on his way toward the kitchen. "What was that noise?" she hissed.

"Canna say, Miss Rose. I hope there weren't food on those trays that dropped."

She pushed through the swinging door and rushed down the servant staircase. The heat and aromas grew stronger as she descended. In the kitchen, three maids were cleaning soup off the floor. A second tureen had shattered, the porcelain smashing into tiny pieces and its contents now all over the ground.

"What happened? Is everyone all right?"

"I am so sorry, Rose," Ida, one of the maids, said. "There was a rat." She held out her hands wide, then wider, as if sizing a dog. "It was huge. Ran right across my foot."

Rose pinched the bridge of her nose with her thumb and forefinger. "Ida, you've seen a rat before. This is New York City, for heaven's sake."

"Yes, but one's never run across my foot! Gave me the shivers."

"We still have a little more soup." Bridget, Henry's fiancée, showed Rose a smaller bowl. "I'll take this up in case someone wants seconds."

"Thank you, Bridget." Rose turned to the other two women. "Should I be worried? The kitchen must be spotless after dinner. The entire group is descending to watch me make those ridiculous cookies."

"It will be, I swear." Ida kept sopping up soup. "Don't you worry, Rose."

"What about the next course? Are we still on time?"

Ida pointed to the platter, still covered on the counter. "Broiled salmon, ready and waiting."

"Thank goodness. Would you like any help cleaning up?"

The two young women glanced at Rose as if she'd lost her mind. "And ruin your borrowed dress?" Ida said. "No, indeed. Tonight you are the mistress of the house. We'll deal with this."

"I am so grateful to all of you for helping me. Honestly, I haven't a clue what I would have done without you."

Ida grinned. "You are family. We always help family. If this helps you keep your fancy job at that newspaper, then we'll gladly do it. You're famous."

Rose nearly snorted. *Famous* was a relative term, especially considering few people knew she and the author of Mrs. Walker's Weekly were one and the same. "I am grateful nonetheless. I will return to the dining room, if you are settled."

"Good as gravy, Rose. Now, you get up there and charm those board members."

* * *

Seconds after Mrs. Walker's departure, Mr. Walker also pushed away from the table. He excused himself and strode out of the dining room.

"Hope our food ain't on the ground," Cameron murmured at Duke's side.

Duke agreed. Tonight's meal must be perfect. He continued the small talk at the table, acting as host as best he could. Yet his attention kept wandering back toward the corridor. Where were the Walkers? A weight built up in his gut, a growing concern over the lingering absence of their hosts. What had gone wrong?

". . . to replace Pike?"

Duke swung toward the board member who had spoken. "I'm sorry, what?"

The man's mustache twitched. "I asked if you have anyone in mind to replace Pike. I was thinking maybe someone from the outside instead of one of the other senior editors. Fresh blood, you know."

Duke did not want to have this conversation now. Not at this dinner party, and not while the two hosts were missing, tonight's other courses possibly scattered on the kitchen floor.

Perhaps he should follow, see if he could be of any use. Waiting patiently for bad news was not his strong suit. He had to *do* something.

He hadn't expanded his family's publishing empire tenfold by sitting around.

Pushing his chair back, he placed his napkin on the table. "Excuse me. I'd like to check on our hosts."

A footman stood at the hallway door. "Which way to the kitchens?" Duke asked him.

The man's skin turned the color of plaster. "Sir, Mrs. Walker asked that the guests—"

"Never mind that. Just point me in the direction of the kitchens or I'll find it myself."

The footman pointed a shaky finger to the right. "Stairs are behind the second door."

Duke moved into the corridor. He was no idiot; this was overstepping his bounds as a dinner guest. No one should leave the table to wander about the host's home, especially to wade into a domestic matter.

However, this was no normal dinner party. This was business, and everything connected to HPC tonight, even Mrs. Walker herself, was his concern.

Nearing the second door, he heard . . . heavy breathing. The rustle of clothing. A giggle. What in God's name . . . ?

He slowed and peered around the doorjamb into the landing. Duke jerked in surprise. At the top of the stairs was Mr. Walker . . . kissing one of the housemaids. Walker had the girl pressed against the wall, his lips locked on hers, hands greedily roaming over her uniform-clad body.

That bastard.

Anger flooded Duke's veins like lightning, quick and fierce, and he shook, fighting the urge to punch Walker in the face. It was not uncommon, unfortunately, for the master of the house to dally with a maid, but Duke was fucking furious to learn that Walker fell into this disreputable group. Mrs. Walker deserved better.

Had Walker no respect for his wife in her own home, especially tonight of all nights?

As much as he longed to beat Walker senseless for this, Duke backed off. He had no right to get involved. He marched to the dining room, his head spinning with what he'd witnessed. As he retook his seat, Cameron asked, "Well, did you learn anything?"

"No." Duke wasn't one to gossip, and this was a private matter between husband and wife.

Perhaps she takes lovers, as well.

Lust raced along his spine, the possibility causing his skin to grow both hot and cold. Yes, that was a very real possibility. He'd been fascinated with her, yet stifled the interest out of respect for her husband and her position at HPC. Turned out the husband didn't deserve such consideration.

Have you forgotten? Married women are not worth the trouble.

Indeed, he'd learned this fairly early. As a young man, he'd bedded a married woman for a short period of time before her husband found out and tried to blackmail Duke for an obscene amount of money. Duke had hired an investigator, who uncovered many infidelities on the part of the husband, dalliances his wife hadn't known about. She hadn't been pleased.

But Duke hadn't stopped there. Further digging revealed the husband was stealing funds from several top Wall Street investors, the details of which Duke happily printed in the *Gazette*. That was the last he'd heard of blackmail.

From that point on, Duke had sworn off married women and also vowed to remain faithful to his own wife should he ever marry. Otherwise, why bother standing in a church and repeating the vows?

A man's only as good as his word.

What were Mrs. Walker's views on marriage? Her columns brimmed with joy over a woman's lot in life. She wasn't inspiring rebellion or calling for women to join the suffrage movement; rather, she encouraged her readers to run a tidy and efficient household, to please their husbands through good food and well-mannered children.

Did she know of, or even suspect, her husband's infidelity? Perhaps she encouraged lovers outside the marriage bed; many married women did, after all. Yet he'd read each of her columns, even the ones that dealt with relationship advice. He could not foresee a situation where Mrs. Walker would approve of such an agreement. She seemed a romantic at heart.

Though he had to say, meeting her in person, he was having a hard time reconciling her with the woman who wrote the column. She seemed strong-willed and independent. Outspoken. Ready to cosh the unenlightened Cameron over the head with a blunt object.

While he admired Mrs. Walker the writer, he found himself entertaining other feelings—physical feelings—about the fierce and fiery woman behind the column.

It was a terrible idea, taking her as a lover. He never mixed business with his personal relationships. Yet he couldn't help but imagine those clear blue eyes clouded with desire. Her pale skin flushed with pleasure, slim limbs wrapped around his frame . . . He was shocked by how much he wanted that.

Stop. Remember your purpose tonight.

The Walkers returned just as the soup course was cleared. He shifted closer. "Is everything all right?" he asked under his breath after she settled.

"Oh yes. Nothing to worry over," she said, loud enough for everyone to hear. "Just a minor slip with some porcelain."

"Good help is impossible to find nowadays." Cameron shook his head regretfully. "It's all those middle-class jobs available. The good servants are being wooed by the false promise of independence."

Duke frowned at the comment, which smacked of the social entitlement and privilege that he'd come to hate about New York society.

"And how is that promise false?" Mrs. Walker asked the question innocently enough, but she leaned in, like a fencer awaiting an opponent's next parry.

"Putting ideas in their heads," Cameron said with a wave of his hand. "Tell me, what could be better than working in a household? They have a roof over their heads, meals to eat. Clothing provided for them. There is a sense of security in domestic service not found in other employment."

Mrs. Walker's gaze narrowed on Cameron. "Have you any idea of the hard work that goes into being a footman or a maid? Have you seen the aches and pains, the gnarled fingers? A servant's life is grueling and unrewarding, with little to show for it except exhaustion at the end of the day. At least with an office or shop position, you retain some semblance of freedom, leaving the job behind when you clock out."

An uncomfortable silence descended as the footmen appeared with the next course. Duke lifted his wineglass and drained the contents, all the while contemplating her answer. She seemed intimately aware of the perils of domestic service, as well as unexpectedly progressive in her attitude regarding the status of servants. What would she think if she learned her husband was screwing one of the housemaids?

Mr. Walker laughed at something down the table, a comment from another guest, and Duke's jaw clenched. The adulterous bastard . . .

Duke shifted toward her. "Will you and Mr. Walker be traveling this holiday? Visiting family nearby?"

She stared at him blankly for a few seconds before saying, "Oh no. We remain here for the holidays. I like to be surrounded by familiar things, I suppose. And you, Mr. Havermeyer? Will you travel?"

"No. The papers keep me quite busy."

"Over the holidays?" Her brows drew together. "Come now, even publishing magnates surely deserve a break at this time of year."

"Havermeyer works so the senior editors are able to celebrate with their families," one of the board members explained. "It's a Havermeyer family tradition."

Instead of appearing impressed, her jaw fell open as she locked eyes with Duke. "Are you saying your father never spent Christmas with you and your family? That is . . . terrible."

For as far back as Duke could remember, Havermeyer Christmases had lacked fanfare and affection. His father would depart for work at dawn, leaving Duke alone with his mother. She hated rising early, so Duke had been forced to wait until after luncheon to open presents. The anticipation had nearly killed him as a small boy, but it seemed a silly thing to complain about now.

Not to mention his father's dedication had strengthened the *Gazette*, which developed into one of the country's biggest and most influential newspapers. It had become the foundation of Duke's publishing empire. Hard to belly-ache over his father's absence during his childhood when he now understood what had driven the older man.

Duke straightened. "He was devoted to the company, as I am. I didn't acquire eight newspapers in the last five years by taking vacations and relaxing at home. Everyone who works at HPC depends on me—including you, Mrs. Walker."

"Depends on you, certainly, but also on those you have hired to oversee the operation. There must be others who could take your place?"

No need to argue about a practice he had no intention of changing. "Perhaps, but it is tradition. Just like how you always plant a new hydrangea shrub each spring."

An appealing flush stole over her cheekbones and she bit her lip. This time, he made no effort to look away or quash his reaction. Heat wound through him, and he contemplated pulling the plump wet flesh of her lip between his own teeth.

"You truly are a devotee of my column," she said.

He reacted on instinct, ignoring all his good sense. He shifted toward her and pitched his voice low. "I am indeed. It is one of the highlights of my week."

When he heard her swift intake of breath, his skin prickled with satisfaction. This exchange was the height of recklessness, yet he was not sorry. Not sorry at all.

Chapter Five

$\mathcal{D}$inner continued with two more stellar courses: delicious broiled salmon and perfectly braised beef. Wine flowed, and lively conversation filled the elegant dining room. Duke watched Mrs. Walker carefully through his lashes, transfixed by how her expressive features changed as she ate. She relished each bite and he wondered what she'd look like in bed as he pleasured her. Would her appetites remain as strong in bed?

Her eyes met his and she blinked, wiping her mouth with her napkin. "Have I food on my face?"

"No," he murmured for her ears alone. "I merely enjoy watching you."

She grabbed at her wine and drank deeply. Good. He'd unnerved her. For the next few moments, she avoided looking at him and engaged in conversation with the two elderly men on her left. Though disappointed, Duke could hardly hide his smirk. Unfortunately for her, those two particular board members were extremely loquacious. And boring.

When she finally shifted toward Duke, he leaned in. "Were you able to get a word in edgewise? Board meetings always run an hour longer than necessary when those two attend."

Her lips twitched. "We shouldn't laugh at the expense of others."

His brows shot up. "They are both obscenely rich and have their own teeth. Still visit their mistresses weekly. We should all be so lucky at that age."

"You are lying. How would you know about their personal relationships?"

"I publish ten newspapers. There are over sixty reporters on staff at the *Gazette* alone. There's nothing stopping me from learning every single detail about someone if I wish."

"Like me?" Her voice cracked in the middle of the question. Was she worried over his answer?

Her fears were unfounded, as he had not investigated her. There hadn't been a need, really. Her background seemed straightforward. Yet there had been a hint of something in her voice . . . "Have you something to hide, Mrs. Walker?"

"Of course not." She reached for her wine once again.

"Does the possibility bother you?"

"Yes. Everyone has the right to privacy. I wouldn't care for someone poking about in my affairs."

An interesting choice of words considering Duke's earlier thoughts. "There is an old proverb—if you do not wish for anyone to find something out, then refrain from doing it."

"Everyone makes mistakes. It's unfair to punish people for them."

He thought of her husband, daring to kiss a housemaid not ten feet from the dinner party. "Most people are only sorry when caught, however."

"Now, that is cynical."

"Perhaps, but it's also true. And I would never publish something unverified." He remembered the recent bribery scandal and cringed. "Try not to anyway."

"Does it matter to you, getting the facts right?"

"Of course," he said without thinking. "That's the only thing that matters. The reputation of the paper depends upon its credibility."

She glanced over his shoulder at Mr. Cameron, who was

involved in a serious discussion in the opposite direction. Then she lowered her voice. "So why fire Mr. Pike?"

He frowned. Had she been fond of the old editor in chief? "Because, at the end of the day, he is responsible for those on his staff. The error happened on his watch."

"Yes, but are you not also responsible? The error occurred on *your* watch, too. And they are your staff, more so than his."

He didn't quite understand this logic. "Are you suggesting I fire myself?"

"No. What I'm saying is the person directly responsible has been dealt with. Is that not enough?" She took a sip of her wine. "Are you aware Mr. Pike has a large family? Grandchildren? How will he explain this injustice to them?"

Injustice? "This scandal could ruin me. It could ruin Havermeyer Publishing. Do you honestly believe any of the men sitting at this table or the shareholders care about Mr. Pike's grandchildren?"

"No, but *you* should. Mr. Pike worked for your father. He's been at the paper for more than forty years and is now cast adrift for someone else's mistake. How is he supposed to hold his head up after this?"

A small wave of guilt rode through him. He quickly squelched it. When he'd imagined a private conversation with her, this wasn't even close to what he had hoped to accomplish. She was shaming him for doing his job, for maintaining the integrity of the newspaper.

He didn't like it.

The board expected him to act swiftly and harshly in a circumstance such as this, a scandal that threatened all for which he'd worked so hard.

And yet Pike had been a damned good employee. Had served as Duke's right hand at HPC ever since Duke took over the reins ten years ago. Almost everything he had learned about the practical side of publishing had been from Pike . . .

Christ almighty. *She's got you doubting yourself. Make a decision and keep going. Was not that the Havermeyer way?*

He straightened and leveled her with a glare normally reserved for rebellious editors. "You seem to believe that life is fair, Mrs. Walker. Let me be the first to assure you it is not."

A hint of something—Disappointment? Dismissal? Disdain?—flashed over her face before she schooled her features. "Thank you. I am certain Mr. Pike appreciates that lesson, especially at this most charitable time of year."

He frowned and drummed his fingers on the table. What had happened to their flirting? He didn't wish to argue with her—though he had to admit, the fire inside her appealed to him. No woman had stood up to him before, not like this. "Has anyone mentioned that you are quite opinionated?"

A smile twisted her lips, transforming her from lovely to breathtaking, amusement sparkling in her blue gaze. "And yet that quality was precisely the reason I was hired."

"Indeed, I suppose you're right. Tell me, from where did you gain your impressive wealth of knowledge, Mrs. Walker?"

"I think you may call me Rose, considering no one can hear us." She began lining up the silverware at her setting, ensuring the pieces were perfectly straight. "And my knowledge is not that impressive."

Her modesty was charming. "I disagree. There seems to be no topic on which you are incapable of opining. Plants and shrubbery, cooking, household matters, relationships . . . You are truly a marvel."

"An adventurous upbringing, I suppose. I'm not afraid to read and ask questions, as well."

"You know, I once asked Pike if he selected the questions for you, to find the easy ones. He told me the questions were chosen at random, that you had insisted on it."

"That is true. Otherwise, the column would grow boring—for both the readers and me. I'm frequently forced to investigate or research my answers. That is what makes it interesting."

"Have you ever been wrong?"

"Once."

The tone of her voice changed with that one word, revealing a quiet sadness underneath. It was rude to pry, but curiosity urged him on. Besides, he was her employer. Hadn't he a right to know? "What happened?"

"I . . ." She reached for her wine and took a long swallow. "In the early days, before I received as many letters as I do today, I used to write every single person with an answer, whether it was printed in the paper or not."

He stared at her, astounded. That must have taken hours and hours. How had she managed such a feat? Instead of asking, he kept quiet, not wanting to interrupt.

"A woman wrote to tell me about her husband. He was older and did not treat her kindly. She refrained from sharing intimate details, but much can be read between the lines when it comes to relationships. She said he had recently grown more violent and she feared him. Feared for her life. However, her religion told her to honor and obey him, so she asked me what to do."

Duke's stomach sank. "You do not have to—"

"Yes, I must." Rose ducked her chin and focused on her plate. "I told her to leave him. She had a sister in Queens and I advised her to move there immediately. That God would understand putting herself and her safety above her marital vows. Never mind that he had promised to honor and cherish her, and how is beating a woman cherishing her? Anyway, I read about her in the newspaper not long after. The husband found her in Queens and strangled her to death in an alley."

"That wasn't your fault."

Tears shimmered in her eyes, and the sight felt like a punch to his solar plexus. Her pain revealed a different side of her, one he suspected not many ever saw, and it affected him like nothing else. Something turned over in his chest, a shifting of some kind, as if puzzle pieces were being rearranged to create a new picture inside him.

"The logical side of my brain realizes you are right. The fault lies clearly with the husband. However, the emotional part, the part here"—she placed a hand over her heart—"believes you are wrong. She might be alive if not for my advice."

"On the other hand, she very well might have died, living with a violent man like that. You cannot know for certain."

"No one is able to know for certain. That is why, even though I still receive far too many of them, I never answer those types of letters any longer. The consequences are too dire if I'm wrong."

His chest pulled tight with sympathy and something else. Something more. The reaction should have scared him, but he made up his mind right then. He wanted this woman, every bit of her, no matter who stood in his way.

* * *

The look on Duke's face changed as the dinner continued, his dark eyes now glowing with heat and intensity, and Rose found herself squirming in her chair.

Was he *attracted* to her?

The idea was laughable, but something was going on inside that clever brain of his. The looks he gave her were hot and intimate, though no one else at the table seemed to notice. His knee even brushed her leg, a fleeting and forbidden touch that sent waves of electricity through her veins.

She didn't know whether to be thrilled or horrified.

Thrilled, because she had admired him from afar since initially spotting him in the Havermeyer building. Horrified, because she had no idea how to proceed. She was supposed to be *married*—and Duke was her employer.

There had been kisses over the years, but nothing more. What would a man like Duke expect from her, a supposed married woman? A torrid affair?

That was out of the question. While Rose might be very, very tempted by Duke Havermeyer, Mrs. Walker of Mrs. Walker's Weekly would never engage in an affair. Havermeyer had to know that, seeing as how he read her column each week. Mrs. Walker was about propriety and manners, not brazenness and infidelity. As much as Rose longed to test those forbidden waters, reacting favorably to his advances would be completely out of character. Worse, it meant he might discover her deception.

You must ignore him. Put any ideas about you and Duke Havermeyer firmly from your mind, despite how long you have thought about—and lusted over—him.

She caught Henry's gaze and tried to impart the need for escape. Considering they had all finished eating, it was time for the ladies to separate off into the drawing room. Henry nodded and the two of them stood, signaling an end to the meal. The others rose, as well.

"Will the ladies be so kind as to join me in the drawing room for coffee?" she asked the other women.

"Perhaps we could dispense with that tradition just for tonight," Duke suggested. "After all, we're excited to watch you make the famous Havermeyer shortbread cookies."

Exactly what Rose had hoped to postpone.

Dread clogged her throat. These dashed cookies were hanging over her head like the sharp blade of the guillotine.

You will figure it out. Remain confident and they won't suspect a thing.

Yes, but what about when they actually put the cookies into their mouths? Her stomach knotted painfully.

"Everyone would probably rather have coffee first, no?" Rose looked to the guests, trying to persuade them through sheer force of will.

Her will was no match for Duke Havermeyer, unfortunately. Tall and commanding, a powerful scion of New York society, he addressed his board members. "I know this is bucking tradition, but I promise you shall be rewarded when you're enjoying warm shortbread cookies with your coffee."

"And these cookies are your own personal family recipe?" one of the guests asked.

"Yes," Duke answered. "When my mother came over from Scotland, she brought this recipe with her. She'd never say how long it had been in her family, just that the recipe was precious to her."

Oh dear. Rose could feel the debilitating nerves building in her gut, like a looming deadline when she hadn't yet put a single word to paper.

"My dear?" Henry's voice got her attention. "What do you think?"

She appreciated that her friend was giving her the chance to stall but refusing her employer's request would appear odd. Though this was supposed to be Rose's home, it was clear to everyone that Duke Havermeyer was firmly in charge of the evening. "Shall we head down to the kitchens, then?"

Duke's mouth hitched in apparent satisfaction and Henry began leading the guests from the dining room. Rose started to join the crowd when a light touch at her elbow startled her.

"Walk with me."

She glanced up at Duke, who stared down at her from his great height, his arm out. Nodding, she accepted his escort. He stood close, their shoulders brushing. He smelled of a soap she'd never afford, the kind Mr. Lowe and his ilk purchased, one with a scent too complicated to pinpoint. All Rose knew was that he smelled divine.

He dawdled and let the other guests go on ahead. Soon they were in the back of the group, with enough distance between them and everyone else that no one would overhear their conversation.

"I apologize if this has disrupted your plans for the evening."

Not an apology for his high-handed maneuvering, of course. "I sense you prefer to keep control of a situation whenever possible."

"Yes, that's true. It is one of my many flaws."

Many flaws, like his ability to throw her off balance? The dashing way he filled out his black evening wear? Or the imposing self-confidence that drew her like a fly to honey?

Stop. He is your employer and you need this job.

"And do you always get your way?" she asked before she thought better of it.

"Yes—but I'm not opposed to listening to reasonable arguments. Have you a compelling reason not to make the cookies right now?"

No, other than terror over her ineptitude in the kitchen. "I fail to see what is so exciting about watching me move about the kitchen."

"I think there is very little about you that I would not find exciting."

Her heart gave a strange leap at that, her skin going up in flames. No doubt about it, he was definitely flirting with her. But to what end? He believed her married. Affairs might have been commonplace in his social circle, but not in Mrs. Walker's world.

This must remain on a professional level. "Thankfully, Mr. Walker seems to agree."

Duke made a noise, one that had her glancing at him sharply. He held up a hand in apology, though his expression hardly conveyed contrition. "He holds you in the highest esteem, I am certain."

The words sounded flippant. Did he suspect she and Henry were merely friends, not truly man and wife? The idea was ridiculous. They'd been excruciatingly careful tonight to maintain the ruse. Nevertheless, there was a hint of distrust, of superior knowledge, in Duke's careful smile. She didn't care for it. Not one bit.

She went on the offensive. "Have you never considered marriage?"

"No. I am far too busy to pursue a wife. And, in truth, I've never met anyone worth the chase." They arrived at the steps, and he held open the swinging door for her. "All the good women seem to be taken," he murmured as she brushed by him.

A thrill skated down her spine, centering between her legs. *Oh my. You are in over your head, Rose.*

The trouble was, when it came to Duke Havermeyer, she had no idea how to save herself from drowning.

Chapter Six

*R*ose stared at the ingredients in front of her, a bead of sweat rolling between her shoulder blades. The guests were packed into the warm kitchen, standing around her in a semicircle, their gazes rapt. An audience awaiting the master.

Little did they know she wasn't even a novice.

Breathe and follow the recipe. How hard could it be?

The maids had placed the ingredients on the large workspace, as well as a bowl, mixing spoon, rolling pin, and pan. With shaking hands, she tied an apron around her waist and reached for the recipe. Cleared her throat. "All right, let us begin."

The first ingredient was sugar. This gave her a boost of confidence. As a devoted fan of cakes and pies, she was well acquainted with sugar. After measuring the correct portion and pouring it into a bowl, she went in search of the butter. A dish containing a stick of butter was on the other counter, so she retrieved it and added the softened mass to the sugar.

She began mixing, the warm butter easily folding into the sugar. The recipe said to "cream" the butter and sugar, but Rose had no idea how long that took. She kept working the mixture, stirring it, breathing hard, until one of the maids—Ida—said softly, "Is that sufficiently creamed, madam?"

"Yes, I believe it is," she said, having no idea if the declaration were true or not. "Though I do like to be certain." She gave it one more beat for luck, then set the bowl aside. "Now for the flour."

"What type of flour do you use?" one of the female guests asked.

There were different types of flour? Rose attempted to sound knowledgeable when she answered, "Oh, the regular kind. I stick to the tried-and-true ingredients."

"I like Hungarian flour," one of the other wives said.

The woman used flour shipped in from Europe? The extravagance of these high-society types absolutely boggled the mind. Hiding her dismay, Rose added the flour to the mixture, along with a tablespoon of salt.

"That certainly was a lot of salt," someone commented.

Rose peeked at the recipe. She could never remember the difference in the abbreviation for tablespoon and teaspoon. Had she added the wrong amount?

Too late now. Swallowing her trepidation, she lifted a shoulder. "Perhaps that is what gives this particular recipe its distinct flavor."

She began combining the dry ingredients with the wet concoction to form the dough. When it was combined, she dumped the mixture onto the counter and floured it. The instructions said to knead it, so Rose set out to work the dough with her hands. She'd seen her mother and Mrs. Riley do this many times in the Lowes' kitchen. Of course, Rose wasn't as competent as those two, but she soon had a firm ball ready.

So far, it looked good. Perhaps this cooking thing was not that difficult after all.

The recipe said to roll out the dough. Was she supposed to flour the wood first to keep the dough from sticking? She debated this for a moment until she realized everyone was staring at her, waiting. *Mrs. Walker would know exactly what to do.*

With a confidence she did not feel, she took a handful of flour and rubbed it on the rolling pin. Then she began flattening the dough as best she could. The job was harder than it appeared, however. After a few moments, the dough was uneven and jagged. Hmm. Mrs. Riley's dough was always so smooth. Perhaps Rose should start again.

After gathering the dough into a ball once more, she rolled it out as best she could, avoiding Duke's intense gaze the entire time. The shape was not perfect, but it would have to do. Carefully, she lifted the dough into the pan and spread it out.

"Interesting," one of the women said. "These shortbread cookies appear thinner than the standard kind."

They did? Rose hadn't a clue. The dough did look a little thin, but wouldn't they puff up when baked?

"I suppose we'll find out when we sample the finished product," Duke said from the back of the room. The edges of his mouth were curled up in a soft smile, turning him quite dashing. Rose bit the inside of her cheek to keep from smiling back.

"How will you score the dough to decorate them?" another woman asked.

Oh. Rose hadn't considered this, which was silly of her. Of course every shortbread cookie had indents and lines on it. Digging deep for inspiration, she found a long knife on a nearby counter and began embellishing the dough. Sadly, her creativity with words did not extend to the kitchen—a regular joke between her and her mother. When she was finished, it appeared as if someone had stabbed the shortbread dough in a blind rage.

Sighing, she snatched up the pan and hurried to the oven, hoping her audience wouldn't see. Perhaps some magic would occur during the baking process and these would emerge as perfectly as everyone in the room expected.

Oh, Rose. Now you are delusional.

"I'll just put these in to bake and we'll return upstairs to wait." And pray.

She pulled on the heavy oven door and noticed the oven was cool. That was odd. Hadn't she and the maids discussed leaving the fire burning?

Lord above, this was an unholy disaster.

She shoved her miserable tray inside, quickly shut the door, and sent a plea to the shortbread fairies. "Shall we have our coffee in the salon?" The sooner she herded them upstairs, the better.

Ida suddenly appeared, looking as if she were trying not to laugh. "I have coffee ready for the guests, madam."

"Thank you," Rose said, conveying her panic with her eyes as she untied the apron. "We will get out of your way now. Please bring the cookies up when they are done." Ida merely winked in response, confusing Rose even further.

Henry led the guests to the stairs, the group chattering loudly about what they'd seen. Miraculously, Rose had impressed them, though most seemed perplexed about the decorating at the end.

She hung back to ask Ida about the cool oven, but Duke remained, as well, his expression full of a scorching heat that caused Rose's knees to wobble. Goodness, she could melt into a puddle from that look.

"That was quite the demonstration," he said when he reached her side.

"You enjoyed it?"

He lifted a hand and swiped her cheek with his finger, which came away coated in flour. Horrified, she started to rub her face—until he caught her wrist. "No, allow me."

Taking out a handkerchief, he lightly held her chin and dabbed the soft linen over her nose and cheeks, his touch gentle and thorough. She held her breath, heart pounding, as he cleaned her. His chest rose and fell rhythmically, his body close enough that she could feel his exhalations on her forehead. If she pushed up on her toes, she could kiss him . . .

She considered it for one rash minute, unable to prevent herself from staring at his mouth. Would his kisses be rough or sweet? Hard or coaxing? She liked kissing. In fact, she liked it quite a bit. She hadn't kissed anyone in over a year, but she still remembered how it felt, the pleasant joining of two mouths. The shared breath, the slide of a man's tongue against hers.

"There," he said softly, breaking into her thoughts. "You are presentable again."

"Thank you." Her voice sounded strange to her own ears, a deep throaty timbre she had never heard before.

"It was my pleasure." He didn't move away or put distance between them. Instead he seemed to wait, the two of them watching each other as the moment stretched. There were flecks of gold and green in his dark irises, a complex set of colors for a complex man.

The sudden clatter of china behind them in the kitchen startled her, and she took a step back. What had just occurred between them? Her face burned with embarrassment and . . . disappointment.

He cleared his throat and adjusted his cuffs, but his eyes never left her. Rattled, she darted around him and started up the steps. "Shall we join the others?" she asked.

She didn't bother to check if he followed. There was no need. She could sense his presence behind her: the man she longed for but could never have.

* * *

The shortbread cookies arrived not long after coffee had been poured. Duke was surprised the cookies had cooled so quickly, but how could he complain? They were absolute perfection: delicious buttery squares with intricate designs on top. Of course, they hadn't looked this smart going into the oven, but clearly Rose knew her business.

The board members and wives *oohed* over the results, biting into the cookies and rolling their eyes in pleasure. Satisfaction and pride flooded him. Rose Walker was a marvel. He made a mental note to give her an increase in her salary. Whatever he paid her, it was not enough.

He watched her move through the crowd, the perfect hostess. She had paused when the cookies arrived, almost appearing nervous over the results, but now she smiled broadly, accepting the compliments graciously, humbly, her hair shining in the soft glow of the gasolier. Christ, she was lovely. When they'd stood alone near the kitchen stairs, he'd been certain she was thinking of kissing him—as he had been thinking of kissing her. It shocked him how much he wanted her, wanted to feel every inch of her pressed against him. In one evening, the woman had completely charmed him.

What was he prepared to do about it?

"Did you like the cookies?"

Duke turned and found Mr. Walker standing there. Had Walker seen Duke ogling Rose? "They are superb." He glanced at the cookie in his hand. "I must admit, after seeing what went into the oven, I wouldn't have guessed they'd be this perfect."

"Rose is a wonder. She never ceases to surprise me."

Duke recalled Walker's passionate embrace with a maid earlier. For a man who held his wife in such high esteem, his actions certainly were baffling. He studied Walker's face. "Have you known each other long?"

"Nearly all our lives. We've always been best friends."

That was an odd way for an unfaithful husband to describe his wife. Though perhaps this was a hint that the two were more friends than lovers. "There is something oddly sweet to two best friends getting married."

Walker leaned in, his gaze narrowed intently. "Yes, it is sweet. She's always looked out for me and I always look out for her. Always."

"I get the feeling you are attempting to tell me something."

"You're rumored to be a smart man and an excellent journalist. I'm certain you will figure it out."

Duke crossed his arms over his chest. "Then I think it's best I warn you, as well. I watch out for my employees. Everyone at Havermeyer Publishing, from the mailroom clerks to the top editors. If I think they are in danger or at risk of being hurt, I will step in."

Walker appeared confused by this, his brows dipping together. "You're worried I will hurt Rose?"

"If certain things came to light, yes."

"Certain things?"

"I know what you are up to, Walker."

The other man blinked a few times, then his expression cleared. "Oh, so you know about the . . . ?" He gestured toward the kitchen stairs, where Duke had witnessed the earlier embrace.

Duke nodded once. "Indeed."

Instead of appalled, Walker had the audacity to appear cheerful. "What a relief. The subterfuge is damn exhausting."

"But necessary," he snapped. "My God, man. You have a houseful of guests."

"I know that. The entire thing was Rose's idea. You cannot blame me."

Ah, so it was as Duke had suspected: Rose and her husband had an understanding. This was not so uncommon in marriages of the higher classes. Duke's own father had hardly bothered to hide the existence of his mistresses over the years. It was the way things were done, but the wife was not normally so accommodating. "She's quite novel, your wife."

"That is a polite way of putting it. I am surprised she told you, though. We had planned to keep it a secret."

"Yes, well. I've been around reporters too long, I suppose. Always searching for the truth."

Walker chuckled. "We hadn't considered that. I hope you won't hold it against her. She loves writing for your papers."

"Why on earth would I hold it against *her*?"

"Some men are petty that way. At least now I needn't play the jealous husband any longer."

God, this man was revolting. "I suppose that happens often?"

"Come on." Walker elbowed Duke's arm. "I saw the way you were staring at her tonight. Now you know I won't stand in your way."

Duke's jaw dropped, his body tightening in shock. Was Walker so eager to be cuckolded, then?

"You two are awfully tense." Rose appeared, her head turning between Duke and her husband. "Anything the matter?"

"Nothing whatsoever," Walker said. "Just clearing the air a bit. Havermeyer, glad we had this chat. If you will excuse me, I'll visit with our other guests."

Walker strolled away and Duke resisted the urge to follow—and subsequently pummel him. Though he longed to seduce Rose into an affair, she deserved better than a husband who clearly cared little for her. "Interesting man, your husband."

"Yes, he is," she said with a fond smile in Walker's direction. "Were the two of you arguing?"

"No, merely coming to an understanding." An understanding in which Duke was free to pursue Rose Walker. The full implication began to sink in, a rush of excitement flooding his veins. She was here, standing before him, and there was no reason not to make his feelings known. "About you."

"Me?" Her brows shot up. "Why would you need to come to an understanding about me?"

As was his style, he decided to be direct. No tiptoeing around an issue. "Because he knows I've developed an interest in you."

"As one of your valued employees."

"No. This interest has nothing to do with your ability to craft a pithy column. A personal interest in you, Rose."

The idea settled and color spotted her cheekbones. "I—I am sorry. You . . . what?"

"I want to spend time with you. Privately. Originally, it seemed a terrible idea because of your employment at my newspaper, but I've come to think we can handle the situation like two consenting adults."

"But . . ." She cast a glance over her shoulder at the rest of the guests, possibly confirming they were truly alone. When she turned, she licked her lips. "No. This is impossible."

"I realize my timing is poor, as we're still in the midst of this gathering, but I believe in stating my intentions up front. That way, no one may claim to be surprised later on."

"Have I a say in this?" she snapped.

"Of course." He thrust his hands in his trouser pockets to keep from touching her. "But you should know that once I decide on a course of action, I never change my mind."

"Nice for you, but no. Whatever you are suggesting is unwise for many reasons."

"Such as?"

"You are my employer, for one. I cannot risk my position, considering you hold all the power."

"I give you my word that I'm able to separate the two. Whatever happens between us shall not affect your job."

"Even if that were acceptable, I have no plans on being unfaithful to my husband."

"Are you certain he deserves such loyalty?"

She rocked back on her heels, her head tilting slightly. "Of course. Why would he not?"

He clenched and relaxed his hands several times. He'd muffed this. Badly. "All I ask is that you consider it."

"Why?"

"Why?"

"Yes, why should I consider anything improper?"

Because I cannot tear my gaze away from you, not for an instant.

Because your smile thaws out a part of my soul.

Because there is a fire in you, a burning energy that I yearn to feel and taste.

He couldn't share those thoughts, so he said, "Because you will enjoy yourself, I promise."

Her eyes narrowed into slits. "You overstep, sir—"

"Mrs. Walker," a voice said behind them. One of the board members waited there with his wife. "We wanted to thank you for such a lovely evening."

Rose led the couple away, but not before throwing an inscrutable glance at Duke over her shoulder. He watched her go, not deterred in the least. In all her arguments, she hadn't expressed a lack of interest in him. That was telling. If she'd found him unappealing, he would have immediately backed off. Never pursued anything further.

However, the way she'd stared up at him in the kitchen, her clear blue eyes filled with heat and longing, he knew there was interest.

But would she act on it? He couldn't say, but he damn well wanted to find out.

Chapter Seven

Because you will enjoy yourself, I promise.

The words kept tumbling around in Rose's head. Had he been serious? As far as Duke knew, she was a married woman.

Perhaps he'd overimbibed tonight. She hadn't noticed him drinking more than everyone else, but what else could explain his bizarre proposition in the midst of a dinner party?

She quickly said her goodbyes to the guests and retreated to the kitchens for some quiet. And yes, to hide until Duke left.

Bridget was finishing up when Rose arrived. "Is there anything I may do to help?"

"Why aren't you with the guests?" Bridget asked as she wiped down the work surface.

"I needed a break. I'll be relieved when this is over. Pretending to be someone you're not is exhausting."

"Henry said the same thing earlier," the maid said with a shake of her head. "I told him it was only one night and to stop complaining."

"Thank you. For everything, including letting Henry pose as my husband tonight."

Bridget waved her cloth. "Of course. I'm more than happy to help you. Plus, I promised him a reward if he was a good boy—which always becomes my reward, if you get my meaning."

Ugh. Rose put her hands over her ears. "Stop. He's like my brother."

Bridget chuckled. "By the way, the cookies were his idea."

The cookies. Rose had almost forgotten about them in the wake of Duke's proposition. "I have never been so relieved in my life. They were positively perfect. However did he manage it?"

"Henry sent a footman over to the Lowe's kitchen to sweet-talk someone into making a batch of your Duke's shortbread. Turned out Mrs. Riley was still there, seeing as how her daughter's labor turned out to be false. We never baked your tray and used hers instead."

How clever. She would need to thank Henry for such quick thinking. "He is not my Duke."

"My dear, if I had a man staring at me like that big one was staring at you . . ." Bridget fanned herself. "Lord above, I'd claim him before you could blink."

Rose hadn't the faintest idea how to respond. She couldn't claim him—could she?

"By the way, Mrs. Riley said his recipe made absolutely no sense. She said it sounded more like a curse than a cookie. So she made her own version the way she usually does."

"Thank goodness." If the cookies had been terrible, Lord only knew what would have happened. "I must remember to thank her after the holiday. Where is everyone else?"

"I let the others go. I'm just waiting on Henry. I told him he could walk me home." She waggled her brows as if Rose did not already have an idea of what the two would get up to this evening.

"Is there anything left to do?"

"The glasses are washed and dried, just need to be packed in the trunk. Henry and the other boys will come get them first thing in the morning." She pointed to a small room off to the side, a larder they had commandeered for storage. Not many parts of the lower level had been clean enough to use tonight.

"I will finish here." It was the least she could do. Yes, the staff was being paid, but this would have been their night off. "You and Henry go on ahead. I will switch off the lights and lock up."

"Oh, he won't like leaving you alone," Bridget said. "You should have someone here with you."

"I'll stay with her."

Rose's head whipped around at the deep voice and found Duke, large and strikingly handsome in his black evening wear, standing at the bottom of the kitchen stairs. How much had he heard? Her heart began pounding. "Mr. Havermeyer. I thought you'd left." Hoped anyway.

Instead of answering her, he looked at Bridget. "If you will excuse us."

"Of course, sir." Bridget quickly curtsied to them both, eyes twinkling at Rose, and hurried up the servants' stairs.

Then they were alone.

Rose's skin tingled, his nearness causing her to perspire. She had to move away from him, focus on something else. "I have a few things left to do tonight." Lifting her skirts, she went toward the larder and the waiting glasses. "We may speak tomorrow."

Once in the safety of the small room, she pressed a hand to her stomach, exhaling. Goodness, the man was potent. *Because you will enjoy yourself, I promise.* His words, combined with his presence, were enough to send her swooning.

Rose, get a hold of yourself. He is your employer. He thinks you are married.

If she repeated this enough, perhaps she could avoid making a serious mistake, one that could very well get her fired.

Determined, she set to work. With any luck, Duke had returned upstairs and departed. Glasses awaited on the counter, the open trunk on the floor. She picked up a piece of crystal, wrapped it in brown paper, and tucked it into the trunk.

She reached for another glass when his voice startled her. "Why are you doing this? Where is your staff?"

"I dismissed them for the evening. I offered to pack the glasses."

He said nothing and she felt his curiosity like a thick cloud in the room. A lady of the house would never come below and help the servants. If he asked her for a good reason, she wasn't certain what she would say. How many more lies would she need to tell this evening?

Just when she thought he wouldn't speak, he asked, "Why pack them?"

Yes, this was odd, too. In most households the glasses would be stored on a shelf, not packed away in a trunk. "We store these in the attic until we need them."

He drew closer, his towering frame taking up all the space in the larder. "I'll help you."

"That is unnecessary."

"Regardless, I'm still planning to do it."

"You hardly fit in here," she blurted, her body bumping against the open door to avoid touching him.

He stepped in and swung the door closed to make more room. "There. Now the door isn't in our way. Is that better?"

No, it absolutely was not. Now she was confined with an unattainable man who smelled divine and made her body shiver. "Get to it, then," she urged, handing him a glass. The sooner they finished, the sooner she could escape.

He took his time wrapping the glass in the paper before placing it in the trunk. "Have you given any thought to what I said earlier?"

"No," she lied.

A chuckle rumbled in his chest. "You are a terrible liar."

Not so terrible, apparently. I was able to fool you tonight. "I'm married. What you are suggesting is impossible."

"Not when your husband has given his consent."

She jerked in surprise and the glass wobbled in her hand. She clutched at it, fighting to keep a grip on the heavy crystal before it tumbled to the floor and shattered. "What did you say?"

"You heard me. He does not mind. Told me himself. A bit unconventional, yes, but I understand it, considering his association with the maid."

She finished another glass, questions swirling in her mind. How had Duke come to learn of Henry and Bridget's relationship? Yet he'd referred to Henry as Rose's husband, so he hadn't discovered the entire truth. What had Henry said, exactly? Lord, this deception was aging her faster than an opium habit.

"So you think I'll just agree," she said, placing a glass in the trunk to avoid his intense stare, "because my husband has given you the go-ahead?"

Black dress shoes came into view. When she straightened, he was close, his long frame mere inches away. Her mouth turned dry as her gaze traveled north. Every bit of him was appealing, even the way his rumpled brown hair brushed the scar above his eyebrow. He was not perfect, but her body didn't care. The warm feeling in the pit of her stomach swept lower, deeper.

The edges of his mouth curled, and he placed three fingers under her chin. "No, I think you will agree because of what I see in your eyes right now. The flush on your beautiful skin. The hitch in your breath when I move closer."

How had he read her so easily? *The man's a journalist at heart, that's how.* Yet she was a writer, soon to be a reporter. Why could she not tell his thoughts as easily? Then she'd have a better chance at resisting him.

As it was, she was having a hard time remembering why kissing him was a terrible idea.

"I am not one of those women . . ."

He swept an errant strand of hair behind her ear with his fingertips and her words of protest trailed off.

"I know—and that's not why I am here. This is not a game or passing fancy to me. Quite the opposite. You're remarkable, Rose. Unlike any woman I've ever met." He gave a dry chuckle. "In fact, if this were a century or two ago, I might challenge your husband for you."

Her chest tightened, but she strove to keep the mood light. "Pistols at dawn?"

"Always been partial to swords myself," he said with a grin, then sobered. "I know you work for me, but I vow on the future of my company that I will treat you fairly, no matter how long this lasts between us."

"An affair," she said, just to be clear. "You wish to have an affair. With me."

"Yes, I do. I want to take you to my bed and pleasure you until we both drop from exhaustion. Is that direct enough?"

Good Lord, I should say so. If he were any more direct, she'd likely swoon.

While he'd left no doubt as to his intentions, this was new to her. She wasn't a coquette or practiced flirt. Not completely inexperienced, but not *experienced*, either. What should she do?

She advised her readers never to lie, because untruths always had a way of unraveling and causing damage to others. *He'll hate you if he ever learns of what you have done.*

Of course, she'd been lying all night. Why stop now? She should make the most of a situation like this while she still had the chance. This was a fleeting opportunity, not a lifelong commitment. Besides, a man like Duke Havermeyer did not come along every day. She ought to know, as she'd been secretly admiring him for the better part of a year.

Furthermore, when had she ever taken her own advice?

"Please say yes," he whispered, his large hand coming to rest on her hip. The heat of his palm burned through her clothing, branding her skin, and her nipples beaded painfully behind her corset.

There was so much want and longing bubbling up inside her that rational thought receded. A wild reckless abandon overcame her instead. How long had she fantasized about a situation such as this, where she could actually touch him? Kiss him? She wanted to know what it would be like . . . No, she *needed* to know what it would be like. If she refused, something told her she would regret it forever.

All those afternoons spent watching and wanting him— and now he was right here.

In front of her.

Offering a slice of everything she'd craved, a banquet of exquisite maleness wrapped in an elegant evening suit.

He thinks you are an experienced married woman.

Well, what would one more deception hurt?

Sliding forward, she gripped his lapels, crushing the expensive fabric in her grasp. "Yes," she breathed before dragging his mouth down atop hers.

* * *

A dark satisfaction flooded Duke's veins as his mouth met hers. He had no chance to relish his victory, however, because she was kissing him, yielding to him, and his brain could only handle so much, apparently. All he could think about was her mouth, her taste, the slide of her lips over his, the soft press of her breasts against his chest. Lust flared in his groin, blood filling his cock in steady pulses to match the beat of his heart.

He cupped her jaw and parted her lips with his tongue, thrusting inside when she gave him access. She was warm and slick, the taste of her more exquisite than any sweet or spirit he'd ever imbibed. She kissed confidently, eagerly, unafraid of showing her desire, and the bold response hardened him further. Would she be this passionate in bed?

Christ, he could hardly wait to find out.

He swept a hand along her neck and shoulder, then down her bodice to cup a breast. Her back arched, pressing her into his palm, and he tightened his fingers in a feeble attempt at offering relief through her clothing. She gasped, breaking off from his mouth as her body moved closer, seeking, and he grew dizzy, drowning in his need for this woman. He had to touch her, right this minute.

With his hands on her waist, he lifted her up onto the small counter, rattling a few crystal glasses, and then quickly stepped between her legs. Had he ever felt so frenzied, so desperate? He wanted all of her, every bit of her, immediately.

She reached for him, her fingers sliding through his hair to pull him to her mouth once more. He kissed her hard, his hand shoving into the bodice of her dress, searching until he reached the taut bud of her nipple, which he pinched between two fingers. She groaned into his mouth, the sweetest sound he'd ever heard.

He kissed her throat, then the underside of her jaw. He nibbled, teased, and tormented the silken skin on his way to the swell of her breasts. There he spent a considerable amount of time worshipping the skin exposed by her dress, all the while wishing she were completely unclothed.

"Let me pleasure you here," he whispered, and shifted her skirts. "Right now. Then we'll find a bed, so I may see each exquisite inch of you."

She helped by moving the layers of silk and cotton out of the way. When he found the part in her drawers, the heat there nearly caused his eyes to roll back in his head. Her folds were slick and he traced each with a fingertip, learning her, then dipped to her entrance, where even more moisture had gathered. He brought his finger to his mouth, the heady taste exploding on his tongue, and a jolt went straight through him. *Jesus, she was perfect.*

"*Duke.*"

The sound of his name in her breathy plea caused his cock to twitch. He opened his eyes to find her watching him, her blue irises gone dark with hunger. No hesitation, no shyness—just lust and longing. Still, he had to be certain.

"Should I stop?"

"Not yet. Kiss me."

"I plan to," he murmured and dropped to his knees. "Just not on the mouth."

He opened her thighs to make room for him. With his hands under her buttocks, he brought her forward until she rested at the edge of the counter, the perfect meal for his starving mouth. When he draped her legs over his shoulders, she braced herself on the counter, a question in her gaze.

"I need to taste you," he said, parting her folds with his thumbs. The scent of her arousal filled his head, and he swiped his tongue through the glistening moisture coating her flesh. She jerked and he steadied her. Perhaps her husband refused to pleasure her this way. Duke would go slowly, savor her. Let the pleasure build until she was delirious with it.

Her clitoris, swollen and ripe, begged for attention, and he began with gentle circles, using the tip of his tongue. When her hips tilted for more, he increased the pressure and incorporated his lips, teeth, and the flat of his tongue to drive her wild.

"Oh good heavens," she mumbled, one hand threading through his hair.

He slid a finger inside her, filling her, the velvet walls gripping him as he continued to work the tiny button atop her folds. After a few moments, she was rocking onto his hand with abandon, thighs shaking, and he knew she was close. He added another finger, stretching her, and she began moaning deep in her throat.

He sucked hard to push her over the edge. With a harsh cry, she came against his mouth, body trembling, internal muscles milking his fingers. He loved the way she reacted to him, so honest and brave. A woman who knew what she wanted and did not apologize for it. He ignored the need pounding along his shaft and instead concentrated on prolonging her orgasm.

When she stopped shaking, he eased up, kissing and licking her gently, unable to pull himself away just yet. His cock was so hard, desperate for friction, but he continued to pump his hand, her channel even slicker after her climax. "I could do this all night," he murmured. When she grew sensitive he gave one final flick of his tongue and stood.

He kissed her deeply, letting her taste her own arousal. She met him eagerly, her breath still coming in short pants. Small fingers began to work at his trouser fastenings—and he lifted his head. "Wait. We need not go further now. There are many nights ahead of—"

"No, now," she said, and parted the fabric.

He didn't understand the rush. This was madness— even though he was dying to sink inside her. Her climax had fueled his fervor, but he didn't want to do this here. "Rose—"

She put her hand over the heavy length of his cloth-covered cock, her touch tentative, almost shy, and he gasped. Oh *fuck*. Any complaint he'd been about to utter completely disappeared. He broke out in a sweat, his skin burning. He tore off his dinner jacket and tossed the fine wool to the ground. Next, he loosened his bow tie and opened his collar, the gold collar stud dropping somewhere on the floor.

The edges of her mouth curled. She was clearly pleased at his reaction. "Shall I stop?"

"Dear God, please don't. Press hard."

She turned out to be an apt pupil. The rough drag of her palm on his erection over his clothing caused his breath to stutter. He put a hand on the cabinet above to steady himself, struggling for control, trying not to devolve into an animal by ripping her clothes off and shoving inside her. "Rose," he ground out from behind clenched teeth as she worked him. "I am so close."

She parted his undergarment and her fingers wrapped around his bare shaft. *God, yes.* He moved his hand between her legs once more, needing to hear her whimpers, needing her right there with him.

Then she brought the head of his cock to where his fingers teased. "Please, Duke."

He froze. "Are you sure?" They were in a pantry, for God's sake, where any member of her staff could discover them. Her husband might not mind, but society tolerated affairs only if they were discreet.

"Yes." She nodded, her hair tumbling out of its pins. "Tonight. It has to be tonight."

He barely heard anything after the word *yes*, the idea of sliding into her sheath nearly enough to drive him insane. Lining up at her entrance, he pressed the crown inside. His eyelids slammed shut, sensation overwhelming him. Christ, she was tight. Hot. Exquisite.

It was absolute heaven.

"Please, more." Her arms wrapped around his neck and brought him down to her mouth. He kissed her, their lips clashing in desperation.

Canting his hips, he pressed in until he was fully seated. Her grip was snug, pure bliss surrounding him, and he could feel the threads of his control unraveling. One long thrust had them both moaning, her nails digging into his shoulders, and he started to move in earnest, drinking in her sighs and gasps. He held on to her hips, positioning her where she seemed to prefer, and let instinct take over. Within minutes, an electric charge built up at the base of his spine, in his balls, the imminent release he could not stop.

He used his thumb on her swollen nub, pressing and circling, until her legs tensed. "Hurry, Rose." He clenched his teeth. "You feel too perfect. I cannot last."

She threw her head back, mouth open in a wordless scream as her body spasmed around him. Duke let go then, pounding hard, his hips churning. The white-hot release swept up from his toes and his muscles trembled with the power of it. He jerked out of her channel just before spend erupted from the head of his cock, and his hand flew over his shaft as his orgasm went on and on. Finally, his knees buckled and smacked into the wooden cabinet.

Jesus, was he about to faint?

When his brain stopped spinning, he braced himself and attempted to catch his breath. "My God, I cannot focus my eyes. You've blinded me, woman."

Delicate fingers caressed his jaw. "I suspect you will recover quickly."

Was that a hopeful note in her voice? He'd love nothing more than to continue this all night. He kissed her slowly, sweetly. "Come home with me where we may do this properly."

"Tonight?"

"Yes, tonight."

After a long excruciating beat, she nodded. "All right, I will."

Grinning in unholy anticipation, he stepped back to clean up. When they were marginally put to rights, he shoved on his coat and clasped her hand. "You won't regret this, Rose."

Her enthusiasm dimmed for a brief second before she masked it. He wondered over her expression as he reached for the latch. When he pulled, however, the door did not budge. He tried again, yanking harder. Only, he received the same result. "Does this door stick?"

"I'm not sure. Let me see." She slid around him and used two hands to wrench at the door. She shook and pulled, her arms straining. "Oh no. Come on, open! You stupid door." She kicked at the heavy oak with her foot. "How could this have happened?"

"Wait, are you saying . . . ?"

Her eyes were wide with panic. "I'm saying we are locked in."

Chapter Eight

$\mathcal{R}$ose watched as the news sank into his brain. "Huh," was all he said, and dragged a large hand across his jaw.

Somehow, she'd expected a bigger reaction. Perhaps he didn't realize the gravity of the situation.

And why would he? He believes the staff in the house will rescue us at some point.

Cold dread settled in her chest, replacing any warm and tender feelings left from their encounter a few moments ago. Who knew how long they could be trapped in here together?

Morning. Henry is coming in the morning. At least they wouldn't die in this room.

"I cannot see how there is cause for alarm," Duke said calmly. "Someone will come looking for you or visit the kitchens eventually. We merely need to continue a steady stream of noise whenever we suspect someone's about."

He made it sound so easy. No doubt he believed it, too. Everything was easy for Duke Havermeyer, even her. A few kisses and caresses and she'd shamelessly lunged for his trouser buttons.

Stop. You are growing hysterical. She put a hand to her stomach and tried to take a few deep breaths. This night was turning out nothing like she had expected. Moreover, *he* was nothing like she'd expected.

He pleasured you with his mouth. He . . . made love to you. You are no longer a maiden.

And he wanted to do it all over again at his home.

Part of her was thrilled at the idea; the other part wanted to run away and forget this all happened. Of course, she had to escape this room first.

"Rose? Are you all right?"

"Fine," she lied, closing her eyes and struggling for composure. "Positively perfect. I would merely like for this door to open."

His expression said he didn't believe her. "How about if I try to kick it down?"

"Please." He was huge, over six feet. How could one flimsy door withstand the man's brute strength?

He removed his evening coat once more, this time handing it to her. Raising one foot, he kicked at the wood nearest the handle, grunting with the effort. The wood rattled, but held. *Dash it all.*

They exchanged a brief look and then he tried again—only to get the same result. The door wouldn't budge.

Oh God. What would Henry and the other footmen think when they found her and Duke in the morning? How would Mr. Henry Walker explain dressing in the Lowes' livery to Duke? She bent over, her lungs failing to pull in enough air.

"Here." Clasping her hand, he helped her sit on the floor and then lowered himself down. "We'll wait here together. It won't be so bad, I promise."

She arranged her skirts and tried not to dwell on the minuscule size of the space.

"Are you uncomfortable in small places?"

No use dodging the question. He would figure it out at some point anyway. "Yes, I am." She'd been locked in a closet once as a small girl—a prank by another child—and she remembered that fear so clearly. Now she even left her bedchamber door open at night when she slept.

"Ah. That explains it. Do elevators bother you, as well?"

"No, they move, so it's not quite the same. Also, I've never been stuck in one."

"Fair enough. What may I do to help?"

"Other than get us out of here or generate more air, nothing."

"Rose, this room isn't sealed shut. There are gaps around the door." He pointed with a long finger. "And I see a hole down there by the floor, probably where a mouse—"

She sucked air through her teeth. "Please refrain from discussing the vermin lurking nearby until we are safely rescued."

He chuckled, his shoulders brushing against hers. "I never thought the capable Mrs. Walker would be such a frightened little rabbit."

She elbowed him—hard. "Poking fun at me is hardly the best way to keep me calm."

He held up his big hands, the ones that had touched her intimately mere moments ago. The memory caused her lower body to throb with satisfaction and longing. As if he sensed the direction of her thoughts, he drawled, "So what shall we do to pass the time?"

"Not that," she snapped. They needed sedate activities, ones that would conserve their air. She asked the first question that popped into her mind. "Tell me how you got that scar above your eyebrow."

"This?" He ran a finger over the jagged mark, then let out a sigh. "It's not an exciting story. I constantly escaped my tutors as a boy. Hated being indoors and forced to sit through lessons. One day I slipped out to take a swim and got caught in a riptide. Hit my head on a rock and nearly drowned. It bled for a long time."

"How awful. Was it not stitched?"

A joyless sound escaped his mouth. "My father locked me in my room after. Refused to let the physician attend me."

Locked in his room? "My God. How old were you?"

"Thirteen." He lifted a shoulder. "I was subsequently shipped off to boarding school. My father didn't speak to me again for over a year."

Her stomach clenched in outrage over this treatment. What sort of monster had raised this man? "And your mother?"

"She died while I was away at school that first term. He didn't allow me to come home for her funeral." He grimaced. "I've never told anyone that before. I apologize—"

"What a horrid man, your father. I'll certainly never look at his portrait in the *Gazette* offices in the same manner. It should be taken down and burned."

He appeared surprised by her vehemence, momentarily silent as he frowned. "It would be wrong of me to complain. I had more advantages than most."

But you had no love, no support. No wonder all the man did was work. He'd been raised and conditioned to do so. "Not all advantages are material."

"That sounds like the wisdom of my favorite advice columnist."

"Because it is. And, incidentally, if you'd written to me, I would have told you to run away and join the circus."

He laughed, the deep sound filling the small space. "As what? A thirteen-year-old escape artist?"

"Bigger careers have been started with less." They sat in companionable silence until she asked, "Is that why you never celebrate Christmas?"

"I suppose so." He crossed his long legs at the ankles. "I certainly have no memories of holidays by the fire, roasting chestnuts and stringing popped corn for the tree. My father always worked. Then, once my mother died, I remained at school for the holidays with the few other boys who didn't go home. We played cards and tried to sneak out to the local dance halls."

"No presents? No carols? No mulled cider?" All those things made up Christmas as far as she was concerned— along with good friends. She'd never been lonely growing up.

"No, no, and no. I take it your Christmases were quite different than mine?"

"Much different. We had dinners with friends, sang songs, played charades . . . My mother and I enjoyed every minute of our time together. Even now, she prepares my favorite dishes and plays the piano as we all sing carols."

"We all?"

"Our friends are more like extended family." The staff in the two houses where her mother had worked over the last fifteen years remained close. "There was never a dull moment."

"I take it your father is not alive."

"I have no memory of him." Her mother never spoke of her father. Rose had raised the subject over the years, but her mother always had the same answer: *Focus on what you have, not on what you are lacking.*

"So do you believe in mistletoe?"

Her head swiveled toward him. "That bad luck will befall anyone who refuses a kiss under it?"

The side of his mouth hitched in the most adorably playful manner, the one that caused her stomach to flutter. He slipped a hand into his pocket and produced a sprig of mistletoe.

"Where did you find that?"

"I sneaked a piece from the arrangement on your mantel. Wasn't sure if I might need it."

"Turns out you did just fine on your own."

He lifted the plant above her head. "Even still, a man can

never have too many weapons at his disposal—especially when a woman turns him into a desperate, slavering beast."

Her insides melted and she slid her palm over his whisker-roughened jaw. "Then you'd best get to it. I cannot have bad luck hanging over me."

He bent toward her, and she held her breath, anticipating the gentle press of his lips, the fire he ignited in her with a single touch. Her body had barely recovered from earlier, but she could already feel the sweet pulse of desire tugging at her insides. With his lips almost touching hers, he whispered, "I've never met anyone like you, Rose Walker. You have bewitched me."

Lord, this man could be dangerous to her heart. Hoping to prevent any more declarations, she gestured to the mistletoe. "My luck, Havermeyer. You must save me before it is too late."

A noise sounded in the kitchens, breaking the spell between them. Someone was out there. Rose sucked in a breath, leaning back to find Duke's equally startled gaze. He leaped to his feet—he was surprisingly quick for a man of his size—and pounded on the door. "Ho! Let us out of here."

Rose joined him. "Hello! Help!"

After a second, the door flew open and a well-dressed older man appeared, his expression etched with fury. When the stranger spotted Duke, he rocked back on his heels, his anger melting into confusion. "Duke Havermeyer? Who is this woman and what are you both doing in my house?"

* * *

"Your house?" Duke frowned at the vaguely familiar man. "This is *her* house." He indicated Rose, who had gone unnaturally still at his side.

The man sneered at Rose from beneath his large mustache. "I have no idea who she is, but I assure you this is my home."

Rose stepped forward and began to lead the man into the kitchens. "Sir, this is merely a simple misunderstanding. Please come with me—"

"This is no misunderstanding, madam." The stranger halted in his tracks, his tone approaching a shout. "Someone has broken into my home and . . . hosted a party of some sort. I shall bring the authorities here instantly if you don't tell me what is going on."

Duke put himself between the furious man and Rose. "Do not raise your voice to her. It is clear you are confused, but I will not tolerate any disrespect for one second more."

"Mr. Havermeyer." The stranger heaved out a long breath. "I am Mr. Rutherford Miller. We met last summer at the New York Yacht Club. My sister is married to Mr. Jay Cranford, who is cousin to Mr. Walter Cranford."

Walter Cranford was on HPC's board of directors. "Yes, I know Cranford. In fact, he was here earlier. What does all that have to do with Mrs. Walker?" He glanced over his shoulder. Rose had gone pale, wringing her hands as she watched the exchange. Duke lifted a brow at her in the hopes she would clear this all up.

Instead, Miller answered. "I couldn't say, but I do know this house is still legally mine. We've had it on the market for a few months in an attempt to find a buyer. It has been sitting empty for weeks. Then I received a telegram tonight from Cranford telling me he had met the new owners and congratulating me on a sale that never happened."

"Empty?" Duke had to admit, Miller sounded entirely credible—which meant none of this made sense. "I'm confused. If this is your house, then . . ." He spun on his heel. "Rose, did you . . . rent this man's home for the dinner party?"

"Not exactly," she whispered.

"Then you used it without permission?" Even saying it out loud was madness. Surely, he was wrong.

Her lip quivered as she drew herself up. "The house had been empty, and we only needed one day and one night. I never thought anyone would notice. We did pay the real estate agent, if that helps."

Duke's mouth fell open as the words fell into place. This was . . . not her house. But the staff? The decor? How on earth had she managed it?

The details hardly mattered. The relevant part was that she had lied.

Everything tonight had been a lie.

The weight of that statement pressed down on him, his heart beating loudly in his ears. He was stunned, utterly flabbergasted. This was not her home. Were those her servants? Where did she and Mr. Walker actually live? No wonder she had offered to pack up the glasses; they had to vacate the premises as quickly as possible, like thieves in the night.

He rubbed his eyes with the heels of his hands. What if his board found out the evening had been a lie? The possibility turned his blood to ice. Would they assume Duke was complicit, that he'd actively participated in the deception?

Christ, they would roast him over a spit and eat him alive.

The newspapers. The company. He must protect both. Nothing else mattered.

He heard Miller square off against Rose. "It certainly does not help and I shall be firing that real estate agent directly. I don't know who you think you are, breaking into houses and using them without permission, but I will see you reported to the authorities and—"

"Stop," Duke said, his tone sharp. He felt nothing, no anger or fear, merely a bitter resolve for all this to go away.

"You'll do nothing of the sort, Miller. This will be handled quickly and quietly. I'll see you are well compensated for the inconvenience. My attorney will be around tomorrow. In the meantime, say nothing about this to anyone. Do you understand?"

Miller grew agitated, his face turning redder. "I want answers, Havermeyer. Who is this woman? Is she a friend of yours? Did you approve of this scheme?"

He straightened, using his height to intimidate the other man. "I do not owe you answers, so you won't get them. We apologize for intruding and a team of maids will arrive tomorrow to clean your former home. Along with what I plan to pay you, let's leave it at that, shall we?"

Miller appeared like he might argue, then gave a sharp nod. "Fine. I expect to hear from you tomorrow." With one final glare in Rose's direction, he marched through the kitchen and disappeared up the stairs.

Silence descended with all the subtlety of a hammer.

"Was any of it real?" He kept his gaze fixed on the far wall. "Or was it all a lie?"

"Duke—"

"Be honest with me, Rose. I deserve the truth."

He heard her swallow. "I'm unmarried and reside in a boardinghouse on East Fifty-Ninth Street. The man who posed as my husband is just a friend."

He nearly stumbled back at the magnitude of this revelation. Dear God, it was worse than he thought. Absolutely nothing she'd told him earlier turned out to be true. Every bit of it—tonight's dinner party, her persona, and her marriage—had been false. She had lied to him and the HPC readers for nearly two years.

It turned out Mrs. Walker wasn't a recluse. She was a fraud, a figment of imagination. A young girl determined to make a quick buck, spinning lies to further her career.

Jesus, she was unmarried—and an employee—and he'd fucked her on a counter. A strange combination of anger, resentment, and shame rolled through him. He longed to throw something, to smash every glass in that goddamn larder.

Shit, the larder. He closed his eyes. Though he dreaded the answer, he had to ask. "Before the pantry, were you a virgin?"

Her skin turned a dull red and he had his answer. He took a deep breath and counted to ten. For God's sake . . . How had he not realized this earlier?

"It hardly matters." Her voice trembled. "My maidenhead was mine to do whatever I chose with it."

"It matters to me," he said carefully. "I would have been—" He had been about to say "more tender," but if he'd known of her inexperience, the two of them never would have ended up in the pantry together in the first place.

"I don't regret it," she said, daring him to say otherwise.

He let that go—for now. Instead, he had to find out the depth of her betrayal to the company. "Do you even write the column?"

"Yes! Every word. I have friends who help if there's a question I cannot answer myself."

She sounded credible, but he hadn't a clue what to believe. His whole world had just been turned upside down. Anger threatened to consume him, to take away what little reason he had left. The open door to the pantry caught his gaze, mocking him, and his insides froze. He encouraged the sensation, and the ice within him doubled, tripled, to spread throughout his veins, making him impenetrable. Any bothersome emotions were shoved aside, buried, just as he'd done as a boy when his father turned cruel or distant. Or when his mother had died. *I don't need anyone else. Havermeyer Publishing is everything I need.*

"Let's go." He gestured toward the stairs.

"Duke, please. We should talk about this. You've hardly spoken."

You've ruined everything, he wanted to say. *You've jeopardized my company. You've destroyed what could have been between us.*

He strode to the larder and turned the switch, glad to darken that memory. Then he did the same with the kitchen light. "Come."

A soft yellow glow from the upper floor illuminated their way as they climbed the steps. He didn't touch her as they continued on. Didn't yell or even scowl at her. He'd successfully shut down any feelings, become numb to his surroundings. It was a relief, really. The world was much clearer, simpler when emotions were not involved.

Part of this was his fault for believing her. When was the last time he had trusted someone? A mistake he would not repeat.

You were too busy attempting to get under her skirts. You let your cock do your thinking.

"Duke, I'm sorry. I never meant to hurt you or ruin tonight." She hurried to keep up with him, her skirts rustling in the quiet corridor. "I only tried to do as you asked—to host a Christmas dinner for the board."

The result had now given him another reason to hate Christmas. Excellent.

"I'll see that your friends are well compensated for their troubles" was all he could think to say.

"I've already paid them—and I don't want to discuss the compensation. I want to apologize."

Now at the front entryway, he located their coats in the tiny closet. He helped her with her overcoat, then donned his own. There were things he could have said, probably should have said, but he never looked back once a decision had been made. There was no point—and Rose had forced his hand by lying.

He opened the front door. "Is there a key or . . . ?"

She bit her bottom lip, her brows dipping together, and she produced a key from her skirts. Duke took the metal key, closed the door behind them, and locked it.

He returned the key to her. "Shall we?"

She nodded and he offered his arm to lead her down the smooth front steps. His brougham waited at the end of the walk. "Where is your address?"

She rattled it off and Duke repeated the location for his driver. Then he helped Rose into the carriage. He did not follow.

She dropped onto the seat, her eyes bright with unshed tears. "Don't you wish to shout at me? Isn't there anything you want to say? Anything at all?"

He had to keep control, to swallow all the angry words and messy sentiment. Too much was at risk to uncork the chaos swirling inside him.

"I do have one thing to say." With a flick of his wrist he slammed the carriage door. "You're fired."

Chapter Nine

You're fired.

Fired. He had actually *fired* her.

Worse, Duke wouldn't talk to her or answer her notes. Refused to see her when she paid a call to his home yesterday. It was as if she had ceased to exist for him.

If only the reverse were true.

Unfortunately, she couldn't stop thinking about him, about the night of the dinner party. Before Mr. Miller's arrival, Duke had been so charming. Flirtatious and fun. Not to mention the way he made her feel in the pantry . . . Good heavens, she broke out in a sweat merely recalling his kisses, the sweep of his large hands over her skin, unlocking all her secret desires and unraveling her with the simplest touch.

Then he'd learned of her lies, and whatever had been blossoming between them had withered. He'd withdrawn, shut her out. Never had she seen anyone go from blazing hot to ice-cold in such a short period of time. Yes, she had lied to him. She had put his business at risk, not to mention those who depended on Havermeyer Publishing for their livelihoods. Though she believed her actions were justified, he had every right to be angry with her.

However, after everything that happened, could he not allow her five minutes to explain?

This was how she found herself at the HPC offices on

Christmas Day. By God, he was going to see her—and listen to her—if she had to strap him in a chair to do it. This was precisely what she would have advised one of her readers to do, and if she couldn't take her own advice, then she had no business writing a weekly advice column.

And if Duke decided there could be no personal relationship between them, fine. However, she wanted her job back. No, she *deserved* her job back.

Though it was a holiday, the main newsroom bustled with activity. Men were checking copy, typing rapidly, and hurrying about as they rushed to put tomorrow's edition together. News never took a holiday—nor did the man obsessed with his empire. Undoubtedly, Duke would be here. That he worked on Christmas to relieve other employees—instead of closing up shop—was an indicator of his priorities.

The door to Mr. Pike's office was ajar and she had a feeling someone had decided to use the office, someone whose own office sat far from the newsroom.

She peered inside and, as she'd suspected, found Duke at the desk, his dark head bent over a proof of the *Gazette*.

"Reggie, this headline on the East Side murder—" He looked up and surprise skated over his features before he masked it behind a wall of cool reserve. Dropping his gaze, he resumed his work. "Make an appointment with my assistant if you need something, Miss Walker. I am quite busy."

"You will see me now, Mr. Havermeyer." She closed the door behind her and turned the lock. The scratch of his pen faltered for a brief second, then continued. Undaunted, she crossed the room and planted her feet in front of his desk. *No fear. No hesitation.*

"Well, get to it. I have an edition to finish."

Her heart squeezed in agony over his wintry tone. Had this been a mistake? The loving, passionate man, the one who'd held her hand in the tiny pantry to help keep her calm, seemed like a distant memory.

"You have three minutes, Miss Walker, before I have you shown out. Were I you, I would hurry."

She took a deep breath. "You never allowed me a chance to apologize properly. Or to explain why I lied."

He made a scornful noise in his throat. "A justified lie is still a lie—and I abhor liars."

The back of her neck tingled, the dismissive words irritating her. Yes, she had deceived him. Yes, she deserved his anger. However, did she not also deserve a bit of compassion? An opportunity to share her side? His rigid judgment stung and her temper flared.

Drawing herself up, she snapped, "How nice for you, this luxury of judgment. How easy for you to remain sanctimonious, a man who never had to struggle or scrape, never had to prove himself to rise above the others. Not all of us have been so fortunate. You don't even care to learn the reasons behind the charade."

He shot to his feet and braced his hands on the desk. "I know you have deceived thousands of people for months. Does their trust mean nothing to you?"

"Their trust—or yours?"

"You think this is about my *hurt feelings*?"

"Are you saying it's not?"

"Rose, there are more than ten thousand employees who depend on HPC for their livelihoods. If no one buys the newspapers, then those people are out of work. People do not buy newspapers unless they trust them. Ergo, it is my job to present the truth. Always."

"Oh, please. Noms de plume abound in journalism—and you know it. Nellie Bly's real name is Elizabeth Cochran, for God's sake. Pike and I made up the Mrs. Walker persona knowing readers would have an easier time accepting advice from an older married woman. However, the advice was entirely factual. I am still the woman behind the words."

"Yes, you and your research partners. Let's not forget them."

She put her hands on her hips and struggled to remain composed. "You probably don't realize this, but I applied for a reporting position at the *Gazette*. I wanted to be like those men out there"—she gestured toward the outer room—"but Mr. Pike told me female reporters would be a distraction to the men on staff. He agreed to let me write an advice column from home, however. It wasn't ideal, scribbling out recipes and solving marital squabbles, but there was no other choice. I needed a position, one that would provide for my mother and myself. A job that will not break me, as hers has broken her."

A flicker of emotion glowed in his dark eyes. "What job is that?"

"My mother is a maid. A housemaid in her younger days, a job that is too rigorous for her now. She works in the kitchens at the Lowe residence with Henry, Bridget, and the others."

"Ah. Your comments at dinner make more sense."

She remembered Mr. Cameron's insensitive attitude concerning the servant class and her reaction. "You were worried about losing your business, but I was worried about losing the roof over my head. And my mother's health. Our future. Telling a fib or two was sometimes necessary."

"You think I only insist on the truth because I am rich."

"No, there are plenty of rich liars in the world. I believe your rigid sense of right and wrong has been tainted by your status. You get to decide the rules . . . and everyone else must play by them."

"My newspaper, my rules. Doesn't seem unreasonable to me."

She clenched her teeth. This was getting her nowhere fast. How could she make him understand? "Duke—"

"You're wasting your time, Rose." He dropped into the large leather chair. "The paper is barely surviving one scandal. Can you imagine the hullabaloo if another one surfaced?"

"Wrong. You are selling the readership short. I read their letters and I know them. They don't like Mrs. Walker because of her wedding ring or her fancy house. They like her because of the wisdom and compassion she displays, the wit and the emotion. That is all right here." She pointed at herself.

Duke was already shaking his head. "I've made my decision, Rose."

She hated that answer, but it was what she had expected—and why she'd written a new column for tomorrow's paper.

"And what about us?" she forced herself to ask. "Have you made that decision, as well?"

He exhaled a long breath and studied her face. "I don't make a habit of ruining innocents. I am willing to do the right thing, however, which is no doubt why you are really here."

Did he think . . . ? Was he insinuating . . . ? The hairs on the back of her neck stood up, her fingers curling into her palms. "I'm here to argue for my job, not to drag you kicking and screaming into a marriage."

He didn't appear to believe her. "You should congratulate yourself. Many have tried to get me to the altar, but you are the only one who has succeeded. Contact my assistant after the holiday and she'll tell you all you need to know." He picked up his pen and went back to proofing.

"All I need to know?"

"Yes, such as the location and date." He waved his hand, still not meeting her eyes. "Where to send the bills, et cetera."

Snow began to fall outside the windows, the sky giving up in trying to hold in the moisture. Rose felt a little the same way, unable to swallow past the lump in her throat as her heart split in two. She'd been wrong about him.

So very wrong.

She couldn't speak, her mouth as dry as dust, tears threatening behind her eyes. As much as she would love to deliver a blistering setdown, one that would reach the heart behind his cold shell, she could not. And really, why would she bother? She'd rather work as a laundry maid for the rest of her life than marry this man. "No, thank you," she choked out and crossed to the exit.

Unlocking the door, she left Pike's office and dug deep for composure. Only a few more minutes. She had one last stop to make before she could figure out the rest of her life.

It took a few tries, but Rose finally located the correct typesetter. "Good day. I am Mrs. Walker," she told the young man. Pulling a folded piece of paper from her pocket, she placed it on the desk. "I have new copy for my column. See that it gets replaced in the morning edition."

"But we've already laid out the entire paper. Mr. Havermeyer'll be very displeased if—"

What was one more lie when she had absolutely nothing left to lose? "Mr. Havermeyer just finished approving the changes. You don't think I'd be foolish enough to go behind his back, do you? On Christmas?" She laughed, though it sounded hollow to her ears.

"I suppose not," the man said and picked up the words she'd written last night. "I'll see this is taken care of."

"Thank you. I owe you a glass of eggnog."

"Gives me indigestion. I'd rather have a cigar, if you want to know the truth."

"Then you shall have it. Take care and Merry Christmas."

"I enjoy your column, Mrs. Walker," he called as she walked away. "Wife and I never miss it."

She turned and thanked him, her head high as she left the *Gazette* for the final time.

* * *

The offices were dark that evening as Duke relaxed in Pike's office with a cigar and a bottle of scotch. The other employees had already departed, the issue long sent to the presses. Only, he had nowhere to go, no one to meet. An empty house awaited him, the thought more depressing than the quiet offices. At least at the office, he might get ahead on his work.

He took a swallow of scotch, hoping to numb the pain he'd felt ever since Rose had walked out of this room. While his proposal may have lacked romance, she certainly hadn't hesitated in refusing him.

What had you expected when you treated her terribly?

He stared at the spot where she'd taken him to task hours ago. *You get to decide the rules . . . and everyone else must play by them.* And why not? With things under his control, then Duke could protect himself from the disappointment and hurt when others failed him. No betrayal. No messy *feelings* grinding up his insides like machinery.

Another mouthful of scotch burned its way to his stomach. Perhaps if he got drunk enough, he'd be able to sleep tonight. The last two nights he had stared at the ceiling above his bed, remembering and second-guessing himself—something he never, ever did.

She had done that, with her sharp wit and striking blue eyes. Her soft kisses and teasing smile. He could still hear her breathy moans in his ear as he drove inside her, his body shaking with need the likes of which he'd never known.

And he'd pushed her away with his indifference.

I needed a position, one that would provide for my mother and myself.

While he didn't approve of lying, he could understand the need for her to pose as someone else, especially after Pike had refused to hire her as a reporter. However, after what happened in the larder, she'd had ample opportunity to tell him the truth. Instead, she'd maintained the lie and now he felt like the world's biggest fool. She'd been a maiden, for God's sake. He would have been gentler if he'd known. Their intimacies wouldn't have gone as far, that was for certain.

A stab of guilt worked its way under his ribs and he attempted to banish it with another swallow of spirits.

The door to the office slid open and Duke's heart thumped hard.

Had she returned?

Pike's weathered face appeared, his body pausing when he spied Duke in the chair. "Mr. Havermeyer . . . I hadn't expected to find you here this late."

Duke pushed aside his disappointment and beckoned his former editor in chief inside the room. "Obviously. You might as well come in."

Pike removed one of the paintings from the wall. "The wife painted this when we were younger. Cannot believe I left it behind." He lowered himself into a seat across from the desk. "I see you found my scotch."

"I certainly have." Duke glanced at the nearly empty glass in his hand, then finished the rest of it in one gulp. "It tastes like varnish."

"Hardly ever drink spirits myself. Kept that in my desk for the editors—and you, apparently."

Duke reached into the drawer and withdrew another glass. He filled it and topped off his own. He held the fresh glass out to Pike. "If I must suffer, then so shall you."

Pike laughed and accepted the crystal. "Fair enough. I must say, you look like shit, Havermeyer."

Duke dragged a hand down his face. "A few long days, is all. Nothing a good night's sleep won't cure."

"Sure about that?" He lifted the glass to his mouth. "Anything you want to talk about?"

It was not an odd request. Duke had worked closely with Pike over the years and had looked up to the man. In truth, Pike had been more of a mentor than Duke's own father. Firing the older man hadn't been easy—almost as hard as not chasing after Rose when she walked out today.

He cleared his throat, determined to stick to business matters rather than personal ones. "Why'd you keep Mrs. Walker's identity a secret from me?"

"So she told you?"

"More like someone told me for her, but yes. I know she's an unmarried girl living in a boardinghouse. What I cannot fathom is why you would think keeping that from me was a good idea."

Pike blew out a long breath. "A bit of what we do is razzle-dazzle, even if you don't like to admit it. Pulitzer certainly ain't above pulling a stunt to gain readers. Look at what he's done with those cartoons and sending Bly into that lunatic asylum. I never compromised the reputation of the paper, not once. I merely wrapped Rose's advice in a bit of sugar to make it an easier pill to swallow."

"The sugar being her supposed age and marital status."

"Of course. Girl's got a good level head on her shoulders, but no one wants to hear advice from one so young. Hell, the *Pittsburgh Dispatch* has an advice columnist who's a man posing as an elderly woman. At least I stuck with the right gender."

"That is not the point," Duke snapped. "And if the public had discovered the lie, the paper's reputation would have been compromised."

"Had discovered it, as in past tense?"

Duke swirled the scotch in his crystal, watching the light reflect off the light brown liquid. "I fired her. After the dinner party she hosted for the board the other night."

Pike winced. "The dinner party failed, I suppose?"

"No. The entire thing was a rousing success. She charmed them all, set up shop in an abandoned house off Central Park. Roped some poor fool into posing as her husband. The board ate it up with a spoon. Haven't heard a peep out of them concerning the scandal since then."

"Yet you fired her?"

Why didn't Pike understand? "She lied—and if it had been discovered, the paper would have suffered."

"You're wrong. Miss Walker is an incredible asset to your company. Have you seen how many letters she receives a week? The mailroom had to hire two additional employees just to handle the volume."

He hadn't known that, but it hardly mattered. "Whoever replaces her shall prove just as popular, believe me."

"Then tell me why you are here so late on Christmas, looking like someone died."

Duke swirled the scotch in his glass, thinking on how best to respond. "Have you ever wanted something so badly, even when it could destroy you?"

Pike remained silent for a moment. "Something—or some*one*?"

"Does it matter?"

"Of course. Things lack the power to love us or hurt us. They also lack the power to change."

"Fine, some*one*."

Pike sat a bit straighter. "I've known you all your life. And never has there been anyone so dedicated or driven to succeed, not even your father. But has it brought you happiness? Your father was a miserable man who made everyone around him miserable, as well. Is that the kind of life you want for yourself? Here on Christmas, instead of home with a wife and children who love you? Believe me, the papers will survive with or without your personal sacrifices. Do not martyr yourself because you think it is what he would've wanted."

Was that what he'd done, martyred himself to make a dead man proud? Duke hadn't a clue, but Pike spoke the truth about Duke's father. "I don't want his life, but a wife and children must wait until the company is more secure."

"A man needs balance, Duke. There'll always be more to accomplish. But when you are old and feeble, the newspapers won't hold your hand. You know, I've had more fun the past week with my grandchildren than I ever did with my own children. I missed all those years because I was here every single minute, and I regret not stopping to smell the roses now and again."

Duke considered this, trying to recall if his father had ever attended a birthday or holiday . . . or a picnic? A ride in the park? He couldn't remember spending time with his father outside of these offices.

"Any chance I'm familiar with this woman?"

"Yes, you know her," he mumbled.

Pike's expression darkened. "Wait, you do not mean . . ." Duke offered up no denial and Pike blurted, "Absolutely not. She is not for you."

The reaction startled Duke, an argument instantly on his lips. "Why not? You just finished singing her praises. She is an asset, you said."

"An asset to the company, yes. A candidate for your . . . whatever, absolutely not. She is kind and decent. A proper young lady, not a strumpet. She does not deserve to be—"

"Calm yourself, Pike. I'm not talking about that."

"Then, what? Your wife?" When Duke didn't answer, Pike huffed an angry breath. "That is worse! I'll not see you saddle that woman with a lifetime of loneliness and heartache. She is too good for the likes of you."

Was it the scotch or were Duke's ears deceiving him? "Too good for *me*? The woman flimflammed the national newspaper-reading public for nearly two years! She's a liar and charlatan."

"No, she's a woman who desperately wished for a job at a newspaper. Nothing more. I talked her into the advice column because she had an overabundance of common sense. I liked her, dammit. And you may not know this, but her mother has worked as a maid for years. She's in poor health and Rose is saving money to help her retire. How are you able to fault her for that?"

Duke understood, but his stupid pride kept getting in the way. She'd lied to him. Made him feel like an idiot. "Borrowed" someone's house for a dinner party. Jesus, the woman's moral compass was as flexible as wheat stalks in a storm, bending to suit her whim. How could he ever believe anything she said?

My maidenhead was mine to do whatever I chose with it.

She couldn't mean that, could she? He assumed she'd been angling to marry him. So why would she refuse his proposal today?

Pike drained his glass and slammed the empty crystal on the desk. "You know what your problem is? You don't care to admit when you are wrong. Keep moving forward, never look back. Because to reflect on your past means you might come to regret some of the decisions you've made . . . and you'd be forced to admit you are not perfect." He stood and collected his painting under an arm. "What you don't realize is that the world does not need more perfection. It needs more compassion and empathy. And if you cannot learn the difference, my boy, you have a very lonely future ahead of you."

Pike spun on his heel and strode toward the door.

A strange sensation filled Duke's chest. He missed Pike and didn't care for things to end this way.

He's been at the paper for more than forty years and is now cast adrift for someone else's mistake.

Rose had been right, dammit.

"Wait," he called. "I'd like you to return to the paper."

Pike stopped, a frown on his face. "You want to hire me again?"

"Yes, I do." The decision seeped into Duke's bones with a surety he'd not experienced before. "I was wrong to fire you."

"Indeed, you were. Never thought I would hear you say it."

Neither had Duke. He'd never gone back on a decision before. "Perhaps I am learning compassion and empathy."

Pike's mouth twitched. "Fair enough. I do miss working here, but I have no desire to put in ninety-hour weeks any longer. I like spending time with my wife and grandchildren."

"What about part-time?"

A grin spread over the older man's face. "Twenty hours a week for the same salary as before."

Duke chuckled at the ridiculous bargain. Pike had him cornered and they both knew it. "Fine, but you start back tomorrow."

"Only for an hour or two. Taking the family to the Central Park menagerie tomorrow." Duke didn't argue, so Pike continued. "Now, what are you going to do about Miss Walker?"

"I suppose you want her rehired as part of your negotiations."

"That would be nice, but I didn't mean her column. I meant your intentions toward the girl."

"I don't know," Duke answered honestly. "I haven't decided."

"Well, you'd best decide quickly. But, if you aren't prepared to place her happiness over your precious newspapers, then you need to let her move on."

Duke's mouth turned to ash as he contemplated Rose moving on without him. Who would teach her to ride? Who would stand up to him and tell him he was wrong? Who would show him how to sing carols and drink mulled cider? Who would corner her under the mistletoe to sneak a kiss?

He drew in a deep breath and admitted what had been staring him in the face for days. He had to win her back.

Chapter Ten

*R*ose nibbled her nail and watched as her mother and the others read Mrs. Walker's latest column. They were crowded into the Lowes' kitchen, the newspaper spread over the flour and salt atop Mrs. Riley's workbench.

Bridget gasped, while Henry covered his mouth. Rose's mother said nothing, but the flattening of her lips spoke volumes. When the group stopped reading, no one spoke.

Finally, Henry broke the silence. "You told them."

"Yes, I did."

Her readers now knew the truth about Mrs. Walker's age and marital status. Without giving her mother's name, Rose had explained her reasons for pretending otherwise, apologized, and pleaded for understanding. Then she told them this was her last column.

Duke would have a difficult time finding someone else to pose as Mrs. Walker after this.

"Why on earth did you do that?" her mother asked, her eyes bright with unshed tears. "You loved being Mrs. Walker."

"I did. Unfortunately, I was recently fired." More gasps filled the room. "This was my final column and I wanted to be truthful. And I needed to say goodbye."

"I cannot believe he fired you," Henry snapped. "What happened between you two that night?"

Rose had eventually told her mother of the dinner party,

which had earned her an hour-long lecture on the stupidity of the venture. She hadn't, however, told anyone of what occurred in the pantry at the end of the night. That stupidity was hers alone. "He was upset that I lied, said my deception could jeopardize the entire paper."

"So instead of keeping the secret, you've spilled it all over the pages of his newspaper." Her mother shook her head. "I do not understand how this helps anyone."

Bridget said softly, "It's called having your heart broken and needing to clear the air before moving on."

Rose gave the maid a wan smile. "Something like that." *Exactly like that.*

"But you have ensured he'll never give you your job back."

"Mama, I don't want my job back. I'll find another newspaper to work for." One not owned by Duke Havermeyer.

"Anyone would hire you," Henry said. "Havermeyer is a fool for letting you go."

The vehemence in Henry's voice nearly had Rose in tears. She threw him a grateful look and said, "I'll be fine. Do not worry about me."

"Then how was your heart broken?" Her mother glanced around at the faces in the room. "I feel as if everyone here knows something I don't."

"There is nothing to tell," Rose said. Not only were her feelings for Duke unrequited, he'd insulted her further by saying she was attempting to trap him into marriage. Better to forget him and move forward.

"Excuse me." Mr. Chaplin, the Lowes' butler, appeared at the base of the stairs. "Henry, there is a man here asking for you. A Mr. Havermeyer."

Duke was here, asking for Henry? *Good Lord.*

She and Henry locked eyes. "No doubt he's looking for you, Rosie," he said.

Questions bounced in her mind, making it hard to think. "I cannot . . . see him here." She raised her brows at her mother, silently asking for help. Her mother said nothing, however, her attention focused on the newspaper.

"Mr. and Mrs. Lowe are not in," Bridget pointed out. "And I think you should hear what he has to say."

"Still, it doesn't feel right to commandeer one of the family spaces," Rose said.

"I told him to come to the servants' door around back," Mr. Chaplin informed them. "If he wants to meet with one of us, then he shall do it on our terms . . . not his."

Rose could have kissed the butler right then. No doubt Duke would balk at being sent to the servants' door. Most likely he was headed home at this very moment.

"What do you think he wants, Rose?" her mother asked. "Perhaps he is here to give you back your job."

Impossible. Duke never admitted to a mistake, never changed his mind once it had been set. And even if he did, she couldn't work for a man who'd accused her of scheming to marry him.

A bell sounded and Rose started. Had he actually come around back? "Allow me," Henry said and strolled off toward the servants' entrance.

She heard the latch turn and soft words were exchanged. Henry returned—and then Duke Havermeyer appeared in the kitchen, a large hand sweeping his bowler hat off his head. His gaze bounced around the room until it landed on her and, though she had prepared herself, a jolt went through her as their eyes connected. She sucked in a breath, unable to move her limbs as she stared at the familiar planes of his handsome face.

"Mr. Havermeyer." Rose's mother marched right up to the tall, imposing man in a black overcoat. "I am Mrs. Walker. I understand you fired my daughter."

He grimaced. "Yes, I did. It was a mistake, madam. One I have come to rectify."

A mistake? Rose could hardly believe her ears. "Have you seen today's column?" He clearly hadn't, or else he'd know there was nothing left to rectify.

"I have. Clever thing you did, switching it out without me knowing."

"Then how . . . ?" She frowned. "I thought you'd be angry."

"As you said, we should not underestimate the readers. They have come to trust you and learning why you lied will only endear you to them. At least, that's what I am gathering from the telegrams we've received today."

"Telegrams?"

Duke nodded once. "They started pouring in once the newspapers hit the streets. I grabbed a few, and left Pike to deal with the rest."

"Mr. *Pike*?" Rose's brows shot up. "Does that mean . . . ?"

"Yes, I hired him back. As a wise woman once told me, I never should have let him go in the first place."

She could hardly keep up, this was all so overwhelming. "I don't understand any of this."

"I came here to ask Henry how to find you. The woman who runs the boardinghouse listed in your employee file wouldn't tell me." He studied the faces surrounding them, the people who were like family to her. None appeared willing to disappear at the moment. "May we speak privately?" he asked.

He'd been to her lodgings? And now he wanted to see her in private? Rose was trying to conjure a response when Henry snapped, "And leave her alone with you? *Again?*"

Duke held up his palms. "How about a walk in Central Park? Would that be sufficiently public?"

Rose studied her toes. She couldn't begin to guess what

he wished to speak privately about. More wedding demands, where she could send his secretary the bills? No, thank you. She wanted nothing from Duke Havermeyer. Not marriage—or her old job. He believed her a scheming swindler and had rejected her attempts to explain. He could stuff whatever amends he'd come to make into a carpetbag and drop it in the East River.

She lifted her chin. "We have nothing to say to one another that cannot be said in front of this group."

"Rose, please. I would prefer to speak without an audience."

"As long as you give your word as a gentleman that you will not take advantage of her," her mother said.

Mortification burned Rose's skin. "Mama!" How could her mother answer for her? Worse, before she could protest, Duke readily agreed. Soon she found herself bundled in her coat and shoved out the back door by Bridget and Mrs. Riley.

"Make him grovel," Bridget whispered right before she shut the heavy panel in Rose's face.

"Shall we?" Duke gestured toward the path that led to the front of the house. "I realize it is cold so I won't keep you long." He held out his arm. "I promise, I shall grovel quickly."

* * *

Neither of them spoke as they crossed Fifth Avenue and entered Central Park. Last night's light snowfall covered the ground and trees, a fluffy white blanket yet untouched by the grime and grit of the city. It was beautiful, like a fresh start for nature.

Or perhaps it was merely Duke who hoped for a fresh start.

Though the park was mostly deserted, Duke led her

toward one of the many stone bridges that adorned the public space. His tongue felt thick and awkward as he rehearsed in his mind what he wished to say. Today was a crossroads, one that would determine how the rest of his life was written.

"There's no need to really walk in the park," Rose said and shook snow off the hem of her skirt.

"I beg to differ. If we don't, Henry might come after me with an accusation of improper behavior."

"He's merely angry that he left the other night instead of seeing me home. He holds himself responsible."

"For which part?"

"All of it." She must have read the question on his face because she said, "I told him about being discovered in the pantry and I am certain he can guess the rest."

"Rose, if I had known . . ." He sighed. "I apologize for what happened. I wasn't thinking clearly. I wanted you too damn much."

"I have no regrets," she said, her chin in the air. "Not about that."

She didn't regret the loss of her virginity while sitting atop a pantry shelf? "Your first time should have been special. And under very different circumstances."

He felt her stiffen at his side. "Have we not already covered this? It was mine, not yours, to dispense with. I am glad to get it over with, actually."

"Why?"

"Because being a maiden is treated as some sort of prize, a commodity. I am more than my body or my ability to bear children. I want a career, too."

"That's part of why I am here, actually."

"Oh?"

She sounded disinterested and he found himself flustered. He didn't know how to say what was in his heart, so he stuck to talk of the business. "Come back to the paper."

"No. Good day." She spun and started in the opposite direction. He dashed around her, blocking her path.

"Rose, wait. Give me a chance."

"Like how you gave me a chance to explain in the days after the dinner party?"

He winced. "I deserve that."

"Yes, and a whole lot more. But I'm busy searching for another position and I don't have time to elucidate all of your numerous shortcomings."

"I'm sorry for ignoring you and not allowing you to explain. I was angry. And hurt. I didn't mean those things I said yesterday."

Her gaze narrowed as she searched his face. "That's quite a dramatic change in attitude. So, you don't believe I was scheming to trap you into marriage?"

"No, Rose, I don't." He closed the distance between them, until her skirts brushed the tips of his shoes, and he reached to cup her cheeks in his palms. "This is new for me, to care about someone this much. To have it happen so quickly is confusing, too. My first instinct was to push you away. I am dashed sorry I hurt you."

She swallowed and took a step back, and his arms fell to his sides. "Thank you for apologizing," she said. "This hasn't been easy for me, either. I never expected for anything to happen between us or to care for you. And now, everything is ruined."

"Don't say that. I cannot accept that I've ruined what was between us."

"Duke, we had one night, one stolen moment together. It can never be anything more."

"Wrong." The strength of his voice rang out in the stark winter morning. "It may have been one night, but it changed my life. I don't want to live like my father, caring for only the newspapers instead of my family. You showed me that.

You showed me how meaningless and joyless my life has been until now, until you came into my world."

She blinked up at him several times. "But you hardly know me."

"I know you. Even if I hadn't read your column each week, I would recognize all the qualities that make up who you are. I know you're smart and loyal, kind and thoughtful. You feel deeply and care about the people who write to you for advice. You're funny and charming, and a part of my soul unlocks every time you kiss me. Most of all, I know I cannot live without you."

Her gaze softened but she said nothing for a long moment. He thrust his hands into the pockets of his overcoat and waited, his stomach knotted with the possibility that she would refuse.

"And what do I get in return?" she finally asked.

Hope blossomed in his chest, the first cracks in the ice that had taken up residence there since she left him yesterday. "The world, Rose Walker. I'll give you whatever you want, whenever you want it."

"But that's merely money. I mean, what will you give me here?" She put her hand over her heart.

"My time and attention. You and the life we build together will always come first, before the company and the newspapers. You'll be the center of my world until I take my dying breath." Then, terrified but resolved, he stepped off the edge of the cliff and acknowledged what was in his heart. "And love, Rose. So much love you will never doubt it for a single second."

She bit her lip, her blue eyes bright with emotion and confusion. "You love me?"

Unable to keep from touching her, he brushed his knuckles over her cheek. "You captivated me from the first moment I saw you. There is no one else for me. You're the most capable and confident woman I've ever met. I think I started falling for you while reading your column each week."

"Really? But my mother and the other staff members supplied most of the tips."

"Perhaps, but the essence of your column, the wit and intelligence, was all you. And that's what drew me in. You have a gift, a way of relating to people that I admire."

"I watched you," she whispered, a pink appearing on her cheeks that had nothing to do with the cold. "I used to stand on the street and wait for you to leave the building. There was something about you that intrigued me. Who was the intense man behind the empire? I found you fascinating."

Now it was Duke's turn to be surprised. "I . . . had no idea. I never saw you. Believe me, I would remember."

She lifted a shoulder. "It was silly. I never thought you would notice me, not in a million years, but I couldn't stop watching. It was that dashed scar."

A smile twisted his lips. "A reporter at heart. That's why you must come back to work for HPC."

"As what? Mrs. Rose Walker is no more."

"Do whatever you want. Write an advice column again or work in the newsroom. Cover games at the Polo Grounds. It makes no difference to me. All that matters is that you come back. And while Mrs. Rose Walker may be no more, I believe Mrs. Rose Havermeyer is available."

"*Duke.*" She wrapped her arms around herself, her lips twitching with what he prayed was happiness. "You are making it quite difficult to remain angry with you."

"Then stop trying. Put me out of my misery, Rose."

"What happens if I only want the job? Will you rescind the offer?"

His stomach sank. Christ, she was going to turn him down. Ignoring how much that hurt, he shook his head.

"The offer at Havermeyer Publishing is yours, regardless of what happens between us."

A grin slowly emerged on her face, one that confused the hell out of Duke. "First," she said, "my mother should take over Mrs. Walker's Weekly. Most of the recipes and household tips were hers anyway."

This was a promising demand. "Fine. What else?"

"I want to work my way up as a reporter, starting wherever Mr. Pike sees fit to assign me."

"He will undoubtedly be glad to have you. And what of the rest?"

She placed her palm on his sternum and Duke's heart pounded beneath her touch. "The rest of what?" The teasing glint in her eyes gave her away and heat slid through him, warming his blood.

"The rest of my life. Will you promise to share it with me?"

"Will you hold up your end of the bargain? You have made promises, Duke Havermeyer."

A man's only as good as his word.

He reached into his pocket and withdrew the small box he'd carried with him today. More than anything else, he needed this woman to be his wife. "I intend to keep them. I will never lie to you. Laughter and love, my dear, every day, while the breath remains in my body." He flipped open the box's lid to reveal his mother's diamond ring.

Rose gasped, a hand briefly covering her mouth. "But what of your empire? What will happen to it?"

"I'll entrust it to others now and again. I will never put my so-called empire before you or our family as my father did, not even on Christmas." He dropped to one knee right there in the snow. "Marry me, Rose Walker."

She nodded and launched herself at him. His arms came around to hold her tight, relief and happiness weakening his knees.

"Was that a yes?" he asked, his voice muffled in her hat.

"Yes, Duke. Yes to loving you, and yes to saving you from a life of loneliness and boredom."

Joy filled him, a heady ebullience that felt like a thousand tiny bubbles in a glass of champagne. "I have no doubt you will succeed. After all, I've said many times that Rose Walker is a marvel." He bent his head, his lips hovering directly above hers. "And now she is mine."

About Joanna Shupe

Award-winning author **JOANNA SHUPE** has always loved history, ever since she saw her first *Schoolhouse Rock* cartoon. She writes sexy books set in Gilded Age New York City featuring powerful tycoons and unconventional women.

Joanna's first Gilded Age historical novel, *Magnate*, was named one of the Best Books of 2016 by *Publishers Weekly*, and one of 2016's top romances by the *Washington Post* and Kobo. In 2013 she won Romance Writers of America's Golden Heart® Award for Best Historical.

She currently lives in New Jersey with her two spirited daughters and dashing husband.

To receive more information about Joanna's new releases and to sign up for her Gilded Goodies newsletter, visit joannashupe.com.

The Shortbread

Dear Reader,

The MacLean family has been making shortbread for generations—my mother taught me a few years ago (complete with interesting side notes, which I've left below), as her mother taught her, and her mother's mother before that.

I share it with my mom's blessing . . . and a guarantee that it is far closer to the shortbread in Joanna's novella than it is to the biscuits in Tessa's, Sophie's, and mine.

Though, I should warn you: MacLeans are Scots, so I can't promise there isn't a little bit of magic in here, after all . . .

Much love,
Sarah

Ingredients
330 grams (3 cups) sifted, all-purpose flour
100 grams (½ cup) white sugar
1 cup (2 sticks) soft butter
1 egg (fresh, if possible)

Directions
1. Preheat oven to 350°.
2. Combine flour, sugar & butter by hand. Add egg, knead until the dough comes together. (Note: My mom adds, "The kneading can be tiresomely long, so I often ask your father to do that.")

3. Divide into quarters and roll each into a half-inch-thick circle. Cut into eight equal triangular pieces. Add designs (pinpricks, hatch marks, your pleasure) with a fork.
4. Place on parchment paper or a buttered and floured baking sheet and bake for 15 minutes, then lower heat to 300° and bake 25–30 minutes longer, watching carefully until shortbread is "shortbread colored." (Note: Non-MacLeans would call this a pale golden brown).
5. Let cool.
6. Fall in love.

**Don't miss out on the next books from these
award-winning and bestselling authors!**

The Wallflower Wager

By Tessa Dare

*They call him the Duke of Ruin.
To an undaunted wallflower,
he's just the beast next door.*

Wealthy and ruthless, Gabriel Duke clawed his way
from the lowliest slums to the pinnacle of high society—
and now he wants to get even.

Loyal and passionate, Lady Penelope Campion never
met a lost or wounded creature she wouldn't take into her
home and her heart.

When her imposing—and attractive—new neighbor demands she clear out the rescued animals, Penny sets him a
challenge. *She* will part with her precious charges, if *he* can
find them loving homes.

Done, Gabriel says. How hard can it be to find homes for
a few kittens?

And a two-legged dog.

And a foul-mouthed parrot.

And a goat, an otter, a hedgehog . . .

Easier said than done, for a cold-blooded bastard who
wouldn't know a loving home from a workhouse. Soon he's
covered in cat hair, knee-deep in adorable, and bewitched
by a shyly pretty spinster who defies his every attempt to
resist. Now she's set her mind and heart on saving *him*.

Not if he ruins her first.

Brazen and the Beast

By Sarah MacLean

The Lady's Plan

When Lady Henrietta Sedley declares her twenty-ninth year her own, she has plans to inherit her father's business, to make her own fortune, and to live her own life. But first, she intends to experience a taste of the pleasure she'll forgo as a confirmed spinster. Everything is going perfectly . . . until she discovers the most beautiful man she's ever seen tied up in her carriage and threatening to ruin the Year of Hattie before it's even begun.

The Bastard's Proposal

When he wakes in a carriage at Hattie's feet, Whit, a king of Covent Garden known to all the world as Beast, can't help but wonder about the strange woman who frees him—especially when he discovers she's headed for a night of pleasure . . . on his turf. He is more than happy to offer Hattie all she desires . . . for a price.

An Unexpected Passion

Soon, Hattie and Whit find themselves rivals in business and pleasure. She won't give up her plans; he won't give up his power . . . and neither of them sees that if they're not careful, they'll have no choice but to give up everything . . . including their hearts.

The Duke's Stolen Bride

By Sophie Jordan

An urgent dilemma . . .

To save her impoverished family, Marian Langley will
become a mistress. But she will not be just *any* mistress.
Marian intends to become so skilled, so coveted, that she
can set her own terms, retaining control over her body and
her fate. Only one problem remains: finding a tutor . . .

A scandalous solution . . .

Other men deprive themselves of pleasure for propriety's
sake. Nathaniel, Duke of Warrington, would much rather
be *depraved*. He slakes his desires with professionals who
ask nothing of him but his coin. Marian's proposal—that
he train her without taking her virtue—is an intriguing di-
version, until their lessons in seduction spin out of control.

And a most unlikely duchess . . .

When Marian is blackmailed into engagement by a man
she despises, Nate impulsively steals her away. Though he
never intended to take a wife, he can't tolerate the idea of
Marian forfeiting her freedom to another. But can he bear
to give her what she demands—a real marriage?

The Rogue of Fifth Avenue

By Joanna Shupe

Silver-tongued lawyer.
Keeper of secrets.
Breaker of hearts.

He can solve any problem . . .

In serving the wealthy power brokers of New York society, Frank Tripp has finally gained the respectability and security his own upbringing lacked. There's no issue he cannot fix . . . except for one: the beautiful and reckless daughter of an important client who doesn't seem to understand the word *danger*.

She's not looking for a hero . . .

Excitement lies just below Forty-Second Street and Mamie Greene is determined to explore all of it—while playing a modern-day Robin Hood along the way. What she doesn't need is her father's lawyer dogging her every step and threatening her efforts to help struggling families in the tenements.

However, she doesn't count on Frank's persistence . . . or the sparks that fly between them. When fate upends all her plans, Mamie must decide if she's willing to risk it all on a rogue . . .